Pain and the Secrets

THE
writers
GUILD
Refining passion to satisfaction

Pain and the Secrets

MUGENI OJIAMBO

Published by:

Writers Guild Kenya

The Writers Centre, Nairobi. Email: write@writersguild.co.ke Phone: +254751562750

First Published: October, 2019

Coverpage & Layout Design by:

Eva Mugeni

ISBN: 978-9966-136-92-3

For my amazing parents:
William Ojiambo Ading'o. I still feel your presence in my life;
strongly so! May God rest your soul in peace.
&
Saida Apoya. I can never be grateful enough.

And:

To you all
You who dare to dream
To fight on with unflinching fortitude
And cling on thin layers of intuitive, or futile, hope
For this, at the best of times, will always bear you fruits

Prologue

It was on a frigid Friday nightfall when the clan elders met to deliberate over Jim's fate. Attempts by one of the elders to have the meeting postponed had been thwarted.

Jim was still in critical condition in a Nairobi hospital. His mother's whereabouts were yet to be known, and his father was not known. He had never been known.

"We have to get rid of him! We must expunge any slight trace of a jinx among us!" Okumu, the clan patriarch, thundered in a voice that bore a tensile strength of time, and packed a hefty punch.

"No!" Agnes reaffirmed her silent scolds of reproach for Okumu's illogical stand with a heavy heave. "No, my grandson will never be taken away!" Anger was in every intonation of her syllables.

Agnes was a cousin to Jim's biological grandmother; Francisca. Francisca was also the reason why the elders had gathered. She had passed on while visiting Lily, Jim's mother.

"*Olukhwi Iworenya nilwo lukhusamba.*" The firewood you fetch is the one that burns you; Okumu emphasised, with an air of importance around him, and a tone of finality in his words. Agnes, whose objection didn't seat well with him, remained still on her traditional stool. An old sweater had been folded and placed on it to mitigate the effect of protruding nails. Okumu was three seats away from her, his plastic cup of lemongrass-flavoured black tea steaming beside his foldable wooden chair.

"Have you heard me?" He raised the cup and took a noisy slurp of his tea from the tips of his lips. His Adam's apple bobbed as he swallowed with a gurgling sound.

There was a response this time; an infuriated yet polite nod. "Good," he forced a smile.

"Though, my in-laws..." Agnes searched for appropriate words. None came by.

It wasn't as though it pleased Lily to have a son whose father she didn't know. Everyday, she had craved to have a clue. Even most of the steps she had made in adulthood had been towards finding out who her son's father was, and to provide for him and her elderly parents. This, her top guarded secret, had been the driver of her life.

"Why would you want him to leave? Where to? How is he a jinx?" Agnes paused to take a breath. She railed against Okumu, falsely hoping her brother-in- law, Justus Lubao, would come to her rescue. Lubao just watched, unable to hear what they said. He had lost his hearing in recent years.

"How dare you!" Okumu's face narrowed in agitation.

"It's God who gives," she quipped, her voice raspy as though a strong cold held her throat, yet it was the earlier crying.

"Don't we all believe in God, woman?" Okumu spat droplets of saliva as he spoke.

"Be that as it may, I don't care!" Her hand trembled as she wiped droplets of his saliva from her brow. Okumu's hands itched for a slap. He raised his walking stick, but Lubao held his hand before he could smash it across her face.

Chapter One

It will be a boy.

No, a girl...I mean either," she told him, as though they had only thought of male names. Yet, she yearned for a child of either gender to bruise her nipples. As a patient under treatment, and with the patience of Christian saints of old, Francisca had waited for long to feel the delight of cuddling a child in her arms, or how it feels to breastfeed. As her biological clock ticked, she had anguished about the thought of Lubao marrying a second wife. It had taken many years of trying, praying, hoping, waiting and retrying to conceive.

"I must give him a child," she kept reminding herself as if constantly repeating it would increase her chances of getting pregnant. As a result, their lovemaking, whose frequency increased, was more of a baby search than pleasure. Francisca's frequency to church doubled, and she made silent promises to her Creator.

"No, my sister. I cannot," she even told off a friend who suggested *African Chemistry;* witchcraft!

"What if he brings in another woman?"

"God's time is the best," she responded. And whenever the dark thoughts of witchcraft crept into her mind, she pushed them away, repeating the same words to herself, "God's time is the best." She had said the same words one Friday just before Lubao arrived from work. Eighteen years having slowly thinned out, she now had even more reasons to thank her Creator.

When Lubao arrived, his underarms were soaked in sweat and dust hung onto his worn-out shirt. He had spent the whole day in the fields harvesting acres of maize to earn a day's wage. Francisca had just finished oiling her belly with *Bint El Sudan* jelly, whose green label had a dark-skinned adolescent with pointed breasts and a sling hanging from her neck down to her knees.

"Welcome, Lubao," Francisca said, and repeated, "Welcome, my husband," as though someone would have snatched him away from her had she not. Despite the ominous smell of his sweat, they exchanged emotional warmness, his scraggy beard brushing against her neck as they hugged.

"Are you okay?" he asked.

Lubao was always brief. Even when – years back – his uncle had suggested that he get another woman to bear him children, he had simply objected with a "No, I cannot."

It was the same uncle, and the only other person, apart from Samantha Juma herself, of course, that knew of Lubao's secret of 1973.

In March 1973, Archbishop Maurice Otunga was to be ordained as the first Kenyan Roman Catholic Cardinal. Francisca had left for church in Kitale to celebrate with other parishioners. On that day, Lubao fell into Samantha's arms. Samantha was a business lady in Kitale town who provocatively swung her hips and smiled at Lubao coyly whenever they met. Though Lubao would later nurse pangs of guilt for his infidelity, he would not see Samantha again. But the evidence of their decadent act had been implanted in her womb. She had disappeared soon after the incident, without a trace.

"I'm well, my husband," Francisca responded, getting him a mug of cold water from the pot as she always did when he arrived from his casual work. "Can I serve your food?"

"I'll take a bath first, but thanks." The smell of his sweat still crowded the room.

Lubao had barely finished eating when Francisca started groaning. Labour pains had set in. The prospect of the claim that she had been cursed vanishing into oblivion consoled her. Just like *Mama Adikinyi*, or *Mama Boyi*, or *Mama Sospeter*, she would also be referred to as *Mama Someone*. Lubao had been excited to learn of her pregnancy several months earlier, and with the onset of her labour pains that evening, he rushed to borrow a bicycle to take her to the hospital.

As he pushed Francisca on a borrowed bicycle, even the bicycle pedals propelled it ecstatically. The village paths were quiet save for the creaking of insects and a pedal that gave a regular noisy pattern as it unceasingly knocked the chain guard. Lubao pushed on, his left hand firmly on the handlebar with only small fractions of the plastic handlebar grips attached.

Francisca broke into sudden short wild screams as Lubao dragged the bicycle along the narrow paths that had dry maize stalks on both sides. Francisca's legs, stretched before her, kept knocking the back of Lubao's legs. The *akala* sandals were tight on her swollen feet. But he kept pushing, the cells of his body filled with hope.

Lubao coiled his right arm around her back. Occasionally, he would slide it under her lower body to grasp the bike's carrier. Whenever they encountered a pothole, something he tried circumventing in the settling darkness, her weight would press his fingers against the cold steel carrier. But the inescapable joy of getting a child simply made her weight go unnoticed.

"Don't worry, we'll be there before you even notice," he assured her. Francisca mumbled something but it was held in her throat. Pain raced across her groins and underbelly.

Along the way, they met Angalwa, who in his drunkenness, struggled to rise from where he had toppled. Angalwa lurched in a few strides, halted momentarily to stare at Lubao and Francisca, then said as though to no one in particular, "Are you even sure it's your child?"

Angalwa's words tore through their hearts, but despite Lubao's instant urge to stop and smack Angalwa's face, he pushed on. Francisca tightened her grip and slowed her breathing. Angalwa resignedly threw his hands in the air and staggered slowly in the opposite direction.

"The child is coming!" The air bore the sound of her groan. Some people rushed by the road with either dim torches or glass lanterns to check. Lubao soldiered on.

On arrival at Kitale District Hospital, Francisca was quickly ushered into the maternity ward. She tightened her grip on the bed, absorbing the pain. For several minutes, she grunted and cursed Lubao for being the source of her pain.

Just like her conception, the child's birth was a struggle. A nurse rushed for

a pint of water and B+ blood for Francisca. Expectant mothers flocked around the adjacent cubicles and outside the ward; newly-born babies were rocked in relatives' arms. Some women cried. Some delivered on beds. Others on the floors.

Finally, a baby girl slipped into the world, slicking Francisca's thighs with blood. A doctor held the baby upside down and lightly slapped her little butt, the resultant cry broadcasting to the world her arrival. She would be named Lily.

"It's a girl, you can see her," a smiling nurse told Lubao. Walking into the room, Lubao knelt by Francisca's bedside and buried his face in his palms. *I thank you, God*, he whispered. The nurses cleaned the baby, swaddled her in a cream shawl with flowery patterns, and handed her to Lubao like a delicate parcel. With a tiny face and hidden eyes, she blindly gazed into Lubao's face that sheepishly hovered over hers. But one thing was clear from what Lubao saw; she would be an adorable child.

Five days later, as Lubao listened to the news on Benazir Bhutto becoming the first female head of government in a Muslim world, he didn't say, "Doesn't Pakistan have enough men?" as would be the case had Francisca bore him a son.

11

Days slid by. Lubao and Francisca relished their new title; Baba Lily and Mama Lily.

Days, weeks, months and years flew by.

"Mama, why don't I have a school bag like other kids?" the list of little Lily's infantile questions grew longer every day.

"Don't worry, my baby. You'll soon get one," Francisca licked her thumb and wiped away a streak of dry porridge on Lily's cheeks.

Francisca's memory travelled back to the onset of her marriage when her hope and optimism were full of life. Back to when both of them had moved to Uganda in 1971. *Things will be fine soon.* She had always told herself then, but now, she was not sure she would get Lily the bag. They had relocated to Kitale in 1973; a period around which Lubao's aged father got ill and died. Upon his demise, Lubao was left with a large tract of land whose title deed he couldn't trace. In December of that same year, Samantha gave birth to Juma. But Lubao had no inkling he had a son born miles away.

On Sundays, Francisca held little Lilly as they walked down the village to the church whose roof aimed at the sky. Francisca listened and corrected Lily as she said prayers after her during meal times. She was all they had, and loving her was as part of them as their breaths were. Lily's parents strained to ensure all her needs were catered for. They doubled efforts that mostly bore half the expected outcome. They nurtured her upbringing with a plethora of love and inculcated in her virtues and values of honesty, love, respect, morality and hard work.

Slow by slow, Lily quit chewing pencil rubbers. Just like other pupils, she walked to school barefoot while carrying cow dung for smearing classroom floors and a small jerrycan of water on Friday afternoons. Then she started using pens, and not knife-sharpened pencils and books cut into halves.

One Saturday, she ran to her parents after lunch looking worried. "Mum, I'm sick."

"What's the problem, my daughter?" Lubao said, holding her and pulling her towards him.

"I'm bleeding," she said, showing them a spot of blood on her dress. "I don'tknow why."

Francisca took her to their makeshift bathroom and struggled to explain to her the mystery of the blood. And since small twin swelling started protruding on her chest, too, Francisca warned her that boys were dangerous, and that their pee could get her pregnant. So, she warned Lily not to entertain any boy suggesting a sexual interaction. Francisca would get her sanitary pads from the shopping centre that afternoon with the little money she had. Before long, Lily's hips began to show, and her uniform could no longer fit.

"I want to be a pilot when I grow up," she told her parents one afternoon. Sweat patches that drew a map under her arms were proof that she was growing quickly.

"Indeed!" Lubao said with a smile, and Francisca gave an approving nod.

Lily was a member of the drama club that entertained the area Member of Parliament during their school fundraising. The MP had arrived by helicopter; an inspiration to Lily's dream. In his address, he gladly spoke about Kenya signing the Rome Statute, establishing the International Criminal Court, as if it bore any direct consequence to his audience.

It was in the club that Lily met Barasa.

When Barasa, a new pupil, enrolled at Lily's school, they immediately became friends. She listened to him narrate stories of Mombasa, a big town miles away. His coastal Kiswahili slid with ease on his tongue as he spoke a lot about politics.

Barasa spoke too boldly for his age. He watched the television, read newspapers his father bought, and asked his father questions about the country's politics. He then created topics for discussion in class. Sometimes, Lily thought Barasa had a blood relation with either Jaramogi Oginga or Richard Leakey as he spokepassionately about them. She admired his knowledge of current affairs. She even nursed an envious desire for the big stone house Barasa lived in with his parents. And she imagined her own family living in such a good house too, one day.

It was the year 1999. Boys still glued pictures of the 1998 FIFA World Cup on their used exercise books. While they would discuss Jay Jay Okocha, Celestine Babayaro or Fabien Barthez, Barasa talked about the dark months of August and September, 1997, when Princess Diana and Mother Teresa died.

In the election of that same year,1997, Lubao had sworn to his friends never to vote for Charity Ngilu or Wangari Maathai. *Why*? He had felt the time wasn't ripe to have a female President. Francisca, on the contrary, felt the Presidential bid of both women had signified a major stride in positioning women in Kenyan leadership. Perhaps the women would bring change, she thought, and she wouldn't have to line up in future to receive donated corn as she had done for an entire month before the election. Though it wasn't politics that caused the prolonged drought of that year, forcing her to collect wild leaves and herbs for vegetables, Francisca believed there was a magical way a government led by a woman would have helped.

"This is Mobutu Sese Seko. He was the President of Congo," Barasa pointedout in the 32-page exercise book with pictures glued on it.

"Okay."

"Have you heard of him?"

Lily saw a man in spectacles and a hat that matched his shirt, seemingly made from a cheetah's hide, and nodded.

"Bring, let me see," she took the book from Barasa and flipped through the pages. It had photographs of Jomo Kenyatta, Daniel arap Moi, Patrice Lumumba of the Democratic Republic of Congo, Nelson Mandela of South Africa and many other African leaders that she had heard of or learnt about in class.

"How about this?" she asked, looking at one of the photos.

"It's about the Wagalla Massacre. Haven't you heard of it?" Lily gasped after Barasa had explained in detail and cringed at its imagination.

Sitting under a jamun tree next to the school assembly grounds, Barasa was enjoying her company. He would steal glances at her chest whenever she leant over to look at the photos. Lily enjoyed learning new things and more so those she had not learnt or heard of in class or at home. And so, as Barasa watched the news every evening or read his father's newspaper, he took notes to share with her the following day. He did that on the first day, the next one and the weeks that followed.

Barasa started seeking Lily out during break time or in the evenings after school. He would buy sugarcane for two. Even though Lily received her own, he shared his packet of *"Nyayo" KCC* School Milk, notes and even textbooks with Lily. A few times, he would allow her to go home with one of his books.

He even missed her on the many days she faked sickness to help her parents till other people's lands to raise enough money for her exam fees and other school levies.

"How many seeds per hole?" she would shout from behind, asking her parents when planting maize or beans, their common food crops. With her sweaty forehead reflecting the hot afternoon sun, she would watch her parents bend their backs, digging holes in the dark brown soil with their hoes. With the thick layers of sweat under their clothes, a sign of fatigue, none of them would say a word. As though they hadn't heard her, they would continue striking the ground, exposing insects and maggots hidden underneath, which the chicken would scramble for. A stranger would think they were mourning, with the rest of their countrymen, the victims of the ill-fated flight KQ431 that had crashed off the coast of Abidjan, Côte d'Ivoire. And Lily would resume dropping two or three seeds in each hole and kick heaps of soil, with her bare toes, to cover the seeds.

The next time Lily performed with Barasa in the drama club, they were in class six. Officials of a Non-Governmental Organisation (NGO) from Nairobi had visited. On that day, her legs and forehead shone from the excess cooking oil she had applied. Her blue uniform, with a white collar and a white strap for a belt, was neatly ironed. She had borrowed an iron box from Barasa the day before. As one of the needy pupils who submitted their details, her photographs were taken. In the play, she was the mother and Barasa the father. From then on, other pupils referred to them as a couple. Just like their performance was an illusion, so was the promise from the NGO whose officials went untraceable.

Still, Lily missed classes due to lack of fees, and on some days, she feigned sickness because her parents lacked the money to buy her sanitary pads.

The enthusiasm brought by the political merger between KANU, the Kenya African National Union, and NDP, the National Development Party, swept across the country. There was really no significant change in peoples' lives though. Those without food slept hungry while the sick died in hospital wards. In the village, the majority survived by working on others' farms. Their children would sometimes miss school to help till the farms or due to lack of school fees. Still, the countdown to the next elections had started. The opposition leader, Mwai Kibaki, formed a coalition to challenge President Moi's preferred heir.

Lured by Barasa's in-depth knowledge, Lily's interest in politics sprouted. "And who is Uhuru Kenyatta?" She once asked her teacher.

"Listen, class," the teacher said excitedly. He went on to tell them that President Moi had already vouched for Uhuru, the son of Kenya's first President, to succeed him. Lily would later revisit the teacher's words, just to gauge the weight of that one sentence.

One morning, as Lily prepared for her continuous assessment tests, Barasa ran to her desk. "They say, at last, we'll have a new President next year," he said. She could not grasp what he was talking about because she was distracted. Under her uniform, she felt uncomfortably itchy in the bra she had worn for the first time.

Later that day, Lily was the first to inform her parents about the new political force. "You know another Coalition has been formed called NARC, the National Alliance Rainbow Coalition?" She started. NARC grew in popularity and swept followers across the entire country, especially in December when schools had closed. That same month, elections were held.

Early the next year, when schools opened, the new President, Mwai Kibaki, introduced free primary education. Francisca, Lubao and millions of Kenyans were unstinting in their praises to the NARC government for the move. Chants of *"Yote yawezekana! Kibaki Tosha!"* lasted from dawn to dusk with many praying for him to live a long life. "Everything is

16

possible! Kibaki is fit!"

Thousands of new pupils were enrolled in schools for the free primary education. Lily studied hard for the national examination scheduled for November. After helping her parents with chores at home, in the farms and at the market selling tomatoes, she would study for hours on end. Most Saturdays, she sat with Barasa at the market that burst with green vegetables and fruits, under a big tree, selling while reading the books they carried along.

When a plane carrying MPs crashed in Busia after a homecoming party, Lily dropped her aviation dreams. Busia residents cycled or took boda bodas – an alternative means of transport that has spread to most parts of the world - to go and see the plane crash for themselves. Not long after, Lily changed her mind. "Everyone dies,' she told herself, accepting that even people die on the roads, when swimming, eating, sleeping or praying.

"Which is your dream university?" Barasa asked her one afternoon. They were selecting secondary schools to join by ticking against their choices in tiny boxes on long printed sheets of paper.

"Mmmh, I am not sure. Honestly."

"Mine is the University of Nairobi." He mentioned a few other universitiesbut explained why he preferred the University of Nairobi.

"Wow, I can't imagine myself at the university; my money, room and freedom!" The desires and plans she had for her parents suddenly bulged.

"It's a good thing, only if we're careful. Rumour has it that some students are involved in drugs, prostitution, and even crime. Two days ago, I saw on television students being arrested for hiding guns under beds in their hostel."

Lily raised her hand to cover her gaped mouth. She thought about it for a whileand decided there and then that if she ever made it to university, she wouldn't indulge in any bad company.

"Let's just concentrate on secondary school for now. We aren't so sure of the university, are we?"

In the month that followed, President Kibaki renounced his role as the chancellor of public universities and appointed seven chancellors to replace him. Two months after that, Lubao sat among other elders in his village to console each other after the passing of a son of their soil; the eighth Vice President of Kenya.

One day after the national examinations had commenced, Lily got home to find no food. She felt so hungry that she plucked an ear of maize to roast. Unfortunately, the person Lubao had leased the land to was making a random visit and caught Lily red-handed on his farm. Lily tried to beg for his mercy but he could take none of it.

"I'm just a simple labourer, earning less than fifty shillings a day, you know. Give us time and I'll pay you, please," Lubao pleaded later at the Chief's office. Francisca had accompanied him. Had they not parted with a borrowed two hundred shillings and a promise to pay a further three hundred shillings, Lily wouldn't have been released to attend her afternoon paper.

With only the taste of her hunger in her mouth, she reached the exam room when other pupils had just started the paper.

"I'll give you two hundred shillings to add to what your parents are supposed to pay. I've been saving some money for Christmas." Barasa told her that evening on their way home.

"No!" She was quick to respond, her pulse ramping up and hands prickling. "My parents will know."

Barasa would later use the two hundred shillings to buy her a Christmas gift, a purchase from which he got a forty-shillings-coin balance. The new coin had President Kibaki's portrait! It had just been released into circulation to mark Kenya's 40th independence anniversary.

When the results came out early the following year, Lily had excelled. Her parents couldn't raise the fee to the national school she had been invited to join. They opted for a local school. They negotiated with the person renting their land to extend the lease, but he flatly rejected the suggestion. Pleas to their friends and relatives bore no fruits either.

Finally, Lubao got a businessman from Eldoret to rent the piece of land for four years. He met Mashamba, the businessman, in Kitale where the latter occasionally visited to run a few errands. Lubao paid for Lily's four years' fees upfront, and it was all smiles as Lily joined Form 1.

Time flew by with both Barasa and Lily now in secondary school. During the first Easter holidays, Lily and Barasa sat on a bench outside Lubao's hut discussing

Binomial nomenclature, Agrarian revolution and other new expressions they had learnt in school – unfathomable by Lily's ageing folks. Barasa became so fond of Lily that his mind often revisited their discussions even after he had gone back to his *isimba,* hut. He would visualise pictures of how Lily had grown more beautiful, especially the flesh she had added under her skin.

At times, Barasa thought of her shining eyes and fantasised about brushing his hands against her skin. He thought of her all the time. Even while eating. School separated them, but sometimes, he saw her images in the pages of his books while reading them during *preps* time. He would at times be engrossed in his books reading a sentence over and over without grasping a word.

Chapter Two

From his boarding school, Barasa sent Lily a letter. He detailed his school performance, teachers, new friends, clubs and games. He wrote that he loved her. Before he signed off with his name, he dedicated love songs she never made the effort of finding out. He wrote her one letter, two letters, three letters, and the fourth one – without response. Barasa felt guilty for expressing his feelings and disappointed that she never spared time to respond. The fifth letter took him hours to write. It seemed to get no better with each rewrite. He re-wrote it several times but tore it into pieces at last.

"Why don't you reply to my letters?" he breathed into his spectacles and wiped them with a white handkerchief. It was during the August holidays. Barasa had grown leaner and now wore glasses. His voice had deepened. He looked different; more mature with the glasses on his face – black frames and thin temple tips. Lily could see a hint of beard sprouting from his chin.

"I don't think it's the right thing to do now. But I like you, Baro," Lily replied. None of them spoke in the two minutes that followed. In fact, they didn't talk about it again the next day when they met under the same tree. They just sat quietly reading. In between reading and selling tomatoes and now vegetables, they listened to *Walking Away* and *7 Days* by Craig David, or Cyndi Lauper's *True Colours* on Barasa's Walkman radio. They rewound the tapes until the music dulled with the faltering radio cells – when the sun had gone down.

Back in school, while other students received letters, or held their girlfriend's hands during inter-school visits, Barasa got none. *You are not a man*, his friends teased him. He, therefore, sought alternative ways to redeem himself and service his ego.

On Saturday nights, he would sneak a packet of cigarettes or two across the fence, and would smoke behind the latrines with his two trusted friends. With time, one of his friends easily cajoled him into partaking in sneaked alcohol packed in sachets. Finally, Barasa was introduced to bhang! The pleasure he got the first time gave him flowery illusions of who he was. Of who Lily and him were.

As Barasa's performance dwindled, Lily's kept improving.

Barasa still dispatched letters but never mentioned love or dedicated love songs. He instead wrote about school and politics. He also informed her of the US politics and Senator Barack Obama's visit to Kenya.

"*Ero kamano,*" Barasa would imitate Barack Obama's voice and what he had said when he visited his grandmother in K'Ogelo. Students would heartily clap for him, and Barasa would wish to pen about it to Lily, but his interest in details was now receding to a forlorn memory.

One weekend, an argument ensued with fellow students over President Jacob Zuma's assertion that a shower with cold water, after having unprotected sex, was enough to reduce the risk of contracting HIV/AIDS. Barasa, who was under the strong influence of bhang, supported the assertion while other students maintained that they had been taught otherwise. *You're stupid to support such*, one of the students shouted. He was unaware that Barasa would become physical. And indeed, within seconds of his sharp slap, prints of Barasa's fingers were clearly visible on the student's swollen cheek. Thanks to the teacher on duty, Barasa's behind was thoroughly beaten and he spent the whole afternoon uprooting a tree stump.

21

Around the time they opened school for their final year, President Mwai Kibaki declared his intention to run for re-election even though he had declared prior to the 2002 election that he only needed one term as President. Barasa didn't talk about it. He had realised that years had passed by as he lived up to his friends' expectations. He decided to put more effort into his studies and catch up with the rest. It was his final year in school. Even when, later that year, President Kibaki dismissed ministers Charity Ngilu and John Koech for backing up Raila Odinga for his Presidential ambition, Barasa didn't have the interest to delve into it. All he thought of now was the examinations that were around the corner. He had long stopped sending letters to Lily. Just before their final exams, he decided to send her one. He wished her the best and expressed his excitement towards their completion of high school. For the first time, he received something from her; a success card. The number of times he opened it to read and reread or just pass it across in class and the dormitory were countless.

After nine years of friendship, Lily could now imagine being swaddled in the warmth of Barasa's arms. She imagined his arm coiled around her waist on an evening stride, moonlight lighting up their way, glinting on broken bottles and casting shadows of trees along. How would he react to the success card she had signed off with "*With love*"? Was it the right thing to do now? She had asked herself, and said "Yes!" countless times. She loved him, more than she had probably thought.

* * *

Campaign posters were pasted everywhere when Lily first travelled to Nairobi. She had finished her secondary school studies, and the financial straits in their household had dug even deeper.

"I'll talk to his mother." It was Francisca who had suggested that Lily seek a fortune in the big city. Francisca then spoke to the parents under whose son Lily's service as a househelp was to be engaged. Lily resented the fact that she would be away from her family. From

22

Barasa. However, the desire to see the big city - whose buildings, streets and dwellers Barasa had painted in her young mind - consoled her.

On the day she travelled, Lily's parents advised her to remain the well-behavedgirl she had always been. She wore her best clothes; a yellow top paired with its blue floral skirt. The necklace Barasa had gifted her complimented her chocolate skin as its dark brown beads, the colour of coffee beans, circled the neck that shone with oil.

"Take care, I love you," Barasa told her as the driver ignited the bus's engine. She kept to herself the distant feelings of love – shy to express them. A few times, she had felt jealousy choke her throat when she had seen Barasa talk to other girlsat the marketplace.

"I'll miss you. Take care too." She wanted to tell him she loved him.

The journey was long. Impenetrable darkness immersed the earth early that night. When the moon slowly slithered into the sky later, wisps of cloud stitched around it, Lily looked back on the few nights they had left the market late and Barasa had escorted her up to the entrance to their compound. She now had an ache that came and went; a desire to have Barasa seated next to her. To hold her. She missed him already. But the aspirations and dreams she had had for her parents, to build and furnish a house like that of Barasa's parents, inspirited her.

"How old did you say you are?" James, her boss, interrupted her thoughts. Police officers had stopped the bus at a roadblock. It was common knowledge that even if the vehicle had no fault, they would look for every excuse in a questto quench their huge appetite for bribes.

"Eighteen years." There was an apparent ambivalence in her voice. His behaviour didn't inspire trust in her; especially with the kind of look James kept giving her from the time they left the village. He nodded. She leant against the window, amazed at the billboards, buildings and petrol stations that zoomed pasther view.

The smoky light of dawn and the orange glare of neon street lights welcomed her to the city. Massive tall buildings that graced both sides of the roads claimed her attention as the bus roared on the smooth tarmac, as if sailing on a calm sea.A few clubs blared with music and lights kept on blinking from their balconies like a string of trapped fireflies.

They alighted and literally waded through an ocean of humanity, which shocked Lily for she had never seen so many people in one place. Everything seemed so urgent as people rushed from all directions and traders and matatu conductors shouted.

A small plastic board was by the windscreen of a matatu they took. It read "29/30". The matatu conductor held a similar board and kept knocking the side of the matatu with it shouting, "Mathare North! Thirty bob! Thirty bob! Mathare North!" He repeated it over and over again; not exactly in that order – and sometimes in Swahili. Soon it was full.

As the matatu snaked through traffic, Lily revisited Barasa's tale three days earlier. "While in school, I was told there's an infiltration of thugs from Dandora in Mathare." That had scared her. "You ought to be very careful, lest they become your role models and you start putting on heavy silver-coated chains, or line up your ears with hundreds of rings." They had then laughed it off. But it was becoming real now that she was heading right there.

"They told you how much I'll be paying you?" James asked.

"Yes. One thousand shillings per month," Lily said, imagining how that was a lot of money, and how she would accomplish so much with it.

"Good. I expect you to be a good girl. Right?" She nodded.

"Right?"

"Yes, sir." Her genteel upbringing was vivid.

Ahead of where they alighted, people moved up and down a slope on a rough road. Just near the end of the slope, a group of schoolgirls were buying potato chips. Lily noticed a goat chewing something from a hip of dust across the road. They rushed against the flow of human traffic; some going to work and others returning from night duties. They walked past a woman and her child seated next to a culvert. The woman's cream scarf, green sweater and pink nylon skirt seemed a little dishevelled. The culvert discharged thick sludge into an open drainage full of polythene bags.

"That's where we buy our antibiotics when the child gets sick...and painkillers for her mother." She gave a polite nod.

Had her biology teacher not warned them against over-the-counter or self- prescription of antibiotics? Had he not emphasised that it led to resistance of bugs to drugs and made one more susceptible to even mild infections? A man waved a greeting, but James ignored it, explaining, "That is the pharmacist, Mr Mwaura. I'll introduce you to him next week." Which he did. "Now I'm late for work."

"And that's the shop where we buy from. They're the only ones who give us goods on credit," he pointed out and Lily thought she saw someone's head peering over its counter from inside the shop. A few metres from the shop was a small kiosk from where some young men sat outside on a bench. Loud reggae music pulsated from the kiosk as the young men exhaled puffs of smoke through their mouths and noses. On its door, rolls of *khat* had been carelessly drawn, and the word *"GAZA"* written in big black letters. One of them pointed in Lily's direction. They all turned to gaze.

"Avoid men, especially when you go to the shop or take Junior to school." "Yes, sir." He must have noticed their gestures, she thought.

He paced so fast; in the same manner she had seen people in the streets walk that morning. Lily wondered why he hadn't paced that fast when he went to pick her in Kitale.

"HIV/AIDS is plentiful here...and unwanted pregnancies. The other day, foetuses were found rotting in the sewage there," he pointed at a sewer, a distance away. They were now at the top of the incline. From there, she could see a valley with reeds and grass that separated two inhabited areas. On their side, she saw wooden, metal sheets and concrete walls. On the other side of the valley, there were brown – unblemished – iron-roofed shacks and a few built with new sheets, and an irregular cluster of concrete flats at the end of the climbing incline. A young boy peed near the reed bushes.

"What's the name of this place, sir?" "Mathare Valley."

With a small bag containing her clothes and a pack of groundnuts

Francisca had bought for James' wife, she rushed along the strides of his long legs, struggling to match his pace. "Thank you," she said and did not bother to probe any further, even though she was curious to know what part of Mathare Valley they were striding past.

The view of a child with rugged cornrow lines of brown hair scattered on her scalp and mucus running down her nose did not escape her as she paced behind James. Next to the child, a plate of *githeri* with more maize than beans gathered a swarm of houseflies. A man – probably her father – sat on a pile of building stones nearby, sharpening his knife.

James slowed down and looked back. Lily was a few metres behind. "Come on," he urged her on, "In Nairobi, things are done *chap-chap*, *fasta fasta.*" He had to wait for her. "Please, hurry up! I don't have the whole day to myself," he exhorted her.

They strode farther down the slope past slanted shacks for public latrines. The quietly sinking latrines sloped towards a river, into which they directly discharged. At the bank of the river, tall grass almost swallowed them from behind. In one of the four cubes, a woman washed her hands from a plastic jerrycan whose top had been cut open. She wiped her hands on her woollen sweater and lengthened her pace behind them.

So far, it wasn't the Nairobi Barasa had made her picture, and in whose blueprint she failed to make comparisons. A distant thought of regret crept in. She missed Barasa. She missed her parents. But why Barasa had failed to give her full details of what to expect, she didn't know.

To repulse what was in her mind, she imagined looking at Barasa's eyes through his clear glasses and confessing, "I love you."

They took a right turn and Lily wondered if that was where she would spend two years before joining the University. That's if she would make it. She wondered, too, if Barasa would still hold her dear by the end of that period. A few metres ahead, they neared concrete buildings. Her mind settled a bit. They passed two blocks, and on the third one, from where a lean man was finger- brushing his teeth, James showed her the place from where she would be buying water. Adjacent to the man, a few women had lined up their jerrycans next to a small tap. On the fourth block, he announced they had finally arrived home.

James took the stairs of the building with Lily in tow. The flights of stairs to the second floor were narrow. The corridors were dark, and clothes hung on a clothesline on the second floor.

His house was at the far end corner. A neighbour's child stood by a door, staring as they made their way. He was chewing a piece of yam and smiled when they approached. He was missing three incisors; one from the upper jaw.

The lights there, he told her, were only switched on at night. "Even inside the houses," he was quick to add. *I swear you'll be amazed by the city; cloud-high buildings, good roads, clean tapped water and endless electricity*, the memory of Barasa's assurances irked her.

They had reached his door, and he pulled off his pair of black shoes, whose soles' heels showed square holes with trapped stone pieces. The stench of his woollen socks slapped the walls of her nostrils.

He had scarcely opened the door when his son emerged. He grabbed James' right thigh. "*Karibuni*," his wife stood from a chair, switched on the lights and hugged him. "Welcome, let me keep this for you." She placed Lily's luggage on top of a metal box. "Let's thank God for the journey mercies." And they all bowed down for a long prayer.

James introduced his family to Lily, starting with his wife and then the children. His wife was warm and generous with compliments. However, there was a strain in her smile. The skin on her face looked dry and stretched. The only part that seemed oiled, Lily observed, were the cheeks. Her veins showed at her temples, and a good amount of flesh had sunk a little into her skull. Could the oiled cheeks be a result of washing by frequent tears? Lily wondered.

Lily would soon come to learn that James' wife had cancer. That is why James introduced her to Mwaura, the pharmacist, as he had promised. The illness had entrenched James in debts at the pharmacy, not to mention the shop.

"And this is Junior." The boy neither turned nor said a word. When he finally did turn, Lily made as if to smile, but he turned his head instead,

27

exposing scatters of wounds with some white cream roughly smeared on them. His brown long- sleeved t-shirt had bleached patches and smears of porridge near its collar.

"And that one is Cindy, our last born," he pointed at a sleeping child on the bed next to the only window in the house. Then James quickly added, "For now...in future, we may decide to have one more."

"God willing," chipped in his wife with a distant gaze.

After they had had breakfast, Lily was taken through the household norms.

James emphasised, "You should not invite any stranger to this house." Lily was to wake up at 5 a.m., prepare breakfast, prepare Junior for and take him to school. She would then do other house chores and take care of Cindy.

James worked at a factory in Industrial Area while his wife was a cleaner at the Kiamaiko slaughterhouse down in Huruma. Both of them worked all week except Sundays when they would go to church.

When Lily switched on the lights the first morning, a population of cockroaches that had gathered around the utensils startled her as they scampered for safety. She then went about her chores as she had been instructed.

That became her daily routine.

After finishing her work, she would sit by the balcony, smell the detergent from the flapping clothes pegged by neighbours to dry, and watch the children at Junior's school play. She would also see mechanics at work in the garage next to the school. The campaign period was officially on. Whenever she passed by on her way, either taking Junior to school or to pick him up, she always overheard them discuss Raila Odinga and Mwai Kibaki - the leading candidates in the presidential race. She could tell the election campaigns were strongly ethnicised with Kibaki having a huge support from Central and Mount Kenya regions of Kenya, and Raila having a huge support from Western, Nyanza, Rift Valley, Coastal, Northern and parts of Eastern regions.

It seemed as if business was down. Most of their clients had travelled upcountry for Christmas and to cast their votes. But there was also tension that could be easily picked from people's talks and interactions. With Cindy – as calm as she always was – cuddled on her lap, or toying around with her doll with a missing arm, Lily had enough time to survey the environs. Her view extended to the women selling vegetables on makeshift stalls placed on sewer lines. Her brief encounter with them had proved that they were no different from the women in Kitale market. They always talked about other women and their families, just in a similar manner.

During such moments, Lily reminisced about the moments she had sat with Barasa at the market back home. A wave of sadness and enragement swept over her; she had taken for granted those moments. She missed him, but believed bonds of love would reunite them soon.

Come 27 December – the voting day – James and Madam cast their votes quite early at a polling station at Junior's school. Madam gave her twenty shillings, so she decided to go and buy foolscaps. At the shop, a small TV had been placed strategically on the counter. Many customers stood by to catch up on the news on voting that was taking place across the country.

When one customer shouted, "Someone just did the unthinkable in Pakistan!" Lily was curious to find out who, and what it was. Unfortunately, there was no one to expound. So, when she reached the house, she decided to jot down what she had eavesdropped on, and the words voiced by the customer. She wrote; *1) Benazir Bhutto assassinated in Rawalpindi, Pakistan.*

Provisional results as published by the media a day after the election placed Raila ahead of Kibaki by a huge difference. Even though Lily had more access to information and news than before, she somehow missed Barasa's updates especially the anecdotes. Now that the announcement of election results seemed to be taking long, Barasa would have inferred the reason. Results were being delayed, and when they were announced a day later, two days after the election, the gap between Raila and Kibaki had greatly narrowed. With the tension in Mathare as a result of the delayed release of the election results, Lily longed even more for Barasa's political talks. She wanted to know more about the rumours that the figures were being cooked, hence the delay. And sadly also, she wished to share with him how fearful and uncertain she felt after turning down James' sexual advances! She felt scared, but she could not tell Madam.

"What tribe are you, Lily?" Lily was shocked by Junior's question as they walked from the church, his small hand firmly held by Lily. It was just a day before that Junior had learnt that he was a Luhya since his friend with missing incisors, their next-door neighbour's son, couldn't play with him. Both the kids couldn't understand why being of different tribes was an issue. There was so much suspicion among neighbours and friends, and even the pharmacist kept asking James for his money in a harsh way that made him wonder if he was the friend he had known for years.

That Sunday morning after church, James sent Lily to buy four crates of eggs and ten kilograms of rice while Mama Cindy went to the nearby market to buy flour and enough stock of cereals. James could sense imminent violence, but was very hopeful. And so were Kenyans. In the news, the opposition accused the government of fraud, asked Kibaki to concede defeat, and called for recount of votes. It was a busy day for Lily and Mama Cindy, and while, in the evening, Mama Cindy decided to take a nap from the tiredness and pain she felt, Lily sat down to write about her experiences in her new life on the foolscaps she had bought. She had just finished washing Madam's dirty clothes that smelled of meat. She thought against asking James why they were stocking so much food after it occurred to her that things had suddenly changed in the neighbourhood. The atmosphere was tense.

That evening, when all hell broke loose, three young men armed themselves with crude weapons, wore masks and shot out of a shack belonging to one of them. People shouted from different directions. Gunshots could be heard. From various spots, smoke trailed in thick wreaths, roaring their way with the breeze into the sky. They gathered in low, dense clouds as if to watch the bloodshed that was bound to spill with the tendrils of the residual smoke, and the lives that were to be cut short. *Why*? Mwai Kibaki had been declared the winner!

Chapter Three

It was a lazy Sunday afternoon at Gaza *khat* kiosk along Juja Road, about six kilometres northeast of the Nairobi CBD. The kiosk was on the fringes of Mathare slums.

"*Maze jo*, the day is dragging. Mambo, just imagine if you were with that girl now!" One of the young men said. Mambo did not need anyone to make him imagine Lily and himself in bed. He thought about it almost all the time.

Mambo and his friends were seated on a wooden bench painted with stripes of black, red, yellow, green and black; chilling, as they liked saying. Vaite, the kiosk's owner, was tuning his radio to get a clear signal from Metro FM. He was a die-hard reggae fan and could sing along to any reggae song, albeit off-key. They called him Ras. His right cheek was bulging from a bolus of *khat*, which his tongue constantly kept in place.

"Mambo, I also like that girl…and she comes from home!" Wafula asserted. He referred to Lily as his sister because they both came from Western Kenya, though they had never conversed. He only learnt about Lily from her employer, James. As a matter of fact, she didn't know him. Wafula's demeanour had made Mambo picture Kitale as a small town with a small hotel, a small market, one long and narrow street, and maybe a post office or a dispensary. Perhaps a small bank, too.

"Aaaa, Wafula! Are you sure? Can you help?" the questions streamed in succession.

"*Toa kitu*, then I'll do something," he unleashed a broad grin, soliciting for a bribe.

The Metro FM reception was now clear. Vaite relaxed on a raised stool behind his counter, near the speaker fixed on a wooden box. He started counting a few notes and coins in his drawer as he listened to the music intently. A long black woven hat wobbled back and forth with his head's movement. The red, yellow and green stripes on it revealed its griminess.

"Get me her number, if she has a phone. And stop liking her!" Mambo grunted, then pressed a fifty-shilling note in Wafula's blistered, dry palm. "And please, understand that she is not of your class!"

Wafula was a watchman at a petrol station next to Gaza Kiosk. He did many other manual jobs that earned him an extra coin. He washed cars, helped Mwendwa change tyres, swept the yard and sometimes charged strangers who wanted to use the petrol station's toilets. His scalp was clean-shaven to the baldness of a coot and sheened with sweat.

"I'll try the best I can." He picked his club and stood from the bench, the blue uniform with yellow stripes on the sides fitting him well as though he was born in them. The belly showed, too, and it was promising. At his current feeding rate, in a few months, he would be asking for a new pair of uniform from his boss. "See you guys," he rushed to attend to someone looking for a parking space in the yard.

"Are you serious about that girl?"

"Jonte, do I look like I'm joking?" Jonte's silence served as an answer. Jonte, whose official name was John, was a man of few words. He bisected and scrutinised most of his words before making any utterance. He had just finished his Kenya Certificate of Secondary Education (KCSE) examination and was waiting for the results. In the meantime, he had to chill out at the 'Base' with the crew, chewing what they knew best.

"Don't you think I can make it?" Mambo asked.

"Yes, you can," Myche's unapologetic interruption was brief and curt. His official name was Michael. Lucky Dube's *Hold On* was now playing on Metro FM and Jonte switched his attention to its lyrics. Just like in the song, he made silent promises within him for his mother; a better future. Jonte's mother struggled to fend for her family from a small business of *busaa*, the local tipple, right deep inside the bowels of the slums.

"I will. Watch this space!" Mambo affirmed with a click. He pictured Lily; the beautiful lady whose hips involuntarily oscillated to the rhythm of her strides, gripping men's attentive eyes whenever she passed. Her black hair was always neatly combed backwards and held at the back with a rubber band or a plastic hair clip.

Watching a water vendor pulling his creaking and wobbling handcart down the street, Mambo pulled out a roll of bhang, lit it, inhaled a huge cloud of puff and passed it on, marijuana smoke escaping his nostrils.

"Ssss..." Jonte inhaled through clenched lips, his head leaning backwards, eyes closed and his thumb and finger still holding the roll as if his lips alone couldn't manage its weight. He opened his eyes as the cannabis penetrated the cells of his lungs, and passed it to Myche as it altered his perception. To Jonte, a woman frying *mandazi* across the road, in her once-white dust coat, a piece of cloth tied around her hair, a *khanga* across her lap and dirty, oily slippers now looked like a young, uptown, sexy lady. He felt like walking to her, in his long blue jeans folded above the ankle, a creased short-sleeved chequered shirt hanging above his waist and his open shoes with slanting soles. He felt like going and whispering into her ears, "You are the most beautiful creature I've ever seen."

"I'm still saddened by the thugs who shot and killed Lucky Dube," said Ras as the enticing tune of *Hold On* gradually faded away. No one responded and he sipped his soda through a small nail hole made in the bottle-top.

"That girl is cute. Did you see her curves when she passed here from the shop?" Jonte said to no one in particular, switching his mind back to Lily. "What of her refined Kiswahili? Did you hear when she greeted me "*Habari zenu*?" Jonte rolled the words on his tongue with ease as he imitated Lily's voice.

Before Mambo could protest that the greeting was meant for them all, there was a loud bang followed by an immediate silence in the entire area. Several flats away, a young man was standing on an incomplete slab intended to be the second floor of an already occupied flat. He had on an *Arsenal* T-Shirt, red at the torso with white long sleeves. The *Arsenal* crest was just above his left chest and the words *"Fly Emirates"* were boldly printed in white. He was looking towards the deep Mathare Valley. He seemed to be shouting about something, and a crowd of other people joined him at the top, and some were vigorously pointing towards the road near Mathare North Community Hall.

Mambo jerked out of his seat and ran to look at the long stretch of the tarmac road with a thousand potholes. Down the stretch, the road had been barricaded with burning tyres. Young armed men were gathering in groups. There was a Toyota Probox that had been flagged down and the driver whisked out. Another loud bang was heard along Juja Road and Mambo ran back to Gaza. Five flats away, Mambo could also see James peeping out from the balcony, his wife and children standing behind him. James then led his family down the stairs. There was a mixture of terror and a frisson of excitement charging through Mambo's cells as a result of the marijuana he had just smoked.

Along Juja Road, buses and personal vehicles were hooting incessantly in succession, their headlights in full glare. Young men and women could be seen dangling from the top and sides of the vehicles, chanting. Vendors and hawkers closed their businesses in a hurry and rushed to take cover in the washroom at the petrol station.

At Gaza, Mambo received the roll of marijuana that was still doing the rounds, almost finished now. Ras had already taken the bench inside his kiosk and was now closing from inside. But the radio was still on. Presidential election results were finally out; they had just been announced by Samuel Kivuitu, the head of the Electoral Commission of Kenya. Within a few minutes after the announcement, ethnically-based riots and violence broke out across the country.

Mambo threw his glance five flats and a hundred shacks away again and got a glimpse of Lily emerging out of their single room. Lily, who seemed to be alone now, was trying to search for something from the dustbin on the veranda. The place, suddenly, seemed to have everyone locked in their houses or having ran to the chief's camp for safety. They had been warned of a potential attack by the leaflets that had circulated a couple of days before.

"Let's go, we'll be there in three minutes. I've seen someone like James and his family leaving the flat. I'm sure it's them. Let's go," Mambo commanded. Without even questioning Mambo, as they were all now under the strong intoxication of marijuana, they followed him as he led the way. They snaked their way through alleys containing raw sewage, zigging and zagging past doorsteps of rusting shanties. They squeezed their way through the alleys lined with human waste and polythene bags with excrement; bags which children, with utmost naïve bliss, unknowingly played with more often. The metal cubes were silent as if they had no occupants. As if they'd never been occupied. The stench of the drainage was horrid, the same drainage from which residents fetched water for their laundry.

Mambo led the way as they rushed down the polluted labyrinth to catch up with Lily as she entered her employer's single room. Keenly examining his bleak prospects, it was the only chance Mambo stood to act on his heinous thoughts. He took his last lustful puff of the roll, and the smoulder burned the tip of his lips.

Chapter Four

James' friend called him from Kawangware just a minute after the results had been announced to inform him of riots along the Nairobi-Nakuru highway. Just when they were about to end the conversation, his distant cousin from Kayole called to confirm if it was true that people were being attacked in Mathare as it was happening in Kayole. "Brother, you have to run to the Chief's Camp nearyour place. I'm calling you from a police station right now because people are being attacked and killed! I can't believe..." He ran out of airtime as he was still explaining to James.

Lily saw people lock themselves inside their houses. She ran to their single room. Others ran for safety elsewhere; rushing down the flight of dark stairs and sustaining injuries. It appeared to her that everyone had anticipated something bad. And now that it seemed to have started, they were running away to safer grounds; to relatives in other estates or to police stations.

"Hurry up, Lily!" James shouted as he rushed out with his wife and children, "And ensure you lock the door!" Holding Junior, he signalled to his wife to waitas he rushed to peep from the balcony. "And switch off the lights!" Lily heard James' voice fade as they negotiated down the narrow staircase.

"Okay," she shouted back, throwing clothes on the bed. She searched for the foolscaps on which she had written her experiences. She couldn't find them in her polythene bag. "It must be Junior," she rushed to the dustbin. True to it, Junior had stuffed the foolscaps among cowpeas stalks and rotting avocados. Many a time, he mischievously stepped on washed clothes or scribbled with charcoal on the cleaned floor.

From a distance, James saw a group of youths beating up an elderly woman. On the opposite side of their plot's small gate, three masked armed men were approaching. He pulled his wife and ducked into a dark corridor to hide from the approaching men.

The three men rushed up the stairs. Lily heard footsteps as she tried to clear off the avocado smudge off her foolscaps.

Before she could stuff her clothes and the foolscaps in the polythene bag, the door was slammed open, and three men stormed in. One got hold of her. She screamed as he pushed her aside.

"Do you know any of us?" One asked, and she simply shook her head. He pushed her towards the bed.

"Please don't…" she pleaded. She said *don't* repeatedly. She said *please* many times, and *kindly*, too.

With a stiff palm and swift, vigorous strikes, he fired heavy smacks across her face. With each slap, Lily turned her face this way and that way – still pleading *please* and *kindly* and *don't*. Pain twitched the muscles of her cheeks as they slammed her against the walls. She fought back – and with massive strength– that had it been a game, she would have surprised herself at the post-match self-assessment.

The resistance intensified with the increased beatings from the men, her body thudding with each blow or the cheeks flapping with each slap. Then one of them squared a sharp object at the back of her neck.

She could still hear them, but their voices were only vague sounds. She could figure out no words. One of them ripped her clothes open and sent her reeling against the wall before throwing her on the bed. Unconscious. Unconsenting.

Outside, yards away, a bullet was shot to disperse a mob. It triggered a reaction from the growing armed crowd. "Democracy is unstoppable like the flow of the Nile!" Someone shouted. A second bullet was shot. More followed. Three young men lost their lives; one by a bullet, two from machetes. Properties were stolen, fire razed others to the ground, and smoke came out of almost everywhere. At different spots in the city, gangs attacked people perceived to have voted for or against the main presidential contenders, based on ethnic affiliation. Respect for human life was lost as neighbours killed each other and friends suddenly became foes.

In James' house, the gaffer was the first to unzip his trouser and scrambled to grab Lily. He climbed onto her lap, his knees digging into the thin mattress on both sides of Lily's naked thighs, then threw his weight on her.

Gunshot sounds became louder.

"*Harakisha* man! Hurry up!" The other two men were impatient with their leader.

Suddenly, a loud bang at the gate downstairs and a gunshot sound tore through the air. While escaping, James had met the un-uniformed police officers and informed them of the three masked men he had seen going to their plot. Inside James' room, the gaffer had just softened inside Lily. They held their breath. They listened to movements coming from downstairs. Whether the gunshots were from police officers or not was unclear to them. They bounded out of the room, the gaffer tightening his belt. Behind them, Lily lay unconscious.

There was another gunshot. It left their ears ringing. Just as the gaffer approached a corner, there was another gunshot. The Kalashnikov assault rifle's bullet hissed off just below his nose. The sound was loud. Louder than the initial one; 160 decibels at least. Thick white smoke from the muzzle of the gas-operated AK-47 with a fixed wooden stock choked Mambo's nose. With the taste of steam and sulphur, and traces of urine smell, his eyes moistened and the back of his nose was coarse with irritation.

"Jonte!" Mambo shouted and knocked the gun. It flew above the railing and fell on the roof of an adjacent shack. Myche punched the person who had shot. He hit him heavily on the nose, sending him on a roll down the stairs in his blue jeans and a black jacket.

"Jonte!" Mambo shouted again. The bullet had just missed them and pierced through Jonte's skull.

Mambo's voice was gradually becoming distant to Jonte, who was lying down, blood oozing from the back of his head. Jonte raised his eyelids, but they were too heavy to open, even halfway. With a sharp pang of pain and a state of breathlessness, the rattling voices became even more distant and eventually disappeared as he took his last breath. Jonte's legs were drawn apart, touching both walls on each side of the corridor. His face facing towards his left, his left hand slightly under his left torso and the right hand over his head, he lay motionless.

Before Mambo could bend over to check his pulse, another gunshot sent them jumping on a roof through the back balcony, then to the next roof, circumnavigating electricity lines and TV antennas that shot on top of the rugged brown rusty iron-sheets. They stepped on old tyres that had been placed on the roofs to avoid the wind blowing them away, and disappeared into the slum, leaving Jonte's blood flowing on the floor, staining the concrete holes of the floor.

That night, President Mwai Kibaki – who on 2 January 1998, together with Raila Odinga had rejected the provisional results of the December 1997 presidential election – was hurriedly sworn in by the Chief Justice Johnson Evan Gicheru to serve his second term as the President of the Republic of Kenya. Kibaki called for the verdict of the people to be respected and for healing and reconciliation to begin.

Nairobi became a ghost city. By the end of the first day after announcement of the result, police reported that forty people had been killed in Nairobi and fifty-three in Kisumu, seven in Nakuru and four found dead in Kapsabet. The New Year's Eve came to an end, and there was neither pomp nor celebratory mood anywhere. In his New Year message, Kibaki emphasised the need for peace, stability and tolerance and warned that law-breakers would face the law.

Food and water became scarce. Phone calls could not go through. The attacks escalated to other towns. Rumours of gangs regrouping and politicians and their families flying out of the country spread around. A reporter reported to have seen forty bodies with gunshot wounds in a mortuary in Kisumu. In Nairobi there were more running battles between the police and civilians. More people died. Mambo and Myche were in hideouts. Though it was a result of lust, marijuana and politics, a few days later, they were questioning why they had harmed Lily, yet none of them had even voted. Yet neither Raila nor Kibaki recognised their existence. They silently and regretfully wondered what had become of them. And yet, they spared not a thought for Jonte's mother.

That entire week and those that followed, Barasa flicked through different TV channels. There was news of skirmishes in Mathare Valley, just like Kayole, Huruma and Kibera. There was also news of the head of the electoral commission confirming that he didn't know who had won the election, but had been pressured into announcing the results without delay, declaring Kibaki the winner. With politicians taking stern stands, violence escalated. Women, even those expectant, were raped, and a whole family was killed for being a different tribe. Barasa learnt of passengers being kicked out of buses in Naivasha and mercilessly slashed to death while kneeling, asking for forgiveness for sins they didn't fathom. Many innocent souls were lost, and thousands were displaced. Others locked themselves in their houses, but were burnt alive. And retaliations began in different parts of the country.

Lily's parents kept inquiring from Barasa if he had heard any news about or from her, but none was forthcoming. He, too, kept asking them the same question, but all they kept hearing were reports of other missing children and parents. They dreaded that Lily could be part of the statistics of the dead that continued to increase.

Lily was found when police had come to pick up Jonte's body. She was found naked and her thighs slicked with streaks of blood. Since it was now known that two other accomplices of Jonte had escaped, it was obvious that it could only be his company; Ras, Mambo and Myche. But there was so much happening around the city and the country that the police didn't give looking for them a priority. Meanwhile, the US Assistant Secretary of State Jendayi Frazer met Kibaki and Raila separately to mediate the warring factions and find a solution that would stabilise the country. A day later, the opposition called for rallies to be

40

held on the eighth of January despite the government insisting that it would be illegal.

At the hospital where Lily was taken to, the doctors gave her one look and decided her case was not life-threatening. So, they went on attending to other victims that were being brought in, some by the police, others by their relatives.

When she woke up the following morning, there was a drip of saline water attached to her left hand. Weak and confused, she didn't know where she was and what was happening. She felt filthy. She could feel a bad smell on her. She tried to sit up and there was so much pain between her thighs, on her swollen cheeks, and an excruciating one from the back of her neck. She attempted to whisper a word, but her lips could only rise and fall slowly as her heart thudded against her chest.

The ill-equipped and poorly stocked hospital was congested with injured people, some with chopped-off body parts and some with bandages soiled in dark pulps of blood. She had one at the back of her neck. Hospital staff, just like the hospital supplies, were few.

"How are you?" A doctor asked when she fully regained consciousness. "Good," Lily whispered. "Where am I? How did I get here?" She looked around and asked before the doctor could answer the first question, "Where is Mama Cindy and James?"

"You're in a hospital, as you can see, and you were brought here by the police.

What's your name?"

"Lilian Nekesa," she struggled to talk, each syllable coming out with a sting of pain in her cheeks and a sore tongue. Her dimmed eyes were swollen; red and dark capillaries showed at the sides of the eyeballs.

The doctor asked about her age and home, noted down on a pad, and then finally asked, "Would you please tell me what happened?" She kept quiet. She didn't want to remember what had happened. She was afraid and ashamed to tell the truth. She felt filthy.

"Where is the toilet?" was her response instead. After being given directions, she walked away, slowly, past two victims whispering to each other about the opposition cancelling their planned rallies to give a

41

conducive environment to the mediation that was about to start. John Kufuor, the Chairperson of the African Union and the President of Ghana was to facilitate the mediation. As she walked past them, the doctor just watched her, his eyes full of pity.

At the toilet, she struggled to clean herself up, so much rage and pain running through her. She just wanted to die.

"Feel free to tell me anything you think will help," the doctor said when Lily returned after a long while.

To Lily, no prescription could reverse the rape. No drug could erase the bitterness in her heart.

"Nothing," she calmly said. "Nothing other than the injuries I got from anattack by unknown men."

"Did they sexually assault you?" Of course, from the screening by the triage nurse, the doctor knew she had most likely been assaulted.

"No." She said, wondering how the doctor could not see what was obvious. Had the police not informed him? But to the doctor, this response was a relief for they had depleted their Levonorgestrel pills, which were administered to women to prevent unwanted pregnancies. So, they focused on treating her wounds and continued giving her PEP medication just in case she had been raped by aninfected person.

The hospital was understaffed. Hundreds of patients sought treatments but didn't get a full medical examination. Only a few were, and Lily wasn't among them. Because she had sustained a serious cut at the back of her neck, which after examination, doctors found out had affected some nerves, she was informed that she would be around for a couple more days so as to get more attention fromthe doctors.

During her stay at the hospital, she would walk to the reception with hopes of seeing James and his wife coming to look for her, and would sit by the window of her ward looking out at the gate, but they never appeared. Only more victims kept being rushed in. Sometimes, she would sit outside the ward where a plasma tv had been mounted on the wall and follow news on what was happening. Other than the situation not having cooled down outside, Kibaki appointed ministers and Kalonzo Musyoka was appointed as the Vice-President and Minister for Home

Affairs while Uhuru Kenyatta, Minister for Local Government. The opposition, as a result, said the appointments were illegitimate since Kibaki had not won the election and denounced Kibaki's appointment as a sign of bad faith aimed at sabotaging the mediation facilitated by John Kufuor. Following Kibaki's appointments, renewed outbreaks of violence were reported. This shuttered not only Lily's hopes but those of many Kenyans. Two days later, a day when Kufuor left the country saying that it had been agreed that the former United Nation Secretary-General Kofi Annan would continue facilitating the talks, Kibaki's new cabinet was sworn in.

She was discharged a week later with more PEP pills and a cocktail of antibiotics and painkillers. Some of the tablets left her with insomnia, a nauseated throat and a head that took to aching for hours.

The only place she could think of starting from was James' place. She asked for directions along the unfamiliar, deserted, quiet and lifeless streets and staggered past shells of burnt cars, past looted shops and buildings blackened by smoke soot, past tarmac messy with dry blood or rusty circular wires from burnt tyres. Near the wires, blocks of concrete and large stones scattered by the roadside; blocks that had barricaded roads on the day she was raped.

This was a place only several days back, people had conducted their businesses and children in tattered clothes had played freely; skipping ropes or chasing small balls made from polythene papers. As she staggered along, absorbing the effects of the violence, she turned several times to check if anyone was following her. When two men on a motorbike approached from behind, her heart rate shot to more than 140 beats per minute. Thank God, they just overtook her without incident.

A neighbour, a middle-aged woman, whose name was Ndanu, explained to Lily about her employer's escape. Ndanu had also just returned to the flat.

"They met three masked men just by the gate when they were escaping," Ndanu said. After the incident, word had gone around the area. "Just there," she pointed towards the gate. They were seated on the balcony of the second floor. The playground in Junior's school, or former school, was deserted. The mechanics were also absent from the garage.

Lily nodded. Next to her feet lay Cindy's doll with a missing arm.

"And they were lucky to dodge the three masked men," Ndanu paused, looking with regret at a distant point. Perhaps, at one of the classrooms that had served as a polling stream.

"Mmmmh," Lily prompted.

"They were running along the road heading towards the Chief's camp. But then, they saw a group of young men torching a minibus ahead of them on the main road," Ndanu paused for a few seconds again and then said, "They decided to take a different route."

"Mmmmh," Lily quipped, leaning forward with the pain that raced in her wounded body. There were black patches on Lily's face and a healing wound at the back of her neck. Ndanu then told Lily that, maybe, if James and his family had just taken the main road, they would still be alive.

Lily remained silent like she was listening to the sounds of the departed souls, or as though staring at a watchman in the schoolyard whose form looked like a small wardrobe in her view.

"And how about you; what happened? Where were you?" Ndanu asked Lily, though she knew what had happened. But when Lily said nothing, the neighbour murmured the words in Matthew 6:15, *If you don't forgive others their sins, your Father will not forgive your sins.* Then she asked Lily to visit Kenyatta National Hospital Gender Based Violence Recovery Centre, which Lily nodded to but wasn't interested in. She never bothered to remember the name.

Before Lily left with Cindy's one-hand doll later, which she threw on a heap of dust in confusion, the neighbour pressed her forehead with a cloth soaked in tepid water. She had just developed a fever.

Lily sought refuge at the Chief's camp. She had no one to provide food for her. Even Ndanu had left for a relative's place after picking up her stuff. So, Lily felt even more insecure alone in the flat.

The Chief's camp was a small compound clogged with makeshift tents and the little people had managed to salvage from their homes. She shared a tent with a woman from Gatanga, a young boy from Bondo and another lady from Kitui. The tents were small and unhygienic, but people from different ethnicities, and of different gender, shared them regardless. Though victims at the camp kept talking or reporting the cases, they knew, just like the hospitals they had been to, the police didn't have the proper infrastructure to bring to book the perpetrators. It did not help either that some police would rather protect the perpetrators upon receiving small bribes.

That was the camp James and his family were escaping to when they met their deaths. People nursed smelly gun or machete wounds. People were down with illnesses of all kinds. Most had no families to return to, and no sustenance for their children. Victims had endless questions; why had they been attacked? Why were some of them being raped by the police, the very same people who should have protected them? A few silently talked of having seen police shooting indiscriminately. But one question was common to them all; why did the perpetrators shatter their lives?

People's lives in Nairobi were still being shattered by threats and killings being carried out by what was believed to be an outlawed sect. But politicians moved on. The Tenth Parliament opened fraught with fracas, heckles and cheers, and the opposition candidate, Kenneth Marende, was elected the Speaker, defeating the government's candidate Francis Ole Kaparo.

In that Chief's camp, Lily saw dozens of local and international journalists click the shutters of their cameras and record videos of the miseries and hardships the victims were experiencing. It was just like they had covered the 1994 genocide in Rwanda. But none of them brought food or medication, except for the Red Cross, a few other relief organisations and some well-wishers.

Other than the displeasure and indignity of depending on charity, people at the Chief's camp were always worried about being attacked again. They worried about some of their relatives out there who could as well be taking part in the opposition's protests that had been planned to last for three days in Nairobi and other parts of the country. In

45

Nairobi, police met protestors with force and prevented them from reaching Uhuru Park, while in Kisumu, where police used live ammunition against the protestors, two people were reported to have been killed. By the end of the three-day protests, more people had been killed.

But people at the camp lived each day as it came regardless of their worries. They shared the makeshift cooking area under the shade of a tree in turns where more than twenty families shared a single *jiko*. Still, more injured, helpless, hopeless, hungry and fatigued victims of the skirmishes kept arriving. Hence, more makeshift structures made from cartons and polythene papers sprouted. The newcomers shared stories of their experiences. Some had been sent home without police recording their statements, others were asked for bribes, some were ridiculed or abused, while a majority got no follow-ups on their complaints. Worse, those who had been raped were either served late at night or asked to come the next day or the day after. This was despite the police or healthcare providers knowing the fact that medical evidence to support rape allegations could only be obtained within the first seventy-two hours of the abuse.

When everything calmed down after six days in the camp, the government organised transportation for those who wanted to travel to their rural homes. While some returned to their houses in Nairobi, Lily was among those who opted to go back to their rural homes.

Chapter Five

They were escorted in green army trucks packed with people, their children in tow, and bundles of clothes and bedding; bedding from where bed bugs crawled. They were so crammed that many others had to remain and wait for another day. The journey was fraught with silence and tension as gangs had barricaded many sections of the roads. They didn't talk about what they had experienced, their missing relatives or those whose lives had been taken in cruel manners in the horrid violence. Even those who had no families to return to remained mum. Many had cheated death by escaping and sleeping in trenches or even faking death when confronted by the marauding gangs. Not even the young children, on whose faces flies hovered over smears of dry mucus, or on whose smelly wounds flies perched and flew, said anything or cried. The army officers assigned to escort them watched in silence, their guns strapped on their shoulders.

Lily surmised the men in the lorry could be the same ones who had raped her. They could've done the same to others, and now were heading home with innocence sticking out of their pores. Maybe they had killed, too. She switched her mind to the lurid reality of the skirmishes; the abandoned settlements at the roadsides as they passed

Mau Summit and Molo. Some had been turned to heaps of rubbles and ash.

Lily's parents didn't tire of kneeling in prayer and beseeching God to spare her life. When she finally arrived, it was a big sigh to them and a chicken lost its life to honour hers. It was such a relief for her to be away from the occasional distant gunshot sound and the fear of being attacked again. On that day, they got their heads down after a lot of questions that Lily wasn't ready to answer.

Lily was sleepless, lying on her back and staring at the spaces in the roof from where moonlight wedged through. She felt guilty for coming back with no cent. She thought of what her parents and Barasa would think of her. And when she finally caught some sleep, she screamed so many times in her dreams that it worried her parents the whole night. They didn't talk about it the following day.

When Barasa visited that afternoon, she talked to him with plain indifference. She had since developed an aversion to men and became irate when Barasa visited. *Who does he think he is to me?* She had thought. But he had left in a fit of pique; a disappointed man. The enthusiasm he had for meeting her had been bruised, so was his ego.

On the second day after James' parents visited and she struggled to relay the news, Lily spoke a little more than on the first day. Barasa didn't visit, though something within him kept pushing him throughout the day to make that stride. She told her parents about the attack and found a way to skip the shocking rape incident. Meanwhile in Nairobi, police fired tear gas and dispersed a mourning service organised by the opposition as a memorial service for the victims of the violence. On the same day, Raila and Kibaki would meet separately with Yoweri Museveni, the President of Uganda, who had also come in to try and help in mediation.

Barasa visited on the fourth day on his way from the market and brought with him some bananas. As he sat next to Lily on the bench outside, he thought of saying, "I love you," which he didn't, and instead said, "Eat your banana." He peeled one for her and another for himself. There would have been protests on that day by the opposition, but they had been cancelled.

When Lily took her first bite, she felt strongly nauseated. Quickly, she ran and threw up behind the makeshift bathroom. It happened twice that afternoon, when they were listening to news on the radio that Raila and Kibaki were meeting for the first time since the onset of the crisis. The meeting seemed not so successful. Kibaki said he was the duly elected president, to which people reacted with more violence that broke out in Nakuru, Total Station and near Molo. Buildings were set on fire, more people killed, and many more fled their homes. In the few days that followed, more people would be killed in Nakuru, two slums near Nakuru - Kaptembwa and Sewage, and Naivasha. Towards the end of January, on twenty- ninth, Mugabe Were, a Member of Parliament from the opposition was shot dead and more protests and violence followed. Two days after that, another opposition Member of Parliament, David Kimutai Too, was shot dead in what was said by the police to be a love-triangle related murder. This further fuelled the violence. .

After a week of strong aversion to certain foods, nausea and a missed monthly period, Lily realised she was pregnant; which gave her so much intrinsic pressure to terminate it. She was at war with herself, and didn't even know how she would tell her parents about it; that she was pregnant, and that she didn't know the man responsible for it. She thought of running away from home to a far place where she would be alone and never come back alive, but she could not think of such a place.

Milly, Lily's close female friend, was the first person she told. As Lily narrated her ordeal, Milly would occasionally cover her open mouth and widen her eyes. Lily was worried what her parents would feel, say or do. She was worried that people wouldn't believe her, but instead blame her for what happened. Lily disclosed that she had thought of procuring an abortion.

"No, don't!" Milly took a deep emphatic breath, "It's too risky." She paused to search for words, and when she found nothing to say, she asked, "Can I talk to your mother about it?" Lily was silent as though she didn't hear what she had asked.

"No, thanks, I'll face my fears boldly."

"And did you report the matter to the police?"

"I didn't know I was supposed to. Besides, I don't know the attackers. Who would I have reported then?"

"Mmmh," Milly thought for a moment before adding, "But please don't think of an abortion. Do you know you'll be denying someone a chance to live if you do so? And others a chance to be grandparents…. Children are blessings, you know." Lily remained mute. "I've heard stories of women who died or suffered from botched abortions. We still need you, Lily. Think about your parents."

"Blessing, yes, but in this way?"

Lily still wanted to kill the child growing in her womb whose father she would never know. She felt so convinced that carrying the child would alter her life, and even jeopardise her chances of getting married in the future. And their neighbours, friends and relatives would always talk about her. So, the following day when her parents had left, Lily boiled a whole packet of tea leaves, then downed two full cups of the concentrated bitter drink down her throat. Though she was sleepless throughout the night, sweating and rolling from side to side on her thin mattress, her attempt to abort didn't work. Her parents noticed her discomfort and during the day, Francisca asked to have a word with her.

"I…. I…," Lily paused to wipe a sheen of sweat, then looked up and didn't mince words, "I am…I'm pregnant."

"What?" her mother retorted absent-mindedly, crossed her arms and stared at Lily blankly.

There was a period of silence, which worried Lily.

"We saw it. We just thought it wasn't yet time to talk about it," her mother said with annoyance. Lily could see how heartbroken her mum felt to hear her confirm their fears. She imagined Francisca asking, *Why did you allow yourself to be raped and get pregnant?* as though the rape had been maize seeds which Lily would've chosen to plant three, two, one or none.

"*Obhamanyire?*"

"No. I don't know them, mama. But…"

"If you saw them today, would you recognize them?" Francisca was quick to interrupt.

"...but I'm thinking of terminating it, mum," was her response.

"No..." Francisca paused for seconds then added, "You've no idea the agony thousands of women go through to get a child. Don't worry, God will see you through what you're feeling, and He will definitely provide for the child."

The news that she was pregnant desolated her parents that day, as it would for days and weeks that followed. Francisca imagined the ripple of gossip that would circulate the neighbourhood for a while, and how their parenthood reputation would be at stake.

They stayed awake deep into the night. Silently, they boiled with rage. *Why their daughter? Had she kept herself all those years only for that to happen?*

Lily's mind churned with the same questions as she lay awake on her mattress on the floor of the hut. She recalled, sadly, her first day in Nairobi when James had warned her that there was plenty of HIV/AIDS and unwanted pregnancies at the place. Now she was sure of the pregnancy and didn't care much about AIDS. Perhaps, if she had contracted it, it could help speed up her death. But again, it wasn't her fault that she was raped, and it wasn't the unborn child's fault; she consoled herself.

It also disturbed Lily to imagine where James' and his families' bodies were. Would they ever be found to be given a decent send-off? She imagined of the many people that kept dying, that even despite the Secretary-General of the United Nations, Ban Ki-Moon, arriving to try and mediate in the stalemate, people were still being killed according to the news on the radio. Raila had even called for the African Union peacekeepers to be sent in. Meanwhile, a policeman, Edward Kirui, was arrested for allegedly shooting protesters to death in Kisumu. More delegation came in. The US Secretary of State, Condoleezza Rice, arrived to support the mediation talks. Cyril Ramaphosa of South Africa was to join as a chief mediator to lead long-term talks but the government was concerned that Ramaphosa had links with Raila. That made him withdraw. Fortunately, on the twenty-eighth of February, Kibaki and Raila signed a power-sharing agreement that saw the end of the violence and killings that had been experienced for so many days. However, Lily still had pain and wounds that would stay with her for ages.

Her face, with a puffed-up nose, acquired a fuller shape, and she began adding weight. She was always queasy with morning sickness and even her only pair of shoes didn't fit her swollen feet. Her belly began to swell. She avoided the market. She was however moved by the life she carried in her womb; a life she always kept contemplating terminating, and when she didn't think of abortion, she hoped people would understand it wasn't her fault. It wasn't the unborn child's either.

It was so hard to hide now, and so she observed Barasa's face painted with a lot of questions and hidden disappointments. Though she tried avoiding him, she had to inform him. She narrated the election violence in Mathare and how her bosses had been killed, but avoided the rape part. As Barasa listened to her narrate the ordeal, he wished he could wrap his arms around her so she never gets hurt again.

They didn't talk much on their way as Lily saw him off. "You said you love me?" he asked.

"Me? When?" It surprised them both.

"In the success card. I still have it kept with my school certificates. I look at it quite often," he said and then chuckled.

"Oooh, I remember." That was all she said, and then concentrated on her feet as they ambled along the path.

"Does that mean you no longer do?" The disappointment was louder than the words.

"I don't hate you, Baro." He liked it when she shortened his name. It awakened suppressed memories of the many things they had done together, and the time that had passed since their first encounter.

"I think we have covered enough distance. I need to go back." Lily stopped and stretched her hand, which Barasa shook gently. Without releasing it, he told her that he loved her, only to be met with silence.

They stood there for a full minute looking at each other until the *ngling ngling ngling* ringing of the bell ofan approaching bicycle pinged.

When Barasa learnt about the rape incident a day later, a flood of swirling emotions swept in his mind. The news made him feel as if someone had stabbed the deep chambers of his heart with a blunt dagger. On that day, he aimlessly walked through the village paths, throwing pebbles at birds in the maize plantations and plucking leaves from roadside shrubs. Later on, he went home, lay on the bed under the darkness of his hut and cried for the rest of the day. The following day, he visited her with a small gift. And he said he still loved her. But Lily felt so unclean and unwanted that she doubted if anyone would still love her. If anyone would ever marry her.

Lily now completely avoided people and the market. Her mother, who started knitting a small shawl for the expected child, would go to the market instead. That gave Barasa time to talk to her often. He spoke of many plans before and after the birth of the child. He suggested male and female names, but she laughed it off saying her parents would name the child. She no longer enjoyed Barasa's company but failed to get the right words to put him off. At times, she thought Barasa and everyone else looked at her with judging eyes.

* * *

Early March that year, Koffi Annan left the country, leaving Oluyemi Adeniji from Nigeria to lead talks on pending issues. In Kitale, Lubao lost his tract of land to Mashamba who had forged a sales agreement with the help of the area Chief and land officials. Mashamba had bribed them heavily and illegally obtained atitle deed. Lubao's attempt to have him vacate the land didn't succeed. Neitherdid his efforts through the courts where he filed a case, promising his lawyer part of the land since he had no money. As soon as the case commenced, the lawyer was bribed to drop the case. He tried a few other lawyers, but the story was a replica of the previous one.

Lubao indefatigably fought on. With his persistence, Mashamba got other avenues to finish him. Lubao was served an injunction and court orders never to trespass on the land. One morning, police arrived at his home and arrested him on false accusations of 'trespass'.

For three weeks, Francisca and Lily never saw him despite visiting the chief and the police station umpteen times. The next time they heard of Lubao, he was in a hospital. They were welcomed by a nauseating smell of a disinfectant that sent Lily retching up a stream of vomit. From the hospital fence, *boda boda* cyclists and fruit vendors watched her with sympathy.

"*Emiandu ne liime,*" Francisca told him from his hospital bed. She said it in a soft, nonchalant voice, as if for each sound to land on his ears as soft, and not to change the meaning to anything else other than *riches are dew.*

Lubao didn't respond. He was pallid, as a ghost, and with the silence of a mouse. He looked at them with a taut expression and faint eyes that gazed far past them into stretches of the days ahead. Days that promised misery. Behind Francisca, Lily stood. Barasa was behind her.

"What happened, my husband? Are you okay?"

Lubao's fingers trembled as he struggled to write them a note. From that day, they knew he would never again speak. Whatever they did to his sense of hearing, only he knew. He wiped his face, and Lily ran out of the ward – a large hall that reeked of despair – to cry too. Barasa ran after her and tried to hold her, but she shrugged his hands away, and when he tried again, she paced even faster.

Sitting behind the hospital ward, emotions seeped into her. Lily sunk her lower lip into her mouth and bit it hard that it bled. She cried. Were it not for her, her father wouldn't have even met Mashamba. She cried, and Barasa let her, silently wishing to console her even just for the pleasure of wrapping his hand around her shoulder, or letting her cry into the sleeves of his new blue shirt. Barasa would later bring her methylated spirit and an ointment that she applied on the curved dotted wounds under her lower lip.

* * *

With each passing day, the life Lily carried grew. Many times, she thought of ingesting anything lethal that could eliminate the baby or herself. That rape had intruded into her privacy and she now felt ashamed and afraid. She felt it was better to not be alive. Bending to sweep the house, cooking or picking utensils became difficult. People looked at her suspiciously, further increasing her depression. On her way to an antenatal clinic one morning, she had to dodge her secondary school teacher and duck into the Chief's camp. Villagers had crammed at the Chief's camp to make reports of stolen livestock, and the flag was trundling half-mast because the country had lost Minister Kipkalya Kones and Assistant Minister Lorna Laboso in a plane crash. Still, she felt as though the smell of her shame could easily be picked by those around her, or as though an invisible person among them was pointing at her, "That's the one that was raped".

Time went by, but Barasa's love could not be overshadowed by the stigma, especially created by his relatives who tried to advise him to cut links with her. Though he never mentioned any of that to Lily, she could feel some indifference. By mid-August, Barasa had bought most of the basic things for the expected child to complement what Lily's parents had already bought for her.

"Would you please loan me some money?" Lily requested Barasa, who after asking how much she wanted, promised to give her as soon as he could. Lily was planning to go to a distant hospital where no one knew her. A hospital where she could leave the child after delivery. She harboured a painful feeling that she would have a child whose father she didn't know. A child she didn't want. And to her, leaving the child at the hospital would be better than an abortion. At least the government, or anyone would adopt the child, or so she thought. She was even ready to handle thousands of questions about the child's whereabouts that would arise from her parents.

One Sunday after the mass, Francisca was seated with Mary, a member of her church under a tree within her compound. Lily and

55

Barasa were also seated under an adjacent tree, conversing. Mary hastily whispered to Francisca that she should try to seek justice at the recently constituted TJRC, Truth, Justice and Reconciliation Commission.

"The sooner you do it the better. You know with time details fade as victims forget or the pain caused to them is underestimated by the authorities."

"But it's late, and we don't know any of the perpetrators," Francisca responded while peeling a cassava. "But I've tried to be strong for her, though I can see she has been very affected. I wonder how many other young girls out there have been raped and have nobody to support them."

Just then, Lily started complaining of pain. Luckily, Barasa rushed for a motorcycle that rushed Lily to a hospital.

She spent the whole afternoon in labour pain, which disappeared after a while, and she remained in the ward getting traumatised by the agony of other women in labour.

"It's not yet time," a nurse had said.

Later in the evening, Lily's amniotic sac erupted and she thought the child was coming, yet there were no labour pains. They waited, for several hours, before the doctor finally announced, "Your waters have broken, but there's no sign of labour yet. If we keep waiting, both you and the child are at risk of infection. So, we have to induce your labour."

"Mama! I'm dying, mama! Woooi, mama woooi!" she cried with the corresponding cervical dilation after the induction. Being young and inexperienced, it was a daunting task, and the pain was rending. Francisca patted her shoulders, rubbed her back and said, "Be strong, my daughter. Don't you know you are the only one I have? Push!" For the first time, Lily wished she knew who the father to the unborn child was.

When a nurse handed over the baby to her, she looked away. Francisca took the child as tears started rolling down Lily's cheeks. It didn't take long before Lily fell into a deep sleep from the medication she had been injected with. Her sleep was cut short by the cry of her baby.

"Please, breastfeed the child," a nurse told her. When Lily didn't say anything or even look at the child, which surprised the nurse, the nurse stared at Francisca,who said nothing, then threw a glance at Lily and said with a commanding voice, "You have to!"

When Lily turned to take the baby, she felt an indescribable wave take over her. She breastfed him and he fell asleep almost immediately.

On that day, Jim burst forth prematurely into Lily's world, a month before the expected due date. His birth would shift Lily's dreams, priorities, aspirations and the desires and plans she had for her family.

Had it not been for the delay in Barasa loaning her the money, her unexpected onset of labour pain, and her mother's constant presence, she would have managed to get to a different hospital and leave the child there for the world to take care of. But now that the child was here with her, she had to suppress the depressing feelings she bore within.

Chapter Six

From the onset of his birth, many times Francisca had to force Lily to breastfeed the baby. She would also try to counsel Lily to accept the child. Lily rarely stepped out of their hut, or brought the child out with her. She would hide the child from the world most of the time. And the few times she was forced to go fetch water down the stream, she always felt the loudness of the silence of people she met, and would imagine them saying behind her, "She's the one that was raped."

As the baby grew, Lily slowly started accepting him. Barasa would also visit, bringing with him baby powder, shawls, oil, diapers, and other supplies. After failing in his secondary school examinations, he had refused to repeat as his parents had suggested. How could he go back to a class that Lily had successfully completed? No! He had a better way of proving that he was not stupid, he thought. So, he had set up a shop from where he now got money to support Lily. Apart from the business, he had also pursued a diploma course in electrical wiring at a local polytechnic.

Francisca took it upon herself to teach Lily how to bring up Jim well. And it didn't take long before Lily grasped the basics. The more Francisca taught her, the more she perfected the art.

One time, Barasa was so impressed with Lily's care of Jim, that he wished it were his son. He had gone to their homestead to accompany Lily to Jim's immunisation clinic. He watched Lily apply jelly on Jim's back and butt – the size of two fists clumped together. Jim was lying on her lap, back up. A basin with soapy water, the colour of milk, was beside her on a bench under the tree. His hair was soft and silky. It looked like the immature corn silk Lily used to put on the heads of the dolls she moulded as a child. It reminded Lily of James' daughter, Cindy, and her one-arm doll.

It irked Lily that she was now a mother with new responsibilities, and that she had to think of ways to fend for Jim. Her mother's small vegetable business at the marketplace wasn't doing well even though Lily had thought of joining her. She also thought of manual labour on other people's farms but that seemed so heavy for her.

"Welcome, Barasa," Lily said. She didn't shorten his name this time. She hoped he got the message that his presence no longer excited her. His presence irked her, and the fact that he kept coming.

Jim's arms and face bore swollen, pink marks of mosquito bites. He looked cute and delicate. Lily sucked mucus out of Jim's clogged nostrils and spat it out behind them. She then removed a particle of mucus stuck on the wall of his nostril using a matchstick and then dressed him up. Had Barasa arrived when Jim was being lifted out of the water, he would have taken him and thrown him into the air. Even though she didn't love Jim, such play worried Lily; she worried that Jim would slip from Barasa's hands and smash his head on the ground. Barasa could crush his clear spectacles, too, trying to save Jim. But that was just a thought, an imagination.

"Thanks. Where is mama?"

"She went to the market," Lily said as she fished out her left breast from the bra to breastfeed Jim. At this point, Barasa missed their childhood. A childhood in which, back in 1999, they had sat under the jamun tree and he had taken her through his book, pointing out the names of the politicians whose photos were glued therein.

"Time flies, right?" "Yeah, it's almost eleven."

"I mean we've come from far," Barasa said. He wished he could

59

remind her how small her breasts had been just the other day, but smiled at the intrusive cognisance that it was supposed to be a secret.

Jim curved his soft pinkish lips upwards and outwards as if beckoning for the breast that Lily had fished out. His small fingers twisted in the air. She took the mammilla to the edge of his mouth, and his legs kicked. Elation! Lily moved back a little and gently folded him closer and inserted the nipple into his mouth. Barasa watched as she held the base of her breast for Jim. She leant her head, looking at Jim suck, and listened to the sound of milk as he swallowed in small gulps. Saliva gleamed on Jim's lips and slid down his chin as his cheeks sunk in and bulged out in the suckling process.

"Wow! You are no longer inept." Jim, still suckling, turned to look at Barasa. With no visible eyebrows and tiny lashes, his eyes shone, reflecting the colour of Barasa's shirt. His pupils were black- the colour of charcoal. Smiling at Jim, who held on to his mother tightly, Barasa fanned the young boy with a newspaper.

"Thanks, I'm still perfecting the art." She turned to look at Barasa and added, "What's new in the paper?" Barasa conveniently ignored and flipped through the newspaper. On the first page, there was a story about the Electoral Commission of Kenya. Its lawyers had argued in court that if the basis of sending the ECK commissioners home was the Kriegler Report, then all the 210 MPs should also be sent home. And that Kibaki should cease to be the legitimate head of state. Kriegler had condemned the past year's general election, saying it was flawed.

Lily passed Jim to Barasa as she went inside to change. "You keep on forgetting he's a boy," Barasa said. "Why?"

"All these flowers on his romper suit!"

It didn't take long before they set off to the hospital. On arrival, they found a horde of other mothers waiting. Some women had come with their husbands. Could she have gone there with Jim's dad if she knew him? But there was the indignation of not knowing him. For indeed, her son had a beastly father. A father whose whereabouts she wasn't sure of. Maybe he was a coward who couldn't show up and own up to his mistakes. Maybe he was as courageous as Muntadhar al-Zaidi, the journalist who had thrown his shoe at US President George W. Bush while on a tour in Iraq. "This is a farewell kiss from the Iraqi people," Barasa had imitated al-Zaidi as he related to her the story when it unfolded.

At the clinic, Lily handed Jim's birth notification card to the nurse attending to them. In the card, there was only her name and Jim's; a name which she had just disinterestedly and randomly picked from nowhere.

"What's the father's name?" The nurse raised her eyes to look at Barasa, then back to Lily when Barasa said nothing.

"He doesn't have..." Lily said, feeling so ashamed and choked by a sudden ball of pain in her throat. She wished Barasa had not accompanied her.

"Virgin b..." the nurse almost asked Lily if it had been a virgin birth, a miraculous one, but instead with a weird look, said, "You see, this is important. We can still attend to you without the father's name, if you want, but these documents will be important later in his life. For example, when applying for his birth certificate or in future when he's applying for his identification card or any other...."

"Could you just please proceed without the father's name?" Barasa interjected. "If it's okay with you," she directed it to Lily, who nodded.

Later when they were walking home, Lily asked Barasa not to bother accompanying her to the clinic visits. That was hurtful, but he accepted, understanding how difficult and embarrassing it had been for Lily.

By now, many people had also known what happened to her and some would openly make remarks to hurt her. They mostly consisted of those who had not performed as well as she did in school, those who had dropped out to marry or get married, or those whose children had not been as smart as she was. This was their time to shine, so they imagined. Some would even use her as an example while warning their daughters about men, as though the rape was something Lily had asked for. Some warned their sons from talking to her lest she brought bad omen to their families. She bore a strong hatred for men now, and though Barasa still loved her genuinely despite his family being against it, Lily tried to avoid him. And she felt that raising and providing for her child was too much to bear.

One afternoon, she wrote a letter to Jim and to her parents:

My dearest Jim, I believe by the time you get to read this you'll have found out the details of your conception, and the circumstances under which I choose to do what I did....

She stopped writing as tears welled in her eyes. Composing herself, she wrote a full page, enclosed her only photo with it in an envelope and placed it in a place she was sure her parents would easily see. Since she had no money to buy a rope, she made one from pieces of her clothes, climbed a small table and tied it to the roof of their hut.   Unfortunately for her, the clothes were too old to withstand her weight, and her attempt failed.

She hid the letter for future use. But the following day, she tried to kill Jim instead; by pressing his face against her old mattress to suffocate him, but Francisca arrived just in time to save him, though Lily was quick to pull Jim out before Francisca noticed what was happening.

"Stop crying, my daughter," Francisca said when she saw Lily's teary eyes. She didn't know it was not only the pain of having the child but also the shame and guilt of wanting to eliminate him that was eating Lily from the inside. Francisca took Jim, who was crying on the mattress, "It will be okay, Nekesa. Never lose hope. It shall be okay."

On the Tuesday of Barack Obama's inauguration as the 44th President of the USA, and as al-Zaidi received a 90-minute trial in an Iraqi court, Jim produced sounds as if talking. His growth only served to remind Lily that she was no longer a kid; that her youthfulness had been robbed by his intrusion and that she now had bills to pay, and forever be responsible for another life. That she had a lot to take care of, things that she had no means of fully taking care of. That frustrated her. So, when an old friend, Pauline, met Lily on her way to the vaccination clinic and shared with her about an opening in their company, Lily didn't have to think about it. Pauline had just arrived from the city where she worked for a cleaning company.

"I'm sorry for what you're going through," she said to Lily. "Please apply for this job. You never know!"

Though Lily's predicament had started in the same city where she now thought of applying for the job, she convinced herself that *'a snake didn't bite one twice.'* Besides, going to the city would give her relief from the village and the society that, to her, seemed so judgmental and cruel. She would be away from their eyes and silent whispers. She would be away from their stigmatisation; away in a society where nobody knew of her or what had happened to her.

Before travelling back to the city, Pauline spoke to her supervisor on phone and helped Lily send her application from a cybercafé in Kitale town. Lily was assured of the job, and she was to travel to the city the following week.

Because Lily was sure her parents would not agree with her going back to the city, she lied to them that she had gotten a job in Bungoma; a town not so far from home, and where they had one or two relations. So, it would be easy for her to visit them. When she informed her parents, they were hesitant but understood how dire their situation was at home. They needed a lot more than they could manage to get, so, it only made sense for Lily to get the job even though the very difficult decision to leave Jim behind had to be made.

Chapter Seven

Samantha got married in late 1970. When her husband, Kyalo Godana, had to leave after getting a job as a labourer in the construction of Voi-Mwatate road, she remained home with her mother-in-law and helped her to manage household chores.

Her husband had hoped that she would conceive in the first two weeks of their marriage for no night went by without them making love. Several months later, he got disappointed with Samantha for not bearing him a child. Despite that, he still sent some little cash and wrote letters affirming his love for her.

At first, life was easy. Samantha enjoyed the hospitality of her husband's people. But once they started looking for accusations against her, she started frequenting her parents' home which was also in Tana River, just a few kilometres away. Visiting them invited more insults and accusations. Some of Kyalo's close relatives claimed that she went to her home regularly to bring charms for their son. They averred that she was out to cast a spell on their son so that he could send her all the money he earned. Worst of all was the allegation that she intentionally didn't want to bear him a child.

After the Voi-Mwatate road was completed in 1971, and even

President Jomo Kenyatta had visited, Kyalo was rendered jobless and thus returned home. An outbreak of cholera spread through Tana River that year, and unfortunately, Kyalo Godana succumbed to it. The accusations that Samantha had killed him were too heavy for her to bear. So, she left her husband's home, for good.

Samantha's parents refused to accommodate her. They were more worried about what Kyalo's bereaved family would think or say of them, and the perception of the community than they were for the wellbeing of their daughter. Her father, who drank so much and punched his wife in equal measure, was also aggressively against Samantha's presence in the home. So, they sent her back to her husband's family.

Feeling rejected by both her husband's family and her own, Samantha decided to move to Mombasa and start a new life. She used the little money she had saved. While in Mombasa, she met a lady who introduced her to the business of buying and selling clothes imported from Kampala, Uganda.

After a short while, they diversified into maize and coffee business because it was more lucrative. Samantha bought maize from Kitale while the friend bought coffee that was smuggled into Kenya through the border point at Busia from Uganda. The two ladies shared the proceeds.

The notion about any family relation of hers or that of her late husband was met by nursed anger and hatred. All she wanted was to make money and get a child so as to prove a point to the people she now hated. So, when she incidentally met Lubao in Kitale one afternoon in February 1973, and he hinted at an urge to make love to her, Samantha agreed. Thereafter, she was the one who pursued him. Top on her mind was trying to get a child again, not marriage. And so, a month later, Juma was conceived. To avoid Lubao, and stop him from later claiming the child, Samantha abandoned her maize business, relocated to Nairobi and started running a food kiosk. She swore to herself never to return to Kitale.

* * *

Juma was already in primary school when the 8-4-4 education system was introduced. He was a bright pupil who excelled in class and in extra-curricular activities. Samantha felt proud to have him as a son.

When Juma, among other boys, was selected to entertain President Moi during the Moi Day celebrations of 1990, Samantha bought him a pair of *Sandak* shoes only for them to burn his feet under the scorching sun.

* * *

Years later, thoughts of visiting Tana River crossed Samantha's mind; just so she could prove to everyone back there that she had not been the problem; that it was Kyalo who had failed to impregnate her. She also contemplated taking Juma to Kitale to meet his father. But news of tribal clashes in the Rift Valley made her drop the thought.

When she finally visited her home with her nineteen-year-old son for the first time, a shiver ran through her body on seeing her ageing mother. Their first reaction after greetings was tears. Her father was not at home; he had moved to Likoni for work.

* * *

Juma's earliest memories of his father were imaginations from narrations of his mother. She lied that his father had died in the cholera outbreak in Tana River and that he had no relative that she knew of at the time of his death. When Juma asked her about his father's home, she said they had met in Mombasa town, then moved to Tana River and that he hadn't disclosed his place of birth.

"Where was he buried?" Juma had asked.

"My dear, during that time, I had no money to pay for burial space at the public cemetery. I had to run away and hide from the municipality people. When I went back a week later with some money, I was informed he had been buried by the council. There was no one I could get more information from." Samantha advanced her lies further.

Juma looked at her, confused. And when he wanted to prod further, Samantha warned him never to ask after his father again. He never did even though he had the urge to when they went, a year later, to bury Samantha's parents who had perished in the Mtongwe ferry accident of April 1994.

Juma assumed he had been rejected by his father. Therefore, he decided that yearning for a fatherly figure to look up to had no significance. He consoled himself most of the time with the radio set his mother bought him, listening to the students' programme by Billy Omala, or BBC news in the evenings. Jerome Danford Kassembe and Mwamoyo Hamza of BBC became his favourite radio journalists. He followed the story of the Rwandan genocide closely that it felt like a personal loss when the death of Captain Mbaye Diagne, a Senegalese military officer and a UN Military Observer, was announced.

* * *

Juma grew and joined the Medical school at the University of Nairobi. One day, while at the *Kitchen 1* mess, a lady he had been chasing smiled at him. He smiled back. Three weeks later, he took her out to a dance in town. Her name was Riziki. It was during the dance that Juma swept Riziki completely off her feet. That night, he finally said, "I love you, Riziki."

"Okay," was all she said.

"Riziki," Juma called, two years after they had first gone out to the dance. They were having a drink in town. "Will you marry me?" He proposed with a silver ring, traced her lips with his own that night, and they got married a year later.

In the first months of their marriage, Juma would leap out of bed to prepare breakfast and serve her in bed. But most of the time, they prepared it together. With time, Juma receded from the kitchen chores.

But Riziki didn't cook as much as he had expected. He was forced to employ a househelp. But still, he opened the car door for her, carried her handbag and brought her flowers. He bought a washing machine, but it was the househelp who pegged his clothes out to dry.

Juma didn't like how Riziki slowly morphed with the increase of months in their marriage. She appreciated less what he did now. In March 2007, when Safaricom first launched M-Pesa – a mobile money transfer service – Juma had sent her money through his phone, hoping to surprise her with the new invention. But Riziki didn't show the excitement he expected. She was just nonchalant.

As Juma's career at the Ministry of Health flourished, so did Riziki's demands. They now lived a good life in a good neighbourhood. The office he held came along with a lot of opportunities for bribery and mega-corrupt deals, especially from pharmaceutical companies and related institutions interested in government tenders. With such sources of illicit cash, Juma was able to fulfil not only Riziki's demands but also his mother's needs as well as his business deals. And he had several that he did secretly with his trusted business partners; secrets that only sat on their tongues.

Juma ran most of those errands from places he would less likely be caught, some out of the country. He would meet Lily on one such occasion when he was travelling out of the country to meet an accomplice.

Chapter Eight

The smoky light of Nairobi's dawn and the orange glare of neon street lights reminded her of the first time she had come to the city. Her heart lurched. She didn't want to think of it! Yet she thought of Mathare and the small room she once lived in and the small dark corridors that, for the first time, she wondered how the occupants had managed to get furniture into their rooms. Yet she thought of James and his wife and Junior and Cindy. And she mused at how dwellers in Mathare owned padlocks that were more expensive than their phones. She thought of all the things she didn't want to think of, and how lucky she had been to survive.

People were already rushing to their different destinations, and hawkers shouted for customers in the streets. For the first time, she spoke to the passenger she was seated next to.

"Would you kindly show me where the National Archives is?"

"You know Tom Mboya Street?" She nodded, ashamed that she didn't. As if it was a by-law that every person was supposed to know. "Okay. The best you can do is to get to the city centre and locate your way from there..." Lily was about to ask when he added, "Come, I will show you the city centre."

With her bag, she followed him. They crossed Landhies Road amidst speeding vehicles, then past a bus terminus with many minibuses and touts incessantly shouting "Mayakos! Kitui! Mbooni! Mwingi!" One of the touts, near some brightly painted kiosks playing fast-paced Kamba music, was trying to grab a passenger's luggage. Lily stole a glance at them before walking on, past an old market building that seemed deserted. On the sides, there were heaps of banana leaves strewn next to several handcarts.

"Is it your first time in the city?" The man asked. They were approaching a group of skinny *chokora*, street urchins, playing cards at a roundabout. Two of them, with brown hair the colour of countryside soil, had transparent bottles of glue, hanging by their sore lips. With black stains of dust on the bottle, the glue inside looked dirty as well. The glue, which had formed small bubbles inside the bottle, looked like undiluted honey. Their clothes were filthy. Houseflies rose in a buzz every time they raised their arms to drop a card on a piece of carton at the centre of their circle.

"Yes," she lied. She didn't want to talk about what happened. They crossed Racecourse Road. The traffic was crawling towards the city.

She made long strides to catch up with him, trembling at the sight of *chokoras*. Had Karisa Maitha - a Minister who had once cleared the streets of the urchins – been alive, things would have been different. One of them noticed Lily's timidness and laughed, covering his mouth with a cupped hand to conceal missing front teeth. He was dressed in an orange campaign T-shirt, a pair of brown khakitrousers and worn-out sneakers. There was one very young boy that made Lily keep looking back as if to see if his mother would appear. She looked until a seething mammoth of humanity blocked her view. At some point, she tripped on a stone and then decided to concentrate on the direction they were heading. "Why them, dear God?" She asked, and wondered, *who then*? "Bless them, dear God," she prayed.

They passed vendors selling SIM cards and handkerchiefs behind *Jack and Jill Supermarket;* past buses opposite Ronald Ngala Post Office – buses determined to rip her eardrums apart with their unrelenting honking. Their engines roared, emitting clouds of smoke behind them as the touts shouted. When the buses' drivers didn't stop for them to cross, they stopped for the buses. Everything seemed so urgent.

"You'll go that way. I'm late for work." Lily didn't know exactly which street he had pointed at. "And be careful with your luggage." When she turned to thank him, the man was gone; vanished into the growing ocean of humanity. It was as if it had been waiting to swallow him up. Luckily, a middle-aged woman showed her where the National Archives was, from where she was to be picked by Pauline.

Nursing her bag between her legs, she wondered how she could communicate with Pauline since she had no phone and could not see a public phone booth around.

And yet as she stood outside the National Archives, hawkers kept coming to her, each appraising their wares. She could only shrug them off. As luck would have it, Pauline finally arrived and spotted Lily.

They left for Pauline's single-room house in Ngara where she would be staying with Lily. The following day, she started a week's training before starting the job at the Jomo Kenyatta International Airport. She was assigned the International Departure lobby, washroom, and corridors around all the duty-free shops. It was a lot of work for her to clean all that area, but was grateful she had a job that earned her some good money. Transportation to and from Ngara was provided by the company. During her stay with Pauline, they had agreed to split the house bills.

Even though the job was tedious, it pleased her that her parents could now afford the privilege of two meals a day and Jim's needs would be met. She didn't get the means to communicate with them often, and it was a relief for her to forget about Jim. But she would send them money through Akamba Bus Services, then send a word to them using Pauline's phone.

She was glad to be so busy that she had no time to think of Jim and the uncertainties of having him. And now that Jim had been forced to stop breastfeeding and taking porridge instead, Lily wondered if she would have tried to poison his porridge. She was still bitter and felt like nobody understood what she felt. She felt like everyone was silently blaming her for what had happened.

Only a few times did she imagine if, like their neighbour in Ngara, or like other mothers, she would ever miss him or look forward to going home every day after work and finding him asleep. If she would, at that moment, sit by his side, looking down at him and watching him sleeping peacefully or sleepily sucking his fingers. If she would watch him for hours and in the process lose track of time. If, like other mothers, she would see a future doctor, a pilot or an engineer in her sleeping son. If at some point she would feel like apologising to him for having taken out her anger and frustration on him. For having tried to kill him and herself too. But she was not the other mothers, and they were not her, and they shared no common experience.

Back at home, Francisca prepared porridge or, a few times, mashed potatoes for Jim. She would then cradle him on her lap, with a bib around his neck, block his nostrils and feed him the porridge from her palm, curved around his mouth. She would then wash him and rock him in her arms, humming lullabies until he slept.

At work, Lily's supervisor started making passes at her, even though he was a married man. It never lured Lily even when he would promise to increase her pay. Her adamant refusal led to her being assigned more duties. Lily never gave in. She also didn't tell Pauline about it. Despite all that, Lily dispensed her duties with unabated ease. The picture of her family at the back of her mind always refuelled her determination.

By now Lily's parents had received, on her behalf, an admission letter to the University of Nairobi. The letter had been delivered to them by Lily's former school's head. When she got the letter, she was worried and excited at the same time. She would now skip her lunches to save money for her university education basic needs, though she was to get a student loan from the Higher Education Loan Board, HELB. Although saving most of her earnings also meant less money sent to support her family, especially her father who had been in and out of the hospital oftentimes, she was motivated by the chance she had to uplift their standards of living in the distant future.

While her local school celebrated her for making its name shine, her mother was hesitant about her daughter's stay in Nairobi, which was even worsened by her being invited to join the University of Nairobi. By now, they had already known she was in Nairobi and not Bungoma.

"Any sane person that went through what my daughter experienced would not think of going back to that city." Francisca would lament to her friend Mary. "But if that's what she chose, and is sure of it, so be it. It's a consolation that she gets something for her son and us," she would add.

"You shouldn't worry, Francisca. God will protect her." Mary would reassure Francisca.

"What about what happened to her? Why was she not protected?" Francisca would ask, looking away with a film of tears in her eyes.

"I understand...." Mary would search for words before adding, "Please hold on to faith. Have strong faith that nothing bad will happen to her again."

Back in Nairobi, Lily was still afraid of men and would always try to hang around her friend when they were not at work. She never went out. At work, she rarely talked. She never even got awed by the planes that kept taking off or landing; her mind was always preoccupied by her past experience and the responsibilities she now had. She would do her work silently and swiftly, except when someone talked to her; like this day when a gentleman needed some help.

"Excuse me, ma'am, good afternoon. Would you please show me where the gents are?"

"Good afternoon, sir," Lily said, turning to look at the person whose sweet scent of *Versace Eros* cologne had first announced his presence even before Lily saw him. He was a middle-aged man in a sharp expensive grey suit, chequered with faint dark grey lines. "Actually," she paused, searching for the right words, and when she recollected herself, she pointed, "this way sir." She was stunned and confused by the soft seductive look in the man's eyes. The distant, airy and sensually intoxicating scent of his cologne made her wish she could hug him and rub some of it on her dress. For those few seconds when she looked at

73

him, she forgot about all the problems she had ever had.

"Thank you, ma'am," he said with a few slow blinks. "Have a pleasant day,"he added very politely; careful with his choice of words.

But even after he had left, and Lily felt like he turned to look at her, she suddenly became aware of how much she was inhaling the air filled with the scent of his perfume. From then on, Lily would go to the duty-free shops selling perfumes to just window-shop during her breaks. And while she window-shopped andgot ignored in those shops by the sales ladies who continued browsing on their phones, the man with a sweet scent of *Versace Eros* cologne would be thinking of Lily and wondering why he hadn't asked for her number.

* * *

After ten uneventful months and having saved enough to help her with her university admission, it was time for Lily to go back home. When her dad, Lubao, got ill just a few days before she travelled home, she sent part of her savings for his re-admission to the hospital.

Jim was so grown up and looked so healthy. Francisca must have taken good care of him. Lily wasn't so excited to meet him. At first, Jim didn't recognizeher and it took a whole day before he could allow her to hold him without him crying. Lily wasn't excited about meeting Barasa either, who kept passing by rightafter he learnt that Lily had arrived.

Barasa helped Lily to move from one office to another, filling in the pre-admission forms, and to open a student bank account for her HELB stipend. He also assisted her to shop for a few essential items.

For those few days she was home, Lily visited her father frequently. On that specific day, she spent the entire afternoon beside her father's hospital bed. She even silently wept when her father had fallen asleep, imagining how she would miss him and the kind of burden her mother, whose health was also deteriorating,was forced to carry. She cried at the thought of her mother struggling to get money to buy food, his father's medications and Jim's supplies. And still, she had to attend to chores at home and a backlog of other duties that would be piling up every splitting second. Lily silently wept beside her father's bed until another patient's caretaker called her aside and admonished. "My daughter, don't do that. It's very wrong! You're killing the old man while he's still alive!"

"I haven't seen Barasa today," Lily's mother said one mid-morning.

"He must be busy, but I'll pass by his shop on my way," Lily responded. As a matter of fact, Barasa spent the entire morning in his house saddened by her looming departure. It was as if he hadn't seen it coming. He went to his shop later in the afternoon.

A chicken, which would be part of their meal later, clucked loudly as it ran around the hut almost knocking down *mukherekha,* traditional lye that Francisca had set outside.

"*Cha okule uto,*" Francisca called from outside, sending her to buy *uto*, cooking oil. Lily left with a plastic cup and five shillings. Francisca was preparing vegetables, her legs stretched before her as she sang a Catholic hymn in a monotone, *Hodi hodi nyumbani mwako bwana, ninabisha nifungulie.* On the traditional winnowing tray were a mixture of cowpeas, nalta jute and squash leaves. She was still removing the prickly squash vines when Lily came back.

Later that evening, before she left for the *green city in the sun*, mother and daughter embraced in a prolonged hug and both of them soaked their faces with sullenness.

"Please, don't be sad, mum. All will be well," she assured Francisca that she would be coming home as often as she could, provided she got time and money. "And when I finally complete my studies, things will change for the better. Everything, I promise," she said with a distant gaze, before adding, "I'll build you a good house. You'll no longer be casual labourers. I promise to reclaim our land, and we'll employ people to work on our farm at good wages." She wiped the tears streaking her cheeks and pulled back the mucus that was peeping out of her nostrils. Lily didn't know how she would achieve that dream, but deep inside her, she knew she would.

"I know, my daughter. I pray for you a lot. My little girl, I know you've gone through so much in your short life. And I know, for sure, better things are in the future for you. I'm happy I brought forth such a strong woman! Many wouldn't have managed the trouble your tender shoulders have carried, and that which your heart has sustained…" Lily wore a forcible smile, and wondered if they were tears she saw in her mother's eyes or were they her own? Francisca pulled her *khanga* and wiped her face. "Have a sit Nekesa," she said at last.

They sat on a bench, a log fixed on forked pillars on the ground under a tree in front of the hut. The sun's warmth patted Francisca's back and shone on Lily's hair. She had plaited it a day before at the market.

"You see, my daughter, you may still face challenges at the university. Let it not discourage you or make you feel like the world has come to an end." She paused. "Nekesa, you know that we love you, right?"

"Yes, mama, I know."

"We always will," she bent to pick a dry stalk. "Please, let nothing induce you to indulge yourself in any unlawful acts. Stick to what is taking you there. Don't worry so much about us. We have always managed. Besides, there's so little you can change for now." She chuckled. "And Jim is very fine and safe."

"I know, mum, and I don't know how I'll ever thank you enough."

"You already have, my daughter. When you go to the university, don't strain because of anything that concerns us back here at home." She said. When Lily said nothing, she added, "In 1 Corinthians 10:13, it is written that *No temptation has overtaken you except what is common to mankind. And God is faithful; He will not let you be tempted beyond what you can bear. But when you are tempted, He will also provide a way out so that you can endure it.* Do you understand?"

"Yes, mum."

"Good. Don't worry much about us. So, Lily…" with reluctance in her tone, Francisca started before she paused, and then with the edge of a crispy mango leaf that produced a cracking sound against her fingers, wiped a bird's droppings from her *khanga*. Looking up, the hawk that had pooped screeched as it flapped noisily into the distant sky. Throwing the leaf away, she continued, "don't worry about us. In case of any eventuality, please be strong and continue to pursue your dreams."

Lily bit her teeth so tightly that her jaws showed and her eyes moistened. Francisca kept quiet for a while, wishing she hadn't instilled worry in her daughter.

"I hear you mum, but I pray that everything will be alright." Her mother's request had sent deep twinges into her nerves.

"Sure, my daughter. *Omanyiree yolile mwo siifwao bhuloho*?" "You know the animal that gets to the river cannot die of thirst?" Lily nodded. "Your father will be happy to learn that his child has joined university. You know what?" Francisca paused before continuing, "There is nothing that has ever given us pride, except you and your achievements. So, my daughter, keep on making us walk with our heads high!"

Francisca softly patted Lily's shoulder and flashed a broad smile, ear to ear, only blurred by the tears on both of their faces. Faces that bore many similarities, both in beauty and smile.

There was a brief silence. "Come close," Francisca said, unwrapping her *khanga* from the waist. She then untied a knot at its edge and took out a folded one-hundred-shilling note, smiling. She clasped her daughter's hand, pressed the note into her palm and closed Lily's fingers around it.

"Nekesa, this is just one hundred shillings…" Lily unfolded her hand and looked at the note in her palm. The portrait of Mzee Jomo Kenyatta, Kenya's first President, was conspicuous on the left-hand side of the note. The dominant shades of blue and violet, among other colours on the margin, formed a nice pattern on the note. The Court of Arms – printed at the centre –with shades of pink and green looked beautiful. The date *1ˢᵗ July 1978* was printed just next to the court of arms; on the right-hand side.

"Yes, mum, one hundred shillings," she nodded in agreement.

"I've kept that note for…" Francisca stopped, looked at Lily and asked, "How old are you?" Lily responded, and her mother continued, "Yes, I've kept it for exactly the number of years you've lived." She wiped a thin film of tears that hadn't even formed well before continuing, "…it was a painful experience yearning for a child, and

77

when I gave birth to you, we drowned ourselves in an ocean of happiness and gratitude to the Almighty. That was long ago, and that note was my gift from your father. That was the best he could afford back then, and it really meant a lot to me. That's why I kept it till now. When he gave me the note, he asked me to buy with it anything that pleased my heart. And it was a lot of money back then!" She chuckled at the memory. "You see my daughter, but I didn't use it. I told myself that this note would be a personal and very special gift to you from your mum. I had thought of an occasion like your wedding day or something...but we can't be sure if we have much time left to witness that..."

"God forbid, mother! You'll even carry Jim's children," Lily was quick to chip in, her heart swelling, that even words escaped her tongue. Had Francisca resigned in hopes of her getting married? She wondered, or worse still, had her vision of witnessing Lily complete her university studies, get a job, and then have a good marriage, vanished with Jim's birth? Did she believe, like many others, that the prospects of a woman whose 'leg had been broken' getting married were close to zero?

"Amen," Francisca responded. "Besides, this is a very special day for our family. That's why I offer you my sincere gift. Do you accept it, my daughter?"

Kneeling in front of her mother, she said, "With all my heart, mother."

"Okay, stand up...and stop crying. We should be rejoicing, you know!" Lily smiled amidst tears. The clock was ticking off the minutes so fast. "Hey, you should be catching up with the evening bus."

They proceeded to the hut, had a long, detailed prayer and Lily prepared to leave.

They talked as Francisca leapt along. She had an injury from a hoe cut she sustained while weeding around the hut. It was a long distance. When they met Milly, who was on her way to pick up Lily, they embraced. Lily looked at Jim, who Francisca had tied on her back, one last time. The innocence in his eyes held her captive. She kissed her son for the first time. Jim looked at her, half crying and half smiling. She saw her reflection in his eyes and felt like she was leaving a part of her behind. But somehow, Lily was happy.

"My daughter, *so do not fear,* Isaiah 41:10 says, *For I am with you; do not be dismayed, for I am your God. I will strengthen you and help you; I will uphold you with my righteous right hand.* May God be with you, and may He guide you. Be the good girl I know, and work hard to be the pilot you want to be. This is the time, okay?" Francisca spoke in a hushed voice, slightly louder than a whisper.

"I'll be a good girl mum, but I already told you it's not aviation I'm going to study. This is something different," she responded in her usual polite timbre. At a road junction, they stood as though waiting for someone to permit them to bid each other farewell. Lily felt her eyes betraying her feelings. Before she left for the *green city in the sun*, they once again embraced in a prolonged hug, and both of them soaked their faces with sullenness. "Okay, travel well," Francisca said before they parted.

Lily made her way with Milly as Francisca went to the hospital, Jim on her back and a tin of food in the basket she carried with her left hand. Francisca didn't look back until she was sure Lily was gone. She mourned for the boredom and loneliness that would chore her, and the uncertainties the future promised. It was a future in which Lily would remain oblivious of her parents' worries and prayers. Only God knew if they would see each other again. Lily passed by Barasa's shop to bid him farewell. Barasa pressed a white envelope with red and blue stripes at the edges in her palm. He then escorted them to the bus stop.

When Lily finally boarded the bus, Barasa waved as he watched it slowly pick up momentum. Passengers pressed their palms to the glasses of the windows, or whispered a *bye-bye* to their kins; whispers that left the glasses fogged. But Lily didn't. She didn't even turn to smile at him. Barasa wished he had told her he loved her, as he had done before. As he stood at the bus stop watching the bus spew a massive cloud of suffocating exhaust smoke, he whispered to himself that he loved her. Very much.

Every kilometre Lily made away from home marked every kilometre she made towards her new life. She had had different aspirations with her first journey to the city. The same journey had eventually altered her priorities. For this third one, she was moving towards the bold step of searching for Jim's father; an intention known only to her

Chapter Nine

The bus Lily was travelling in ripped through the dark hills and valleys in the countryside on its way to Nairobi. The sound of its old engine thrummed in the frozen silence of the starless night, venting a cloud of exhaust smoke behind as it tore through the night's darkness. The glut of passengers and luggage were packed like sardines along the stretch of an aisle on whose end Sam Mangwana's *Bana Ba Cameroun* boomed from a speaker conveniently placed by the driver's side.

In the crowd of suffocating passengers on board, Lily sat quietly by the window staring blankly at clusters upon clusters of dark silhouettes that were shrubs and distant trees. Or maybe even zebras. Her eyes were glued to the vastness of the outside darkness. No passenger bothered to open a window. In effect, layers of their breath condensed on the windows. There was also the smell of hair oil and soiled diapers. The wind howled in through the loose spaces between windowpanes. It slapped her face with cold, but her brow remained on the window with a clear circle around it. The rest of the glass was covered with layers of vapour.

Lily's nape faced the shoulder of the next passenger. She thought of her parents and how much they had sacrificed to see her through school.

How would she reciprocate? Not even giving them the whole world could be sufficient. And she imagined her life on campus; her only chance to change their lives. She would excel in her studies and scoop awards. She envisioned herself making friends; God-fearing and bright students whose ambitions reflected her aspirations. Her mind churned with pictures of herself networking and getting valuable contacts, securing a good job, building her parents a mansion and hiring servants for them. She pictured herself driving them to Nairobi for a treat, and paying for their air tickets back to Eldoret; the nearest airport to Kitale. Imaginary images of Jim's father begging for his son and her calling the police also came floating.

Meanwhile, in room 17 of Hall 4 hostel in the University of Nairobi, a student called Halima was alone. Her roommate had not reported yet. With the excitement of being at the university, sleep wasn't coming by. She decided to call her mother and tell her about her first day's experience on campus. The phone rang, repeating over and over the dull beeping sound, but there was no response. Calling her sister with the same story would be boring, so she recited a *dua*, an invocation, and some Quran verses then slid under her duvet. But even before she had been immersed in a deep sleep, a scary yowl of a cat woke her up. "*A'udhubillahi min ash-shaytaan-irrajeem*," she said and repeated in English, "I seek Allah's protection from *shaitan*, the accursed one." She never slept again that night. That was the norm whenever she was scared or frightened. Luckily on that night, her roommate was on her way to the city.

The song in the bus changed to Aurlus Mabele's *Liste Rouge*. At that point, Lily remembered Barasa's envelope. She would read it the following day, she told herself. The bus raced up a hill, shortening the distance between Lily and her dreams, or so she thought.

"I'll soon pay for Baba's cochlear implant," she whispered to herself as the bus approached Nakuru town. The street lights cast orange beams some distance ahead as the bus slowed down into a petrol station for a stopover.

With the next passenger leaning on her for the rest of the journey, and the smell of his sweaty armpits, the journey seemed longer than it should. Tankers and trucks loaded with farm produce or bags of charcoal overtook the bus as their brake lights blinked. Cars and Nissan matatus shone indicator lights as they dangerously overtook the trucks. The bus driver's foot was less generous with the accelerator, keen to avoid knocking down zebras that grazed and monkeys that made love by the roadside at Gilgil.

* * *

"I'm telling you, in all honesty, I have no problem with Riziki. She's the problem; always doubtful and disrespectful...Yes, she doesn't treat me like her husband... Aaaa, no! I provide for her...everything...I try so much to treat her as best as I can...but she doesn't seem to appreciate...anything! Since the birth of our daughter, she has just changed...yes. And do you know how many times she has called today? She claims I'm at another woman's place. I think one of these days, I'll do exactly that...No...No!" Juma was outside the Hilton Hotel whispering on the phone in a conversation with a confidant. As he spoke, his mind swirled with various images of his wife, leaning against the bedroom door, as she addressed him disrespectfully. "So, you see....," he was abruptly interrupted by the image of a beautiful lady he saw across the street. ".... wait.... wait, I'll call you back shortly."

Juma had just arrived at the Hilton Hotel for an early breakfast. But just as he had started the conversation, while waiting for his driver to park, he saw the lady he had once met at the airport and who had not left his mind since. His heart lurched.

He looked on both sides of the street for oncoming vehicles before crossing. It was improper of him, he thought, but that was his second chance, which he wouldn't just let go of.

"Hello madam, it doesn't strike me that you're okay. Do you need any assistance?" He politely said when he approached her. He was careful with his words. The lady seemed a little confused, trying to figure out something on a piece of paper. It was directions to the University of Nairobi scribbled on it.

"Why?" She found herself mumbling. The man smiled. He looked calm, and she quickly picked up the scent of his *Tom Ford Black Orchid*

83

cologne. Lily was trying to recollect where she might have seen him.

"Just simple curiosity, and you look like you need some help." There was a timbre of genuineness and warmth in his brief smile. Lily raised her head and their eyes met. His eyes glinted with the sun's rays struggling to penetrate the morning clouds. "You helped me once, and it would be a pleasure to be of whatever small assistance to you…. We've met before, remember?" His cheeks filled out nicely as he spoke.

"We've met before?" She patted the cornrow lines to ease an itch. Her scalp, pulled by the cornrows, still shone with coconut oil she had rubbed on it along the rows of plaited hair the previous evening. The skin between her cornrows also gleamed with the chocolate colour of her skin, just like those in glossy magazines.

"Beautiful hair," he complimented her.

"Thank you, sir." But it was still itchy. She felt like inserting a stick under the cornrows and scratching the scalp.

"So, you don't remember helping me with directions at the airport?"

"Oooooh," was all she managed.

"So, where are you headed with such heavy luggage? I can help…"

"Actually," she paused, searching for the right words, and when she failed, she continued, "I am trying to find my way to Chiromo." He moved closer to look at the piece of paper she was holding. The clean, soft and sweet scent of his cologne filled her nostrils. Just like the *Versace Eros* she once smelt on him, the *Tom Ford Black Orchid* was distant and airy.

"Aaaa, in fact, I was heading in that direction." There was fresh mint in his breath. "My office is in Kileleshwa." Lily was at a loss as to where that was.

"Okay. Could you please show me how to get there, sir?"

"Sure, I can. But there is no harm if I save you the burden of getting lost. And besides, with this luggage and the many street urchins, I doubt if you can make it there safely." He paused to look at her. Lily raised her head without uttering a word. Their eyes locked again. His height guaranteed her safety. *Wow, you are beautiful*! He almost said, but coolly extended his hand for a shake, "I'm Juma."

"Lily is my name, sir," she responded with a warm smile that Juma hadn't seen even from his wife for a long time.

"Has anyone ever told you that Lily is one of the few most beautiful names?" Both of them were silent for a while before he added, "It's a pleasure meeting you."

From a brief and rushed conversation they had, Juma found Lily to be strikingly intelligent and beautiful. The glamour in her gait struck him hard, and he disregarded the feeling of guilt that came with the thought of infidelity, as though, like a male's nipples, it was nothing worth attention. Her stylish grace and quiet demeanour were innocently genuine. He was completely enthralled by her beauty. He couldn't resist the waves of attraction she radiated.

After some persuasion, she gave in to be assisted. Lily was hesitant at first. But she found Juma irresistibly persistent that she connected with him. Besides, Juma seemed so civilised, exposed, gentle, and wealthy, and there was no way he could harm her. But first, he requested that they have breakfast at the Hilton before they could proceed, and it only seemed respectful for her not to say no, she thought. He carried her luggage and she found herself flanking him as they crossed the street. At the hotel's entrance, he handed Lily's luggage to a concierge and requested him to take it to his driver who was still in the car waiting for Juma's instructions.

Juma called the driver to ask him to receive the luggage, after which he could leave the car keys at the hotel reception, and then he – the driver – would be free for the day.

"So, where exactly in Chiromo is your luggage destined? And where are you coming from?" Juma asked as they were being ushered in the hotel.

"I've just arrived from Kitale. I'm heading to the University of Nairobi's Chiromo Campus for my first-year admission."

The eyes of a few young men present followed her to her seat, yet she didn't find it awkward, it surprised her. Juma's nerves pulsated with pride. What with being in the company of a lady whose beauty stripped

85

men of their composure? A waiter welcomed them and pulled a chair for Lily. He then brought a menu and stepped aside. It humbled Lily.

Juma helped her choose from a menu she barely understood.

"*Pole, safari lazima ilikuwa ndefu,*" Juma inquired about her trip. He watched her blow the steam and then sip from the edge of her cup. She silently cooled the tea before swallowing, and said, "Thank you, sir." Then silence. Both were thinking of what to say or not say.

"Call me Juma, please." He watched her struggle with the cutlery. Though hungry, Lily nibbled at her food, twice wiping her mouth with her palm. He asked her about her home and her parents as they ate. While she responded, she was keen not to mention Jim, which made her feel guilty for secretly disowning her own. They didn't take long before heading out.

The strong lemongrass fragrance in Juma's car was even stronger than his cologne. Lily seemed distracted by the crisp aroma. "Feel free." Juma said. Lily was leaning against the door, feeling the cool leather seats on her arm. She was trying to keep some distance between them.

"So, what do you look forward to on campus?" Juma switched a button that slid the sunroof to closure.

"Aaaa," she paused to think. Beads of drizzle slipped up and down the windscreen, as the car moved, forming thousands of tiny 'tadpoles'. The intermittent wipers drifted them off as a popular hit of TPOK Jazz played from the car stereo. A waft of light steam rose from the bonnet.

"Do you know this music?" He asked.

"I have no idea, Sir." She watched a hawker run after a car with his merchandise firmly clutched in his hands.

"But isn't it beautiful?"

The wipers were still diving left and right on the screen, making a smooth screech. Traffic was building up, and the tarmac was becoming wet. On the verandas of shops, with a thousand signposts with 'browse@50 cent', 'M-Pesa Available', 'KRA PIN', 'Quick Loan on Items', people raced against time. The Nairobi weather had changed abruptly. It always did, and so some people wore thick jackets while others held tightly onto their umbrellas that kept knocking the signposts above.

"It's a beautiful song. Do you understand what they are singing about?" "Yes," he said.

She picked the newspaper on the dashboard and flipped through the pages. She now became a little comfortable in his company and was easily giving her trust. And she felt something fatherly in him; something relatable to her father, but one she couldn't clearly unravel.

"So, you were asking about the song?" She nodded. He translated each verse of *Massu* to her. At Riverside Drive, two traffic police officers were busy directing traffic. As they approached, Juma asked her, "So, you're only three in your family?"

"Yes, Sir." A lie! The drizzles had ceased. Her eyes followed the water drops sliding down the side mirror.

"Juma," he said. "Call me Juma." He informed her that he had been raised in a humble home and knew what it meant to be destitute. "I've gone through thick and thin, but I thank God for her."

Lily nodded.

"She is one hardworking woman." "Who is *she*, Sir?"

"My mother. Her name is Samantha Juma."

Lily wanted to ask if he had siblings, but found herself asking, "What of your father?"

From a distance, on the opposite side of the road, cranes swung back and forth in the air from inside an enclosed area. She kept her eyes glued to them, hoping she hadn't irritated him with the question that went unanswered.

"You see that place enclosed in iron sheets painted, *'Crown Paint'*?" She bobbed her head, lifting it a little high. "There is construction going on there. It will be a big hotel." Then he paused. He pressed his power window control, rolled down the glass and greeted the traffic police officer who saluted back. "I once worked at a construction site; mixing gravel and cement. I did that!"

Maybe one day I'll also be served in a big hotel, Lily thought. Who knows?

He turned left and came to a halt near a signpost that read "Chiromo Mortuary". A lad was dragging a beggar towards his car. His hand was outstretched with a polythene bag that flitted back and forth. He had on two worn-out sweaters. There was a gap in his front brown teeth, and streaks of dirt ran down his face towards the unkempt greyish beard. When the beggar was almost getting to his car, the traffic cleared and the drivers behind him impatiently started hooting. Juma returned his one hundred shillings in the car console, near his iPhone and Blackberry, and drove past flatly trimmed hedges and the hidden homes behind them, to a blue gate; the Chiromo Campus. The gates were flung open, the security guards saluted, and he drove in.

On that Thursday morning, Lily entered the University of Nairobi with abundant hopes and expectations. She felt the cool air of the serene green Chiromo environment as they drove in. She quivered with a flare of pride. Proud that she would be admitted to the campus that fed Kenya and the world with thousands of scientists, doctors, diplomats and government officials. But most importantly, she felt proud that it was the only chance she had to change her parents' lives and make them proud. She wasn't sure, though, about the uncertainties ahead in her life on campus.

She wasn't sure what to say when Juma, finally, whispered, "I know no father."

Chapter Ten

"Welcome to Chiromo Campus," Juma said, his lips stretching into a smile. He slowly nosed the car to a parking lot a distance from an old building opposite the Chemistry Laboratory and cut the engine.

"Thanks," her dimples crinkled as she responded with a smile that sent a warm rush through him. That was a good sign, he felt accomplished. With Riziki, too, it had started with a smile. Things seemed to be unfolding as he had hoped. After close to an hour of going through clogged traffic, she now smiled back. She didn't say *Sir!*

Young ambitious men and women, future doctors and scientists, crammed the campus. The admission process was still on for latecomers. Those undergoing orientation were being taken around in small groups from one building to another and from office to office. A few feet away from where he had parked, there was a queue of students with A3-size parcels containing x-ray slides, envelopes and admission booklets. Most had small bags strapped on their shoulders, a few conversing on the queue that coiled into the administration block of the Faculty of Physical and Biological Sciences.

"I have a son who knows no father," Lily would have told him, and asked for help to search for Jim's father. But he was a stranger. Guilt ran through her; she hadn't even mentioned that intention to her mother.

But now she imagined Jim also growing up knowing no father. Would other children make fun of him and laugh at him when they ask him what his father's name was? How would it feel knowing there was someone responsible for his existence roaming the streets like nothing ever happened?

"Okay, here we are," he signalled her to alight, and picked her bag from the open car trunk.

"Thank you so much, sir." He wasn't pleased by the intrusion of "sir" again.

Lily fished two envelopes out of her bag. Juma slung his grey coat on the passenger seat, adjusted his seat, and lay on it as he watched her fumble with her bag and the envelopes.

"Let me help you," he said, getting out of the car. He leant to pick an x-ray parcel that had slid from her armpit. "I'll help you with the bag too." Juma offered. "On second thought, I better keep the bag in the car," Juma continued, "then once you're done, you can pick it."

Lily queued behind a young man in formal attire; shiny black shoes, black pleated trousers, a silky pink shirt and a blue-striped necktie. He had a red pen in his right hand and a few printed A4-size papers and an admission booklet in the left hand. His left leg rested on the kerb adjacent to a neatly trimmed flower hedge reaching his waist. The young man turned to Lily to pick a conversation. "Hi, I am Dave, you?"

He inquired which course she was being admitted to, and from which high school as he told her his.

"God must have taken a lot of time to create you," Dave joked. Juma was still in the car. "By the way, is he your brother?" He asked, smiling. But Lily wasn't sure if it was a smile. His teeth had been showing from the very first time she saw him.

"Yeah, thanks." First day on campus. First student to speak to. First lie.

When it was her turn, a staff member drew her chair noisily and took Lily's documents from Juma, who had just joined her. And then she asked them a question, and Juma nodded, yet Lily, surprised that Juma was the one holding her remaining documents, just said *okay.*

* * *

He rushed her to the Barclays Bank branch along Muindi Mbingu Street and helped her pay tuition and accommodation fees. Back to Chiromo, they submitted the deposit slips at the admission desk. Lily smiled with gratitude. She acquiesced to his help because he said he was helping her the same way he would have helped his sister; if he had one. She felt sorry he didn't.

"I have to rush to the office. When you're done, please, give me a call." Before leaving, he looked at her documents and took note of her date of birth. He then handed them back to her, together with his business card.

* * *

Lily walked down to a *Simu Ya Jamii,* a public telephone near the tuck-shop kiosk to call home.

"Can I buy you a soda, please?" Dave intruded, tapping her on the shoulder. Lily recognised him. He looked at her at an angle, his mouth slightly open as if he wanted to add something.

"No, thanks," she said, "In fact, I had already paid for one. Next time!" And she proceeded to order a bottle of soda and a piece of cake; both of which she hadn't planned for. Shortly after, Dave walked up the slope onto the main road towards the hostels. On his way, he kept looking back and peeking over the hedges until she disappeared.

At the telephone kiosk, Lily gave the attendant a piece of paper with Milly's number. It would be easy to get to her parents through Barasa, but she opted for Milly. Lily knew Barasa was expecting an answer to the letter he had given her. But she hadn't bothered to even open the striped envelope. She also thought it better to create a rift between them. Barasa loved her; that was evident. But the little affection she had nursed for him had dissipated, like a wisp of light smoke on a windy day. As a matter of fact, she had never thought, after the rape incident, that she would have any feelings for any man. But it surprised her that she had felt safe around Juma that day.

"Hello Milly, this is Nekesa," she said. Milly was enthusiastic. "Yes, I arrived safely. I've just finished the registration process. And now, I'm going to my room." Milly told her how happy she was for her and asked how she felt, what the campus was like, and several other questions which Lily nodded to, only to realise in time Milly wasn't seeing her.

"Of course, I'm so glad…Yes, I already know. It's called Hall 4," she told her plus the number of the room she had been allocated. After inquiring about Jim and her parents, Lily requested Milly to pass her greetings on to them and inform them that she had arrived well. "Tell them I miss them already."

"And Barasa?" Milly snickered.

"I'll call him myself." She toyed with the receiver for another minute, thinking silently. When the attendant threw a puzzled look at her, she felt as though the attendant had been eavesdropping on her entire conversation. Lily recalled a few Sundays she had gone with Barasa to the Post Office in Kitale town after the mass. They would proceed to the tall, red public telephone booths and Barasa would insert a few coins and dial random numbers from the directory. When a call was picked on the other end, they would drop the receiver and take to their heels. Quite often, the booths were in bad shape, broken glasses and ugly crusade posters were their hallmarks.

The attendant inquired if she wanted to make another call, which she affirmed. She informed Juma that she was through with the admission. With her envelopes, a bottle of soda and a snack, she went past the BLT lecture halls and sat on a smooth concrete bench in an open field with a green expanse of grass. The concrete benches were sandwiched between the Department of Biochemistry and the Biological Sciences block. From where she sat, a group of Asian medical students were seated on the grass in a circle, having their lunch. Juma had said he would be in Chiromo in fifteen minutes. A distance from where she was, Muslim students were making their ablution. A slight breeze rode through and rustled purple jacaranda flowers, dropping them on their backs and heads as they prayed. Lily was impressed by their commitment to prayer.

* * *

"How is it so far?" Juma asked after picking Lily. He pulled out of the parking lot and drove off down Prof. Mourice Alala Road. She was surprised to see students walking on one half of the road, while vehicles squeezed on the other half. They didn't seem to find it fit to use the sidewalk and leave the road for vehicles. But she liked the environment. She saw herself gracing the same road with interlocking blocks every day. She would be feeling the scent and fresh air of the flowers and different species of trees along the way, and listening to the soothing sound of the river that passed under the thick foliage of the trees.

"You'll most likely have a roommate pursuing a similar course as yours, or in the same faculty. That's one of the considerate things I like this university for," Juma broke the silence. What if he hadn't returned? Lily was now wondering why she had trusted him with her luggage

"Sure?" She asked, surprised. Pictures of her possible roommate crossed her mind. She pictured a young girl in her early twenties, as naive as she was. She imagined them together in their room after lectures talking about their families, among other topics. They would do their laundry on Saturdays and then go for the first mass on Sundays.

"Yeah. It's very convenient. Imagine having someone who's in an entirely different faculty. That would mean different timetables, and worse, examination timetables!"

"Is it bad to have different timetables?"

"Look at a scenario where one of you loves music. Loud music! How would one manage to revise for exams from the room while the other, whose exams are probably months away, is listening to loud

93

music?" He pulled over next to a gate, and a security guard emerged.

"*Kuna baridi, mkubwa, hata chai sitakataa.*" The guard smiled at Juma, to enhance the 'tea', a euphemism for a tip that he was soliciting. His smile broadened after Juma squeezed a hundred shillings in his palm.

"Have a good day, Moses," Juma said, tapping the guard's name tag on a strap around his veined, thin neck.

"Thank you, sir," he saluted, then rushed to swing the gates open.

"He could be having a lot of dependents or no fare to get home, you know." Juma said as if to justify his gesture. Lily was jerked by the noise the metal bridge produced, immediately after the gate, as Juma drove past. The green bamboo leaves, hugging the roof of the car from both sides of the road, swung with the stir of the moving car.

"You have a nice car," she finally said what she had been holding since morning. Outside, students played on football pitches on both sides of the road.

A few sat in pairs, watching cars pass by. Lily looked, in disbelief, at one of the pairs wrapped in each other's arms a distance away, like a couple.

"Thanks." They drove past the Graduation Square where a choir was practising. When they reached the University Chapel, he pointed and said, "This is St. Paul's. You're a Catholic, right?"

"Yes, I am." She pulled out the rosary from her neck and fiddled with it for a while. He could see the gleam of excitement in her eyes. Lily stuck out her head to look at the chapel again when Juma took a right turn to join Lower State House Road. "How far is it from our hostels?"

"Not far. In fact, these are the hostels." He pointed at Lower State House hostels on his right and Hall 6 on their left. They had just passed the Architecture, Drawing and Design Building (ADD). "It's only that we have to go around because of the car. If we were on foot, we would be in the room already," he added, taking a left turn to join Mamlaka Road.

At her hostel's entrance, a woman with heavy round glasses weighing on the bridge of her nose directed them to the custodian's office. Juma registered himself as her brother. Lily felt a twinge of surprise as if she wanted him to indicate something different. As if she had told him what to say or write. She shouldn't have taken it that far, she thought. For that reason, he wouldn't have come with a full shopping bag that Lily had rejected and left in the car. She wanted to thank him and let him know that she wasn't comfortable with him following her up to the room. But she didn't know how to.

The room wasn't locked. She pushed the door open, only to see a lady in a black silky *buibui* and a blue hijab prostrating. Facing north, her forehead was pressed on a mat on the floor. Lily's heart gave a lurch. She took a few steps backwards, confirmed the room number, and then pushed the door open again. The lady didn't turn.

"Let her finish." Juma's voice was just an audible whisper. He gently pulled her by her wasp-waist. His hands were warm on her. Lily felt his breath gently brush against her ear. She turned to look at him, and their eyes locked, his head a little bent towards hers. She felt a shiver run through her and quickly detached herself from him, almost knocking him.

He closed the door as Lily leant against the opposite wall. Avoiding his face, she buried her head in her palms and whispered to herself, "Jesus!" She could feel the echo of her heart pound in her chest as her mind churned with pictures of three men slamming the Mathare door open. Her hands trembled. Her chest moved up and down as she intermittently heaved. Juma could tell she was struggling to breathe.

"I'm sorry, did I scare you?" Juma whispered.

"No...no...no," she said nervously, still breathing heavily. She had mixed feelings about her reaction. But her face still showed naked fear, which took her some time to rid herself of. She started thinking that perhaps they had both taken the help too far.

Their attention was drawn to a voice from behind the door, next to the wall where Lily was leaning. A lady was on the phone, speaking in Luganda. For about three minutes, she kept intonating, and every now and then she would quip an "*iii*" or a "*bambi*" or a "*kakati*" or "*munange*", followed by a burst of short laughter and claps or slaps.

95

Lily imagined the lady slapping her thighs as she laughed or how she clapped in surprise. Afterwards, Juliana Kanyomozi's *'Kanyimbe'* song poured from the room at full blast.

"I'm sorry," Juma apologised. "I didn't mean to scare you. I just wanted to let you give her space to pray. You'll probably be excusing her five times a day, that is, if she minds your presence when praying."

The door to her room swung open before Lily could ask, *Five times a day for four years?*

"*Karibuni,*" the lady welcomed them. Her soft voice and coastal Kiswahili reminded Lily of a young Barasa. Still in her *buibui* and *hijab*, she smiled warmly as she ushered them in.

"Please, have a seat," she said, pointing at her neatly spread bed for Lily and the reading chair for Juma. In her soft voice, she spoke slowly as if counting each word she uttered. She was a beautiful, young, brown girl with a gap between her upper incisors that glistened when she smiled. She was still smiling several minutes after she had ushered them in. Lily felt a little safe now that there was someone else present. It would have been a different feeling if only Juma and her were in the room.

"Hi," she extended her hand politely to Lily, but just said a polite "Hello" to
Juma without shaking his hand.

"Hi. I am Lily, and he's my brother..." Second lie.

"Juma," he finished as he toyed with his car keys. Lily felt sourness run down her gut for lying to her roommate in their first encounter. She hated herself for that; for the certainty of the lie being told again. For the uncertainty of how long the lie would be told. And even the following day, when they went for the Vice Chancellor's address at Taifa Hall, Main Campus, she still thought of how to tell Halima that Juma wasn't her brother.

Lily kept abreast with Halima. At the function, there was a lot of excitement. Male acquaintances hugged and patted each other on the back. While some busied themselves with photo-taking at the *Fountain of knowledge* – the concrete that spat tinkling water over giraffe statues – Lily was preoccupied with thoughts about Halima's impression of her, if she finally came to know the truth.

Chapter Eleven

"I studied at The Kenya High, you?" Halima asked Lily. Juma had just left.

After more chit-chat, she watched Lily unpack. She didn't have much. Halima was intrigued by her red-and-black-squared blanket. Outside, the clouds were low, full of rain. Lily unpacked a scrubbing loofah, a pair of red *Umoja* sandals, a few panties, a packet of sanitary pads, A4-size notebooks, a small blue Bible and a few dresses. She had, for years, kept the Bible which she and her schoolmates had received from *Gideons International* representatives who had visited their primary school. She placed her admission booklet under her clothes in the closet. In there was the envelope Barasa had given her.

"Can I excuse you?" Lily asked when she saw Halima spreading the mat on the floor. They had just had their first supper together.

"No need, unless you're planning to interrupt my prayer. I don't expect you to cross in front of me as I pray, talk to me, or play music. I mean…anything that will distract me." She smiled.

After her *Isha'a* prayer, the rain started pelting the windowpanes relentlessly like a hail of grains. They had to speak louder. Late that night, Lily listened in as Halima made her supplications. Lily also prayed and switched off the light, leaving Halima's *misbaha* glowing in the darkness from the reading table. She was now less worried about staying with a Muslim. As she lay quiet, she thought of Jim, Francisca and Lubao until she slept.

When she opened the window on Saturday and felt the cold smell of soggy soil in the air, they were even closer than they had been on the first day. Halima took Lily to a cybercafé at Hall 6 to register for her course units. After that, they left for Club 36, an open-air market where students bought affordable items.

Halima bought an anti-pick for their door locker, what students called 'anti- genitor' and tumblers of fresh banana juice. There was the petrichor, for it had rained at night, which mixed with the smell of chapati and boiling beef. They sat on a worn-out bench, among other students, and drank their juice.

Lily wanted to use a public telephone booth to call home, but there was no network coverage around the market; so, Halima lent her her mobile phone. She agreed to Lily's request that her family could be reaching her through her number. When she made the call, Lily let the thought of telling them about Juma slip away.

On their way back to the hostels, Lily and Halima met Dave. He was in a group of other four dark guys. Three of them wore identical brown leather jackets. Lily conveniently ignored him.

"*Achame chepto inon.* I like that lady," Dave said in Kipsigis. They all turned to look at her.

Lily had a feeling that Juma might reappear just like Dave. "Can I see you again, Lilian Nekesa?" Juma had asked. But she had remained silent, so Juma had changed the subject.

She now regretted letting Juma into the hostel. She was afraid he might turn out to be just like the men who had raped her. Worse of all, she regretted having lied to Halima. *I'll tell her the truth before we reach the room,* she thought. She didn't. Instead, she became curious to find out about the occupant of the opposite room who played mostly Ugandan gospel music.

As Lily settled in on her new life on campus, she would learn of buildings and parks in the city. She was amazed by the KICC, the Kenyatta

International Convention Centre, from where they took a couple of photos.

"This is the August 7th Memorial Park," Halima said. They were standing next to a wall with many names on it.

"Okay. What is it about?" she asked innocently.

"This place is where the American Embassy used to be, before the fateful day.

You remember the terrorist attack of August 1998?"

"I remember having heard about it. A friend called Barasa told me about it..."

She suddenly stopped and hoped Halima wouldn't probe further about him. "Cool. This is where it took place. And you see this?" she pointed to a name.

Lily leant forward, squinting while shading her eyes from the sun's reflection on the plaque. Then she read the name Halima was pointing at. "That's my dad. He was killed in the attack. I was still very young."

"I'm so sorry for that loss." Lily felt inadequate of words.

"It's fine, my dear. We're already used to life as it is." Halima bought two bottles of soda by the park's gate and paid sixty shillings entry fee for two people. "So, we come here to reflect, remember, and relax. There's also a peace centre where we learn peaceful coexistence and the need to condemn acts of violence."

"Yeah...and I see it's such a beautiful place." They sat on a bench in the green garden.

"I think it's unfair to associate Islam with terrorism, yet that isn't the case. Young people are nowadays being brainwashed by people who don't even know what Islam is all about. They are asked to be suicide bombers so that they can ascend to paradise. I hear about virgins too. But my question is, why are the people telling them to be suicide bombers not doing it themselves if the reward is paradise? Don't they need paradise too? See, my dad was killed, and he was a Muslim." Halima paused and looked at Lily, who had hunched close to her.

Lily nodded.

Halima continued, "You know, if I commit a crime, it is Halima who has committed it. Not my religion, right?" Lily nodded. "Just the same way you can commit an offence. It is you, not christianity, right?" Halima paused again,and then said, "I think all these acts of terrorism are just something else other than religion. And when Mungiki, or Joseph Kony or Wycliffe Matakwei, or Chinkororo or Taliban or ISIS or Boko Haram commit crimes, it's just them, not their religion."

While ambling back to the campus, Halima showed her the stage from whereto take a matatu to campus.

"And how about the matatus to Mathare North?"

"They park along Tom Mboya Street near the Post Office. Route number 29/30. Do you have relatives there?"

"No. I was just asking." Lily thought about the question; was it not an uninvited, unwanted relative she was after? Wasn't Jim's father now one?

They strolled to the Main Campus to take photos at the *Fountain of knowledge* with Halima's phone. Each shot came with a different pose. After several shots, they sat down to analyse them. You would have mistaken them for twins. They curved their necks, and their heads leant on each other's as they blocked sunlight with the back of their hands to get a good view.

They checked to confirm if the water the block spat was visible in the photos. They also looked out for the statues of the giraffe and those of other animals standing next to the water-spitting block. They deleted a few pictures in which the pool of water collecting at the base had not been captured and also one which didn't capture the elegant white hotel in the background whose design looked like maize cobs stalked together. They took more shots at different parts of the Main Campus before heading to the Student's Centre for their early supper.

The following day, Lily woke up to find Halima on her mat, mumbling a prayer in Arabic. She mumbled the same words Lily had heard her mumble before; words Lily thought Halima knew so well, but whose meaning she didn't. But why would Lily want to know? Besides, wasn't there freedom of worship?

As Lily got out of the room, she met a lady whose shoes' heels made an

101

irritating noise on the corridor's Marmoleum floor. The lady had just been dropped in a posh car a few minutes back. She looked tired and swayed in her movement like a scampering ten-minutes-old calf. With a towel wrapped just above the suppleness of her breasts, Lily stopped to look at the lady.

"Hi," the lady greeted Lily. Her eyes were red and puffy, but they shone with surprise as if she had been lurking in the corridors, avoiding bumping into anyone.

"Hi," Lily greeted back and walked past her towards the bathrooms. How could the lady comfortably walk around in such a dress way above her knees? Lily wondered. A sizable chunk of her flesh, especially the brown thighs, was just exposed for everyone to see! And wasn't the morning too cold for such dressing anyway?

"Excuse me, please," the lady called after Lily. Lily stopped and made two strides back. The lady was now leaning on the wall, her left hand stretched. Her face had a thick layer of foundation. "I'm Babirye...Rose Babirye from Uganda," the lady said. The smell of alcohol swept across Lily's face.

"Oooh, you must be the one who plays nice Ugandan gospel music." Babirye looked down. She had long toes that keeked through her peep-toe shoes. "My name is Lilian Nekesa, from Kitale."

"Nice to meet you. *Oba* can we catch up later?"

"Sure," Lily said, more worried about what they had to discuss. Behind, Babirye shuddered in a loud yawn as she struggled to insert her key into the keyhole.

* * *

"How was the mass today?" Halima asked later when Lily returned from church. Halima was composing a poem on her desktop computer.

"It was nice. I prayed for you too." For lack of a better adjective, Lily would always say the mass was nice. Whenever she went to church every Sunday, she always looked back on the events of her childhood. The mornings when she would accompany her parents to church clad in her best dress, her hair adorned with a white hairband, with a plastic flower over her brow.

"By the way, do you write?" Halima asked.

"Not really, but I once tried." Lily had seen her scribble stuff on an A4-size notebook whenever she wasn't reading, listening to religious teachings, or praying her *misbaha*.

"Oooh, sure? I'll be glad to read them."

Lily didn't want to tell her that she lost those pieces the day she was raped. She was not ready to talk about it yet, that, apparently, those pieces of paper had gotten her raped though somehow they had saved her from the death James and his family faced. Instead, she asked to read Halima's poems. After reading through, she made comments and suggested some changes that astonished Halima.

"Wow, you can make a good critique."

"I wish I could," Lily said. Halima was elated. She now had someone to genuinely critique her poems. And that made her happy.

In the afternoon, Lily bumped into Babirye at the tuck shop. Babirye seemed sober, mature and friendly. But Lily excused herself, she didn't feel like making her an acquaintance. They would in the subsequent days meet a few times at the tuck shop, washrooms, corridors, cafeteria and even in the TV room. Babirye religiously smiled at her and they would exchange the usual "Hi" or "How was your day?" or "Do you have an electric kettle you lend me for a few minutes?" or just asserting, "You have a nice dress!"

Out of curiosity and Babirye's persistent invitations, one afternoon, Lily knocked on Babirye's door. Babirye welcomed her with a glass of juice. Lily found Babirye so charming and funny she made Lily tip back her head and laugh the better part of that afternoon. They talked and laughed until late in the evening.

As the days slid by, Lily's bond with Halima grew just as the quantity of their coursework increased. Lily forgot about Barasa. The feelings she had once harboured for him were quickly ebbing away. Barasa felt despised and looked down upon by Lily. She had not even

103

called to say she had arrived safely, or just to thank him for all he had done for her.

One day, he asked Milly, "Please, give me the number you usually use to call Lily." He then called Halima and requested to speak to Lily. The conversation was brief. Lily sounded reluctant and disinterested. After disconnecting the call, Lily said nothing about him. Halima knew there was something amiss, but didn't want to probe. That night, Barasa didn't sleep well. *What had happened to Lily?*he wondered. And he didn't mention a thing about it to Milly, to whom Jim had developed a liking more than anyone else. Jim enjoyed being carried around by her, as though he knew she was the one who had saved him when Lily thought of flashing him out with abortion pills.

That night, Lily was also engrossed in thoughts. Why wasn't Barasa giving up on her yet she was miles and miles away from him? She didn't know the answer. If there was any man she had thought of, more often, it was Juma. Juma, too, thought of her every day. He kept resisting the urge to pay her a surprise visit. He wanted to apologise for pulling her close to him at her hostel door. But uncertain about her reaction, he kept on postponing. He wished she had a phone.

Lily didn't have enough money for her meals. So, to avoid sharing Halima's food, she would leave the room early for her lectures and come back late. Even when they started cooking from their room to save on costs, Halima noticed that Lily rarely bought foodstuffs. And whenever Halima was cooking, she would always disappear to the ADD building or the library. She enjoyed the smell of books around her. But the few times Lily cooked, she ensured they ate together or kept some for Halima. She also noticed that Lily never called home as often as she did at the beginning.

"Can you try to apply for the SONU Bursary?" Halima asked one evening. They were seated outside the Chiromo Library, on greyish concrete benches where medical students enjoyed sitting with their white lab coats while revising for their frequent examinations.

"SONU Bursary?" Lily asked, turning her eyes to the noticeboard. Almost all the notices pinned on both sides of the library door were outdated. The only recent poster was a picture of a man suspected to be on a stealing spree and therefore students were being warned to be careful. "I don't see any."

"No, that one is rarely advertised there," Halima informed her. She applied for the bursary, although she didn't get it.

That evening, when she dodged Halima's supper, she was disappointed to find that no studying was going on at the ADD Building. The venue was playing host to a *Fresha's Bash,* a party organised by SONU to welcome first-year students to the university. She went back to her room, and after sharing supper she'd tried to dodge, went – together with Halima – to see how things were going down at the ADD.

You caught my eye as you walked towards my pathway

And I couldn't turn away my eyes won't let me

I thought I was dreaming but you stood right near to my way

And all my eyes can see is you.

The song, *You caught my eyes* by Judy Boucher, welcomed them at the ADD. The words of the song echoed in Lily's thoughts. It reminded her of a past scene with Barasa under the tree at the market.

"Let's get out of this place; I'm not comfortable here," Lily snapped even before they could get inside the ADD Building.

"I almost told you the same thing."

As they were leaving, two students, Geoffrey and Tom, watched them from a distance.

"Have you seen that lady well?" Geoffrey asked.

"Of course, though not very clear. I just caught the figure."

Geoffrey's eyes followed Lily and Halima until they receded into the distant darkness of Hall 7 hostel corridors as they headed to Hall 4.

"My friend has invited me for a bash in Prefabs tomorrow, please come along." Babirye's roommate extended the invitation to Lily when she visited their room three days later.

105

***

Geoffrey and Tom were roommates in a Prefab hostel. While Tom concentrated on his studies, Geoffrey discovered pubs that sold cheap alcohol in town; where he would always be surrounded by the smell of urine, cigarette butts and vindictive drunkards who hurled lewd insults at anyone and anything that crossed their path. Though just a few months in the University, Geoffrey now knew nearly all the nightclubs and strip clubs by their location and full names.

Most of the time, after lectures, he would grace the pubs downtown, arriving even before the tables were full and when the music wasn't playing yet. He would spend the entire evening drinking and groping naked thighs of the scantily dressed barmaids and hookers. He marvelled at the sight of old men licking barm from their beer bottles or the outbursts of profanity, late into the night.

A few times, he would toss himself on the dancefloor under the dim light, faltering against sweaty bodies. He would dance with random women, his drink clutched tightly in his hand. At least, he was conscious that someone would spike his drink. He would then return to his room and sink into his thin mattress.

On the days that Geoffrey didn't go to town, he hosted female friends in their shared room. A few were ladies he knew from back home, while others were his classmates. A few of them also smoked. Sometimes, they would drink and wipe their plates of food down to the last morsel.

Tom, on the other hand, spent his time reading. His afternoon reading was not free from interruption. A few girls would knock on the door looking for Geoffrey, or hawkers selling vests and boxers, or students selling onions and tomatoes.

That was campus life. A few times, he would go to shop in town, especially when he still had loose change from his student loan.

In the lecture hall, Tom always sat in the front row. He was always among the first to shoot their hands up whenever a question was asked. His grasp of *Inorganic Chemistry* was superb. During one of the lectures on the topic at Millennium Hall 1, he shocked the entire class with his knowledge of the subject. Yet it was a topic all other students seemed to grapple with. The lecturer was impressed and showered him with compliments. That entire week, Tom walked around the campus with an air of brilliance. He set a target for himself to always read ahead of the lecturers in all the units so that his growing ego – as huge as a jobless man's miseries – and pride could remain gratified. However, his roommate couldn't give him ample time. He kept inviting ladies and playing loud music. Such high decibels were the thresholds to which Geoffrey and his army of visitors would effortlessly swivel their waists in weird dances. They would step on the beds and shake their bodies like they were performing frenzied gymnastics or as though their bones were soft cartilages.

The more Geoffrey's visitors infested Tom's jurisdiction, the more Tom became impatient. He derived no excitement from the endless stories and shrieks of laughter every time the visitors were around. Geoffrey seemed arrogantly inconsiderate. Tom thought it was high time he stopped licking his wounds of dissatisfaction and confronted him.

"You know what?" Geoffrey asked Tom one morning. He stood by the window smoking.

"I know."

"What?" He quipped, a cigarette clenched between his lips.

"That it makes little sense, if any, you are smoking from outside while the entire cloud of smoke still comes into the room!"

"Nkt!" Geoffrey clicked, taking a drag of the cigarette. He then stubbed out the remaining butt under the sole of his *akala* sandals. "Sometimes," he said, "you behave as if you're an unblemished saint."

"Okay, I didn't know." Tom said, opening a new page of his *Biomolecules* notebook. The Hs, CHs and OHs of whatever Tom was drawing made no logical sense to Geoffrey. Why would someone travel all the way to the institution to be drawing such? Geoffrey wondered.

"Why don't you get some life outside books?"

"Mmmh..." Tom raised his head and looked at Geoffrey. Tom's face was smooth and his eyebags a little swollen from having read late into the previous night. The corner of his right eye was reddish, and his black

107

jacket swished as he moved to faceoff with Geoffrey.

"By the way, listen. Today, I'll have a very special guest; forget about Judy and Doreen...even though Doreen and I..." Geoffrey paused and smiled. "You remember Doreen, my classmate?"

"Mmmh..."

"I visited her room at the Metropolitan hostels in Chiromo, and we kissed for a long time. If it weren't for her friends who paid a visit, who knows what would have happened? Probably this week, she'll be coming over. I tell you, man, her lips are just as sweet as she looks." Geoffrey licked his lips at the memory.

"Okay, I've heard you. Congratulations, man! Now, can I continue reading?" "But I haven't told you about today's visitor, have I?"

"How different will the story be from Judy's, Pauline's or Ann's?"

"If I get this one, I'll surely settle down with her. I've been chasing her since the first week I stepped into this university. I'm even surprised! Many beautiful ladies fight for my affection while this single soul is proving to be a solid rock."

"I hope so because you said the same thing about Pauline a while back. Besides, maybe this single soul knows what she came here for."

"For Mary, it will be a different thing altogether."

After days of the Nairobi chill and drizzle that had sucked the air, the egg-yolk- like sun finally emerged and shone above the sky like a hot inferno. Inside the hostel that bounced latent heat off its walls and roof, Geoffrey cleaned the room after days of untidiness.

In the evening when Tom arrived from the library, the room was filled with intense heat from an unregulated cooking coil. Geoffrey had borrowed a few more cooking pans. Perhaps, some wouldn't be returned if the owners forgot about them. He was cooking rice and beef stew. Several bottles of liquor and soft drinks stood on one of his closet shelves. The room was cleaner than ever. A sweet fragrance could be picked above the spicy aroma of steaming beef stew.

The disinterested Tom pulled his reading chair and sunk into it. On his table, a voluminous *Organic Chemistry* book by Morrison and Boyd was on top of Lehninger's *Principles of Biochemistry*. Next to them, there were a few printed handouts from the previous lectures' PowerPoint slides.

"But listen, brother...you have to reduce your visitors' visits. You inconvenienceme a lot," Tom finally spoke.

Geoffrey nervously ran his fingers through his unkempt hair, reached for a cigarette and sent a good content of nicotine down his lungs. How he felt itsettling! His eyes squinted against the smoke. Contented on the dosage delivered to his alveoli, he expunged the remaining nicotine through his dilated nose in a bolus of stinging smoke. Through his coiled lips, another cloud swirled into the room. A breeze blew through the broken windows and wafted a whiff into Tom's face, sending him into bouts of coughs.

"Sorry man..." Geoffrey said as he twisted a few of the scattered strands ofhair on his chin. He then took another puff that brightened the smoulder in a fine orange umber as the ground tobacco leaves burnt.

"But I hope you heard me," Tom said, still recovering from the choking cough that had moistened his eyes. Another fine sheet of white smoke spread from Geoffrey's twisted lips. He swung the cigarette stick aside. The ember flicked ashe did, and there was a flake of ash threatening to fall on his bed.

"I hear you, man." The ember was still eating up the tobacco rod. Just before the ash could fall on his bed, he flicked it off. He opened his mouth to add something. But his tongue stuck. He paused for a few seconds with the tongue hanging in his mouth and ended up saying nothing.

Chapter Twelve

The images of big self-contained concrete hostels Lily had pictured when she thought of the Prefabs hostels slowly faded away as they were replaced with wooden structures that stretched before her eyes. The wooden walls had a lick of brown paint that seemed freshly painted. She banished the thought of brushing her fingers against the paint, just to see if it would stain them.

Lily and other ladies met young men along the pavements who would turn to look at them, as they went past the custodian's office. They then turned left, according to the directions Geoffrey had given Babirye's roommate, and at the end of it, they saw Prefab 10. As the ladies walked through the dark corridors of Prefab 10, whose air smelt of emptiness, Tom was unaware of the role a beautiful lady, whose skin shone with the colour of coffee beans, would play in his life. Just like a lily flower, the lady was tall with an adequate endowment of smooth feminine curves rightly placed on her fleshy self. While her presence in his campus life was to have a significant impact on Tom, his roommate wasn't going to make life such a swift walk in the park either.

A pristine silence hung over the room as the guests entered, Tom forgetting what he was reading and absent-mindedly drumming his pen on the table; *tat tat tat tat tat*!

"What? Didn't you expect us?" one of them asked. The two young men couldn't admit that it was the presence of one new face that had left them speechless.

"This is my friend Lily. We aren't in the same faculty, but I met her through my roommate, Babirye."

"You're most welcome, Lily. And this is my roommate Tom, my brother from another mother," Geoffrey finally added.

"Oooh, you're the Tom?" Mary asked in a manner that betrayed the gossip Geoffrey had whispered to her before about him.

Tom, with a smile that showed off his shining, cotton-white teeth, rushed to greet them, imagining how difficult Mary had been for Geoffrey to win over.

Geoffrey's investment in Mary's visit to their room was worth the effort and cost, Tom thought. Her beautiful face was smooth and her eyes pure white with a coal-black iris. The eyes, like two immaculate precious stones, curved nicely on her lids with slight eye bags. They shone with a soft glimmer like a limpid lake reflecting sunlight on a dull afternoon.

"Welcome, Mary."

"Thanks, Joe," Mary referred to Geoffrey as Joe. She drew back a soft wisp of her stray black hair with her smooth, slender finger and tugged it behind her ear. The hair caressed the skin of her upper shoulder as it shone with the white illumination from the fluorescent bulb. Every time she tilted her head, shiny silver studs glistened with the reflection of the bulb. But Mary didn't capture the interest of the two young men in the room as Lily did. In the seclusion of his inner feelings, even Geoffrey wondered why he hadn't met Lily before meeting Mary.

Geoffrey rushed to dangerously prod the live wire of the cooking coils' cords into the socket under his reading table, which had already been half-burnt by the room's previous occupants. Tom closed his books and sat back in a relaxed manner. He was hoping that one of the visitors would start off the conversation he so much ached for. A conversation he was ready for. Besides, aren't our friends' friends our friends? He asked himself.

"It's quiet in here," Lydia finally commented.Low music was playing.

"How about you increase the volume, please?"

Tom quickly bent under the table and turned up the volume of the *Ampex* speaker. The sub-woofers were fixed on nails dug into the wooden wall. From his bent position, he noticed Geoffrey had carelessly piled all their shoes in one corner under his bed. Just smile and pretend all is well, he advised himself.

"Better?" Tom asked. The ladies were surprised that he wasn't immersed in volumes of books as usual. On most of their visits, Tom would ignore them and sandwich his chin in his palms as he read through pages and pages of textbooks.

"Such big books!" Lydia couldn't resist commenting. Tom retracted back on his chair for her to scrutinise the books and his small personal study timetable glued on the wall next to his table. Her face came close and she smelt of some cheap perfume, he thought. *"Organic Chemistry,"* she muttered more to herself as she balanced one book in her stretched right hand. "I am lucky all this ended in secondary school." She placed the books back, then took out a handkerchief from her pocket to fan herself with. The room, whose cream wooden walls had patches of other colours, a handwritten timetable and a campaign poster, blazed like it was meant to store heat.

"Aaa, you also study *Organic Chemistry*?" Lily asked Tom, looking up. Their eyes locked for a full second. Lily's small eyes surrounded by erect eyelashes drilled into Tom's, steering emotions that tore through the marrows of his bones.

"Yes, I do. You too?" Lily's presence utterly awakened Tom. He was glad that her question had catapulted him into the centre of the conversation.

"Okay, and that would mean you are also in Chiromo Campus."

"Sure," Tom then fumbled to say something that didn't come through in his mind. "Nice to know I'm not alone here," he quipped. "So, Prof. Emmanuel Yudah is your lecturer?"

"No, I haven't heard of him. My *Organic Chemistry* lecturer is Dr Daniel

Wefwe." Lily felt a solid happiness sink in her with the realisation that she had just possessed the lecturer.

"Which course?" Tom asked, adjusting the chair at the reading table, in which he had squeezed himself in. The visitors sat close to each other on the beds. They had pushed their legs a little under the beds; away from the heat of the cooking coils at the centre of the room. Lily's legs sparkled; a little shiny from a pumice stone scrub and the jelly she had applied before leaving her room.

"Look at these *Chiromites*, trying to reduce all of us to mere spectators in their

Q & A session," Geoffrey's joke didn't provoke the humour he thought it would. But he was glad that both Lily and Mary smiled at it. Lily's smile revealed her gleaming teeth. They were white like the sap of unripe papaya. In a split second, the conversation intensified. Various topics were randomly thrown around. Soon, the food was ready. Tom participated actively in the discussion and even helped Geoffrey arrange the plates on the table.

Geoffrey served the rice and beef stew, sprinkling a few pieces of meat on his plate. Under the grains of rice in his newly bought melamine plate, a huge dry bone lay buried.

"Where I come from, they say a person of great appetite is the first to wash their hands," Lydia said. They all laughed. Lily's soft laughter thrilled Tom's heart.

"Lydia," Mary started, then stopped halfway to lick the soup at the tip of her finger, "I hope you realise you aren't in your village in Msambweni, but rather in the university."

Tom glanced at Lily. He caught her just raising her head, her right cheek bulging with a spoonful of rice. Their eyes locked again. He noticed that her eyes were shining with the reflection of the fluorescent bulb, notwithstanding the few insects that flitted and flapped their wings against the tube. The flapping sent fine flecks of dust particles down their heads and sometimes on the food they were eating. Outside, the earth was bathed in moonlight. A swift breeze blew inside through the open window like a flamboyant neighbour who strides in at lunch without an

113

invitation.

"I can attest you are a good cook, Joe," Lily said with a soft, sprightly voice that bore discernible traces of shyness. At that point, a bed bug crawled up the wooden wall, and Tom caught it in time to spare them the embarrassment. He removed the cap of his pen with his teeth and crushed the insect hard against the wall. It burst, forming a red spot around it, which he quickly wiped with tissue paper.

"Thank you."

The suggestive look Tom gave Lily brought a spell of silence. Except for the sound made by the water Mary was drinking, all was quiet. Even the music had stopped. Mary placed the glass on the chair from where her food had been served.

In the new glass before her, the remaining water sat cool and clear. A crescent shape of her lower lip had formed on the glass. Her fingernails and toenails, just like the lipstick and open shoes she wore, shone with light shades of pink.

"You're welcome." Lily's voice gradually evoked deep-seated emotions in Tom. He feared that with the constant beating, his heart would leap out from his chest.

"I guess we are yet to sample Tom's," Mary said.

"Sure," Tom felt more at ease now. He liked Mary's exquisite cream top with sprinkles of a pink floral pattern. But he admired Lily most in her simple dress. There and then, he knew he had fallen for her. Had he been closer to her, he would pretend to be slightly moving, and then extend his hand to run over the smoothness of her arm and feel its warmth.

Tom's eyes refused to leave Lily, on whose face an infectious smile kept lingering. He kept admiring a pair of dimples that never left her cheeks until Mary caught him and said, "Tom, just feel free to talk to her." And they all laughed, making Tom feel a little embarrassed.

Tom and Lily talked about Chiromo Campus, the common units, and a bit of national politics and current affairs. A few times, she smiled, igniting strange feelings in Tom that he could least explain.

"Where are your washrooms?" Lily asked. Tom offered to take her.

In the washrooms, he helped her wade through the flood of dirty water overflowing from the sinks amidst food remains.

"I never thought that on campus students would have to put on swimming costumes to visit the toilets," Lily joked. There was ethereal magic in her voice.

"Now you know," Tom spluttered. Lily smiled. He smiled back.

When Lily returned to Hall 4, Halima was still awake. "Barasa called earlier," she informed her. "He requested that you call back. Your mother would like to speak to you tonight."

"Is there any problem?"

"He didn't say. Here," she offered Lily the phone.

"Hello," Francisca said from the other end after the phone had rung for a few seconds. "We were so worried about you Nekesa, are you okay?" They talked for a while, catching up on many things.

"Does he eat using his right or left hand?" Lily asked. Francisca had told her that Jim had now started eating on his own. Later, Lily spoke to Barasa before ending the call.

"And these are for you," Halima said, pointing at huge shopping bags and a gift box. They were heaped on the floor under her reading table.

"What? From whom?"

"Surprise gifts from Juma. He was here a while back. He said 'hello' to you." It was 11th November, and there was the perplexity of how Juma knew. "Happy Birthday, dear roommate," Halima added and rose up to hug her. She wrapped her arms around Lily's shoulders and pulled her closer in a tight embrace.

"You too...ooh, sorry...Thank you," she said. She gently rubbed Halima's back. She then sat on her bed and looked at the heap of gifts with mixed feelings. Halima was observing her reaction. *It is high time I told Halima the truth*, Lily thought. *No, I will tell her tomorrow*. Without moving from the bed, she pulled the blanket and slid under it. She hadn't touched the gifts.

In her dreams, Lily saw Juma and Tom approach her in a dark washroom. They had masks, but she could discern them. They knocked her down with clubs into a pool of dirty water. They then tore her dress

115

apart. In her nakedness, she became paralysed and cold. From behind them, she could see Barasa watching. She raised her hands and tried to shout for help, but her own voice betrayed her.

Chapter Thirteen

"You were calling Barasa in your sleep," Halima said, calmly without inflexion in her voice, when Lily finally woke up late that morning. Halima drew the curtains into two thick, generous folds at both ends after swinging the windows open.

"It was just a bad dream," she said and watched Halima walk from the window. She hadn't put on her *buibui*, and her pair of shorts and a T-shirt perfectly traced the hourglass figure that was always hidden under the *buibui*. Bright light streamed in from the window, and a black prostration mark on her forehead was conspicuous on her brown skin. Her deep philtrum and the brownish henna on her toenails were noticeable, too.

"Yeah! It must have been a horrible one. I could tell from your frantic movements. I almost woke you up, but then you slowly receded into a deep, sound sleep."

"Was I snoring?"

"With a terrible rumble!" "Are you sure?"

"Seems you expected a specific answer," Halima paused to allow her to ransack her thoughts then said, "I was kidding. You don't snore; at least not yet."

Lily had felt a little tired when she woke up. She was unaware of how her encounter with Tom had left his skin prickled and his mind unsettled. That entirenight, Tom thought of her.

The polythene bags full of Juma's gifts were still lying on the floor waiting for her attention. Still, she harboured a strong negative feeling against all men. The dream had just rekindled sad memories. "You haven't touched your shopping.""What?"

"Your gifts; you haven't touched them."

"I don't want them. I'm not comfortable with them.""With?"

"The shopping from Juma," Lily answered tiredly. "But why? He's your brother?"

"Aaaa..." she started, but then cupped her face with her palms, her elbows burrowing into her thighs, and buried herself in contemplation. "I am sorry, Halima," she started, "I should've told you this long ago. I've always been meaning to." When she finished narrating her encounter with Juma, she told her all about Jim, and her parents too. They shared quite much of what each had kept secret.

Halima insisted that there was no way she could throw away the gifts. Lily, thinking about the past two Sundays when she had borrowed money from Halima for church offerings, felt the same too. It would be illogical for her not to take the gifts, she thought.

That entire week, Tom looked forward to bumping into Lily along Prof. Mourice Alala Road, or even under the green foliage of Chiromo Campus trees from where students idled, talking about the ICC, the International Criminal Court's Chief Prosecutor, Luis Moreno Ocampo. Apart from the official duty he had come for, Ocampo had taken time to appreciate the country's wildlife. A few times, Tom roamed the parking lot between the two blocks of Biological Sciences – where lecturers parked their cars, mostly old un-tinted Peugeot 504s with decorated seat-covers or Datsuns with stretched noses – but he never met her.

Lily would disappear behind the Biological Sciences Block during lunch hours. She would take with her a few books so that, while other students had lunch, she would be reading in isolation. The building was reserved for *Insect Science*, just behind the Biological Sciences Block.

But as much as Tom didn't bump into her, he was better off than Barasa who just wanted to hear from her. He wanted to know about the new friends she had made. How was her newfound freedom and lifestyle? What company did she keep? Were the stories about illegal arms, prostitution and drug abuse real on campus as he used to hear or was it just hearsay? How about male students having forests of *Afro* hair on their heads and trousers that swept the roads as they walked? How was she surviving? Did she have enough money to live on? And if not, how would he send her some? Had she fallen in love? Barasa had a ton of questions that he couldn't easily answer. But just like Tom, he hoped that over time, he would get in touch with her.

"She is in Chiromo. I bet I'll get her soon," Tom had sworn to Geoffrey as he placed his right foot on the chair he was seated on. He cut his toenail and looked up at Geoffrey.

"You? The teetotaller bookworm?" Geoffrey asked as he picked an electric kettle and a pile of dirty utensils in a basin from under the reading table.

Sniffing the cheesy pungent of the toenail, Tom said, "Perception is one thing, and action another."

At the Chiromo Campus mess, and the restaurant below it too, Tom scanned through the long queues of hungry students, just in case she could be among them.

A week after Lily's first encounter with Tom, thoughts of changing her course came with a stronger impulse. She asked Halima if they could have an early supper at the Students' Centre.

"I think soon, you'll be attending classes alone," Lily finally told her, jokingly.

"What do you mean?" There was a feeling of dejection as if Lily had called for the last supper whose cost she had no reasons not to believe Lily had either eked to save or had borrowed. "What is it?" Her fingers rested back on the plate with a chunk of thickly stewed *pilau* she had squeezed between them. Halima ate from the tip of her fingers; a *'sunnah'* – a practice ascribed to the life and teachings of the Prophet.

119

"I've finally decided to apply for the Inter-faculty transfer I once told you about."

"Whaaat! Have you done it already?" "Tomorrow."

Tom met Lily at the Department of Biochemistry. Tom, alongside the class representative, had gone to find out why a lecturer had missed a lecture that morning. Lily had come to submit her Inter-faculty transfer letter before the deadline. As she walked out of the reception, Tom was walking out of the Chairman's office.

"Hello, beautiful one," Tom greeted her, extending his hand. "Hi," she said without taking his hand or turning to look at him.

"You have to be careful with these stairs." She didn't respond. "Unlike the washrooms back in the hostels, where you have to put on swimming costumes to visit, you have to put on firm gloves to hold on to these handrails, lest you roll down the stairs. A few have!" Lily stopped at the first landing and turned to look at the persistent voice.

"Aaaha, here comes Morrison, or should I call you Boyd?" She laughed and extended her hand. They were now on the same stair level. "Hi, long time!"

"Hi," he held her gaze as he shook her hand with a gentle squeeze. His breath suddenly became shallow, and his voice shaky. The things love does! Lily moved aside to pave the way for the class representative who was behind them. "This is my friend Alex," Tom said.

"Pleasure meeting you, Alex," she smiled.

"The pleasure is all mine, Lilian..." Alex's handshake was a little prolonged, creating a vacuum of silence before he said, "Nekesa...Nekesa."

"Interesting guy," she said, as Alex paced down the grey concrete stairs while brushing his fingers against the black plastic handrail. Lily turned to Tom. "So, how is the electron configuration or the ionic and simple bonding helping you in..." she said, "Your Bi-chem, Mr Boyd?"

"Morrison sounds a little more African than Boyd. I would prefer it," Tom said, unwittingly knocking the back of his shoe sole against a baluster.

"So you say, Mr Morrison,"

"But Lumumba is not only a little more African than Morrison, but as a matter of fact, it's African."

"I hear you, sir. So, how is it?"

"I would say fine, especially the covalent bonding that holds amino acids in our bodies. Or even the simple bonding that binds hydrogen and oxygen molecules in water." Lily shook her head. They sauntered down the stairs, towards the Histology Laboratory on the ground floor.

"How about the other side?"

"All is well, only that I'm thinking of crossing over. That's what brought me here. Though I am not sure of my prospects. Any advice?"

"It's almost lunchtime," Tom said, looking at his wristwatch. "Why don't we have lunch together as we talk about your prospects? I can share the little I know." Lily thought about it for a moment, but Tom quickly added, "on me," before she could say "yes" or "no".

"So long as you don't drag in the conversation on neural and hormonal regulations on digestion. By the look of the books I saw on your table the other day, I can tell you're one person who will start explaining how the food we'll be eating is being metabolised as we eat," she said with a chuckle.

"Maybe just a little bit of how the autonomic nervous system contributes to the regulation of the blood pressure, gastrointestinal response to food, contraction to the urinary bladder and focusing of the eye. And especially my eyes on you!"

"Yeah, I noticed the other day how they could pierce into someone else's. And I wonder how many people your eyes have pierced into." She felt surprised at how words rolled off her tongue with ease. "But if Biochemistry turns one into this kind of a zombie who can only hold a biochemical conversation, I rather remain with my plants and animals, and you stay with your prospects' advice for now."

"No, no, no! I was just trying to cultivate your interest in the course."

"Then you failed at the attempt. Besides, I already have an interest. That's why I came to drop the application." There was a pause as they both thought of what to say next.

121

"Tom?"

"Eee?"

"A more proper way to respond would've been, 'Yes, please'." They both smiled.

They took a left turn at the Department of Medicine, from where she had, a few times, peeped into the mortuary a few metres away and seen first-year medical students unwrapping cadavers from polythene body bags. Their white lab coats and latex gloves fascinated her. As they took a right turn along the hedges of the pavement leading to the entrance of Arziki Restaurant, the astringent smell of formaldehyde from the morgue was quickly fading. A few steps ahead of them, an Asian guy carried his girlfriend's handbag. Tom wasn't pleased by the gesture; that was the kind of challenge he wasn't ready to face and whose attempt would prove futile.

"Can I?" Lily asked, reaching across the table. She picked something from the collar of his grey shirt before he could even permit her, and flicked it off her finger before he could see what it was.

"Thank you." He wanted to ask if it was a bed bug, which he highly suspected, but he didn't want to make her aware of his room's state, just in case it turned out to be a beetle or something else.

Tom observed how slowly she ate, gazing longingly into her irresistible eyes.

"How do you feel being part of this institution?" Tom asked, and watched her bend over her plate, and then she raised her head and said she was proud and humbled. Tom talked mainly about himself, and how excited he was to meet her again. Then there was silence. "I think you'll one day make a good mum, Lilian Nekesa," and the quiescence prolonged.

She avoided his eyes, and he kept secretly looking at her. Lily's real beauty, etiquette and composure dazzled him. He was astonished by how he had gotten the guts to approach her at the department.

Lily never left Tom's mind that week. He couldn't see her in the crowd of students and civilians who avoided Waiyaki Way and took the shortcut to town on foot through Prof. Mourice Alala Road. In the evenings, as he walked down the road after lectures, he still couldn't fish her out from the enthusiastic crowd. There were several young and old men and women headed for their evening lectures at the Millennium lecture halls.

After meeting Lily at the Department of Biochemistry, and knowing that there were prospects of her joining them, Tom morphed into a new version. He started looking at himself in the washroom mirrors more than necessary and took more time brushing his teeth with *Sensodyne* in the morning and after supper.

In addition, brushing his shoes took a more deliberate effort. He also ensured that the iron remained on his clothes properly before stepping out of his room. It was as if he was preparing to meet Lily every day. He even started using *Nivea for Men body wash,* face wash and body lotion, and *Veet* cream to shave his underarms clean.

The next time Tom met Lily was in a *Mammalian Physiology* lecture.

"It's such a nice feeling to have you here. I'm glad that my prediction about your prospects came to pass." Tom told Lily on the first day of her transfer after her first lecture. They were headed for lunch. A few male students interrupted them just to say hello to the new comrade. The ladies were more gracious; they just waved a random "Hi" on their way out of the lecture hall.

"Thank you," Lily said just at the same time when Tom suddenly sneezed. The muggy cloud of foul-smelling sneeze and a drop of phlegm settled on Lily's face. Tom could smell it. He felt mortified. He had a recent sinus infection and the antibiotics were not acting as fast.

"*Sasa hii ni ujinga gani na wewe*!" One of the male students admonished him as those who were nearby made a few steps backwards. The student pulled a white handkerchief from his pocket and extended it to Lily. "Sorry, Lilian," he said, "I wish Tom had welcomed you to this Faculty in a better way. As you'll come to learn, that's not how we all are."

Lily instead pulled out her own handkerchief and wiped the phlegm and the smelly droplets of the sneeze from her face.

"I am sorry. Please." Tom couldn't look her in the face.

"By the way, they call me Emmanuel," the male student interrupted.

123

That night, the incident fazed Tom. He still revisited the scene the following day, too. He secretly watched her in class. He observed Lily's deskmate, Doreen, copying a sentence the lecturer had just rubbed off the chalkboard from Lily. He noticed Brayoh "accidentally" dropping a pen and asking Lily to pick it up for him. Then Brayoh scribbled a note and slid to her. On that day, Tom didn't say much to her. But in his silence, she stayed in his mind. She always would. At night, he slept late fantasising about a relationship with Lily.

Lily only started thinking seriously about Tom when she joined the
Biochemistry class. He became her default source whenever she needed notes to photocopy. She could also inquire from him about the location of lecture halls or laboratories, or about timetables and lecturers. Other aspects that Tom gave her information about were where to make a name tag required during the *Histology* laboratory practicals, comparing results after a laboratory practical and writing the reports. In the evenings, she couldn't wait to tell Halima about the progress in her studies. She also called home more often.

Their friendship slowly picked up, at times, Tom almost acting to his impulse feelings. It was him who took her to the Post Office on Tom Mboya Street to buy postage stamps that she didn't need, and she mastered the route they followed through the Jeevanjee Gardens. Several times, he wanted to tell her how much he adored her, but banished the idea.

However, there was always a nice feeling whenever they were together. Tom wondered why time flew twice as fast only when she was around. And he always looked forward to the next lecture, practical or the next day. Whenever he was free in his room, he thought or talked a lot about Lily. Geoffrey's ceaseless smoking or the many friends he hosted for drinks in the room now seemed to bother him less.

Lily's weekends were now predictable. On Saturday's, she did laundry and later went for studies at ADD. With time, Tom joined her and Halima at ADD for regular studies and revision. Later, because Tom and Lily mostly discussed Biochemistry, Halima gradually withdrew from the ADD and opted to read from her room.

On Sundays, Lily never missed the holy mass. The front pews were her favourite so that students who whispered from the backbenches wouldn't disturb her, and she would feel closeness to the Garden of Eden. A few times, she would turn and throw blank glances at those who whispered behind.

She followed all the three readings and the song from Psalms by the choir. The entire congregation would join in the singing. Apart from the sermons and the articulation of the priest, she enjoyed the songs by St. Paul's Students' Choir that bounced off the thick walls and echoed in the hall; way up to the rafters which were so high they seemed like ladders to heaven.

From outside, a man on a wheelchair selling sweets, chewing gum and credit cards would, from time to time, sing along the hymns that flew out of the church.

A few taxi drivers in their cars parked outside the compound would sometimes switch off their stereos and listen to the mass. There was always a revived energy whenever she stood to recite the creed. With the crucifix right in front of her, she always felt lighter and lighter; with every weight that left her body carrying with it her sins.

Later, she would keenly watch the priest sprinkle holy water on the altar and on those at the altar. Lily's eyes would intently follow him as he walked slowly on the aisle, his shiny, sharp black shoes poking out of his long alb as he moved. She would wait for the holy water to land on her before making the sign of the cross and wait for the water to dry. She would then pray that the water dries with temptations from Juma and other campus lads sprinkled on her path.

As the priest raised an aspergillum from a metallic tray carried by an altar boy, water would sprinkle on the boy's chest, and the spots of water on the boy's chest would increase as they moved through the congregation. At the end of the mass, she would bow her head and make the sign of the cross, as the priest named the Trinity, and she would think less of the altar boy, but more of how lighter she felt.

During some of the services, she remembered Barasa accompanying her to the church.

"Go in peace," the priest would then add.

"Thanks be to God." The congregation would reply. Lily would leave for the campus, after giving the Lord her soul, with hope and happiness in her heart to take her through the coming week.

* * *

"Can I please talk to Lily?" Juma called Halima one evening. He had taken her number the day he had brought the birthday gifts.

Lily was hesitant, and Juma could hear her whisper from the background in an attempt to refuse to get the phone from Halima.

"I am so sorry for pulling you close on that first day," Juma apologised when Lily finally picked up the phone. They talked briefly before Juma said bye-bye and take care and goodnight to Lily. And then he called the next day, and the next.

Lily thought it selfish to be receiving more calls on Halima's phone. She pondered on whether she should caution Juma to minimise the calls or stop altogether. Then calls from home also started flowing in. She forgot about it.

Jim was very ill with pneumonia. He had been admitted to the hospital; they told her the first time they called. The subsequent calls were updates that indicated Jim's health was deteriorating. Fortunately, they were breaking for Christmas holidays in a few days. As she borrowed bus fare from Halima, Lily knew she needed her own phone when they resumed school.

A day before she travelled home for the Christmas holidays, she took a matatu to Mathare North. On arrival, she stood at the bus stop near the Chief's Camp for about thirty minutes. She was contemplating whether to go back or to proceed with her mission. The scars left by the events of 2007/2008 started palpitating with a distant ache.

Chapter Fourteen

Juma hoped he would bump into Lily as it had happened twice. If she had a phone, communication between them would be easier. But still, he didn't stop calling her using Halima's number. So, when he called and Halima informed him that they had closed for their Christmas break, he felt like going after Lily in her rural home.

When Lily went home on that first visit after joining the university, she didn't carry anything as would be with her subsequent visits.

Short rains had recently soaked Kitale. The grass on both sides of the path to their home had grown knee-length so that her feet were swallowed as she walked along. Francisca was happy to see her, and so was her ailing father. When she arrived at the hospital to see Jim, she found Barasa there with a small bag of fresh fruits. He had also just arrived.

"I read your letter, thanks. I liked what you wrote," Lily ashamedly told him later. Although Barasa knew Lily no longer considered him worthy, he chose to ignore thoughts that she might have as well torn the envelope or thrown it during her journey. He was very disenchanted with her. She never even took her time to just appreciate his effort. Even if the content was worthless to her, she should have appreciated the time he took to buy the envelope, lick and seal it!

During that holiday, Lily couldn't sufficiently describe to her family how campus life was, and the university. She had carried two photos she had taken on campus. She told them – including Barasa and Milly – about Halima, Tom and her other acquaintances on campus. But she was very careful not to talk about anything that would bring Juma's name into the picture; lest they judge her as having started to entertain men into her life and forgetting what had taken her to the campus.

After Jim's discharge from the hospital, Barasa and Milly helped them offset the hospital bill and bought them food. Milly operated a cybercafé. Lily created time for her two friends, though she felt detached from Barasa. She focused on helping her mother with the household chores and busied herself with things that would make her not bond with her son whom she still didn't like much. She also tried to be indoors most of the time and didn't like going out where she would meet with people. So, when the short holidays came to an end in early January, Lily was glad that she would be away from Barasa for a while again. From the whispers and eyes of her villagers again.

* * *

"Lily, come on, my dear," Babirye told her a few days after she had arrived from Kitale. Lily remained silent, giving Babirye enough time to reposition herself on the bed. She looked straight into Lily's eyes and said, "You'll never plough a field if you only turn it over in your mind. Never! You have financial challenges. For you to address them, you need money. When do you think you'll get a job to do so?" Lily didn't respond. "But just look at you; here you are, and there's someone who can, and is willing to help. You must choose between the present opportunity and the uncertain future."

Back in her room, Lily found comfort in what Babirye had said. She now felt convinced that things could only get better with Juma's assistance. From then on, Lily would visit Babirye regularly. They spent most of their free time sharing tips and ideas. Though baffled by how

Juma now became a primal figure to her, she started making calls to him "to just say hey". With time, the duration of the calls increased. Juma would get out of the house to receive or make discreet calls. Either would call any time, sometimes even in the night though she knew it was inconveniencing Halima whose phone she still used. Halima didn't mind lending her phone, but was not happy that it was a man on the other side of the line.

One evening, Juma arrived with goodies in a huge shopping bag. In it, there was a phone.

"Isn't this too much, Juma?" Lily feigned surprise.

"It's nothing for someone like you. Besides, this is just a little help. I would've done the same for my sister; if I had one." Lily's beauty had intoxicated and confused him. It had tickled his philanthropy and he had to win her affection by all means. "And I think it's okay to help someone if one is in a position to, right?" Juma continued. A wave of gratitude swept over her when she saw the phone. She could now communicate home at any time without inconveniencing Halima.

A few days later, she went shopping in town with Babirye with the money Juma had given her. With Babirye's help, Lily bought several tight dresses, tight trousers, and mini-skirts. They were both sure the tight clothes would impress Juma even more. Back in the room, Lily tried to fit them on, one by one. They all firmly hugged her curved hips. Goodbye old Lily, welcome new Lily, she whispered to herself.

Halima was shocked by the extent Lily had transformed which she didn't need to be told was just to impress Juma.

With her new elegance, she turned heads and raised eyebrows on campus. Even her traits changed. When walking, she threw back her hair every now and then, flexing her neck as though it had no bones.

Juma bought her airtime to call home, shopped for her and gave her cash for her upkeep. She started making plans for Jim. She would send some of the money home and also to the upcoming youth group which her former teacher had introduced her to during the holidays. Though she had not been comfortable meeting the group, she accepted out of respect for the teacher whom she had bumped into on her way from the market. She now talked to her mother for longer and would end the call by passing her regards to her father.

Soon, it was the end of February; the end-of-semester examinations were quickly approaching, and so, the library was busier than usual. Students no longer went to the library just to run their fingers across the spines of books. They crammed outside the library waiting for it to be opened. They would then rush in to secure seats.

It was the same story at the ADD Building in the evenings. The seating spaces would fill up quite early. The few studios were reserved for use by architectural students. They would block the entrances to keep away other students and busy themselves with either drawing or writing projects as they listened to cool music.

Tom and Lily would book suitable places for study in advance. They would discuss past examination papers or revise lecture notes together. Early one evening, an unanticipated blackout occurred. Students were reading for examinations while some were cooking in their rooms at the time. Lily was having terrible cramps and she had called Tom to postpone the discussion. So, Tom was reading from his room.

Within no time, students had gone on a rampage; it was a bad time to have a power blackout. That evening, windscreens of vehicles using the Lower Statehouse Road were smashed. That was just a precursor of what was to happen the following week. Petrified, Lily watched from her room's window.

"Hi Lily, are you fine?" Juma called after seeing the breaking news about the riot on TV.

"I'm fine, Juma. Thanks for your concern," Lily murmured. "Indeed, there is a blackout, but I think the riot is now dying down."

"Sorry, I got worried when I saw the news." There was silence. Unlike other days where music would be playing from Babirye's room across, or laughter and chit-chat from rooms and within the corridors, there was pristine silence. Lily imagined Halima eavesdropping on their entire conversation, which she would otherwise not agree with. Lily walked out to Babirye's room.

"Are you still there?" Juma asked. "Yes."

"Fine. I'm sending you some money to buy candles."

Tit-tit, a message came through Lily's phone. Juma had sent five thousand shillings! Since there were no lights, Babirye suggested that they go shopping. Lily protested, saying that it was late, and she was also not feeling well. Babirye insisted, arguing that many students walked to and from town 24/7. And that was the first of the many times that Lily went to town at night.

Lily gave Babirye a one-thousand-shilling note from the money as an appreciation for her pieces of advice. In the supermarket, Babirye bought drinks and other niceties.

"Why don't you buy more dresses and shoes to pamper yourself so that you can impress him even more?"

"Sure, that's an excellent idea," Lily agreed, adding, "tomorrow." They walked back to campus.

* * *

Lily skipped her morning lectures. Babirye took her out shopping at Gikomba market.

They walked past the Machakos Country Bus Station, past a few banks and a throng of M-Pesa shops. In the several hardware shops along their way, sellers wore either dirty navy blue or green dust coats. A few steps ahead, two young men were loading thick, heavy wooden doors on an old Nissan pick-up car.

"And how did you know all these places?" Lily quipped. "You have to."

"Oooh, okay. And do you know Mathare North? I mean, do you know it well? No?"

The day Lily had visited Mathare before she travelled home, she had just taken a bus back to town without having stepped an inch inside the slum.

They roughly brushed shoulders with people along the way, past a preacher shouting in *tongues* to no particular audience. He would often

131

raise his Bible with the right hand as if calling on the angels to drop from the clouds.

Soon they were at the market. At the entrance, young hawkers rushed towards them shoving all manner of merchandise; polythene bags, dresses, handbags and other wares.

They went past the makeshift stalls that lined the cramped path, fine layers of bed sheets, curtains and carpets piled on wooden tables or hanging on the stalls.

"*Beba mia*," a seller shouted in Lily's ear, calling out to buyers. *Beba mia*, it rang a few times before someone else shouted from the opposite direction, "*Hamsini bei*!"

"*Hamsini*?" Lily asked.

"Yes, only fifty shillings," Babirye confirmed. They bent down and joined other buyers making their selection from the pile of skirts placed on a low wooden stand.

"*Dhati! Dhati!*" someone shouted from behind them.

They bought a few skirts and tops from different sellers before proceeding down a muddy path that slurped at the soles of their open shoes, past a group of cabbage sellers chatting in rapid Kikuyu – which she thought could be Jim's father's tongue. Or could it be the Dholuo the women with skins that bore thick hues of dark melanin, from whom they bought *omena*, silver cyprinid, were conversing in? They then proceeded to an old woman from whom they bought a few tomatoes and onions.

Back on campus, Lily tried on her clothes again from Babirye's room. Among them were two pairs of shoes, several dresses, and several mini-skirts. Both of them agreed that they were perfect.

Lily knew the miseries of her family were soon coming to an end. She would do whatever was possible to save her family from abject poverty. And Juma was key. *I cannot get to the top by sitting on my bottom*, she told herself.

Lily didn't respond to Tom's calls that day. And Tom didn't visit her either. Geoffrey was away that day, which gave him a good time to read. Geoffrey turned up the following day only to take a shower, pick a few books and disappear again.

The next time Tom saw Geoffrey was when campaigns for SONU elections commenced. Geoffrey had come to the room to request him to join a group that was campaigning for one of the candidates. The group was about to leave for campaigns at Kabete, Kikuyu and Kenya Science Campuses. When Tom turned him down, Geoffrey placed the bottles of beer he had in his closet and disappeared to the Students' Centre from where a bus would pick them up outside Hall 9 hostel.

He returned late that day, and the day after. Geoffrey was engrossed in campus politics for the entire of that week. He always came back drunk, carrying bottles of beer or packets of milk. A few times, Tom saw him sliding folded notes of two hundred shillings or one hundred shillings under the newspapers spread on the wooden shelves of his closet.

There were frequent *Kamukunji* gatherings in front of Hall 9 that week. The candidates were charged. There was a strong wave against the incumbent because he was purported to be pro the university administration. There were posters along the roads and pavements, in the hostels, on the tuck shop, on gates and at Club 36. The posters at the city clock at the roundabout of Nyerere Road, University Way, Uhuru Highway and Waiyaki Way were the most prominent. Some found their way into town, on the walls of several buildings and the lampposts that lined the University Way and even the gates of Kenyatta National Hospital. Small stickers were also put on the university buses' seats, on mirrors in the washrooms, and even on desks in lecture halls.

On a drizzling Friday morning, candidates and their campaign teams were making the last efforts to woo voters with fliers. Lily ambled along the road early in the morning as she made her way to Chiromo. After casting her vote at the department of biochemistry, she went back to her room to rest. Once in a while, she would peep outside her window to catch up on the happenings.

At around six-thirty in the evening, a group of students gathered outside the Students' Centre. Tension was building up after rumours spread that the incumbent team was manipulating results from the Main and Kikuyu Campuses. It was said that the vice was also spreading to other tallying centres on other campuses. Then information trickled in that the Mamlaka ballot papers had been stolen during tallying, and the administration had aided the incumbent in disrupting the process. With the news spreading like a bushfire in the halls of residence, students immediately shot out of their rooms.

At the Main Campus, the Jomo Kenyatta Memorial Library's windowpanes were brought down, the bookstore broken into and property stolen. Several offices lost their windowpanes before the destruction spread to the halls of residence. From her room, Lily heard a surging crowd chanting from the dark tunnel under Lower State House Road. They were heading towards the Kamukunji grounds in front of Hall 9. The tension gripped every nerve in her as they came close to Hall

4. The unfolding scenario brought back memories of her horrible experience in Mathare slums. It seemed just like yesterday as she recalled the lives that were lost. Feeling helpless, she rushed to sit next to Halima. They hugged and stayed in the embrace for a long time, with Lily trembling terribly.

Tom rushed down from Prefab 10 and joined the crowd that materialised at the *Kamukunji* ground.

"Students power!"

"Power!" the crowd roared back. "Studeeents power!"

"Power!" The crowd roared, louder and stronger than before.

"Comrades ryaaaa!" The aspirant charged them even more as they responded to the chants.

Tom could feel the charge sweep through his veins. For him, each minute spent standing there was a waste of time. "Action now," he said inaudibly. But as the students dispersed to cause more mayhem, he receded to his former coward self and rushed to his room.

One group rushed to the Students' Centre where, within seconds, all windowpanes were down. The plastic chairs were hauled about and some broken, before the door to the bar behind the restaurant was forced open for students to get free beer and sacks of foodstuff.

Another group of students swarm towards the Lower State House Road. At the gate of the YMCA, a car was stopped, and its occupant was ordered to get out and run for his dear life. He did. Shortly, a cloud of dark smoke billowed from the belly of the car as the students turned it into ash and scrap. The chaotic activities extended up to the nearby highway and the roads around the halls of residence. More cars were vandalised.

It was not until midnight when things began cooling down. A few students returned to their hostels. Some were still huddled in groups outside the hotels when Tom came to check on the situation. Though late in the night, tension still hung in the air. Outside the Prefabs, Mamlaka and other hostels, some students relished the looted beer as they shouted, "Osiany must go!" Some were smoking bhang.

Some of the returning students flocked to *Kamukunji* grounds. It had rained earlier in the day, but none of them felt the cold. The place was unusually lively.It was like on Christmas Eve; with white thermal papers stolen from the Students' Centre hanging in hundred stripes from the trees. Hordes of female students watched from their hostel windows, worried about the unfolding events.

Lily had nightmares the entire night, and Halima kept calming her down and silently praying for them all.

Tom returned to the room later that night, only to find Geoffrey in bed with adrunken lady, caressing. "Ooooh sorry, Tom. I should've informed you earlier," he apologised. That night, Tom had to share a small bed with Mwangi, their neighbour.

"Do you know that Ruto and Ongeri have been part of this great institution before?" Geoffrey asked Tom in the morning. He behaved as if nothing had happened, forgetting that he had inconvenienced Tom. "Yesterday, they said that Raila has no authority to suspend them." Tom didn't say a word. Whether William Ruto had dismissed his suspension from the Ministry of Agriculture or Professor Sam Ongeri from his Education Ministry wasn't his business.

Saturday morning was a replica of the previous evening, though the destruction was minimal. Most of the potential targets had already been destroyed. Tension continued to build up. It was odd that most students were pleased with the prospect of the university being closed down and examinations postponed. Students had long depleted their loans. And

135

what was more; they hadn't revised enough to sit for the exams.

When the memo finally came, that all the students vacate the campus immediately, most of them ran from room to room, preparing to depart, in merriment. Tom called Lily to break the news, but she didn't answer. Tom packed a few things and rushed to Hall 4. He was met by a GSU, General Service Unit, battalion deployed to vacate the students, near the hall. He took to his heels.

Lily didn't hear her phone ring, not even when Juma called. Like Halima, they learnt about the memo to vacate after the GSU entered Hall 4. Lily's stomach rumbled with hollow, loud sounds. So petrified, so destitute!

Two teargas canisters were shot outside to disperse the students. Adrenaline welled up in Lily. The shots awakened images of Mathare in her mind again. Then she heard screams of female students from the corridors and the stairs. They hadn't packed their belongings! Scenes of her rape ordeal swept through her eyes in vivid illustrations. She felt the air she breathed becoming cold, solid and inadequate.

Composing herself, she put her phone and the money she had in her pocket. Someone shouted from the corridor. A second later, the thick choking tear gas smoke slithered and writhed under their door. Lily felt choked; her eyes could no longer see well. She could no longer hear whatever Halima was saying. Halima moved to the floor where Lily had collapsed. Halima held her by the shoulders and struggled with her weight.

Chapter Fifteen

Lily and Halima arrived in their room almost at the same time. A few of their belongings were missing, but the room was cleaner and more organised than the way they had left it. She was grateful to Halima for having saved her. Halima had struggled with her out of the hostel on that day the school had closed indefinitely.

"When I got the news that we were reopening, I was glad that we'll finish that examination once and for all," Halima said. They were heading to the Barclays Bank to deposit money; the fines the university had slapped the students with for the damages caused during the strike, an amount Juma had sent her.

"I just hope the SONU guys won't interrupt our studies again."

"I hear there are no SONU officials now. Some of the aspirants were arrested.

An interim body has been selected to run the office."

"Better," Lily said. They met Babirye who had just arrived from Uganda. She looked elegant in her black and brown rolls of unwound *mambo* braids, tight black jeans that curved her butt, a green and brown flowery blouse, and a brown coat. They exchanged pleasantries and went their way.

Tom arrived in the afternoon and immediately rushed to Lily's room.

Halima told him that Lily was washing her clothes from the ground floor outside the hall.

"I missed you," he told Lily. He had told her a few times before, though he had intended to tell her how much he was falling for her, and how much her presence aroused feelings he couldn't clearly describe. His own silent thoughts making him shy away, he picked a piece of paper and shredded it into smaller pieces.

"I missed all my friends, too," Lily said.

"And you look beautiful in that dress," Tom enthused. Lily looked spectacular in the light, tight white *dera* dress that was being soaked with dripping water. Every time she pulled out her clothes from the basin to hang them on the lines, more water dripped on her chest and belly. The more clothes she hung, the more the dress clung to her skin and Tom could see hazy traces of her skin and the exact sizes of the sharp pointing nipples.

"How was your holiday?" Lily asked, looking away in search of a distraction. She poured the water after rinsing her clothes and rushed to the tap to refill the bucket. Tom sat on a slab covering a sewer line as he watched her bend over the tap.

"I don't think that was a holiday at all. The uncertainties of when the university would reopen, and the thought of looming exams made it dreary," Tom said.

"I thought I was the only one concerned about the uncertainties," Lily said as she took the water to continue with the washing.

Not long, their routine of evening study, revision and discussion picked up. Exams were two weeks away. At the ADD, a few students carried thermos flasks, tins of coffee, packets of sugar, and plastic mugs to keep away the cold.

* * *

An invigilator shuffled into the examination room, the size of a

138

football pitch. He looked at the CCTV cameras that poked from all corners before saying good morning. There was an aura of self-importance in his voice as he read the exam rules and took slow, staggering steps around the room. His eyes dug deep into students' eyes to identify suspicious faces on which he would concentrate on during the examination.

In the afternoon, the paper was even harder than the morning one. So were a few of the subsequent papers. But when results came out in late March, Lily was overjoyed for she had scored straight A's in all the papers.

* * *

Lily boarded a matatu to Mathare North after the two-weeks break between the first and second semester. She returned to the campus having just wasted her fare; she couldn't gather enough courage to get into the area.

Mary didn't come back for the second semester. She had deferred her studies. A year earlier, when she had just reported as a first-year, Mary had also deferred her studies due to financial constraints. She had however applied for a scholarship with the *Kenya Airways Ab Initio Pilot Trainee*. So, when Lily and other students were reporting back for the second semester, Mary was reporting for the training that was to take place in South Africa. That gave Geoffrey more time to channel his efforts on chasing after Lily despite knowing Tom was also interested.

As much as Lily started avoiding Tom, and instead talked more with Juma, Tom was still determined to win her over. Though the strains of his efforts seemed fruitless, he wasn't giving up, now that Geoffrey had also shown interest.

With their meagre students' loans, both men competed to impress Lily with random dinners. They would separately take her for fries and chicken at a fast- food restaurant along Moi Avenue, or for *chicken biryani* at the Students' Centre.

Occasionally, they brought her packed chips. With such stiff amateurish competition, Tom decided to step up his game. He befriended a SONU interim official, who slotted him regularly in their several trips to different parts of the country, and one in Kampala, Uganda and Kigali, Rwanda.

Then there was also the trip to Diani Beach, Ukunda, at the Kenyan South Coast. The trip was so fascinating that Tom resolved to pay a second visit with Lily using his own money. True to it, three days later they were in Mombasa.

The Portuguese, he told her that weekend, *built this building in 1593*. They were at Fort Jesus, Mombasa. Lily was wearing dark shades and a wide weaved hat. "But in 1698, it was captured from the Portuguese by the Oman Arabs."

"I know, I've read about it before," she politely dismissed, watching over his shoulder at a group of tourists a distance away. Before getting into the museum, they stood by a concrete block at the shore and watched white water waves sweep over the blue ocean water in ascending layers. The waves softly crushed against the concrete breakwaters and bounced back in rumbling ripples. "I had a friend called Barasa…"

"You've told me about him before," he replied curtly. It was quick, and her glance widened with the shock of his impulse. A warm breeze blew. To avoid an altercation with Lily, he pretended to be concentrating on the sound of a small engine boat in the ocean that the breeze carried with it. Twice, he blankly stared at the shallow waters of the shore where three young Arab boys were swimming in identical pairs of black shorts; the colour of their hair.

"Sure, but I've never mentioned that he once told me that this museum becamea colonial government prison in 1895."

"True, but can we talk about something else?" Tom couldn't hide his impatience. Lily thought she had caught a streak of jealousy in Tom's voice.

After taking a photo together, with the faded, black-patched cream wall of the Fort Jesus in the background, they remained quiet for a while. They walked past two boys sitting on a scrub of moss at the foot of the wall. They silently walked away from the shore, past a group of students disembarking from their schoolbus at the parking lot.

"Just like these caves imprisoned slaves, I feel my heart has been detained for months now," Tom broke the silence. He was pointing at the caves inside the museum. Lily conveniently ignored him. He took her right hand and interlocked their fingers as they moved towards the small windows facing the Indian Ocean. Slightly offended by his public display of affection, she slowly withdrew her hand when they reached the window.

"Tom?"

"Yes, please."

"Can I ask you a question?""Go ahead."

"Why do you do all these things for me? You take me out, you are concerned about my lectures, you change your mood whenever I mention Juma, and now you feel offended because I mentioned Barasa's name."

Of course, Lily knew the answer, but she wanted confirmation. Then she would use the opportunity to tell him that she had no intention of starting a serious relationship with anyone. As days passed, she liked him more and more just as a friend. But there was always a deep fear and resentment whenever thoughts of men crept into her mind, which Tom and Juma were somehow managing to penetrate. For Juma, it was mostly due to his assistance to ease the huge financial burden she had.

He held her by the wrist and said, "I like you." She felt something unexplainable, and confusedly wished he could prolong the grip on her wrist. He wanted to say more, but he felt she would judge him. So, his mouth failed to articulate the right words. He looked at her face, and heard the silence of the rooms and corridors, and the sound of water waves outside. He was now breathing a little faster. He hoped she didn't notice.

"Okay," she said as they stepped out into the courtyard. They sat under a tree and she sipped from her bottle of juice in silence. With his right hand timidly resting over her lap, Tom stared at a tour guide addressing a group of tourists around him; every now and then blinking his sunken

141

eyes. Tom's mind pictured Lily without the tight black skirt and the yellow top that left the entire of her arms exposed to the sultry coastal air.

"You're the most beautiful lady I've ever set my eyes on," Tom said with an intrinsic timidity. His voice was slightly more than a whisper. Lily remained mute, listening to birds that chirped and darted over their heads in the courtyard.

Tom repeated the same statement minutes later as they squeezed through the narrow streets of Old Mombasa Town. They walked past men drinking ginger tea under the awning of old buildings. The streets were thronged with Coastal traders selling spices and Kamba traders with sculptures and wood carvings.

"*Kalimbu mblother, mandam*," they welcomed Tom and Lily in a fusion of heavy Kamba and the polite, slow Swahili accents. But Tom moved on without saying a word.

"Thank you," Lily finally told Tom. From behind them, in the busy street connecting to the narrow alley, three-wheeled, *tuk tuks* and matatus scrambled for passengers with their endless honking. Tom led the way.

They joined Ronald Ngala Road and proceeded through busier streets, past Nawal Centre, past a mosque whose opposite side stood a half-demolished building – which nobody mentioned, but she knew it must have been torched the same way and time it had happened in Mathare – with heaps of dust and thick black soot painted on its open walls, and walked to a hotel around MwembeTayari.

Along the Mombasa Road, verandas of buildings were clogged with pedestrians; women in *buibuis* and hijabs and men of different races, accents and tribes. Near the mosque, they passed a group of tourists, trailing behind a tour guide as they paced down the street towards Digo Road with big cameras. After their lunch, they took a matatu to Likoni ferry – under which water lapped – from where passengers slid out as though coming out of a torn sack. At Likoni, they took another matatu to Ukunda.

The entire evening was spent along the beach. They buried themselves in the fine white sand and ran with swimming tubes into the warm salty water, inside which he peed and felt the warmth of his urine against his groin. Whenever a mild wave swayed water to the beach, they saw it approaching from a distance, and they would run to the shore before the white foam of ocean waves reached them. Tom always remained behind. He watched her run and traced the curves of her body on the soaked light t-shirt and white linen pair of shorts. As the pair of shorts dripped water, it clung tightly to her skin, and Tom's eyes followed the hems of her knickers as they showed on the pair of shorts. Tom would then run after her, a pile of seaweeds that came with the wave impeding his movement.

They threw themselves on the ground and lay facing each other, their bellies and chests resting against fine grains of the white Diani sand. Breathing heavily into each other's faces, they watched each other and looked away into the ocean, or at the throng of tourists who had come to the coast for the sand and the sun, their skin already reddened by the coastal heat.

"Do you know how to play?" She asked, the taste of salty water still on her tongue. She admired the tourists who jumped high and slapped a volleyball, or shouted each other's name; names that the breeze blew away, and they had to repeat a few times, *Here, Pavlichenko. Give me the ball!* Or, *Vladimir, that's mine. I said that's mine!*

Water waves gently caressed the sides of a moored boat that swayed with the waves. They watched in silence. Tom occasionally looked deep into her eyes which were aglow with the golden rays of the setting sun. He made a few random whispers, and after tidewater imperceptibly ebbed, and the water calmed a distance from the shore, they sauntered towards the ocean. Tom walked behind her, stepping on each of her footprints as they picked cowrie shells from little pools or the wet weeds left by the waves along the stretch of the shoreline.

Beach boys stooped down and reached for cowrie shells too, and coconut shells whose meat had been scooped out.

Later, when it was dark, Tom was disappointed when Lily insisted that she would sleep in a different room in the same hotel, which Tom still had to pay for. When she went to her room after dinner, Tom was unable to sleep, so he left the hotel.

He went out in search of a hooker whose perfume would entice his olfactory receptors. He yearned for a soft voice that would please him and flesh that would quench his lustful thirst. He took a taxi and headed back to Mombasa town and then to Mtwapa.

Lily felt a little scared alone in her room, just moments after they had parted. She decided to go and ask Tom if she could share his room, with her sleeping on a mattress on the floor. Once at his door, she held the doorknob, thought better of it for a couple of seconds, and changed her mind. She did not even twist the knob or knock. She tiptoed back to her room and silently closed the door behind her. An hour later, she was sound asleep.

In Mtwapa, Tom asked some *boda boda* riders, and one of them quickly pointed at a distance away, asked for 'something small', and when Tom pressed a twenty-shilling coin in his hand, the guy said, "It's an interesting one. You will enjoy it!"

Tom strode across the road to the club that smelt of too much ambient scenting. The faces of the semi-naked women glowed in the dim light. He hadn't expected it to be a strip club, but the show was so tempting that he couldn't resist the urge to stay and watch. He found space on a table full of old men sipping beer from their glasses and smoking cigarette rolls endlessly as they ogled at the strippers dancing provocatively.

"Coke, please," Tom told the waitress. She hadn't allowed him even a minute to settle.

"A hundred bob," she shouted into his left ear. Tom smelt the scent of her deodorant. The distant look in her eyes betrayed untold agonies, only hidden by the soft dreadlocks on her head and her shiny skin.

Tom sipped his soda slowly, ogling at the two dancing ladies. The ladies swirled in graceful arcs, in tandem with the music, rubbing their naked flesh against the cold shiny metal rods. The men also continued to sip their beers slowly. With their eyes on the girls, a few missed locating their glasses until they were prompted.

* * *

Tom arrived back at the hotel around 4:15 am. As he walked towards his room, a young man beckoned him from a room next to the reception. "She was looking for you late in the night," he told Tom. Lily had been captured on CCTV. The young man was on the monitoring screen, having retrieved the footage.

"See, she knocked on your door, but walked back when there was no response," the man said.

Back in the room, all was silent but the fan. Tom shifted in bed from one side to the other trying to get sleep. He thought of her. He thought of the feelings he had ignored for weeks. He feared she would ask why he didn't open the door when she knocked, or where he had been. He regretted having left for Mtwapa, and imagined what they would be doing now if he hadn't gone. Images of the strippers still crossed his mind with conjuring ideas. Should he go and knock on Lily's door?

Twenty minutes after a distant *adhan* for *salat al-fajr*, he walked barefoot to the shore. He was dressed in a pair of shorts and a singlet. The watchmen at the beach were surprised, for it was barely twenty minutes past five, but opened the gates. He said 'thank you' and slowly strode down the sloppy sandy terrain. The ocean water had receded even further, but he could still hear the soft hum of its distant waves. A few rocks popped out of the white sand.

The air was humid and smoky, the colour of Europe. He squinted to look at the sand, but he couldn't trace their previous evening's footprints. He made steps into the damp sand and sat on one of the rocks. He felt cold dampness on his soles as wet sand pushed up the spaces between his toes.

From a distance, the sun's rays appeared far below the dome of the calm and gentle waters. With his phone, he took pictures of the sky, the calm waters, and later, the sun's brilliant glow. He then thoughtfully watched the waters flow back in mild waves, slowly tonguing his feet until they were submerged. He sat down to look at the photos he had

145

taken.

"I pray that you, Lily, will shine such brilliant rays in my heart the way this sun shines on the earth," he said to himself as he strode towards the hotel. He pictured Lily waking up to the gentle hum of the ocean and the chirping birds. The first thing he would do when she opened her door was to whisper, "Good morning, sunshine," and then get her a glass of juice, or a cup of lemon tea. What he didn't know was that Lily had had a nightmare that scoured her memory and exposed her fear of men. Again!

In the days that followed, she would have more nightmares. She dreamt of violence and mutilated bodies, and of perpetrators of violence walking scot-free, some serving in the same government offices that were supposed to dispense justice to the victims. In those dreams, she would see flashbacks of what had happened and would shout and get traumatised for days.

"Good morning, sunshine," he said when Lily opened the door for him.

Chapter Sixteen

Umpteen times, Geoffrey hosted different ladies, and Tom had to get used to being *exiled*. That coerced Tom into efforts to prove his courage and manhood. He struggled to chase after Lily, but there were no signs of her giving in to his attempts. So, at last, intrigues of cushioning himself from cracks of heartbreak by getting another lady in his life finally swept him.

"Look for someone else," one of his friends had once whispered to him as he was placing a call to Lily, a call that went unanswered.

"I think I need to," Tom agreed. So, the friend introduced him to a phone chat application through which Tom met a lady called Eve. He would now spend most of his late nights chatting with Eve.

More feelings burgeoned between Lily and Juma. Although Lily had agreed to the relationship with the aim of getting money to meet her needs, there was the subtle pleasure in flirting with a mature, rich man.

Tom, on the other hand, became a closer friend so fast that she started confiding in him. She even told Tom that she was seeing Juma. But the deluge of feelings Tom had for her excessively crazed him that he didn't mind clinging on a thin layer of intuitive hope. He knew he was very impecunious when Juma was in the picture and that his lack of money contributed to watering down his efforts. But he wasn't going to give up.

"What did he say yesterday when he called?" Tom asked Lily one day. They had just finished their *Evolutionary Biology* lecture and were heading for lunch.

"Who?"

"Juma, of course; I'm sure he called." Tom held Lily's hand as they crossed the Riverside Drive and walked to a lad selling roasted maize by the roadside. As they then sauntered towards the Prime Bank Building at the junction joining Ring Road Westlands Lane, Lily veered away from the subject. Deep in her heart, however, she was impressed that at last, Tom was accepting things the way they were.

And the positive signs Lily showed pleased Tom. She would gladly hug him or accept his offer for a cup of coffee at the Students' Centre in the evenings without hesitation. Tom would also visit her room frequently. Most of the lunchtime interludes, they would walk together slowly. On a few afternoons, they would sit on the benches at Chiromo Campus and watch tree leaves fall. One day, Tom picked a flower and placed it at the edge of her top. The flower dropped into her cleavage. When Tom attempted to remove it, she slapped his hand so hard that it kept tingling with pain for minutes.

When Juma came that evening to pick Lily up for a drink in town, she rushed to Juma's car leaving Tom slightly frustrated and embarrassed. Tom wished he had seen Juma's face through the car's tinted glass; just for the consolation of placing a face to his struggles.

Juma would call Lily, and in the evenings, they would go for coffee or a movie in town. And every time she planned to go to Mathare to search for Jim's father, Juma would pass by or call. She never said no to his coffee dates. Tom and Lily no longer had frequent discussions. Halima missed Lily as she spent more of her time in Babirye's room making plans.

In Tom's pursuit of Lily, he gradually grew away from hitting the books as much as he did before. Her beauty had invited emotions in him whose thirst couldn't be easily slaked. He had fallen head over heels in love, and it was driving him round the bend. Tom even tried to evince his feelings to her, but his efforts did not bear any visible fruits. Were it not for his money, he knew, Juma's wheel of life wouldn't rotate with such ease. But Tom's efforts were not completely vanquished.

In the first week of May 2010 when Nigeria was mourning the death of their President, Tom went to Lily's room to tell her that he loved her. He had to tell her the truth that day, he told himself. She wasn't in when he arrived. He found Halima who wasn't pleased with the decision a three-Judge Bench of the High Court had ruled that the inclusion of *Kadhis'* Courts in the current Constitution was illegal and discriminatory. She told Tom that Lily was just within the hostel and so he decided to wait.

"I'm worried about Lily," Halima said with a disturbed look on her face. Tom listened keenly, not knowing what to say. Halima continued, "She has changed so much; we don't even talk as much as we used to."

Thoughts of Juma crossed Tom's mind. He clenched his teeth at the intuition that Juma was now the centre of Lily's life.

"Lily doesn't even attend church like she used to, nor call home as often.

Please talk to her about it," Halima implored.

A "No..." escaped Tom's lips. Halima raised her eyes to meet Tom's.

"No, I mean, you are the best person to talk to her," Tom explained.

As he waited, more courage and ideas, some which had kept brewing in his heart and mind for so long settled in. He visualised how, finally, he would say, "I love you. I always have."

"Lily, we should try applying for the clerks' positions advertised by the Interim Independent Electoral and Boundaries Commission," he told her when she finally arrived. She had been at Babirye's room. All the courage and ideas that had formed in Tom's mind disappeared with her arrival.

When Tom left later, he felt stupid for not having expressed his love to Lily. Lily started searching for her certificates in her wardrobe. It was then that she came across Barasa's envelope and the one-hundred-shilling note gift from Francisca. She opened the envelope to find a one-thousand-shilling note.

"Lily, you're like my sister," Halima said that night. "I know."

"How would it be if your happiness didn't solely depend on someone else? You know men can take advantage of our situations to make us and our feelings hostage; so they can use us when and how they want…"

"I don't understand you, Halima," Lily's heart lurched.

Deep into the night, Halima tried to convince her to get an alternative means of livelihood without depending on men. Halima suggested that Lily could start and run a small business at the campus. She mentioned photocopying or printing from their room, or selling tomatoes and onions to other students in the hostels, or selling scratch cards or dresses from Gikomba. Amid their conversation, images of three men ripping her clothes in Mathare came floating again in Lily's mind.

Lily thanked Halima for sharing her thoughts and the options she had suggested. Halima prayed for Lily in a prayer of supplication.

For the first time since she reported to the university, she called Barasa in the morning. "Thank you for the money, I really appreciate it," she said, and they talked about each other's health and that of their families. Barasa informed Lily that in Nigeria, Dr Goodluck Ebele Azikiwe Jonathan would be sworn in as President after the death of Umaru Musa Yar'Adua. And they left it at that.

Tom woke up very early and wrote his application letter and made copies of his documents. He then rushed to the dark bathroom with dirty walls. He drenched himself in frigid water, and carefully stepped out with caution not to get in contact with the gross walls, wading cautiously through the flooded water as if he could float, and in the next ten minutes, he was already leaving his room. He passed by Lily's room and together, they left for the offices of the electoral body.

Lily's call gave Barasa a new lease on life. He whistled and sang the entire day. Even when he dialled Lily's number but she didn't respond, he didn't feel slighted. Later that night, he called her again twice, calls that remained unanswered. He then sent her a message telling her that she meant everything to him. Part of his long message read: *I love you; a love that would always be tested by the sands of time. I genuinely love you to the depth, breadth and height my soul can stretch to. I loved you once, I love you still, I always will.* Lily didn't respond, for she liked him just as a friend. Nothing more. Nothing less. Nothing else. But she was grateful that he still cared.

* * *

Lily would now spend most of the time in the library after heeding Halima's advice. With Halima's advice and the memory of her rape etched in her mind, she switched off her phone most of the time to avoid Juma. She had minimal contact with Tom and even reduced her visits to Babirye's room. Whenever they met on the stairs, corridor or the washroom, she would tell Babirye that the coursework was weighing her down. But once or twice when she stayed late reading at the ADD, she felt it would have been better if Tom were there because news of Philip Onyancha whose craving for women's blood had shot the roofs. Lily feared there could be many other unknown serial killers roaming around the campus.

* * *

Friday nights at the campus were always a spectacle. So, having not met Lily for days, besides during lectures, Tom went to see her. He found her sitting by the window watching students moving up and down. Those from wealthy families would park their cars outside Hall 4, waiting for their girlfriends. Once the ladies slid into the cars, they would zoom off at top speed while the cars vibrated with booming music.

Some male students were at the staircase of Hall 9 discussing politics in loud voices. Lily took an interest in their dressing: jeans trousers, tight-fitting T-shirts and sharp blazers. Some were shouting vulgarities from across Hall 9 and Hall 5.

Most of the Political Science students stayed in Hall 9. They sat by the benches near the Students' Centre, with their big smartphones, watching the smartly dressed campus ladies walking past. They would comment on

151

the ladies' dressing, appearances and even endowment as they passed by.

In between, they discussed the murders of JM Kariuki, Tom Mboya, and the death of Ronald Ngala. When the debates got heated, the most vocal supported their arguments with a quote or two, and even digressed to talking about Martin Luther King Junior, Mohandas Karamchand Gandhi, Barack Obama or Benazir Bhutto.

"There'll be a football match just outside there," Tom pointed to the crowd forming outside. Both Lily and Halima knew about the match.

"We knew it even before you," Lily said and stood to get a better view. It was already dark and the place was already crowded. Some students had carried chairs from their rooms.

"Please, come along, let's go and cheer for our team," Tom said as if it were indeed theirs.

"And which team is this?" Halima asked.

"It's the quarter-finals between Uruguay and Ghana," he said. "The game is starting in twenty minutes at the Soccer City Stadium."

Her response wasn't longer than an "Okay."

"We now have ten minutes to prepare." Tom got up and walked towards the door. "Let's secure a good place in the crowd. Are you joining us, Halima?"

Halima said she wasn't sure she would, and she didn't.

Tom and Lily watched the game from the periphery of the crowd. Some students wore Ghana jerseys. Whistles pierced the air from different spots in the crowd whenever Ghana attempted to score. Slowly, an electrifying, profound passion and tension built up in Lily. The mood swirled through all the fans. Students watched silently, with brief shouts and exclamations of, "Aaaa!" whenever Ghana missed the goalpost. Some even kicked their feet slightly or pushed their torsos forward as if they were the ones attempting the scores.

The cold breeze that swept through the crowd didn't surpass the little warmth Tom felt when Lily moved closer to him. She could unconsciously cling to his arm but quickly thrust her hands back into the pockets of her sweater. Her magical touch gave him a sense of worth.

The game ended in a draw after full-time. So, they went into penalties. Ghana's goalkeeper was tricked to dive in the wrong direction, resulting in a loss to Uruguay. A disappointed Tom whispered goodnight to Lily as he went mourning to his room.

Before the start of the match, Geoffrey had strolled into the room with his classmate, Lydia. He caressed her skin with a light touch as if a little heavier touch would dig into a fresh wound. It hadn't been the first time they had intimate contact, but he trembled with nervousness, and she looked away from his narrowing glare. She groaned with passion, and before her mind fully synthesised the pleasure, Geoffrey rushed to pull down her knickers. They curled into each other's body enough to feel their heavy heartbeats.

When Tom pushed the door open, the feet that dangled from under Geoffrey's blanket first met him. He stopped to confirm that he was right. Annoyed by another *exile*, he stepped back, making a loud click and slammed the door. He was irritated and emotionally charged in equal measure as he walked to the main entrance of the hostel. He stood there for a few minutes, thinking. He then walked back and stood closer to the door. He could not stand the sounds of moans and the creaking bed. After a few seconds, he locked the door from outside and walked away.

On his way to Hall 4, he called Lily. She descended the stairs and joined him on the benches outside the hostel. They talked about how it had been fun to watch the match together, and a little of nothing and everything.

"I think I have always nursed feelings for you," Tom finally said. He felt as light as a feather in a windstorm when the words came out.

"Thank you," Lily said. She didn't even question the fact that he 'thought'. He thought he nursed feelings for her? But the hidden truth was, unlike Juma to whom she had developed feelings, she didn't feel the same for Tom. His efforts to engage her in a calculated conversation came to naught, with Lily avoiding the subject with precise deliberateness. A cold breeze laced through Tom's hair after she left. He continued thinking about their encounter. He didn't hear from

153

her again that night; neither did she pick up his calls. After calling her thrice, her phone went dead.

* * *

That weekend, Lily went to Mathare North for the third time. This time, she went deep into the area where she used to stay. Children still walked half-naked. Mwaura's pharmacy was no longer there and the Gaza shop was now a charcoal store. Many of the faces were not familiar, except a few of the vegetable sellers. She did not get into the plot but went to say *hi* to the few women she could recognise.

They briefly talked about their current life experiences, but they avoided discussing the 2007/2008 crisis. She was afraid and ashamed; she could not compose herself and ask if anyone of them knew her rapists. She didn't even want them to know that she had been raped during the chaos.

But they mentioned to her that Mambo, Myche and others had been arrested thereafter. It was common knowledge that Mambo's uncle had approached Marto, a wealthy businessman, for a loan. He had used the money to bribe judges to secure Mambo's freedom. But the women never talked about the rape. They pretended they knew nothing of that sort ever happened, but instead emphasised how Mambo and the team had been arrested for injuring victims and looting property. They said this repeatedly, as if it would purge them of a guilt they didn't understand; it was their way of telling Lily of how much they were sorry, and that justice had been served.

* * *

A dejected, grumpy and depressed Lily returned to the university with her emotional hurricane in full force. She didn't want to speak to anyone. She didn't have the energy for any interactions. Tom's attempts to reach her were all in vain. Her phone was off that day, and the days that followed. During lectures, she avoided him like a plague; and Juma, Barasa and Babirye too, all of them.

The following month, after Tom found a pair of dusty red knickers under Geoffrey's bed while sweeping, and fought temptations of sniffing its dusty scent, he went to her room. Lily wasn't in the room. Halima, who was not in her *buibui*, was shocked to see him. She hadn't expected a male visitor.

Halima was wearing black jeans that hugged her curved hips. Her light blue top had open slits at the shoulders, and her breasts dug sharply into the top. Tom noted her brown toenails with henna, protruding from her open leather shoes.

"Wow, you are beautiful!" Tom genuinely commented.

"Thank you," she said with a smile before mumbling a memorised sacred verse under her breath. Her face looked smoother and lighter. Her lips were moist with a pinkish hue and her eyes sparkled with white and black. Tom admired Halima's long, smooth and black wispy hair, tied behind in a ponytail and tiny golden studs that shone from the lobes of her ears. "I'm sorry, I didn't know you were coming," Halima said, quickly reaching out for a *khanga* to cover her head.

"You are better that way. In fact, all my visits will be unannounced." Tom joked, but quickly realised that she was uncomfortable with the discussion.

"Where is she?" he changed the topic. "She went to the library in the morning."

"Please, ask her to check with the IIEBC guys. They just called me. I'm supposed to report for training tomorrow."

The following day, he sat next to Lily in a training hall. A week later, they were conducting the Constitutional Referendum as polling clerks in the same polling station; a primary school from whose opposite side, across the fence, men whistled at her from their tall bar stools.

Images of Halima in her tight jeans would, from time to time, flash in Tom's mind. "Hi," he wrote her a text one night. Halima replied promptly. Feeling jubilant, he texted again, "Hope u had a good day."

She didn't respond! He had to delete the third text he had already drafted. Besides, she knew he loved Lily. She would not fall for his antics.

When the new constitution ushered in a new political dispensation in Kenya, on a Friday in August, there was an air of elation. People's faces shone with pride. Students gathered at the entrances of their hostels to discuss the momentous development. Expectations were high; they talked about the fruits of independence trickling down even to the folks in villages. Lily had the same hope; that her parents would also benefit from the devolved government enshrined in the new constitution.

She followed the proceedings at Uhuru Park from the hostel's TV room. It was the day of the promulgation of the constitution. Tom went to Uhuru Park with a number of his SONU friends. They found themselves squeezed in a mammoth of sweat-smelling humanity. The happy mood cut across the whole country. Everyone praised the electoral body for managing the poll well.

That night, Lily received a call from home. She read happiness in Francisca's voice. She knew it was about the referendum, but it was partly something else.

"Jim recognised you. He called out 'Mama' when he saw your photo," Francisca said excitedly. Jim had just turned two years that month. *How about baba? Did Jim utter anything of the sort?* Lily wanted to ask. "Does Jim still stickhis thumb in the mouth?" She asked instead.

After the Holy month of Ramadan, Halima invited Lily, Tom, Babirye and other friends to celebrate Eid al Fitr.

"*Eid Mubarak*," a friend, Hanifah, greeted her on arrival.

"*Taqabbalallahu minna wa minkum,*" Halima responded; a response Tom tried to memorise but forgot even before the celebrations were over.

Students formed tribal and regional unions and associations. Tom became active in regional politics. He would attend the Kisumu County University Students Association more often. He was also directly or indirectly linked toother associations.

"Would you mind us having dinner tomorrow in town?" Tom asked her. The electoral body, IIEBC, had paid them a month earlier, and that meant his pockets were quite loaded. Unfortunately for him, she wasn't in the mood. In another attempt, Tom requested her to accompany him to a reggae concert where Alaine was performing at the show, and they talked about a 25-year-old lady from Samburu, whose name – Naisula – meant victory. Naisula had been decorated with the Presidential Order of the Grand Warrior Award for her efforts in advocating for peace amongst warring communities. Naisula's work and peace initiatives undoubtedly inspired Lily.

Slowly, Lily started hatching ideas on how she could empower the girl-child. This had been at the back of her mind for some time. She would draft proposals to NGOs and local leaders requesting funding.

Lily sent half the amount she earned as a polling clerk home. She used the remaining amount to start the business of selling tomatoes in the hostel. This was the only business she had had experience in. After a few days, she realised that it was consuming her study time. It was also tiresome. Not many students bought from her, and Babirye persistently discouraged her.

Lily had left for Gikomba one afternoon to buy more tomatoes when Juma visited. When she returned to the room, birthday gifts from Juma were waiting for her. It was the 11th of November again. Juma had also left a note asking her out for dinner. She didn't confirm. When he called, she didn't pick up. She was sure she would have trouble explaining her recent silence. Instead, she just sent a text thanking him for the gifts. She shared the gifts with Babirye. Babirye insisted that there was no harm in going out for dinner with Juma.

* * *

In the scorching heat of that afternoon in December, Lily lengthened her strides through Nairobi's bustling streets. The sun burnt down on her skin as though she were a delicacy and it wasn't part of the recipe. A few times, she squinted to check if there was more than one sun. Juma was top of her mind. Tom was somewhere at its periphery, but Barasa had long receded into oblivion. And so, when she got to her room and saw an incoming call from Barasa, she thought it was his political talks, perhaps the most recent one of Côte d'Ivoire where there was an imminent crisis. But it was not about both Alassane Ouattara and Laurent Gbagbo claiming victory after a Presidential election. It was about Jim. He was seriously ill, again. Lily sent her mother all the remaining money and was leftwith nothing to buy tomatoes.

That same afternoon, Tom swapped with Geoffrey's roommate. They had moved to new separate rooms in Hall 2 hostel for their second academic yeartwo months earlier. How happy Tom was to finally stay in a real hostel and not the wooden structure first years lived in! Halima and Lily remained roommates, but now were in Box Hostel.

* * *

While Lily travelled home for the December break penniless, Babirye was flying to South Africa.

And even when they resumed studies, Lily was even more broke than before. She didn't have money for food; not even enough to buy sanitary pads. The only money she had was the one-hundred-shilling note her mother had gifted her. For two days, she had gone to get cotton wool and tissue papers from the students' clinic, which she used in place of sanitary pads. In despair, she started calling Juma again for frequent "hellos". And Juma did not disappoint.

With time, Juma's help cemented their relationship again. Lily and Tom continued being confidants despite Lily's relationship with Juma. She would spend a little more time with Tom now than in the recent past.

With Juma providing almost everything that she wanted, her life started pacing ahead of her income.

Chapter Seventeen

"Lily, you can manipulate him in your favour," Babirye's words rang in Lily'sears.

"This time around, I'll give it a serious thought," Lily said. She was tired ofher financial struggle.

"Look," Babirye stretched her hand and picked her brand-new handbag from the reading table. Thin silver hoops of her earrings dangled with a distant clank. "I get around a lot," she added, picking her space grey iPad from the handbag. It still had the scent of the Asian shop they had bought it from at Shaka International Airport in Durban.

Lily moved closer to look at the photos from the iPad. Babirye's finger swiped the photos across, the golden cutex on her nail and the green-strapped small wristwatch coming into Lily's view as she swiped. It was the same watch she wore in the first photo; with a black top and a pink coat with black stripes at the pockets and around the zipper. On her right hand, she held a glass of white wine, her eyes whittled as though deprived of sleep. "You must have taken a lot of wine here," Lily joked.

"It's true; I had drunk quite a lot." Babirye paused to push a strand of hair obstructing her right eye and continued, "And this was in a very nice restaurant in Johannesburg. We had driven to and from Pretoria, then went on a shopping spree at Sandton City when we returned to Johannesburg in the evening." She then swiped through the photos until she landed on one that she was lookingfor. "Here," she pointed, "this is Sandton City." They had taken the photo at the entrance of the mall. She swiped to another photo taken at the 6-metres tallstatue of Nelson Mandela. "And this is Nelson Mandela Square."

Lily remembered the stories Barasa would tell her about Rhodes Island and Mandela's imprisonment. Her mind flashed back to the day she had escorted Barasa from their home, feeling lighter. He had told her about how he used to sneak at night to watch the cinemas shown twice a month by the Kenya Film Corporation. He had told her of a flying rotten egg that had landed on his shoulder, of actors like Billy Blanks who was as black as he was, or Bolo Yeung whose broad-split chest vibrated with ease and Cary-Hiroyuki Tagawa who had the fury of an angry tiger. Barasa's way of describing the actors surged her admiration. She had also admired how he had worked hard to build his hut. And now for a moment, she missed him.

Babirye showed her more photos she had taken at the Kruger National Park, with lions in the background. There were more photos showing the blue ocean and hazy, humid air of Durban, spectacular beaches and low clouds that engulfed the Table Mountains of Cape Town.

"Look at us here!" Babirye pointed to a photo and narrated to her the experience.

Lily visualises Babirye with the MP standing by the window of their hotel room. Standing behind her, he places his hands around her waist and runs his lipssoftly around the back and sides of her neck. Watching the greenish water under a long exquisite footbridge connecting the Canal Walk Shopping Mall and the hotel, he whispers endearments into her ears; how he adores her in a thousand declarations of love. Lily further imagines him sweeping Babirye swiftly to the bed, and how an aroma of the blooming flowers greets them at the Kirstenbosch National Botanical Garden. She sees them touching the leaves and flowers that leave a sweet fragrance on their fingertips.

"Wow, you must have enjoyed your holiday," Lily sighed at the notion.

"Sure. I did, and you too can. You can enjoy it even more." The statement ran over and over again in Lily's mind. It was true, she believed. It was only that she hadn't given it serious thought. If Juma did what he did without her asking, how much would he do if she showed open willingness?

That evening when she watched Babirye put on her make-up in front of her mirror, she thought of Juma. "You look beautiful," she told Babirye.

And the following day, she asked Babirye how to use different shades of make-up, the rationale of colour and type of make-up to use. Babirye showed her the shades, explaining every detail on how to use them.

Back in her room, Lily went through every step for the next two consecutive days to start off the process of learning her new interest in make-up. Slowly, she started borrowing Babirye's make-up items. She began by applying faint lipstick. Then the NYX eyebrow pencil followed. By the end of the month, she was pretty well familiar with moisturising, priming, use of eye shadow concealer, foundation, eyeliner and even mascara, and their purposes and effects.

When Juma pressed dinner invitations on her the following month, she had learnt to apply the make-up considerably well. After thinking about Juma's invitation over and over, she was sure that's what she wanted. She didn't want to avoid him anymore. She wanted to have a relationship with him. She wanted to travel to places and be treated like Babirye, if not more. Most importantly, she wanted to get money for her needs, and to aid her hidden mission; searching for Jim's father. She needed that money for her planned trips to Mathare and wherever the search would take her. She wanted to find Jim's father. She wanted him to take his bastard son. She wanted him to face the law and pay for his crime. But above all, she wanted him to answer her "why?"

By four o'clock in the evening, she was meeting Juma, Lily had completed her class assignments and even written her laboratory report.

Lily sat by the mirror in Babirye's room and moisturised her face.

Babirye had escorted her to a cosmetic shop where Lily bought make-up that matched her skin colour; high-definition primer by *MAC*, *Maybelline Dream Lumi Touch* Highlighting Concealer, *NYX* Eyeshadow Base, a *Dior* lip glow and a few other selected brands.

Babirye leant forward and made perfect lines on the upper and lower brow with a black eyebrow pencil before making light strokes between the two lines. She brushed the brows upwards before she started applying *Graftobian HD Glamour Crème*.

"I look like a Zulu traditional dancer," said Lily as she laughed at her imagein the mirror.

"Wait until I am done; you'll look like the famous guests the Zulu dancers entertain."

Babirye applied spots of the concealer under Lily's eyes, over the cheeks, alongthe nose and over the forehead, before she started applying the foundation. She applied the eye-shadow base on top of the eyelid with incredible ease.

"Come on, give me a smile," Lily's lips spread into a forced smile, her cheeks protruding. With that skew, Babirye easily brushed on the cheeks towards both ears. She finished with the eyeliner and dark mascara that erected Lily's lashes.

Lily picked the red lipstick and drew fine lines on the edge of her lips before applying a thick layer. The lips were red as a ripe watermelon. Satisfied, she smacked her lips rapidly to create evenness in the red smear.

"Am I not beautiful?" Lily asked, turning to admire her new look before the mirror. She had come from far, she self-admitted. Many changes had taken place in her life. She thought of the days when petroleum jelly was alone enough and laughed. Her skin looked softer and shinier than before. She had even started to add weight.

"I'm surprised you are just discovering that," Babirye said.

"Wow, you look stunning," Halima told her later when she went back to their room to dress up for the evening. Her nails shone. She placed her feet, one at a time, on her bed and squeezed thick lotion onto them.

"I love the scent," Lily whispered to herself, rubbing the lotion against her left leg; from toes to thighs.

"That makes the two of us," Halima said.

"Try, you'll like it," she threw it on Halima's bed.

Halima watched Lily put on a knee-length red dress that curved with the shape of her body. She then emptied her old handbag on the bed before transferring a few items to a black pouch. She stood before the mirror fixed on her closet door, patted her hair with her palm, applied perfume to her underarms, and smacked her lips again.

"Will see you later," she said and left Halima watching a religious video on her desktop computer. The heels of Lily's stiletto shoes clanked on the floor as she walked down the narrow stairs. At the entrance of Box hostel, she greeted Geoffrey who was signing the visitors' book. And with graceful strides, Lily walked outside the compound. A couple of students, Geoffrey, and even the watchman turned to gaze at her when they were sure she wasn't aware.

Lily's heart paced faster, and her breath grew louder with each pounding heartbeat. She was somewhat anxious and fidgety, unsure of how the situation would unfold.

"Wow! You look gorgeous, Lily. Really," Juma commented as he caught a whiff of her perfume as she approached. She was resplendent in her dress. He opened the door for her before going round to the driver's seat.

"Thank you," Lily said with an obvious blush, inhaling the familiar fragrance inside the car.

"You're welcome," he leant against the centre console. Her dress had rolled up and he admired her shiny thighs. Thoughts of placing his hand over them crossed his mind, but he immediately slapped them away. He started the engine, and soft music played from the stereo. She nodded rhythmically to the music, tapping with her feet and humming along carefreely.

"Nice music," Lily said. She threw the black pouch she had on her lap on the back seat and rested her head on the leather headrest. From the corners of his eyes, Juma continued to steal glances at her as he drove on.

There was something incredibly beautiful about her new carefree nature.

"So, how are your studies?" "So far, so good."

Their conversation centred on studies, politics, novels they liked, movies and the places they had visited. Lily wasn't so well informed about the current politics and even the novels Juma mentioned.

"And from the few novels you've read, which ones did you enjoy the most?"

"*Half of a Yellow Sun*. I loved that novel. I wish I could write...I would love to be like Chimamanda. I love her, yet she doesn't even know I exist." Lily wanted to say more, but her mind went blank. "I am..." the words stuck in her throat. Instead, she looked out. Some of the cars had men driving with ladies by their sides. She tried to make out who a relaxed girlfriend, an excited concubine or a napping wife was among them.

Juma swerved to avoid hitting a matatu that had stopped instantly without signalling. "Look at him now," he said, "what does he think he's doing?"

Although he had a driver, Juma drove himself every time he visited Lily.

At the hotel, they took the elevator and waited for the *"Door's closing"* recorded voice, and then stood silently looking at each other.

"Welcome sir, madam," a lady smiling gracefully welcomed them. The staff standing nearby also smiled, a few adding "Hello, sir".

"Thanks," Lily said, smiling back. Has he been here before with some other lady or ladies? Lily thought.

"*Karibuni sana,* Welcome," the lady said again as she led them to the reception desk to check in. Her short black skirt hugged her wide hips tightly. Her voice was soft and cheerful as she spoke in a distant coastal accent.

At the reception desk, Lily noted the painting of a woman with wide hips on an abstract split piece that hung on the wall behind. There was a framed portrait of President Mwai Kibaki next to the painting. The reception desk was shiny, reflecting the clocks on the wall slightly above the painting and the portrait. One clock showed the time in London; the others showed time in Paris, Washington DC, and Nairobi, respectively. The local time showed 7:20 p.m.

"How many others have you brought here?" Lily asked as they sat down after taking the stairs to the second floor. There were traces of jealousy in her voice.

"A number of my business partners. Both genders."

"And how many have taken you out? Not necessarily here." Juma asked injest.

"One. Today." She whispered. She looked into his eyes.

"Good evening. Sorry, would you like to have the menu or would you prefera taste of our day's special?" A waitress interrupted them. She was dressed in an impeccably sleek short black skirt and two-pocket black vest, a sparkling white long-sleeve shirt and a black cravat.

For drinks, Lily ordered a cocktail of orange, pineapple and banana juice, blended with fresh ginger. Juma settled for basil leaves blended with fresh apple and lemon juices and olive oil.

"This one," Lily pointed at an item on the menu when the waitress asked her to pick an appetizer. The waitress jotted down, *Smoked salmon, balsamic onion, mixed lettuce leaves and with balsamic dressing.* Juma ordered *thin slices of cured air-dried beef with arugula, and truffle olive oil.*

They were served with a sumptuous lamb kebab, lamb shish kebab and lamb cutlet served with oriental rice and a dessert of sponge cake, layered with ricotta and chocolate topped with marzipan.

The skyline outside was delightful, augmented by the spectacular aerial view ofbuildings and thousands of neon lights and bulbs, not to mention the headlights of vehicles snarled up in traffic. Juma kept on looking at her as she enjoyed the sight. Images of when Juma had driven her through similar traffic as he tookher for admission in Chiromo flashed in her mind. Back then, the hotel was still under construction. She had hoped that, maybe, one day she would patronise the hotel. Who knows? She had asked herself.

"Time flies," Lily said. Juma was silent for a few minutes. He then

165

broke the silence with stories about his job at the ministry, and about his mother. Then he asked her more about her studies and life's ambitions. They talked about random stuff, but Lily did not ask him why he didn't know his father.

They continued to eat slowly, with Lily handling the cutlery like an expert. Babirye had taught her how to use them. She laughed at a memory of her first meeting with Juma; how she had struggled to use cutlery during breakfast. The ambience was pleasant and soothing with the breezy fragrance circulating. Lily thought the food was very delicious.

For the first time, Lily noticed a wedding ring on his finger and his imported *Montblanc* wristwatch. His fingernails were neat and short. Why had she never noticed the ring before? She wondered.

"Why did you decide to help me on that day?"

"I think I already told you." Both their voices were sprightly soft. "So..." his phone rang before he could continue. He excused himself to pick up the call. Lily overheard him talk about surveillance data, epidemiology, circulating serotypes and other medical jargon.

"Sorry about that," he said after disconnecting the call then switched off both his cell phones. As they continued with their conversation, a medical student she had met several times at Chiromo Campus passed by, headed to the elevators in the corridor. Minutes later, an MP followed. Lily recognised his face; he was the one who had taken Babirye to South Africa and whose photos Lily had been shown. His security detail sat in the restaurant and ordered drinks as they waited.

After dinner, Lily and Juma went to the bar on the upper floor. A live band was playing rhumba music. They sat on a white leather couch in the foyer. There, the view of the city was equally spectacular; the lights twinkled and gleamed from the fringes.

Juma ordered wine for both of them. They nodded to the music as they watched men and women shift their bodies on the dance floor. The men guarded their women around their arms as they rotated in circles. Some of the women wiggled their hips and shook their butts provocatively.

The waiter brought their drinks and served them. Lily was hesitant with the first sip. After that first attempt, she took the second, third and fourth until the glass was empty. As the wine took effect, she got more jovial. They both traded suspicious grins, with Lily laughing at every witty remark Juma made. He refilled her glass.

"Thank you!" Lily said, smiling. She continued sipping from her glass as she listened to his stories.

"You have a family? A wife and children, I mean...?" The question finally slipped through her mind to her lips.

He refilled her glass of wine again and asked for a toast to their new friendship.

He moved closer. "Can we dance?"

"Sure, why not? But you have to teach me the moves."

She walked to the floor with caution. Juma held her waist. He watched her for a moment, dancing out of sync, swaying her waist left and right. He moved closer and held her closely by the waist. He moved her round and round as they danced slowly to TPOK's tunes.

"You remember the song I played the first time in the car when we met?

Massu?"

"Yeah," Lily said, swinging to her right. She lost balance, but Juma swept her weight before she could taste the floor.

"Beautiful!" Juma beamed, pulling her up as they resumed their dance. "Is it beautiful to watch me fall?"

"Never! It's beautiful holding you in my arms and seeing you dance."

"And it's beautiful to dance with you. Especially to these TPOK's tunes," Lily said with a radiant smile.

"Ahaaa, I'm surprised you know."

"You just asked if I remember the song *Massu*. It's easy to place their voices. I knew you would ask which group sang this song."

"Brilliant! Brilliant!" he said with a raised voice.

As they continued dancing, with Lily feeling Juma's eyes tour her body, a man walked in and sat at their table. A shiny gold necklace glistened around the man's thick layer of rolling flesh slabs that passed for a neck.

The top three buttons of his expensive nifty white shirt were open. A waiter approached the man politely. Before even placing an order, the man pulled out a bunch of notes, counted five thousand shillings and slapped them, with blithe arrogance, on the table.

"Sir, this table is occupied," the waiter tried to explain to the man, but he ignored him. The man went ahead and placed his order before lighting his cigar.

"Let's go and talk from inside a room now that we have company at our table," Juma whispered. He had watched the little exchange between the waiter and the man. He took Lily's hand and led her out of the floor. On their way out, Juma tipped the waiter generously for the benefit of Lily's eyes. He then let her walk ahead. Lily could feel his eyes on her. When Lily couldn't tell from the hallway which way to take, he held her waist and led her to the elevator.

The well-designed and bedecked corridor that led to the room was warm and cosy. Beautiful paintings of flowers and wild animals hung on the walls. Juma ushered her inside. The room too was warm and impeccably lit with dim lights that bounced off the crimson walls. She first saw the huge bed with white pillows nicely arranged on it. There was also a table and a sofa set with multi-coloured cushions and embroidery. Juma took her pouch and placed it on the table.

She turned to look around the washroom. It was spacious, well-equipped and sparkling clean. It smelt of a sweet fragrance; unlike the dirty toilets on campus. There were magazines on a small table, several rolls of tissue and a telephone extension. What a life!

"*Je t'aime*," Juma heard a heavy voice say outside their door. A lady stifled a chuckle as the voices disappeared in the hallway. Then there was a distant door banging. He locked their door, too, and went to the bed where Lily sat. From his standing position, he could see her glowing cleavage.

"I love you," Juma said, leaning forward. Was that not the word a man had just told his lady as they passed by their door? Was it not the same word men told ladies without meaning it? Juma moved closer to her. Lily moved away, her hands hugging her midsection. Juma stretched his hands to touch her elbow, but Lily stood up from the bed, her back to him.

"What's wrong, Lily? I thought this was okay with you," Juma quipped."I'm not sure if I want to do this. I...I..."

"Whatever is bothering you, you can tell me. I'm here for you. We can take it slowly. We don't even have to do anything tonight. We can just cuddle," Juma interjected, walking towards Lily, his hands flexing on his sides.

"Did you mean it when you said you loved me?" Lily asked, turning to look at Juma.

"Yes, a thousand times more than you think, more than life itself," Juma assured her, finally releasing the breath he didn't know he was holding.

"Th- th- then show me how much."

"Are you sure Lily? You sound agitated. Are you okay?" Juma took Lily's hand into his and drew her to his chest. "You are shaking."

"Don't be silly. I am fine, just excited with your closeness." Lily leant into Juma, wrapping her hands around his neck. "Love me Juma," she whispered into his chest.

He kissed the tip of her lips, swept her off the floor and carried her to the bed. He laid her nape on a fluffy pillow, then leant in and gently kissed her. There was the taste of her lipstick on her lips. He slowly ran his hands all over her body, feeling her out. He remembered the first time he met her and the instantaneous attraction he had felt, followed by the long arduous days of patience as he wooed her. He could not believe that finally tonight he would have Lily in every way.

As Lily felt Juma's hands all over her body, she tried not to stiffen. She let her body feel. She allowed herself the pleasure of feeling his lips graze hers as he lay fully on top of her. She felt his hands lift her dress, probing, and her body stiffened, her mind fighting to remind her of that day when grabby fingers took a hold of her, forcing her to submit.

Juma stiffened on top of her as if sensing her turmoil. Lily grabbed his neck and kissed him, not sure if she was doing it right. She did not

169

care; she wanted this - Juma and her, like this. She could not allow that day to take this night from her.

"Don't stop," she whispered.

"I don't intend to," Juma whispered back as he removed her clothes, stopping to kiss every exposed inch of her body until she lay bare before him. "You are so beautiful Lily, every inch of you, do you know that?"

"You make me feel beautiful, Juma."

And as Juma joined her in bed after stripping his own clothes, Lily opened herself to him. He grazed his fingers around her nipples and she allowed his fingers' stroke to break goose bumps all over her body. She stroked his back as she arched into him when he lay on top of her. And when he moved inside of her, she moved in tandem with him, grappling to reach for something that every stroke brought her closer to, listening to him whisper to her of her beauty and how amazing she felt. She allowed the words to wash all over, soaking them in, believing in them. And when that feeling she didn't understand overwhelmed her, she let go and screamed Juma's name, smearing his neck with the colour of her lipstick. From a distance, and while pulling the sheet under her with both hands, she heard Juma say, "That's it, let yourself go."

Afterwards, they lay on the bed for some time, just relaxing and listening to the hum of distant traffic outside. Then she stood up from where her oily hair had formed a mark on the sheet, and switched on the air conditioner. The air felt cool on her skin. Suddenly, Juma watched as she staggered nude to the bathroom barefoot. The crapulence in her sent her to the toilet. She bent over the bowel, holding her belly as she threw up. Tired, she knelt and threw up a few more times. Thereafter, she sat there for a couple of minutes. Juma came to check in on her but she shooed him away.

Looking at herself in the mirror, Lily had mixed feelings. Voices of their Sunday school teacher echoed in her mind. *You shall not commit adultery. You shall not covet.* Had she not failed her parents again? Wasn't her startling pregnancy in 2008 enough shame? Had her morals died the moment she had stepped into the city? She looked contrite.

Leaving her thoughts behind, Lily went back to bed. In Juma's arms, static currents started traversing in her again. Her hormones were surging and the beast in her came out yet for another round. This time when they came together, Lily felt alive and free.

Later, she sat on the bed and pulled a pillow to her lap. She bowed, leaning on her palm, and turned to look at Juma. He moved close and nipped at her earlobe.

"I need to go," she said after taking a shower, tugging her fingers through her messed-up hair as she reached for her pouch and took out a comb, lipstick and mobile phone.

Lily and Juma camouflaged their intoxication with mint on their way out. They didn't speak much. She hoped Halima and Babirye wouldn't ask her much. Besides, she had carried a bottle of wine for Babirye.

Soon, Juma hit the highway, and as he ran his hand along her thigh, traffic police flagged them down for speeding. He almost knocked down one of the officers as he pulled over to the side, with hazard lights already on. Two police officers rushed to the driver's window with fury. Noticing that it was Juma, they muttered an apology, saluted, and allowed him to proceed.

Verckys and Veve's *Ndona* was playing on the car stereo.

Nalingayo mingi Ndona eeh, Obandolinga motema eeh, sang the lead vocalist. "Beautiful!" Juma whispered.

Nakobanza mobanda ya ngai naye eeh Ndona Ko kolinga ngai mingi ooh

Nalinga nalulayo tobanda naye.

Lily just nodded, and increased the stereo's volume, provoking Juma to increase it even more. In fact, he decided to restart the song and sing along the English translation of the lyrics:

I loved you so much Ndona
But your beauty discouraged me from loving you
I always feared thinking about sharing you with other men I loved you so much.

Lily did not care whether Juma played the song intentionally.

171

"Thank you for the dinner," Lily said as Juma pulled over the car outside the Box Hostel.

"Can we have another dinner tomorrow?" Juma asked.

Lily held her breath as she entered the room. She did not want Halima to sense the wine smell. As if reading Lily's mind, Halima didn't ask about the outing.

Lily and Juma had fish and *ugali* at a restaurant along Kimathi Street in town the following day, when she wore a tight dress that clung to her hips and showed details of her body, and roasted meat and *ugali* in Kiserian the day that followed. A routine had been inadvertently set. Or intentionally, maybe.

Chapter Eighteen

As Lily was fitting herself well into her new status, Tom felt she was pushing his existence in her life to the periphery. Geoffrey too saw her less often on campus. He was finally giving up on dreams that promised nothing. It was during the month that followed that he met her in Box hostel, two days to Valentine's Day. He was sticking posters of SONU aspirants, wishing students happy Valentines, on the noticeboard and the washrooms, and handing out fliers.

"I wish Mary was around this Valentine's. I would have spent the money I'm getting out of this job to treat her," Geoffrey jested, patting Lily on the back.

"Don't worry; I'll find her for you," Lily said, smiling.

That evening, Lily met Juma in town. She returned late in the evening and went straight to Babirye's room, where they drank a few glasses of wine. She didn't tell Babirye about the MP and the medical student at the hotel.

It had now become a habit. Babirye would bring expensive wines after her outings and the two of them would drink to their merry. Occasionally, Lily would reciprocate. Lily now openly hugged Juma whenever he came to pick her. And on the evening of that Valentine's

Day, when he came with a bouquet of red roses adorned with ivy leaves, he openly held her by the waist and pecked her on her left cheek.

That February, Lily travelled home. She wore a dress that grazed her ankles; it could sweep through morning dew or the afternoon dust. She didn't spend much time with Jim who seemed to be growing fast. She actually beat him up many times for very minor childish mistakes like urinating in his clothes. She would scold him many times too. One time, she beat him so hard that he cried for a long time and caught a fever, but she didn't care to calm him down.

"Nekesa, you can't do this!" Francisca was so angry when she arrived from the market. "Just look at the child…. he looks sick but you haven't cared to give him any painkillers. You haven't given him food as well. Surely…." She held Jim and took him inside the house. Later, she would tell Lily, "My daughter, I understand you don't like him. But you don't have to treat him that way. He's as human as you are, and we can't fault him for what happened to you." Lily started crying because she didn't want to be verbally reminded about what had happened.

Just to be away for a few hours, Lily decided to visit Barasa. Barasa still loved her even though she had been avoiding him. He was surprised to see Lily that he removed his glasses to confirm that they were not deceiving his eyes.

"Lily!" was all that Barasa could say, continuously blinking.

"Yes," Lily responded, searching around the room for the source of the ominous marijuana smell.

"You have a nice house," Lily said. Barasa didn't say another word. His eyes were itchy; the skin around them had darkened from the long use of the glasses. *If Lily had finally visited*, voices in his head, inspired by the marijuana he had smoked an hour earlier, told him, *then she would most likely allow me to lift this dress and touch her breasts.*

Barasa itched close to asking her about her silence, where she now placed him, and what happened to the feelings she had for him. But the fear of her response clutched his throat.

Barasa's mother was equally happy to see Lily. She slaughtered a cock with a piebald comb. Of all Barasa's relatives, it was only his mother

174

who had no problem with Lily, so long as both Lily and Barasa loved each other.

On her way back home, a distant uncle pulled over his bicycle by the roadside and summoned Lily from across the road. After greetings and a small chit-chat about the city, he said, "It has been a long time, my daughter; you should also pay your aunt and cousins a visit." He then said goodbye with a smile and started pushing his bicycle away, only to call her back again.

"And when you get back to the city, get me a mobile phone," the uncle said, smiling again before jumping on his bicycle and disappearing at a bend of the ragged road. Deep inside Lily, she knew the smile was not genuine; that uncle was among the people who had said so many bad things about Lily when she got raped. He had even blamed Lubao for not having married a second wife who would have given him a son instead.

* * *

Jim tried avoiding Lily who openly showed her dislike for him. But sometimes, Jim would be just happy to see Lily and would come to her with a big smile and a jovial mood only to be met with a frown on her face. All that bothered Lily; she wondered how, when in the university, she would somehow miss her child and want to see him and carry him and play with him, but things would be different whenever she was home with him. With such an adorable kid, it bothered her that she always got agitated so fast over nothing. It bothered her that she sometimes still thought of the easiest and painless ways to kill Jim. Lily would get so angry at herself too for being cruel to Jim. Why would she not be grateful for what she had?

* * *

"*Masha'Allah*. You look happy today. What's up?" Halima inquired from an excited Lily one day back on campus.

175

"Let me treat you to lunch today, and I'll tell you."

After Halima had finished her *dhuhr* prayer, they went to Arziki Restaurant. Halima was anxious to know the new development in Lily's life. Was she getting married to her new brother- cum-boyfriend? Halima hoped not.

"The good news is that..." "Mmmmh?" Halima listened intently.

"They killed Osama yesterday," Lily said with a broad smile.

"Are you serious?" Halima asked exultantly to please Lily, though she alreadyknew about it.

"Positive," Lily replied. She wished she could tell how Halima felt now thather father's killer was dead.

"*Bismillah*," Halima dug her fork into a piece of meat and chewed silently.

Lily raised her glass for a toast.

In the hostels, the TV rooms were full with students watching the news of Osama bin Laden's killing. In the evening, students gathered outside Hall 9 to discuss the USA *Navy SEALs* and how they had cornered Osama. In between, the discussions veered to the terrorist attack in Nairobi and Dar es Salaam in 1998, Kikambala at the Kenyan coast, and the 9/11 bombing of the Twin Towers in the USA. The students even shared pictures of President Obama and his security team watching the killing of Osama from the White House.

"You're eating well, huh? About time you hit the gym," Babirye said, laughing, after the zip of Lily's dress burst open. They were passing by a group of students gathered outside Hall 9 discussing the killing that evening.

Soon, they both joined a gym and also started swimming at the YMCA. Theywent on for three months until Babirye moved out of the hostels to live in an apartment outside the campus. The night Babirye moved, Lily was bored in her room. She undeniably felt Babirye's absence. She called home and talked to her mother for a long time. Jim was now three years old. "He asks so many questions nowadays, and he calls me *Mama* and your Dad *Baba*," Francisca told her.

When Lily read in the dailies the following day that Naisula had scooped another award, this time from the International Labour Organisation, Lily's resolve to empower girls was re-activated. She immediately sent follow-up emails for the proposals she had earlier drafted with Tom.

Lily and Babirye still hung out in the evenings. A few times, Babirye would tag her along when going to meet her various men friends. Most were senior government officials or prominent businessmen. They always met in big hotels or members only clubs. At such gatherings, it was evident that Lily's beauty attracted men's attention. Sometimes, she would try to pitch her *girl-child empowerment* ideas to the people, but they changed the subject even before she could delve into the details.

On one occasion, they attended a party where South Sudanese were celebrating their cessation from Sudan and becoming an independent state. By now, Lily could gulp long draughts of wine or beer with ease. It had started as a few sips with Juma, but now she was slipping deep into it. She could even differentiate between the white wine that tasted like apple juice or light yoghurt and red wine that left a strong red grape-like aftertaste in her mouth. She even knew about the latest music and trending musicians.

On another occasion, Babirye's man, a wealthy businessman in a coat with elbow patches, took Lily's number.

"Hi beauty, what are you up to?" Juma said when he called Lily. She had just arrived from that outing. As usual, she had passed by Babirye's apartment to gargle with a strong mouthwash to get rid of the smell of alcohol. She never wanted Halima to know.

"I am watching *Three Idiots*," Lily said.

"Doesn't that make you the fourth one?" Juma teased. "It depends…"

"Anyway, how are they and what are they doing?" "It's a movie, come on!"

"Oooh, I should've asked first," he giggled over the phone. "It makes me look like the fourth one now."

"Sure. All is well," Lily said, and they veered off to other topics before she ended the call. Later, she wished Babirye were there to advise her on

177

how to get more money from Juma.

Babirye's new house was well-furnished. Lily would visit her, especially on weekends, and they would drink wine together. There was always something new in the house whenever Lily visited.

Slowly, Lily started forgetting about her intentions of searching for Jim's father; even though she had the resources to facilitate it. Her mind shifted to the things Babirye owned. She would spend hours thinking about how she could get the same, and her own house too. Jealousy had seeped in. She began demanding more money from Juma and her visits to Babirye became infrequent. For the first time, October, the month dedicated to the Most Holy Rosary, swept by without her realising.

At the stage to Umoja in town one morning, unexpected rain sent people scampering for shelter. Hawkers made a killing selling umbrellas. Women with no coins to part with had to fish out polythene bags from their pouches to shield their hair.

"May I shelter under your umbrella, please?" A young man asked Lily; she accepted. The man was untidily dressed. They both squeezed under the small umbrella. Lily faced the opposite direction, embarrassed by the contact of their arms. Both were quiet as they waited for the next matatu to arrive or the rain to subside. She looked at a *Charity Sweepstake* kiosk a distance from where they were. With its yellow and blue paintings, and a smiling cartoon on it, it brought to her mind a day in her childhood when she had been given fifty shillings to buy sweet potatoes in Kitale town. Instead, Lily had spent the money on a *Charity Sweepstake* lottery and lost. Barasa had to bail her out.

The rain was subsiding. The young man pushed his hand out of the umbrella to confirm if it was considerable so that he could continue with his business. As he drew it back, his elbow knocked Lily's breast, causing a sharp pain. Lily squeezed her eyes for a few seconds to defuse the pain.

She had been feeling a lump on that breast for a long time, but it was only a month earlier that Lily had felt a slight pain. She had felt the pain for a few days but eased it with painkillers.

I am really sorry for that, he said.

No, you shouldn't worry. It's okay. But it wasn't okay.

People were now emerging from the verandas and shelters to the streets. The man thanked her and disappeared into the crowd. Lily still felt the pain.

The pain continued even in the narrow-aisled noisy matatu she had boarded to Umoja. Passengers rubbed their behinds against her shoulder as they passed. The ache was taking time to ease off.

"Which style do you prefer today, sister?" A woman asked Lily as she entered the section that hosts salons at Umoja market.

"We'll make it quick for you, madam," another woman implored Lily. Many others tried to woo her, but Lily knew exactly the salon she was going to. She had been there several times, so she shrugged them all off and walked to the salon of her choice.

Two girls attended to her; each rolling her braids on their shiny thighs as she sat quietly listening to their pep talk. Opposite the salon was an old dreadlocked man whose key-cutting machine made screeching noise. Next to the man was a woman in her early thirties selling *samosas*. Lily wondered how much she made in a day. If one or two hundred, Lily thought, how did she manage to pay her bills, buy food and pay school fees for her children? And did the children care to help?

On her way to take a matatu back to town, Lily passed by a Toyota Probox advertising pesticides parked near a pub. The entire area hosted several small pubs and wine and spirits shops. In Umoja, it was said, pubs and bars outnumbered retail shops.

Once in town, Lily decided to do some shopping at City Market. As she walked along the pavements and verandas, she admired her image in the mirrors of shops.

She knew Babirye would say, "Aaaau, I love your hairstyle," and ask, "Who plaited your hair?" She had told Babirye a couple of times, but Babirye would definitely not go to a salon in Umoja. She preferred the classy ones in town where she would be served with beverages of her choice as she waited to be plaited, and treated to warm body massages afterwards.

179

"Madam, what will you have today?" Lily was welcomed by a vendor at the City Market along Muindi Mbingu Street. She bought chicken from a trader who was alternating between whisking away flies and wiping the sweat on his brow with the length of his sleeve. She also bought a few other groceries before making her way back to campus.

The following morning, when Tom came to help them fix their short-circuited cooking coil, she still felt the breast pain.

"A revolutionary wave is sweeping across Tunisia; the *Tunisian Revolution*. Have you heard about it?" Tom asked. He narrated to both Halima and Lily what it was about. As he explained, Lily prayed that Jim should never revolt against her with a demand to know his father.

Lily's pain persisted with a vengeance for four consecutive days. Juma advised her to check with an obstetrician gynaecologist. She didn't go to check with a doctor but instead eased the pain with painkillers as she had done before, and normal life resumed. Lily drank and went out more often, having completely forgotten her pursuit of Jim's father. She even ignored calls from Milly and Barasa because they mostly called when she was out with Babirye in noisy places and in the company of men. Even when she was certain that it was her mother who wanted to speak to her, she would still ignore the call. Francisca was so worried about Lily's safety, especially because of the investigative story of *Paruwanja La Mihadarati* that everyone was talking about in Kitale. The story exposed dealings in drugs and related murders. And since one of the victims hailed from Kitale, it triggered memories of 2007/2008 in Francisca's mind and got her distraught. A few times, Lily would pick up her mother's calls and Francisca would complain bitterly, demanding to know why she was indifferent. "I usually have no credit to call back whenever I get the missed calls. That's why I haven't sent you money in a while now," Lily would lie. But it was only that her focus now was to dress well, patronise fancy restaurants and live a life like that of Babirye that she didn't send money home.

As a result, Francisca searched for a job to supplement her tomato business. She finally got one; cleaning latrines at a dispensary in Kitale town. She would report with Jim and sit him on the grass nearby. Jim would watch her wash the dirty and smelly latrines as she too kept an eye on him.

Francisca would send most of her meagre earnings to Lily through Barasa every month. Whenever Lily failed to call back, even just to acknowledge receipt of the money or say a word of gratitude, Francisca would imagine the cash wasn't enough and would send even more the next month.

Every evening, after the cleaning job, Francisca would walk home from the market with Jim strapped on her back, swapping her small basket of the remaining tomatoes from shoulder to shoulder while hawking from homestead to homestead. She topped up her earnings with money from her tomato business and sent it to Lily, her only daughter. But Lily never bothered to call back. She assumed that it was Barasa sending the money with hopes of winning her over.

New clothes and shoes were Lily's top priority; she wanted to be like Babirye, if not better. She wanted a house of her own, not the rooms in the hostels which she now thought had no privacy she needed. She started making more demands of Juma. Juma tried to fulfil most of them, but he could clearly see a change in Lily; a change that left him displeased.

When, in 2012, the MP took Babirye to the Maldives on Valentine's Day and Juma took Lily to Naivasha, she wasn't dazzled. Juma even bought her a laptop that day, but she felt that wasn't good enough. She deeply desired to travel to faraway places like Babirye. So, by Easter holidays, she had managed to convince Juma, and they left to holiday in the archipelagos of Zanzibar.

When the taxi came to pick her up from the hostels, she had already packed a few of her clothes for the trip. The cab glided through traffic and in no time, she met Juma who was waiting for her at the airport. The flight was delayed. It gave her time to take photos and update her Facebook profile, just like everyone else, as if it was a mandatory immigration requirement. *Lilian Nekesa at Jomo Kenyatta International Airport Departures, Zanzibar here I come!* She posted.

They sat alternating between watching the plasma screen mounted on the wall and the planes landing and taking off, but Lily couldn't place down her phone. Facebook comments and likes had started trickling in, and she had to *like* and *reply* to some. Once in a while, she would look around at other travellers, airport cleaners, duty-free shop salespersons and other staff, wondering if Jim's father could be among them. If not, where was he? What was he doing? She didn't want to remind Juma that she was once a cleaner at the airport, and neither did he want to tell her what was in his mind at that time; of how they had met at the same airport. When it was finally time to board, they were among the first people in the boarding queue, their shoulders hunched as they examined their boarding passes before some could start removing their belts and shoes at the security check.

Lily sat by the window of the plane. She was amazed by the dim light that illuminated the interior of the aircraft from behind the overhead luggage rack and below their seats. *The Pride of Africa* indeed! Outside, the wide-stretched wing with the colours of the Kenyan flag shone in the afternoon sun, and the wing engine created a mirage around where it rotated. A lady on the ground, in a green reflective jacket, waved paddles to guide the pilot.

In a warm, soft and polished voice, the pilot greeted passengers, introduced himself and gave a summary of the trip. A minute later, he said, "Flight attendants, please prepare for departure."

When the wheels hit the runway, Lily's heart leapt. She stuck her head on the plastic windowpane and glued her eyes to the runway's side where red and yellow images of the runway signs flipped past her view. She listened to the sound of the plane as the wheels beneath rubbed furiously against the runway. Lily felt weightless when the plane's nose rose on take-off. She was constantly pressed against the back of her seat by the impact until the aircraft maintained a stable altitude.

"Juma," Lily whispered.

"Yes, my dear." Juma had been quiet, observing and admiring her demeanour.

"You're the best," Lily said. She turned to the window to look at the clouds below them, the miniature buildings whose iron roofs shone from a distance, and the earth shrinking below. They were now buried in the clouds. For a moment, recalling the Busia plane crash that had almost made her change her aviation dream, she imagined their fragility. She wondered where exactly in the vastness of the clouds heaven was. Then the signature bells of the plane interrupted her. She turned to look at Juma, whose eyes were still on her. Then she just smiled. And he smiled. And a cabin crew came from behind them pulling a jiggling cart with an endless smile.

In Pemba, they were welcomed with an enticing scent of cloves and other spices, and the warm weather, which she had thought would be colder for it was an island surrounded by water. They spent the first evening being entertained with Pemba songs and dances; songs by women dancing as they rotated umbrellas over their heads with their right hands. They wore *buibuis* and scarves over their heads.

The second group was even more entertaining. The men entered the stage blowing their trumpets incessantly, a group of young men and women trailing behind, dancing to the tunes. The men had red caps and white wrappers around their waists while the young girls had flowery *lesos* around their waists. The girls danced by taking two steps back and forth as they swivelled their waists with incredible swiftness, then pulling out the *lesos* and swinging them left and right over their chests. Their soft, high-pitched voices tore through the hall as they sang with utter enticement.

From her chair, Lily moved her head and shoulders from side to side; knocking Juma's shoulder every time she leant towards him. Both their feet thumped the floor softly with the flow of the dance. The female dancers receded to the background, swinging their bottoms right left and centre as they made their calculated steps. The men danced towards the front with long wooden sticks before they formed parallel lines with the female dancers; the female at the far right and left. Their bare feet and skins shone in the stage light. Sweat formed under their arms and their white T-shirts clung to the skin of their furrowed backs. They danced and danced, and Lily fought the urge to join them in the circle they made as they twisted their groins back and forth.

"I know you're good at that," Lily whispered into Juma's ear. And that night, he twisted his groin on top of her. Barasa kept calling, but she kept rejecting the calls.

"You're a stupid village idiot!" Lily shouted into her handset when she finally picked up Barasa's call. Her words crushed out tersely.

"Were it not that your mother sent me to check on you, I wouldn't have visited your room." Barasa retorted. And so, Lily clicked, a crunchy click, after which Barasa heard the disturbing tone of a disconnected call.

The brutal words from Lily were too painful for Barasa to withstand. He remained dumbfounded for some time.

"You shouldn't have ...You were so harsh on him," Juma admonished Lily.

Back in their room on campus, Halima watched Barasa move the phone away from his ear, shock written on his face. It was as if he was looking at the screen to confirm that it was Lily's number he had dialled. Both Halima and Barasa were shocked. Barasa regretted having travelled all the way from Kitale. He nursed resentment for Lily. His innards collapsed inside, with his heart bristly snapping from its cage. But were it not for Lily's ominous silence and failure to communicate with her family and friends, he wouldn't have travelled to Nairobi. Were it not for the worry she had instilled in her parents, they wouldn't have sent Barasa to check on her.

"Please, help me with a piece of paper and a pen," Barasa requested Halima, but once he got them, he didn't know what exactly it was that he wanted to write.

Halima was immensely tempted to call Lily and quarrel with her but opted to silently recite a prayer of redemption, "*Astaghfirullah, astaghfirullah, astaghfirullah.*"

On their second day in Zanzibar, Juma hired an aircraft to take them around the island. As they flew above, Lily admired the long stretch of green clove vegetation and Ufufuma forest separated from the serene blue sheet of the Indian Ocean by a long strip of white sand. Later, they walked through the town and markets, despite the crowds of people. Some cycled their bicycles carrying bags of cloves or other farm produce, thrusting their torso forward with every left or rightpush on the pedal.

Lily was fascinated by the distinctive culture and how almost all schoolgirls draped themselves in white *hijabs* to school; long veils that stretched down their backs. They arrived at Zanzibar City, west of Unguja, when an *adhan* was calling Muslim faithful for their afternoon prayer. On their way to the tourist hotel they were booked in, they passed by a shop playing traditional *taarab* music, donkeys pulling heavy carts, and police in bright white uniforms.

Lily and Juma swam together at the beach after lunch. The ocean breeze whispered past their ears as Lily inhaled the warm salty breath of Zanzibar with her eyes closed. They splashed salty water on each other's face, chased after each other on the sandy beach, and then sat and basked in the baking heat of the sun that was hot on their bare skin.

When they boarded the tour van to take them around the villages, she opened the windows to let the warm humid air whistle past, "*Sssssssss!*" loosening her hair strands and slapping her face. "If you get time, I can take you into the Ufufuma forest to watch the endangered Cox Red Colobus monkeys; they are only found here in Zanzibar," the van driver said that night after they had had dinner at an open market. Unfortunately, they didn't get time because they were flying back to Nairobi the following morning.

"I'll miss the aroma of their tempting delicacies, and the warmness of the people," Lily told Juma when they were departing at Jomo Kenyatta International Airport, Nairobi, that morning. "Thank you so much for everything, my dear," she added, and they embraced in a long hug before each one took a taxi and they left.

Lily went straight to Babirye's apartment to show her the pictures they had taken.

"I'm so happy for you, girlfriend. That's how you should enjoy life," Babirye beamed at Lily.

Later in her room, Lily asked Halima what Barasa had said or wanted. "He was sent by your parents to check whether everything is fine with you since you don't pick up their calls. He also left behind foodstuffs and money for you."

185

When Lily called Barasa's number, it was off. From the disappointment, Barasa– who now felt completely dejected and alone – puffed marijuana for solace. She called again late at night. It was still off. It was off the following day too, but when she called Milly, a wave of relief swept through her to know that Barasa had arrived home safely.

Then Lily said, "Okay.""Okay," Milly said.

"Okay," Lily repeated, and then there was silence before Milly giggled. And though she didn't know how to ask about it, Lily hoped that Barasa hadn't mentioned it to anyone with whom she had gone to Zanzibar. Lily believed Halima must have told him.

When the call was disconnected, Milly sat with her back against their kitchen wall and thought about her friend.

A month after her return from Zanzibar, Tom brought up Barasa's visit and how she had been rude to him. Halima had shared the story with Tom. Lily argued with Tom about it and ended up insulting him. *I'm not a child, and I'm not your sister for you to be concerned with my life!* She had finally said and walked away. They didn't talk again for the rest of the day and the weeks that followed.

Tom would now spend part of his evenings either chatting with Eve or watching TV. He followed the ICC proceedings until the day former Liberian president,Charles Taylor, was sentenced to fifty years in prison.

During lectures, Lily and Tom ignored each other as if they were strangers. Lily didn't call home either. She pressed Juma with more demands for money, outings and the need to move out of the hostels.

"Hello sweetheart, how are you?" Juma called one afternoon.

"Better than you, and if I weren't, you wouldn't have missed it in the headlines."There was a chuckle before he asked what she was up to.

"Just watching a movie; *Sometimes In April*." "Try *Slumdog Millionaire*," Juma suggested."Will that make me one?"

"It depends…""On what?" "If…"

"If?"

"If you're working hard enough to be," Juma then laughed. Towards the end of the conversation, Lily demanded more money and Juma promised to deliver that evening. And he did.

Lily started making plans of moving out of the hostels too. Her demands surpassed what Juma was willing to offer, she thought. So, she thought it was the best time to call Babirye's wealthy man – Marto, the businessman who had once asked for her number during one of their outings. Marto had been pestering her with endless calls; something she hadn't mentioned to Babirye.

She made that first, which led to many calls and endless favours from Marto.

On a chilly Saturday 9 June, Lily moved out of the hostel to a one-bed-roomed apartment in Ngara. She chose the first of the three-floor-apartment block overlooking Thika Superhighway. Its construction had only taken two months. What people didn't know was that the owner of the building had bribed the relevant government officials, and also the MP with whom Babirye had an affair with so he could skip proper construction procedures. The MP had instructed his bribe to be wired directly to Babirye's account so there would be no way to link him to it in case things failed. Not even Babirye knew that it was from the same project that the MP had loaded her account with cash, and only asked her to usea very small amount from it and keep the rest for him.

It was a sad day for Halima when Lily moved out. The day that followed was also a sad one for the whole nation because Professor George Saitoti and his Assistant Minister, Orwa Ojode, died in a plane crash. A similar date, four years back, Lily had dodged her teacher into a Chief's camp where flags were flying half-mast because Kipkalya Kones and Lorna Laboso had perished in a similar accident.

Halima didn't see Lily until during the Eid Al Fitr celebrations. Halima was still kneading the dough for making *mahamri* when Lily knocked on her door. It was on a cool August morning and Lily walked around the room, reminiscing on the past days she had been an occupant. The room now seemed spacious.

Later, Tom joined them, but after the usual pleasantries, there was no more conversation between him and Lily. Halima had invited her friends to celebrate with her, just as she always did, and they said *Eid Mubarak*,

187

and talked and laughed as they ate the *mahamri* and tea and later *pilau* that she had preparedfor them.

* * *

Lily had tried to avoid Tom, even when she needed him most. Such an occasion was when she needed to buy a new sofa set. She flipped through the pictures of furniture in an album at a store, looking at different colours and designs, but was muddled about the choice. She thought of Tom, of how helpful he would have been in choosing and bargaining. She settled for a brown and cream sofa set. Even during the transportation, she knew, definitely, that Tom would have been of value. And it was not only Tom that she looked down upon. In her frustration, she had once yelled at Juma over the phone, though she later apologised.

* * *

One afternoon, Babirye wanted to pour out her heart to Lily. Marto had not been picking up her calls. Babirye was distressed because she had no money and she wanted her man to help her out. The MP had long asked her to withdraw all the money for him, and she had obediently done so, remaining with nothing.

Babirye called Lily, but Lily didn't pick up her calls or call back, so she decided to go to her apartment in Ngara. Marto's car was parked at Lily's compound in Ngara. Her heart pumping, Babirye rushed upstairs, and on knocking at Lily's door, there was no response.

"Lily! Lily! Are you there?" Babirye called out loud. Still, there was no response. "Lily!" She called, peeping through the thick blinds, but the only thing she could see in the windowpane was the reflection of the compound and the tall buildings behind her. She rushed for her phone.

"Lily!" She called out. No response. Both their phones – Lily and Marto –were now switched off.

When Babirye got back to her house, she threw her purse on the sofa set and took Lily's photo from her album. She imagined what could be happening in Lily's house in Ngara. "*Kale*, you'll see me, you slut!" She furiously growled, folding the photo into a small creased ball, like a report page full of variances and mistakes, and buried her face in the cushion of her sofa.

When Marto later came to Babirye's house, his presence alone sparked rage in her. The bell had rung, and Babirye had rushed to open the door, only to find him standing there looking remorseful, his left hand resting against the wall. Babirye wished she had checked first in the peephole; she wouldn't have bothered to open the door.

"Hello babe," Marto extended a gift bag and a bouquet to her. Instead, Babirye removed the necklace and the earrings she had and launched them on his face. The earrings missed him, but the necklace bruised his nose and fell at his feet. Babirye closed the door in his face, and when she heard his footsteps disappearing, she rushed to the kitchen window and peeped through the space where her two thick curtains separated.

Babirye was livid that he had left. It hurt her. And once his car disappeared, and the smooth sound of its engine faded, she broke down. She opened the door, picked the necklace and earrings and the gift bag and the bouquet, and then threw them in her clean dustbin at the end of the veranda. She locked herself inside her house and sat on the doormat, her left shoulder leaning on the door, and cried. After that, she went out to the dustbin to check what gifts he had bought for her and retrieved her jewellery and the flowers.

Babirye now hated Marto because she thought there was no way he would have chosen her friend; a friend she introduced him to. He had broken her heart into pieces and betrayed her and taken her affection for granted. But to her, Lily was worse; she had no shame in stealing her man.

When Lily arrived at Babirye's apartment, Babirye was playing loud Ugandan music, *Mpambatira Mukama. Omutima gunnuma, guyayaana guyayaana...* the voice rented the air.

When the bell rang, Babirye thought it was her next-door neighbour whose voice she had heard talking to the watchman. But she peeped through just to be sure. Babirye's body shook when Lily's face came into vision. Lily was straightening her dress as she waited. Babirye rushed back to the sofa where she was taking her wine, but the bottle was still half-full. She hurried to the kitchen and grabbed an empty bottle, her hands shaking. The kitchen still smelt of spices she had burnt earlier while preparing lunch.

Babirye slowly opened the door, calculating how she would strike, her eyes filled with hatred. She just needed one good strike and Lily would be gone. For good! When the door finally went ajar, Lily quickly noticed the ire steaming in Babirye's face and made two strides back, wondering what Babirye held behind her.

Babirye didn't strike first, but lashed out in Luganda, her words shooting like bullets, *"Gwe malaya gwe nali ndowoza oli mukwano gwange!* You slut, I thought you were a friend! I never ever want to see your face!" Lily made a step forward, but Babirye banged the door in her face to the extent that the windows vibrated and the watchman came out of his small room by the gate to check what was happening.

"Okay, but be aware that you're not the only one with Hon. W." Babirye heard Lily's faint voice saying. That gave her even a stronger itch to go after Lily and crush the bottle on her head, and finish her once and for all. Was it not enough for Lily to have Marto that she had to go for the MP as well?

"Go to hell!" Lily added as she ran down the stairs.

Chapter Nineteen

"You're a stupid man!" Every word Riziki spouted stung like a bee.

She had just confirmed that Juma was cheating on her; even when he lied that he was going to Zanzibar for a business meeting over the past Easter, and avoided taking her and their daughter to visit Riziki's family in the countryside. She now knew it was a lady, Lily, who was snatching her husband. The many nights Juma had returned home late was because of her. The many nights Juma hadn't touched her was because of Lily. Riziki resented him for that!

"Juma, why?" she asked, leaning on the kitchen fridge. From the door, their daughter watched, resting her cheek against the doorframe. There was silence but for the refrigerator's humming compressor that automatically went on and off. "Juma, am I not talking to you?" Were it not for their daughter's presence, a glass would have been smashed against the wall. Still, he didn't know what to say. He left the house, and their daughter ran after him, giving Riziki space to smash a flower vase on the floor, cracking a piece of tile.

Juma not finding a word to defend himself was not the Juma Riziki met on campus; a Juma that would fall short of expectations at times and annoy her as much as he would surprise her with charm. But above all, he would realise his faults and say, "I'm really sorry, sweetheart. Please find it in your heart to forgive me."

Riziki was keen to note the many nights Juma had come late, or made long whispered phone calls from outside the house. He rarely left his phone on the table. He didn't take them out during the weekends as he had always done, and whenever Riziki questioned him, he would say he had a heavy workload in the office that consumed most of his time. Even when he noticed that Riziki would talk to herself in the house more often, it bothered him not.

One day, Riziki asked Juma to take her out for shopping, but he declined, stating that he was busy. Instead, he gave her one of his debit cards and asked her to drive herself to the mall. She bought a lot of unnecessary items, but the card didn't have enough balance to pay for all the items. Could there be something wrong with the system or the bank? Riziki thought. Juma had made her a signatory to the account too. So, she went to the bank and was surprised by the bank statement she was given. It showed several hotel bills Juma had paid for in Nairobi, including hotel rooms. A lot of female stuff had been paid for too; shopping she was sure wasn't his mother's.

"You've been buying a lot of female stuff with the card, whom for?" Riziki confronted Juma. He defended himself that the hotel bills were job-related while the hotel bookings were for clients he had invited from Arusha, Dodoma, Kisangani and Mwanza, on different occasions. He explained that those were business friends with whom he was trying to strike business deals.

"The rest of the stuff is Mum's shopping, of course!" Juma beamed, walking away from her.

"So, you buy your mum knickers, bras, sanitary towels and even morning pills?" Riziki blurted with venom, shoving at him the bank statement and a receipt she had picked from his jacket a day earlier. Juma buttoned his shirt, picked up his car keys and walked to the kitchen to get a glass of juice.

On one occasion, Juma forgot his phone in the bedroom. She had already pried and peeped several times that she now had the password. She took it, and rushed to check the call records, text messages and

WhatsApp chat, which she quickly took screenshots of and sent to her phone just so she could have evidence. Later, she printed them all. She was infuriated that she decided to punish Juma. She would decide to go to the Ministry of Health and report his corruption deals that she'd kept secret for long; one of which was a major scandal. By doing so, she was sure that would cut off the source of money that Juma and Lily enjoyed and travelled around using. She also took Lily's number from his phone, just in case she may need it; which she fought the urge to call and have it out with her for interfering with her marriage. *Let me wait for the ministry's decision*, she would advise herself, however.

"We'll investigate this matter and act accordingly," Riziki was assured at the ministry.

* * *

Two days after Babirye had closed the door on Lily's face, and rushed to her with a bottle, she still wanted to know what exactly Lily meant. So, she pretended to have buried the hatchet and went to visit Lily at her apartment in Ngara.

"How have you been?" Babirye asked as if nothing happened.

"I've been well," Lily paused, "And by the way, if you think anything happened between Marto and I, then you're wrong, my sister." A subterfuge.

"If I thought so, I wouldn't be here. Come on!" She gave Lily a slight slap on her arm. As they sipped their fresh mango juice, Babirye asked, "By the way, you said something about Hon. W. that day. What was it?"

"Ooooh, sorry, dear. I couldn't just hide this from you," Lily paused. Babirye felt like strangling her for snatching Hon. W. from her but controlled her anger. "I saw him at the hotel on my first date with Juma. He was with a certain medical student. I think her name is Winnie; she stays in Hall 12." Babirye had heard rumours about Winnie and the MP, and someone had even shown Babirye the lady.

Two weeks later, Marto apologised to Babirye. Juma had stopped picking up Lily's calls for four consecutive days, re-assessing himself and trying to committo the promise he had made to Riziki that he would not cheat on her again. The month was quickly coming to an end, and Lily didn't have enough savings to pay for her rent. Trouble was brewing.

"So, you want to take care of Lily's son and neglect your own daughter?" Riziki had shocked him. After learning about Lily, Riziki had searched for her on social media and found her profile and photos on FaceBook which she had taken good time to go through. It was in two different photos in which Milly had tagged Lily that Riziki had found out about Jim. In one of the photos, Milly had taken a photo of Francisca and Jim while in the second one it was Milly and Jim. Though Lily had wanted to delete the photo from her profile and the comments on each of the photos that clearly showed her relation with Jim, she knew deleting them would clearly tell of how much hate she bore for her son. So, she had let them be. And since she had never told Juma of Jim, Juma had later confronted Lily about it. When Lily had finally confessed to him about Jim, he had suddenly gone cold on her and cut communication. At that moment, Lily's hatred for Jim had instantly shot, and she had silently cursed his presence in her life.

Riziki's cousins and Juma's mother also talked to Juma at length and advised him not to break his family because of a random campus girl. Juma promised never to repeat the mistake. He was just as human as everyone else was, and was prone to err, so he said. And so, he always fought the temptation to call or visit her or pick up the many calls she made. Actually, he would switch off his phone whenever he was at home or near Riziki.

Lily thought of going back to her campus room but brushed the thought aside. Tom wouldn't mind helping, she thought. Sure, he wouldn't mind especially now that he was hosting a female guest, Eve, in his room. And as Lily sat by her bed that night, she knew Tom might be comfortably reading, Halima praying and Juma making love. Tom wasn't reading.

After meeting through the phone chat application, *2go*, Eve always suggested paying Tom a visit to campus. But he always postponed until he finally gave in and invited her for the first time.

Earlier that morning, Tom woke up early to do a thorough room cleaning. He spread the bed and folded his clothes in the wardrobe. He bought food and drinks. He picked up the phone, dialled Lily's number, but again dropped it. He prepared to welcome Eve, a student nurse at the Kenya Medical Training College in Murang'a, several kilometres from Nairobi. The frequent *exiles* Geoffrey subjected him to and the campus decadence had incited his new step. So, Tom first felt like calling Lily on that day; he still loved her.

Eve brought with her a nice, new shirt for him. Tom fumbled, "When I heard before, I never believed that nurses are very caring. I have today. Thanks for the shirt." She was comfortably sitting on his study chair, running her eyes around the small room. "Wow! It's such a nice choice," Tom said, placing the shirt in the closet and then quipping, "Which drink can I offer you?"

She sipped from her glass of mango juice. Her voice was soft and low as she spoke slowly, "It's such a pleasure to finally meet you. I've longed for this day."

"Not as much as I did. All the pleasure is mine." Tom moved close; only an inch remaining between them. Their shoulders touched. "You have beautiful eyes," he complimented when he turned to look at her. When she turned to look at him, their lips touched by instinct. Tom felt hot despite it being cold outside.

"You look amazing in that trouser," Tom complimented her later that night. They had just eaten rice and chicken stew, which she had given a thumbs-up to, praising Tom's culinary skills. They were now seated on his bed. He moved close again, just like he had done during the day, and looked her in the eyes. "You have beautiful eyes," he said again, holding her hand and running his fingers along the length of her arm. Eve's breath smelt of mint, and his shirt, of fresh lemon-like cologne.

"Thank you," Eve sighed as she closed the gap between them.

"Anytime, babe." They sunk into a turgid silence before Tom said, "I wish you knew how long I've longed to be next to you, Eve. And how your lips are soft and tender," he said as he gently grabbed her and leant towards her, pressing his lips against hers. He framed her face with his hands as he leisurely glided his lips against hers, sucking in every tiny noise she made.

He gently laid Eve on the bed as he ran his hands all over her body, trailing kisses from her mouth to her neck and back again to her lips. He let his hand glide over the mound of her breasts, loving it when she arched her back.

Tom let his hands roam on Eve's trouser-cladded thighs, loving how his hands filled out with her. Her thighs were thick and she had flesh packed in the right areas. Before letting his tongue glide into her mouth, he nipped Eve's lip, deepening the kiss as his hands languidly wandered to her behind. Eve arched into his arms, moving restlessly beneath him, her arms kneading his back while her tongue laved his neck.

"Tom, please," Eve said, biting his lower lip.

Taking Eve's plea as an invitation, Tom let his hands drift away from her behind to the pesky zip that blocked him from baring her nakedness. His sweaty hands kept slipping over the zip. Smiling, Eve pushed his hands away and stood beside the bed, facing Tom.

She lifted her shirt inch by inch, giving Tom a glimpse of skin here and there. Tom sat in rapt attention at the edge of the bed, his heart beating too loud for his ear. Eve let the shirt fall on the floor, her eyes glued on Tom's as she slid off her bra. Tom pounced.

As if anticipating Tom's move, Eve side-stepped him, laughing.

"Not yet, Tom," she said, returning to the edge of the bed. Tom leant on his elbows on the bed, his hands slowly opening and closing, mimicking how he wanted to touch Eve's breasts that were staring right at him.

Eve lightly skimmed her hands over her nipples; Tom held his breath. "Eve, this sitting here while you touch what I want, is getting hard," Tom confessed, letting his eyes rove over Eve before going to his hardness.

Eve just smiled as she unzipped her trouser. With her legs slightly apart, she removed her trousers and silky panties in one swoop. "You don't have to wait anymore," she said.

Tom, for a full minute, just took her in. He took in her sizable breasts and her soft skin that seemed dewy from where he sat; it begged him to kiss it. He loved the way her hips tapered into curviness, giving the illusion that Eve had the narrowest waist he'd ever seen. "You are sexy," Tom said, standing before her.

"Thank you, Tom. It's your turn," Eve said, kissing Tom softly on his lips before climbing onto the bed.

Tom did not need a second invitation. Within seconds, he had stripped and joined Eve in bed, his nervousness forgotten, especially when Eve leant and kissed him, her hands exploring his body. In that moment, Tom forgot about Lily and his undying love for her. He even forgot that for a second, he had wished to dial Lily's number and just let her listen in to them making out; an act he would say was by mistake. It was actually a good thing he didn't call for it was the exact moment, in Ngara, that Lily thought of calling him to come to her aid. Instead, Tom got invested with the movements of Eve when she moved to meet him halfway and got drunk in her soft feminine moans when he leant forward and took a nipple into his mouth.

And then Eve stretched her arms and legs, flexing her thighs, as the sound of her breath kept changing. She moaned silently in sublime pleasure, weaving and writhing her body. And when Eve held him tight whispering his name, as he muffled a moan and softened inside her, Tom gleaned what it was like to be wanted and desired. He pulled himself down, and she rested her head on his chest. She listened to his heartbeats and their breaths, awkwardly thinking of how it would have been had Eve not rebelled in the Garden of Eden.

"Good morning, beautiful one?" Tom whispered into Eve's ears. When she turned to look at him, there was a smile on her lips, and her eyes were half-closed. Below her, on the creased bed sheet, two bedbugs crawled to their hideout. "How was your night?"

They went to shower together in one of the small concrete cubes with thick green waterproof vinyl curtains at their doors. Walking back along the corridor, Tom met Geoffrey; he felt guilty for the squeals Eve had made at night. But just like Geoffrey did to him more often than not, he hoped Geoffrey had pressed earphones into his ears and increased the volume of the music from his handset. If not, he must have dug his fingers into his ears.

Tom moved closer to her when she was dressing and brushed his cold fingers against her frame. She pushed him away.

"Next time," she said.

But when Tom escorted her to town to take a bus back to Murang'a, he was never to hear about her or see her again. "You are the best!" she whispered to him as the bus pulled from its parking. And when he later tried to look for her to no avail, he wondered what she had actually meant by those words.

That whole week, and the two subsequent ones, Tom wore the shirt Eve bought for him at least once every week until it was unpegged from the clothesline outside the hostel. For the rest of the semester, he kept looking for any student wearing it. He saw none. Not even on those days he dreamt of her and woke upto wash his sullied pants and bed sheet.

Chapter Twenty

Juma was slowly drifting, and as much as Lily tried to bring him closer, it seemed as if she was nagging him. Whenever she asked him what was wrong, Juma just replied that everything was okay and that he didn't see any difference in their relationship. But he no longer sent her money or showered her with gifts. The few times he sent her money, the amounts were small compared to the previous times. And with time, the money became less and less.

Whether it was the raising of her voice or her persistent demands, Lily couldn't tell exactly what it was that kept Juma away from her. She was, however, sure that the future she had envisioned and her expectations would crumble down. Soon. On his side, Juma couldn't gather the audacity to face Lily and tell her that it was over between them. Whenever she called, he had no words to adequately explain to her his coldness. So, he ended up ignoring her calls and even text messages. But she kept glancing at her phone several times a day with hopes of getting a response.

Lily hated herself for the expensive lifestyle she had elevated herself to. She had a new status that she had to find money to maintain and also keep abreast with people like Babirye. From the way things were going, there was little promisethat Juma could help her maintain it. Both Juma and Marto had left her in the middle of nowhere – completely neglected. She had a son and parents who had no guaranteed source of income, she now recalled. She also had her personal needs at school and her apartment.

Lily started skiving classes, stressed about what she would do. One evening, Tom called because he hadn't seen her during lectures that week, and he was worried about her. Lily took a long time contemplating whether to pick up thecall or not. Even after five missed calls, she decided not to call back.

For the next two weeks, she cut down her expenditure by eking out her meagre savings on only basic items. However, her bedroom stifled her with lonesomeness. She missed the sense of security she always had whenever Juma was around. She missed the scent of his cologne. She wanted him, but he was nowhere to give her even just a little less than what she wanted.

The silent drift left Lily soaked in coldness, and intimately malnourished. She sobbed herself to sleep on some days. Her heart nursed a solid hatred for Juma. He shouldn't have introduced her to an expensive lifestyle only to leave her hanging without an anchor; she regretted. She felt Juma may just have dumped her after knowing her in the biblical sense; like Tamar and Amnon. She swore notto call him again and never to pick up his calls. But despite all those affirmations, she still missed him and updated on her Facebook wall emotional quotes about love, relationships and breakups. She was tempted to call him and indeed called afew more times; each time convincing herself that it was the last. Still, Juma neverresponded to her calls.

Lily spent most of the time locked in her bedroom. Her ears could now easily pick up the sound of an approaching car from a distance. Every time a car passed by the gate or drove into the compound, she would run to the window and peep through the silky white blinds. Neither Juma nor Marto visited. She would also sit by the window, fiddling with her phone in her hand, hoping that a call would come through from either of them, but all was in vain. Her days sagged and the nights seemed like

200

ages. There was always an ache that came and went whenever she thought of the valuable friendships she had broken, the people she had despised and the genuine concerns she had disregarded. "How do I survive without money?" She asked herself. She had long asked her mother to stop sending her money, and she was sending them instead. It was already difficult for her now, yet she was bitter with herself for letting her happiness depend on a man; Halima had warned her about it. But again, she was itching to find out exactly what the problem was so she decided to visit Juma at his office.

"Good morning," Lily greeted the secretary who was perusing files in a cabinet.

"To you too," she said, still going through sheets of paper in a red file. "How can I help you?" The lady asked, looking at Lily.

"I would like to see Mr Juma."

"Your name, please?" The lady asked, retrieving her diary. "Lilian."

"You don't have any other name, my dear?" The lady asked disinterestedly, turning pages in the diary without looking at Lily.

"Nekesa...Lilian Nekesa." Lily said. The secretary ran her finger from the top to the bottom of the diary twice looking for the name without success.

"You said your name is?" She asked after failing to trace Lily's name on the previous and subsequent pages. Lily repeated her name.

"You have an appointment?" "No, madam,"

"Then it would be difficult to see him; he's not in now," the secretary said, putting back the diary and adding, "But you can leave a message for him."

Lily could hear someone flipping through the dailies behind the thick wooden door.

"Actually, he knows me, and he wouldn't mind me visiting even without an appointment." The secretary looked at her for a moment, mortified.

"Wait," she said and went inside the office, a thick red carpet saving her from the noise her stiletto shoes would have made. When she came out of the office, she asked Lily to leave her a message for Juma. She didn't.

Lily walked out quietly without uttering a word, a film of tears forming in her eyes. She didn't eat the whole of that day, crying in her bed and thinking about what to do next. When Juma didn't send her any message, not even to explain why he had refused to see her, she was gravely hurt. She had hoped he would at least say sorry.

So, very early the following day, Lily drafted a message to him: *I know I no longer matter, but I hope this gets you in good health because to me, you still matter*, she wrote. She read and reread it a couple of times, and continued: *I send you this text neither to request for your money nor your gifts. I just ask you, please, help me secure any kind of job. You know how much I need the job, and how much my old folks need the money as well. This is the time I need your help more than any other time. Kindly, Lily.*

She reread the message before pressing *send*; *<delivered>* read the acknowledgement almost immediately.

Juma contemplated calling Lily after receiving the text message, but his promise to Riziki held him back. More than once, he walked to his office balcony to make that call, but just ended up putting his phone back in his pocket and making strides back to his desk. For some minutes, he rotated in his leather chair tossing a pen, thinking of the best response.

Three days later, Juma texted back: *Let's meet at 11:00 a.m. in town.* Lily reread the message. It appeared as if he despised her, but the only option she had was to humble herself and heed his call. Maybe help was on the way.

At 10:27 a.m., Lily was already in town. They met in a small restaurant along Kenyatta Avenue. Unlike their previous meetings, there was no hugging and joyous pleasantries. And Juma read the raw anger and hurt on her face, though inwardly, she now accepted that there comes a time when the embers of love burndown to ashes.

"So, how's everything?" Juma asked, turning to look at City Council *askaris* harassing a motorist outside for double-parking.

Lily sipped her mango juice quietly.

"Hey, I'm sorry that our...our intimate relationship has to come to an end. Someone told my wife about us," Juma continued when she didn't say anything.

"Okay," Lily nodded.

Nursing the guilt of being responsible for Lily's situation, Juma promised to help as much as he could. He discouraged her from looking for a job but instead told her to focus on her studies. As for the bills, he promised to help until she finishes school, despite the lack of intimacy between them.

"That is okay," Lily opined. But she knew deep inside that she wasn't being genuine. And since Juma didn't sound so assuring, Lily convinced herself that she would look for a job. Not long, she remembered the airport cleaning job. So, she looked for her supervisor who had now been promoted and had a chat with him at his office. She secured a night shift job at the less busy area of the airport which she started immediately. Lily resumed classes too.

The general election was approaching a year ahead, and aspirants for various seats had already started meeting youths, especially university students, to win their support. Tom attended most of those meetings. Lily came to know of it and it reminded her of Tom's help in proposals to NGOs and local leaders on a myriad of issues such as helping disadvantaged girls in various parts of the country. Though none of them had attracted funding.

Indeed, Juma didn't send her money as he had said he would, but Lily's pay was enough to keep her going. Juma didn't know that she was working now, while Babirye didn't know that Marto had started looking for Lily again and they were now in contact. He even sent her money sometimes. Lily would send some of the money home. There was intrinsic satisfaction and peaceful stillness in her mind and heart, knowing she could cater for the basic needs of her parents as well as hers. But she missed her friends. She missed Tom.

When Juma finally decided to honour his promise, he sent his official driver. His name was Mambo. Unknown to many, Juma included,

Mambo was a reformed man who had taken part in the 2007/2008 skirmishes. He had been arrested, but his distant uncle bribed heavily for Mambo to be freed and the case to vanish. Later, the same uncle bribed so that Mambo would be employed as a driver at the Ministry of Health. He became Juma's driver.

When the driver called, the call couldn't go through because Lily was on a trip to Morocco in Marto's company and they had both switched off their phones so no one, especially Babirye, would learn of their trip.

On that day of August when elections were scheduled to take place, before they were postponed to March fourth of the following year, Marto and Lily were already on their way to the airport.

"Trust me, you'll enjoy," Marto whispered as their driver stopped at a traffic light along Mombasa Road, with several cars trailing behind.

"Sure," she replied with a silent kiss. The light turned green, and the driver stepped on the gas pedal before the drivers behind could start hooting. Two hours later, they were on the flight to Morocco.

The world would've been focusing on the elections, expecting another occurrence of 2007, or worse. But now the media focused on Kenya's achievements at the 2012 Summer Olympics in London where David Rudisha had won a gold medal for Kenya. He had broken the race's record, and it was dubbed, *The Greatest 800 Meter Race Ever.* As a result, he was an ambassador that told the world a different story of what Kenya is; not the clashes and post-election violence that everyone was cynically predicting.

Lily found the climate in Morocco more or less like that of Kenya since the sun rose from the east, the sky was blue and the air was still invisible. On the day that followed, they traversed through Casablanca and Rabat, and ate food laced with a lot of sugar. They then took a flight to Marrakech, Morocco's former imperial city. While there, they enjoyed the cuisine, especially the warm tea served in tiny glasses. Guides took them around the city, enjoying the scenery and architecture. They even visited the *Palais de la Bahia*, a vast palace with hundreds of rooms intricately designed.

"Where are you from, brother?" A guide asked. "We're from Kenya," Marto responded.

"Ahaaaa, Kenya!" He seemed excited, "Kenyatta's country!" "Yeah, you are right."

"How is he?"

"We now have Kibaki."

"Yes, yes, Kibaki! I was confused."

Marto and Lily turned to look at each other, and they smiled.

"This city is called 'The Red City'," the guide said as he drove out of town. They headed to the foothill of the snow-capped Atlas Mountains where they saw Berbers, with massive sheets wrapped around their heads and faces, swinging on the backs of their camels.

They passed several *souks*, markets, on their way back. "And why are almost all the buildings painted ochre red?" Lily asked as they approached the city from the mountainside. The tour guide explained. From a distance, they could see the *Kutubiyya* Mosque's minaret, the tallest building in the city. No other building was supposed to surpass its height. As they came nearer the town, the red colour of ochre on the walls became more pronounced.

"Wow, it was such a nice trip. Thank you," Lily told Marto in the evening as she wiped lipstick off her lips with a serviette. It was 7:38 p.m., three hours behind Kenyan time. They sat sipping their spiced Moroccan tea by the delightful and resplendent garden of La Mamounia Hotel, from where Sir. Churchill Winston used to relax, write and paint. "Thank you for everything," she repeated, placed her foot on her chair and rested her chin on her knee.

"You're most welcome, my dear, this is just the beginning." He smiled at her, a smile that sent her back to a scene earlier that evening. When they had visited the main *Souk* in the city; a market from where people had incense of local perfumes on them, and some scared Lily by kissing trained serpents. Marto just smiled as she sought refuge from the cobras that hovered around the owners' laps. He then held her hand, and they disappeared inside the vast market. Merchandise was on display;

205

traditional textiles, leather products and hides, pottery and jewellery.

"The snakes at the market didn't seem to scare you!" Lily said. "I didn't expect you to be that afraid," Marto responded.

Marto bought an *iPhone* for her at the airport before they took their flight back to Kenya, with a stop at Hamad International Airport, Qatar, from where she could see the runway below shimmering in fluorescent glow.

"Isn't Doha beautiful?" She asked, then turned her focus on the landing lights that flashed by the wing of the plane. As she savoured the last bits of her trip back, and her breast pain re-emerging, she didn't know of Mambo. She never knew of his arrest and release in 2008, she didn't know, and would never know about it.

At the Jomo Kenyatta International Airport, journalists and paparazzi lurked in the corridors of *International Arrivals* to take pictures of a music band that was arriving in the country for a concert. Unfortunately, Lily and Marto were in the same flight and were unlucky to be captured holding hands just behind the band as they were exiting the *International Arrivals*. That photo grazed the following day's dailies with blogs and newspapers writing about Marto, a prominent businessman, moving around with a campus girl. The attention had been switched to Marto and Lily instead of the band. Her lecturers read about it, and even her classmates talked about it. She had to skive lectures until the story died.

When Marto's wife saw it, she immediately telephoned Zainab, her only sister.

"Zainab, do you know what is happening?" Zuhura asked. Zainab worked as a surgical nurse.

"I saw the news, sister," she said, "...and I meant to ask you about it." Zainab could read anger, worry and confusion in Zuhura's voice as they talked.

Okay. Yes? Okay, I'll pass by your place after work and we can talk about it.

"That's fine, but I plan to teach that slut a lesson!"

At the Chiromo apartments, Babirye too was planning how to teach

Lily a thorough lesson; she too had read the blogs about her and Marto.

On the same day, Juma's driver called, and after introducing himself, they agreed to meet outside Lily's apartment. She was lucky that Juma had been busy to even go through the dailies.

Mambo could not be more at a loss for words at the sight of Lily. He was so shocked that he stood there frozen, staring.

"Hi," Lily said, clearly reading so much confusion and anxiety on Mambo's face.

"Hello," he stretched his hand, which Lily could feel a slight tremble from. He was still processing the sudden encounter. There was a suppressed nervous heave from his chest, which he hoped Lily hadn't noticed, but more could be read from his eyes even though he could not utter much.

Chapter Twenty-One

Lily called Babirye to consult her about her breast pain, but she didn't pick her calls.

"It could be mastitis," Halima said when Lily called her. "Are you feeling fever? No? Any swelling? Redness? Okay. Try putting on a loose-fitting bra, and you can massage with hot water."

Lily bought a few pairs of loosely fitting soft bras, but the pain persisted. In fact, for four consecutive days since her arrival from Morocco, the pain gradually increased. The painkillers she swallowed each day didn't seem to help either. It had started as a tingling sensation, and then it became a persistent chronic pain. It hadn't bothered her much initially; she kept on taking painkillers until the third day when she decided to see a doctor.

"How are you feeling?" The doctor asked her at the casualty department. "A little pain here," she touched her nipple.

"For how long have you been feeling it?"

"The first time I felt the pain was close to a year ago. It persisted for a few days; I took some painkillers and I didn't feel it again until four days ago."

"Okay," the doctor said, taking notes in indecipherable handwriting. "Remove your top and sit on this bed," she pointed at the examination bed behind long white curtains. The doctor then explained to her the examination she wanted to perform on her. She looked at Lily's breasts, comparing the symmetry between the right and the left breasts, and searched for any changes in nipple retractions. Then she noted that the nipples were a little creased, the left one inverted.

"Have you observed any changes in your nipples before?" The doctor asked, still noting down her observations.

"I haven't been keen, Doc," Lily said.

"Please, put your hands akimbo, and press them hard on your waist," The doctor noted the skin and nipples' retraction as she observed. She then asked Lily to put her left hand over her head. She observed how the supple breasts elevated a little on her chest.

"You can now lie facing up." She held her by the back and helped her lie down. She then placed a soft pillow under Lily's waist. "Just a minute," the doctor added and went near the door to clean her hands. "Please, place your hand over your head," she requested.

"Any hand," she said before adding, "Okay, let's start with the left hand." Lily placed her left hand over her head and the doctor bent over to palpate her. Gently, she rolled the tissues of Lily's left breast under the three middle fingers. She kept palpating in circular motions, asking every time if it was painful. And it was.

"Sssssss…" Lily hissed audibly, her teeth clenched in pain, "It's very painful."

After finishing palpating the left breast, Lily placed her right hand over her head, and the doctor palpated the right breast. She then made more notes of the symptoms and sent Lily for a mammography exam. Lily paid six thousand shillings for the mammography and was directed to a room where she found a male radiologist.

The radiologist greeted Lily and made her comfortable. He used wet wipes to clean Lily's breasts just in case they weren't or in case she had deodorant on. "This is to ensure we get clear results," he said. After drying them with a soft face towel, she placed her left breast between the two plates of the mammography machine, and he slid down the upper plate to flatten the breast against the lower plate. "You'll feel a little discomfort, but just for a few seconds. This ensures we get clear pictures of the mammogram."

"No problem, I'm okay with it," Lily said. The radiologist changed the plates to take the pictures from the sides too. He continued changing the plates and taking images from different positions and angles. He did the same with the right breast.

"Okay Lillian, you can wait for the results outside."

Lily sat quietly imagining how it would have been if she didn't have the six thousand shillings for the mammography. What of the thousands of sick Kenyans who have no single cent in their pockets? Next to her were other women lined up for the same test. Most of them seemed to be above forty years. From the way they were familiar with the place, procedures, and the way they conversed in low tones, at times giggling, it seemed they routinely came for the test or related services.

"Lilian Nekesa," the radiographer's voice interrupted her thoughts. She shot up and went inside.

"We've found suspicious sites in your mammography," he explained, "and we recommend further investigations."

"Investigations?" Lily asked, surprised. Why was he saying "we" yet no one else had done the test on her? Was he abdicating responsibility as the sole investigator?

"Yes. You need to go for an ultrasound," he said in a soft and polite voice. Lily was directed to a cashier where she paid another two thousand shillings before proceeding to the ultrasound room.

Lily was now left with only five thousand shillings in her account. If the doctor didn't prescribe expensive drugs, she knew the money would suffice to take her through the month. The ultrasound gave positive results. But to be certain and to determine the extent of the disease, an MRI was supposed to be done. Lily was rudely shocked when she was asked to undergo the eighteen-thousand-shillings MRI test.

She had to return home without being tested for she didn't have the eighteen thousand shillings. She was only given stronger painkillers.

210

Thinking of how she would raise the money for the test and why she had to undergo all those tests worried her. That week, she was forced to swallow her pride, and seek help from Halima and a colleague at the airport. Both of them were broke. Babirye was her last resort.

"I'm sorry for whatever happened between us," Lily beseeched Babirye forthe second time.

"We already got over that long time ago," Babirye said, spitting gum she had been chewing into a serviette. Lily sunk into the soft cushion.

"*Bananage* what did the doctor say?" Babirye faked concern and tried not to look gratified. "You can count on me at any time," she continued, "... unfortunately, I have no money now." Lie!

Lily was about to leave, having failed to prise a loan from her.

"Wait! I'll give you what's remaining between me and death," Babirye said, having changed her mind.

"Thank you," she said before leaving with the money babbling to herself that she would never disappoint Babirye.

"Bitch!" Babirye said as soon as she had left. "Were it in my power, I would have added more ailments into that body."

Lily was back at the hospital for the MRI test after raising the required amountfrom both her salary and borrowings. Doctors in public hospitals had gone on strike a week earlier, so the private hospital was congested with patients. She had to wait for hours. Her body was scanned with an MRI machine and details and pictures of the affected area in the breasts were taken.

"You'll feel a little pain," a pathologist told Lily as he prepared her for thecore needle biopsy test later after the MRI. The pathologist lodged a large core needle in her breast and aspirated a small amount of tissue.

"The results will be ready in a week. We will call you," said the pathologist.

Lily left more worried than she had arrived. That month, she wouldn't send anything home. Neither would she call. She feared her mother would certainly decipher worry from her voice.

As she waited for the results, her mind kept sending her to scour the Internet for research about mastitis. This is what Halima had planted in her mind, and Lily didn't want to think of anything else other than it. *More than 50% of women between 20 and 50 years are expected to develop this condition before menopause*, she read. *It is characterised by lumps or thickened areas in both breasts, but usually in one. Most common with lactating women*, she continued. Some of the stated signs and symptoms she read resonated with what she felt.

Lily would also read medical magazines and journals she had picked from a nearby clinic. Whenever she thought of her health and uncertain future, she would either call Marto to check up on him, busy herself with work or she would just sit on her bed after lectures and sleep on the days she wasn't at work. At times, she thought about her friends and family. She would get bored as much as she would get worried, and wished to get in touch with Tom and Barasa and just talk about politics and nothing. And every time she picked up her phone to initiate a call, she would throw it aside and switch to reading her *Immunochemistry* notes, *Biochemical Genetics* or just do something else.

The pathologist called after a week. The doctors' strike in public hospitals had just ended. Back in the hospital, Lily's hopes were dimmed when she was asked to undergo further tests. The pathologist took tissue samples to examine the cells for oestrogen or progesterone receptors. And the tests meant coughing up more money. Lily thought they were just out to milk her of her cash. She was asked to wait for their call, again.

When she picked her phone three days later, it was a different doctor - Dr Esther - calling from her office. Lily immediately suspected that there must be something serious.

At the hospital, a heavy door led to Dr Esther's office with the nameplate reading, *"Dr S. K. Esther, Haematologist and Oncologist,"* mounted on the door. The office was spacious with elegant furniture.

"Have you ever examined your breasts at home? I mean BSE, breast self- examination?" Dr Esther asked as soon as Lily sat down.

"How?" Lily asked, confused.

"Don't worry; I'll explain how it's done." Dr Esther asked her to remove her top and lie on the bed in an enclosed section. Dr Esther already knew Lily's diagnosis, but she thought it necessary to show her. Perhaps she might enlighten others. She explained to her how to look for any physical changes in the breast and demonstrated all the three methods of tactile inspection; the circle, line and wedge.

"The lumps are large, do you feel them?" Dr Esther asked after the demonstrations. She was now examining her breasts. The lump in the left breast was large while the one in the right breast was small. Actually, Lily never felt pain in her right breast. She pressed a stethoscope on her chest and listened to her heart and breath. The stethoscope was cold on Lily's skin. "Your chest is perfect," the doctor said as Lily took her seat.

"The reason I called you is that your results were sent to me for further assessment and advice." Lily buttoned up her blouse as she listened to Dr Esther. "Though there's nothing to worry about, some results aren't out yet. I advise that you come with a family member as soon as you can. By then, all the results will be ready."

Dr Esther then turned to her computer and pressed a few buttons on the keyboard in a deliberate effort to allow Lily time to say something. But Lily remained tight-lipped, unable to digest the doctor's decree.

"We need a family member so that we can collectively discuss the treatment options and make a decision. There's nothing to be scared of." Dr Esther explained further.

"But doctor...," she paused, "My family is very far away from Nairobi," Lily said, still worried and confused. What kind of disease was it that required discussion by a whole family? Was it an inherited illness?

Dr Esther sipped from a glass of sparkling cold water, "It would be better to discuss the treatment regimen with a family member present. It's nothing big, really."

Lily didn't want to think of anything scary, such as a chronic disease. Whenever such thoughts came to her mind, she pushed them as far away as she could. She could feel her heartbeat and the pace at which the blood in her veins flowed.

"It's only that your treatment will cost quite some amount of money;

213

we oughtto engage them, so the earlier, the better," said Dr Esther.

Lily walked quietly to her apartment, scared for herself. The problem that required her mother's presence was as unclear as the illegible prescription the doctor had scribbled on a pad and given her. Was it HIV/AIDS? And still, she was worried because she only had a little money that could only pay for her mother's bus fare to Nairobi. Where would she get the money for her bus fare back to the countryside? And now that it seemed Babirye would be more helpful, Lily didn't want any more trouble with her. So, she opted not to ask Marto for any.

Because it was urgent for her mother to come, Lily went to an ATM and swept her account clean and then called Milly. The coldness she had had towards them evoked guilt, but she called anyway. The fact that Lily knew his father had lost his hearing ability, and there was no need for him to come to Nairobi, made her feel so hurt. She had indirectly contributed to it.

That evening at her house, Lily dragged a seat to the balcony and sat down to reflect on what was going on. The compound was so quiet that she could hear water spattering in her next-door neighbour's bathroom. Still feeling withdrawn, she couldn't tell how long she had been sitting there when it started raining in sheets that were swayed to the balcony by the wind.

From her bed, she listened to the steady pelting of rain on the windowpanes. When it stopped, she folded the curtains, opened the window and sat looking outside.

With the ascension of darkness, the twinkling stars were fast replacing the sun after it had glidingly sunk beyond the horizon. With a cold wind blowing gently, Lily basked in nostalgia; revisiting memories of her having dinner by the beach with Juma. She smiled in retrospect and drew her knees to her chest. Once again, she felt the pain in her left breast dig into her flesh. Later, when sleep was not forthcoming, she browsed the internet for breast-related ailments.

"What is it?" She asked herself. No answer came to her mind. She placed the laptop aside and took her notes. She stared at the pages for several minutes, unable to comprehend even a sentence. "Or could it...no, it can't be!" She could hear her own voice in the silence of her bedroom.

Chapter Twenty-Two

Lily drew up her knees and tightened her legs in a thoughtful hug, her body curled, and chin resting on her knees. By dawn, she hadn't flinched an eye; the walls watching her in silence. Leaning her head against the wall, she watched the eastern sky, with an orange lustre of the sun's paint, without a tinge of sleep in her eyes.

Babirye passed by Lily's apartment that Thursday evening.

"My dear, you know I have no grudge against you, don't you?" Lily smiled, relieved.

After Lily had prepared and served coffee, Babirye asked her to accompany her to a friend's place in Donholm. Lily had heard of this friend before; a Nigerian called Chukukwa Ike. He lived near the Greenspan Mall.

"What's with West Africans and malls? Lily asked.

"It's nice to wake up to a view of huge tall buildings. It gives you the feeling that your life is equally huge, don't you think?"

"No, I don't," Lily answered, and they both laughed. "When did you last do your BSE?"

"BSE? Which unit is that?" Babirye asked.

"It's not coursework my dear, come I show you," Lily led Babirye to thebathroom mirror.

"The last time I checked, you weren't a lesbian," Babirye complained, on seeingLily undress.

"I haven't touched you. I haven't looked at you suggestively! Though I know you're beautiful," Lily joked, and then added on a serious note, "Listen, this is important. What I am asking you is not to allow my hands to touch you but tojust watch me."

Lily stood in front of the mirror and repeated what Dr Esther had taught her, with her shoulders straight and hands on her hips. She pointed out the changes she saw in her breasts as Babirye keenly looked on. "Whenever you do this, ensure you check if the breasts are of their usual size, shape and colour, and that there's no visible distortion or swelling."

"Okay," Babirye said, moving even closer.

"If you notice any redness, soreness, rash, swelling, an inverted nipple, or one that has changed position, dimpling, puckering or bulging of the skin, make an appointment to see a doctor."

"Did you get the results from the hospital?" Babirye asked.

"Not yet. Probably next week," Lily said, raising her arms. "Still, check for the same, plus any signs of fluids coming out of the nipples," she continued.

"Okay."

Feeling her own breast, Lily said, "With the circle method, you move the three fingers in a circular motion like this," she demonstrated starting from the outer side of the breast towards the nipple.

"This is going to be useful," said Babirye, involuntarily trying to do the same without removing her silky blouse.

"Now, with the second method, you do it this way," Lily moved her three middle fingers, starting from the underarm area down below the breast. Slowly, she moved the fingers back upwards repeatedly until she had felt the entire breast.

She further demonstrated the third method. Babirye had even moved closer in front of Lily and leant against the wall next to the mirror. She intently watched Lily demonstrate the third approach. Moving from the outside of the breast towards the nipple, Lily repeated the procedure from every wedge until she felt the entire breast. "As you do it, check for any abnormal changes in the breasts. Normally, the breasts should be soft and smooth to touch. You can read more about this, right? Prevention is better than cure, you know!" It pleased Lily to have demonstrated to her the BSE; if only for the simple knowledge that Babirye had now buried the past.

* * *

Lily and Babirye took a taxi to Donholm early that night. They branched to the Tuskys Supermarket at the Greenspan Mall to buy a few gifts for the birthday boy. The area was congested with revellers who had come to have fun at the *Cubano Club* on the rooftop of the *Nairobi Java House.*

As they were getting to the house in Donholm, tunes of Gregory Isaacs boomed through the corridors. Laughter and chit-chat by the people in the house wafted through the lyrics.

Please give me a chance, so I can make my confession, the song played as if addressing Lily. After greetings, Lily took a seat at a corner. *I must apologise, coz I'm so sorry to treat you so cruel*, the song went on playing from the *Sony* home theatre. Lily had heard Tom play the song before. She hadn't talked to Tom for a while now. She felt the need to apologise for her irrational behaviour.

From her corner seat, she quietly scanned the crowd. All the faces were new to her. Most of the people sipped their drinks hunched over the screens of their phones; sending and receiving messages. A few times, someone would whisper to his or her partner.

"Can we *stsop tsoking* for a few *minutse* please," the host demanded after pausing the music. Lily noted his strong Nigerian accent. He introduced Babirye, then himself before asking others to introduce themselves. In their loud conversations, the Nigerians seemed to add "aaah aaah" or "now" almost at the end of every sentence.

218

As the night progressed, drinks and food were served. People savoured and danced. Lily just watched. Once in a while, Babirye would emerge from either the kitchen or the bedroom, talk to her for a few minutes, mingle with others, and then rush back. And with Gregory Isaacs' songs playing back-to-back; *I gave her back the key to her front door, 'cause it seems she didn't care about me anymore* lyrics sinking in after other lyrics, Lily's mind shifted from Tom to Barasa and back to the house. She thought of them and how she had treated them, despite all the efforts they had put into her life.

Two hours later, Babirye emerged from the bedroom straightening her skirt and rotating it by the waist. "*Twende*," she whispered, smacking her lips freshly coated with lipstick.

On their way, at Kaloleni, a car sped and pulled with screeching brakes in front of their taxi. Two young men – in their early twenties – jumped out of the car while a second car pulled to the side of the taxi and one more guy jumped out. A fourth guy emerged from near a heap of garbage at the foot of the flyover, next to the entrance to the City Stadium.

"Everyone lie down!" one of the guys fished out his pistol and said, pointing it at them. They pulled them out and took their money, pouches, phones and wristwatches before huddling them into the second car, which zoomed off immediately. Though her iPhone was taken, Lily managed to hide her old phone in her bra before they were huddled in the second car.

The two young men locked the taxi driver in the boot of his taxi and got into the front seats. With one behind the wheel and the other pointing a gun at Lily and Babirye who were seated at the back, they drove off. They went to ATMs at various locations where they were forced to withdraw money, before ending up in the basement of a club in Westlands. Fortunately, Lily's account was empty.

Many such incidents had been experienced along Jogoo Road. Lily had heard that young men had guns and young girls became mothers of two or more kids in their parents' houses.

"*Maze jo, tuwamade!*" One of them alluded to the idea of killing them.

Asthey argued in whispers, a young Asian lady drove into the parking lot. They stopped to watch her movements. The scent of her perfume wafted into the taxi as the lady headed to the elevators without noticing them. They then drove off towards the Nairobi Arboretum from where they threatened they would shoot the three dead. Lily and Babirye sobbed, prayed and repented.

* * *

"Let's call Tom," Babirye said after they had been dumped in the darkness and cold of the Arboretum. Their lives, and that of the taxi driver, had been spared.

Tom arrived with other close comrades within minutes. As the taxi driver proceeded to the Central Police to report, Tom and friends escorted Lily and Babirye in a taxi to their separate apartments in Chiromo and Ngara. The two ladies didn't want anything to do with the police. It was enough that their lives had been spared. They didn't talk about what had happened in detail. Every time Tom wanted to ask about it, or about what had happened in his relationship with Lily, he feared he would provoke her and make her continue avoiding him again.

On Sunday that week, Lily spent the whole day indoors with brief snatches of sleep. She had spent the past few nights without an iota of sleep, thinking about what awaited her. For the first time since she moved out of the hostels, Tom visited her that afternoon. He carried with him packed food, and despite her lack of appetite and trying to conceal how pleased she was to see him, Tom forced her to eat.

They talked about school, lectures and her work at the airport. Lily didn't explain in detail the pain she felt in her breast despite using painkillers. They had coffee before leaving to pick her mother from the Machakos Country Bus Station.

At about 6:30 p.m., the bus from Kitale slowly pulled to a halt at the bus station. Francisca was the last one to alight holding her grandson's hand. She looked older than her age, and frazzled like a fisherman by the riverside. Her face looked sad and wrinkled. Her favourite scarf was draped around the back of her neck, exposing the two small holes that rats had eaten into. The fabric of the scarf had weakened with time. On Francisca's shoulder was an old bag Lily recalled belonged to Milly. Why had she never thought of buying her mother a decent bag? She felt embarrassed.

Lily had last seen Jim early the previous year when she had visited them. Though he had grown, he still reminded her of the rape, and the scars and wound it had left in her heart. He looked stronger and older than before. His face was a bit dry and pale, probably from the dust and the breath that had kept fogging the bus' windowpane where he had rested his brow as he stared at buildings and trees zooming past.

"Nekesa," Francisca said, enclosing her daughter in an emotional hug. "*Ori Mulamu?*" she asked in a voice only audible enough for Lily to hear. Jim stood holding Francisca's dress. He looked lean in a pair of grey trousers and a blue T-shirt Lily had bought him on her last visit.

"I'm fine, mama."

Lily crouched and hugged him too. There was a familiar smell from the back of his neck where he had dry patches on the skin.

"*Eyo breki fludi niyo, ari nde bhusumwa,*" Francisca offered when she noticed Lily trying to figure out the source of the smell as she hugged him, blocking other passengers' way. Lily could now place the familiar smell. As a child she had either used it, the brake fluid, to treat patches of *bhusumwa, pityriasis versicolor* skin disease, or she had rubbed leaves of some weeds on the affected areas.

"How are you?" Lily greeted Jim, still clasping his hand softly to her bosom and rubbing his small back. He didn't show any signs that he had missed his mother. Standing up, she said, "Welcome, mama. How's dad?" She held Jim's small hand, and his fingers disappeared into her soft palm.

"We're all fine. He said hello."

"Oooh, and this is Tom. He's a close friend."

"Hello mum," Tom extended his hand politely, smiling. He was

221

conscious notto say any word that would brew questions.

"Hello, my son," Francisca said then turned to Lily, "And Barasa said hello, too."

Lily wanted to say, "No mama, it's not what you think," but then, she didn't know what Francisca thought. Lily didn't know how Tom felt; now that Barasa's name had been mentioned openly. Anyway, Lily thought, Francisca simply didn't know about Tom's feelings.

"*Ori mulamu*?" Francisca asked again, wiping a layer of dust from her face with the edge of her *khanga*. A few hawkers shoved biscuits, groundnuts, watches, cigarettes, *ready to drink* juices and other wares to passengers in the vehicles next to where they stood. Some also approached them.

"Yes, I am, mum," Lily said, taking the bag from her mother.

"Wait," Francisca said and pulled out an old woven sweater. "This town of yours is very cold; I don't want him to catch pneumonia." Francisca helped Jim put it on. Lily made a mental note to find out about the relationship between cold and pneumonia.

"Okay, mum. Let me help you." Lily took the bags from her.

"And it's noisy too. I wonder how you people communicate with each other."

There was a music store selling CDs and playing loud music next to where they stood. Touts shouted. Vehicles hooted. Hawkers called out for buyers. Along Landhies Road, matatus heading to Eastlands hooted noisily as they blocked each other and nudged private cars or climbed on the pavements.

"Are you okay, Nekesa?" Francisca asked for the third time. "Yes, how about you? How is baba at home?"

"I am well, and your dad too. Only this backache, and my bone pain has proved resistant to the *diclofenac* tablets I swallow endlessly." The rate at which her parents were ageing was saddening. Lily felt sorry that the painkillers they took didn't help as much in reducing the bone pain, especially with Francisca's legs. Was that an onset of osteoporosis? She questioned herself.

"Sorry, you'll feel better mum.""Amen. But are you fine?"

"Of course, mum," she retorted, a little irritated now.

They talked briefly, a few times involving Tom in their conversation. Tom took the bag from Lily as they walked towards the town centre. Though Jim was grown up now, Lily carried him on her chest, his feet bouncing from her lap. They trod the congested streets, passing young girls selling bananas on the pavements. Francisca turned metres after they had passed to look at them. She sympathised with them. Once in a while, Francisca would strike up a conversation with Tom, inquiring about where he came from, and whether he was pursuing a medical course, or he would be a future lawyer or teacher.

In town, they got into a matatu. Lily sat next to her mother and held Jim on her lap. Tom sat behind them. On Lily's left hand sat a young man who kept throwing glances at her as if he wanted to initiate a conversation. Lily didn't acknowledge any of his attempts and instead concentrated on Jim's fingers whose nails he had nibbled down to the skin.

"*Huyo atawachanganya, huyo atawachanganya wana shangazi na kaka. Tena kisha akipenya, tena kisha akipenya na baba atamtaka,*" East African Melody's *Paka Mapepe* taarab was playing.

A lady with huge lips, seated next to the young man who was staring at Lily, sang along in implausible whispers. She swung her head back and forth in response to the tunes of the song as the matatu moved through the bustling streets. She went on warbling along, "*Njoo kwangu, nakudhamini asikupeleke puta huyo,*" until she alighted at Fig Tree in Ngara. Francisca watched as she slapped her open shoes against the tarmac and disappeared in the crowd of touts and hawkers descending on cars with peeled pineapples and watermelons.

When they reached the first flight of the stairs, Lily worked the door lock, and a sweet fragrance slapped their nostrils as they entered. Francisca's eyes surveyed the neat living room. Streaks of light streamed in when Lily drew the curtains. Francisca admired the house, which was painted cream and matched the colour of the curtains.

Though it was now five months since Lily moved in, the building still had a distant smell of paint. A few cracks already showed on the white concrete ceiling and the walls. But Francisca was impressed by the well-furnished house. She said a prayer to thank God for His protection and journey mercies before they settled in. The question as to where Lily got the money from was tugged in Francisca's throat, but she didn't ask.

"There's some foodstuff in the bag," Francisca said, asking Lily to bring her the bag. "I couldn't carry more, my daughter," she said, as she unpacked. "You know how money has disappeared. I wonder if it's because of the forthcoming general elections!"

"Don't worry, mum, we're okay."

Lily had planned to borrow money from Halima but forgot. Tom had paid their bus fare to town and back. He also gave her some money for groceries. He also offered to help her in preparing the meal, but the gas had run out, and when he bent to light the kerosene stove, Lily asked him not to bother.

"No, let me help as you talk to your mum," Tom insisted, adding, "Just show me around your kitchen." Lily showed him the salt in the coffee tin, a small tin of cooking oil, a wooden rack where she stored onions and tomatoes, a matchstick, and *pilau masala*. She then called her gas supplier and requested for delivery on credit.

After taking tea, Jim looked at the fridge and stood by the TV, surprised by the miniature people he saw. He then joined Tom in the kitchen, from where Tom was watching them out of the corners of his eyes.

"*Sasa*," Tom greeted Jim, wiping the sting of onion from the corner of his eyes with the back of his wrist joint. With a knife, he pushed the slices of chopped onions into the frying pan. Jim watched the blue gas flames roar under the pan as the onions Tom was frying hissed.

"Jim," he called again, and turned to rinse the knife and the chopping board, but once he heard Francisca and Lily lower their voices and switch to speaking Luhya, Tom turned off the tap and reduced the amount of heat to listen in, just in case his name, or that of Barasa, would be mentioned in the conversation. He had not been at ease that evening; he kept asking himself if the way he shook Francisca's hand, or how he stood, or sat, would invite judgement from her.

Jim crouched to watch the fire from the gas, amazed at the flames emerging from the tiny nozzles and painting the base of the pan yellowish-blue. "I hope Jim is not disturbing you," Lily said in a loud voice from the living room, jerking Tom to attention. She had noticed the silence emanating from the kitchen, recalling her childhood when she would just look at her mother, or how she would remain awkwardly silent whenever she did something wrong.

"No," Tom said, turning to Jim who seemed to be worried that Lily could punish him, "Come, let me show you something." He touched Jim's wrists gently, so delicately, as if afraid of some bristle bones breaking, as though Jim would resist and scream, knocking off the frying pan. Though timid, Jim didn't resist. Tom tickled him as he giggled. He then lifted him into his arms, and then switched on the second cooking panel and showed him the flames. Tom showed him the gas cylinder and the connecting pipe. Thereafter, Jim laughed easily at Tom's tickles. Then a spoon clattered to the floor, and Jim left immediately before Lily could find a fault to punish him for.

"Are you okay, or do you need my help?" Lily stirred him up minutes after Jim had left the kitchen. She was leaning on the frame of the kitchen door. The room now smelt of steamy spices.

"You will; once I'm done with the beef stew." Lily left. Through the kitchen window, Tom secretly watched them and eavesdropped on their conversation in Luhya. Were they talking about him, or his cooking, or how Francisca won't eat his food? He could see truth in how Francisca talked, how the words, calmly, came out of her one after another, how intently Lily leant in and listened, and yet he couldn't tell what it was they were talking about.

Tom was pleased to watch Jim scoop spoon after spoon of his meal until he finished the last morsel, pushed the plate away, licked a few morsels that tugged at his fingers, and came to him. "*Asante kwa chakula*, uncle," Jim said, as though he wouldn't have thanked anyone else.

After eating the evening meal together, Tom left for the campus clinic

225

to check on Geoffrey. Geoffrey had been in and out of the clinic due to random infectionsor fights he carelessly picked. Rumour had it that a few of his girlfriends had aborted and one had almost died in the process. Tom had promised Lily that he would send her more money by the end of the following day.

And as his shoes kissed the tarmac on his way to campus, Lily and her mother sat next to each other, with several questions in their minds drawing endless blanks on what the following day portended.

Lily spread a mattress for Francisca to sleep on in the living room. Francisca led them in prayers before they called it a day. Attempts by Lily to talk to Jim came to naught. He didn't say much. He politely shook his head vertically or horizontally, depending on the question she asked. And when there were no more questions to ask, she watched him fiddle with her hair band until he dozed off. And the band fell from his hand, then she pulled a blanket over his head.

* * *

By 8 a.m., Dr Esther's receptionist warmly greeted them and ushered them to the waiting couches. A nurse took Lily's vital signs and encouraged her to relax. They watched the muted television, which was tuned to *Citizen TV*.

"Welcome," Dr Esther ushered them into her office, shaking Francisca's hand then softly brushing her fingers over Jim's clean-shaven head. She perused through a few files then hit a few keys on her keyboard, before continuing, "My name is Dr Esther. I'm happy you responded to the call on such short notice."

Dr Esther took a few candies from a small glass bowl on her table. "Here, for you," she extended her hand. Jim turned to Francisca.

"Yes, take. And remember to say 'thank you' to *Daktari*."

They talked about the countryside, and Dr Esther inquired if it was dry or as rainy and chilly as the city was, and how the crops were doing and other small talks.

226

"So, coming back to why you're here," Dr Esther said, jolting them to rapt attention. Their ears were now sharp, and Lily's heart skipped a beat. "I hope Lilian has already told you that she has some lumps in her breasts. We did tests on her to ascertain what the precise problem could be." Dr Esther spoke softly, gently and slowly to ensure they got every word.

"Yes, she informed me already."

"Great," she nodded. Then she turned to Lily and said, "Did the radiologisttell you anything about the MRI?"

"No," her heartbeat increased again.

"Not to worry, but have you thought of what could be the problem?

Anything..."

"I haven't thought of anything, Doctor," Lily was curt. She felt more nervous. Actually, this wasn't true for she had thought of many things. She had evenscoured the Internet for certainty.

"So, the mammography and MRI results showed lumps in your breast." Dr Esther took a sip of water, giving time for the bits of information to sink slowly into their minds.

"Okay," Francisca incomprehensibly started, but stopped immediately. Her voice was low. The room was silent. The plastic rolling window shades swayed with the fan air.

Dr Esther digressed a bit and told them about advancements in technology and the resultant availability of a variety of treatments for various diseases. She cleverly threw bits of encouragement in her words and a bit of medicalconsolation and counselling.

Dr Esther was a great talker, and after skirting around the subject for some time, she finally leant forward and said, "Lilian, we reviewed and evaluated your results," she turned to Lily's files and flipped pages as if she were studying it for the first time. Lily's vital signs taken that morning by the nurse were first on top of all the other papers; *temperature – 37.2⁰C, pulse rate – 92 beats per minute,blood pressure – 110/70.*

"Would you like to see the results?" They both nodded.

Dr Esther took out an x-ray and moved around her table. "You see these?" She pointed out spots on the x-ray slides.

"Yes, doctor," Lily responded as Francisca nodded in agreement.

"After keenly evaluating all the results, it is clear that you need immediate medical intervention," Dr Esther told Lily as she had done many times to other patients, walking back to her black leather seat. Even though she bore bad news, it was her duty to inform them. She settled down into her chair, gave them a few seconds to absorb the results and relax before hitting it home, "I'm sorry, Lily, you've been diagnosed with breast cancer. Those spots I've shown you are cancer cells."

For a moment, Lily just stared at Dr Esther blankly. She couldn't see her. Couldn't hear her. The smile that was always planted on her face suddenly creased into deep thoughts in a world none could tell. The weight of the news was huge! She felt the earth beneath her caving in to swallow her. She opened her mouth, but whatever she wanted to say dissipated. She could only hear her own breathing; huge gulps of air rushing in and out of her respiratory tract, and her heart pounded. The sound of it had stung her deeply.

Blood rushed into her head, and silence ensued.

Chapter Twenty-Three

When Riziki questioned Juma about Lily, he was so embarrassed that he stormed out of the house, unable to give any convincing reason. That day, he came back home late in the night drunk. Riziki was asleep in her daughter's bedroom, with the door locked.

"Riziki," Juma called; the smell of alcohol on his breath and his eyes painted with guilt. He wanted to mend fences and, if possible, apologise, but Riziki kept quiet.

"You mean you prefer that girl over your daughter and I? Your own family?" Riziki again confronted Juma in the morning when she woke up to find him waiting for her at the couch where he had slept. When Juma said nothing, she shouted, "Okay, are you saying it's over between us?"

Their daughter came running to the living room.

"Sorry," Juma said calmly, "...let's talk about it." He was afraid that her shouting could attract the attention of neighbours. It would be a scandal if they knew the source of the disagreement. So, he kept his cool and left it at that.

"I shared it with my mum and uncle. They'll be coming over so we can talk about the issues we have." Riziki said without mentioning her visit to the Ministry of Health.

Juma picked his phone and went to their bedroom. A message came through from a neighbour inquiring if all was well. He didn't reply and was glad he didn't bump into the neighbour that day. They met with the neighbour at the parking lot; the same day Lily was with her mother in the hospital.

The cracked tile on the kitchen floor reminded Riziki of the coward she had for a husband; a man who could not face her while sober. And now she was desperate to get someone to fix the tile so that she could forget the incident.

* * *

At the hospital, the silence that came after Dr Esther's disclosure lasted for minutes. The chilling message fell on Lily's ears with an overwhelming shock that her mind went blank. She sat there, her legs heavy as though a wheelbarrow of wet concrete had been poured on them. Her throat was dry. *This could only betrue in a dream*, she thought. The symptoms had been there a while back when Juma had advised her to visit a gynaecologist but she instead got for herself painkillers. She regretted not visiting a doctor early enough.

"And the earlier we start treating it, the better," Dr Esther's words echoed in her mind.

Lily had read and heard people talk about cancer, and was engulfed in awhirlpool of emotions and bitterness.

"You may feel like this is the end of your life, and that you will never fully recover again, but that isn't true. People have created lots of myths and misconceptions about cancer, which have a potent influence on the feelings of patients. Being diagnosed with cancer is not a death sentence," Dr Esthercounselled Lily, "Don't think of what you've heard from people that have littleor no knowledge about the disease."

"But what exactly is this cancer?" Francisca asked because she didn't know much about it.

"This is a type of cancer that is most common in women," Dr Esther started. "But it's the easiest to manage." Lily moved closer. The doctor explained to them how it grows slowly and how it can take years before one feels the lumps. "Some cancers grow quickly. Others grow gradually," Dr Esther said. She detailed the basics of what a cell is, then how cancer develops from a single cell to millions. "And this is the breast, right?" she asked, holding a plastic model of a breast.

Francisca repositioned Jim to face away, but he turned to watch as Dr Esther demonstrated. She further explained the development of breast cancer using a model showing cancer infection.

"So, what's the treatment or what are we supposed to do?" Francisca probed. Dr Esther explained all the tests and procedures that had been performed and what needed to be done.

"Based on the assessment and prognosis, this cancer is in its third stage. Fortunately, it hasn't spread so much to other parts of the body. This is indeed rare!" Dr Esther paused to read a few pages from Lily's file and then clarified the type of breast cancer Lily had. "Before we start treatment," she said, "We must consider Lily's age, health and menstrual cycle, given that this is her first cancer treatment."

Francisca nodded.

"Generally, we would like to consider combining surgery with chemotherapy." Dr Esther mentioned radiotherapy, and why she chose not to use it. She also patiently explained the pros and cons of each option and the cost.

"Oooh my God!" Lily exclaimed in a tremulous voice. It had taken her minutes for the lump in her throat to soften. There was no way the family could raise such an amount.

"Oh. My. God!" Lily repeated. She cupped her face in her hands and remained tersely silent.

"As I said, cancer has spread to her breast tissues. The only treatment is mastectomy..." Dr Esther's voice was softer than before. Both Lily and her mother pulled pale blank faces. The doctor quickly registered their incomprehension. "I mean, the only appropriate treatment is to ablate, sorry, I mean to surgically remove her breast tissues, followed by chemotherapy."

"Mmmmh," Francisca shook her head.

"Chemotherapy is the use of medicines to weaken and destroy any remaining cancer cells at the origin. And those that might have spread to other parts of the body, but the tests did not reveal. The procedure targets cancer cells, but in the process, rapidly growing cells in the bone marrow and hair follicles are affected too."

Noticeably, it was going to take time for Lily to get her head around theshackles of misfortune her life had just been tied with.

Much of what the doctor said wasn't in the realm of their understanding, but all they wanted to hear was that there was a solution. Dr Esther explained all the steps of chemotherapy, the side effects and the total cost of the entire process. Their emotions and thoughts spoke louder than words. She ended by asking them to seek a second opinion, that is, if they were in doubt. But Lily knew their options were limited, especially with the financial implications. They would go with the treatment suggested by Dr Esther. After all, Lily had learnt that she was the hospital's best oncologist.

* * *

Lily took a deep despondent look into her life, a life that had just begun to mime normalcy. It seemed like a nightmare. The revelation had just shredded all her ambitions into a million fragments that could not be pieced back together. Had she, and her family not gone to church? Had she not given money and food to the needy on the streets a few times? Had she not accompanied Halima to a children's home once? Then why was her Creator denying her a space to catch a breath? Had she not avoided smoking? Or was it the wine she had been taking? Or was she being punished for the multiple sex relations she had?

Many questions pinged over and over in Lily's mind. Stealthily, cancer had decided to choose her as it had chosen James' wife in Mathare North. If the post- election skirmishes hadn't claimed their lives, would the woman have fought the bout of cancer? A pang of bitterness stubbed her heart, as dark ideations darted into her mind. She silently prayed the rosary; something she hadn't done in along time.

Lily thought of committing suicide. Then she noticed Jim pull a sad face at her as if he was reading her mind. How would he grow without a parent? What ofher parents? She then quickly expunged the thought.

Had they run afoul of any laws laid down by their forefathers? Had Lubao or Francisca offended their ancestors? Where were they to get 1.2 million shillings for the treatment?

"God will provide the money," Francisca kept saying.

An hour later, after a long persuasion with the doctor about the cost of treatment, they left her office.

They walked silently, past an open space with white thick linen drying on washing lines. They then passed a group of women mourning a dead relative along the corridor. Had the deceased died of cancer? Lily wondered.

As they boarded the matatu back to Ngara, which was not very far from the hospital, both Francisca and Lily were engrossed in their thoughts. The matatu moved so fast that they only realised when they had passed the stage where they were supposed to alight. Lily even forgot to ask for change from the conductor whom she had given two hundred shillings.

* * *

Lily felt like her bedroom was dreary and airless. She took a plastic chair andsat on the balcony where she had spent many hours on most of the previous nights. She needed to digest her thoughts and the advice from Dr Esther. Only thebalcony could provide such an environment.

At lunchtime, Lily's mother went to the kitchen to warm the leftovers of their previous meal. The wind blew thick smoke and stuffy fumes from the stove, but she could not gather enough strength to help her mother. Not even to show her how to use the gas cooker.

233

"Lunch is ready," her mother interrupted her musings. "My stomach is still full with breakfast," Lily said. "Just come and eat a little," Her mother begged.

Lily chewed the beef from her plate of *pilau* absentmindedly; disinterestedly. One would think she had been served a plate of ballast. Even when she went to brush her teeth, she was still distrait that she squirted a lot of toothpaste onto her brush.

"It was not mastitis. It's cancer!" Lily broke the sad news in a call to Halima while on the balcony. After further small talk, Lily continued sitting quietly on the balcony, occasionally glancing at the blank spaces and the numerous buildings sprouting in the area.

Lily's mind shifted to the landlord. He was a middle-aged man living in the leafy suburbs of Kileleshwa. She liked him, and his apartment. It looked classy, except for the small cracks that appeared in the ceiling, and the damp walls. He had promised to work on them as soon as possible. Although he had directly wired a huge sum to Babirye's account, courtesy of Hon. W., he still had a lot. He had just conveniently ignored it. Perhaps the money had become too sweet.

At the time the landlord had promised to fix the cracks and the dampness on the walls, the country was peaceful. There were no ethnic related political differences. But now, the political temperatures were rising, with talk of isolation and discrimination of those who supported opposing presidential candidates in the forthcoming elections. Since she hailed from a different ethnic group from that of the landlord, she was presumed to support CORD, the Coalition for Reforms and Democracy, an opposing political coalition of several parties.

On the other side, her landlord was pro-Jubilee. Therefore, he wanted all his tenants to be from ethnic groups associated with his party of choice. As a consequence, he had recently served Lily with a notice to vacate the house, but Lily had completely forgotten about it. So, when the landlord came to remind her to vacate, she argued her case. Consequently, the landlord promised to give her more time. But still, the day was quickly approaching.

Lily's thoughts shifted from the landlord to the cancer patients who travelled long distances to the hospital and spent nights on the cold floors waiting for either their chemotherapy or radiotherapy sessions. She was filled with a mixture of anger and guilt. Would she face the same fate? She feared losing her sexual attractiveness and even saw death as imminent. She wished she could be phased out to an Elysium painlessly, and be equally forgotten; quickly. Although she sympathised with Jim, she was also relieved that he would remain a constant reminder of her existence. But she feared that he could grow up to be a ruffian like his unknown father, or just do something tragic.

It is already 11 a.m. Lily has not woken up. Francisca is worried. "What could have happened," she's wondering. "Nekesa," Francisca enters her room calling. She's dumbfounded when she is met by Lily's body, dangling on a rope. "Nooo!" she screams. She rushes towards Lily's body. The soles of Lily's feet areas white as dry cassava, and her toenails pale and dry. Her eyes are popped out and bloodshot, and her body swollen.

The window curtains are still closed; Francisca does not know what to do. Should she call neighbours, cry, shout or just wail? Her shouts of "Nekesa! Nekesa! Nekesa!" while shaking Lily's body, wakes up Jim. She hurries to carry Jim out of the room, covering his face with her khanga. She doesn't want him to see the sad sight and to always remember that his mother took her own life. But Jim struggles to push the khanga aside and looks at the body of his mother hanging from the ceiling. Silence. Questions. Pain.

The images of her suicide, her parents childless and her son motherless kept cropping up in Lily's mind. It pained her that she was still alive and would have to face the burden that had befallen her. Though she fantasised about her suicide, she knew she had no courage to do it. It wasn't the solution. It could never be.

After buzzing with endless thoughts for a long time, Lily remembered the one-hundred-shilling note in the small gift box in her dresser. She went into the bedroom, took it out and sat on her bed staring vacantly at it. You would have mistaken her for Cleopatra being painted. The writings on the note and Jomo Kenyatta's image merged into a blurred vision. Then she remembered the change she had left in the matatu; that meant she had no other money except that note. It doesn't matter, she thought. From the living room, Francisca observed Jim in silence as he concentrated on a Cartoon Network television programme.

"I'll be back shortly, mama," Lily said, closing the door behind her. Francisca's attempt to inquire where she was headed was ignored. Lily was on the verge of insanity. She neither cared about the distance she would trek nor the sudden hot defiant sun whose rays glinted mirages on the tarmac. It was 3:30 p.m., but still hot, though it had rained weeks earlier. She strutted along with steady and graceful strides. The slapping soles of her sandals passionately kissed the earth, as if to tell cancer its plans to skew her ambitions would be defeated. She felt like her body was filled with a weightless gas.

Lily made her way back to the hospital to see Dr Esther. The receptionist seated behind the shiny brown desk was clutching a bunch of files from a shelf behind her desk, craning her neck to reach for one more. Those files must be full of patients' hidden pains and miseries, Lily thought.

"Sorry," Lily said, absent-mindedly smiling, wiping beads of sweat off her brow with the sleeve of her blouse. She had almost knocked down a gentleman standing at the reception desk, also waiting to be served.

"Can I please see Dr Esther?"

"Please wait," the receptionist, Ciku, told her. Confusion was written all over Lily's face. She leant on the wall and didn't twitch a muscle. Other patients exchanged puzzled looks. A patient exited Dr Esther's office, and Lily ushered herself in without a go-ahead from the receptionist.

"Oooh, you're back. Welcome, have a seat, Lilian," Dr Esther welcomed her with a warm smile. She could, however, tell Lily was in no good shape.

"Thank you, doctor," Lily said and sat, facing the large window. "So tell me, my dear, how can I be of help to you?"

236

"Doctor, you said my surgery requires 1.2 million shillings, right?" Lily asked, placing the one-hundred-shilling note on Dr Esther's table.

"True." Dr Esther's puzzled eyes moved between Lily and the note. The doctor leant forward, stretching her hands on the desk. Lily avoided her eyes, concentrating on the golden polish on the doctor's nails, and the silver ring she wore.

"I treasure this one-hundred-shilling note. It has been in my family for the exact number of years I have lived." Still, the doctor wasn't getting the gist out of it. Lily explained further before asking, "It is the only amount I have for now, but I'm expecting a very close friend of mine, Tom, to send me some money today. I will add it to this when he sends. Please, doctor, will you take this as a down payment for my treatment?"

"Why not?" Dr Esther agreed with the implausible suggestion. She had noticed that something was totally off the beam with Lily. There was no other reason she could think of other than a psychological problem. "I'll definitely take it, why not?" She took the note, and quickly asked, "Have you taken the painkillers?" before Lily could enquire when the treatment would commence.

"Yes, but they aren't doing so well, I guess." That was the exact answer Dr Esther had wished for at that point in time.

"I'm sorry about that. Let me get you a stronger painkiller." Dr Esther placed a call asking a nurse to bring her an intravenous painkiller plus a drug unknown to Lily. Since the nurses were a little busy, Lily was asked to wait at the reception as Dr Esther attended to the next patient.

In fifteen minutes, Lily was called in and requested to lie on the bed in the office after the injection. Within no time, she became suddenly weak and giddy then fell into slumber.

Dr Esther called a doctor in charge of the wards, and the nurse in charge. She explained to them that she had a patient that she needed to admit for a day. So, admission sheets were prepared, and a nurse brought them for her to sign before two nurses pushed Lily in a gurney to the ward. By that time, all the admission processes had been completed. She only needed to get in touch with Lily's mother. Dr Esther remained in her office searching for the contacts of Lily's mother from her file. Suddenly, she heard a phone beep. It was Lily's; Lily had accidentally dropped it on the examination bed. It was an M-Pesa message from Tom. Lily had mentioned Tom to Dr Esther minutes earlier.

She rang Tom and requested him to come to the hospital with Lily's mother. Tom was preparing for a date when she called; he had skived lectures. After failing to win Lily's heart, he decided to try to hit on Babirye. But Babirye had turned him down several times until a few days before their carjacking incident. Babirye had then accepted to go on an afternoon date with Tom, just so to stop him pestering her about it.

Tom called Babirye. Her phone rang once. Twice. There was no response. The third time, she picked and said, "Sorry, Tom, I was just finishing up preparing. I'll be leaving the room in five..."

"Actually, I was calling to call off the date," Tom interjected. "What do you mean?"

"There's an emergency about Lily, I have to rush to the hospital."

Babirye thought about Lily, and then thought of the make-up, the dress and the time she had wasted preparing, not to mention the lectures she had skipped. Bitterness slithered in her. Why Lily? Was she not the same Lily who had told her to go to hell? How dare Tom chose Lily over her!

Francisca and Tom arrived at the hospital worried; Dr Esther had to calm them down. She explained to them that Lily's mental situation wasn't very good and that there was a need to watch over her closely.

"It's good that you understand Lily's life – and yours too – are going to change. It won't be easy, but you have to be there for each other. In such difficult times, you need to lean on each other's shoulders more than ever before," Dr Esther said. She led them to the ward where Lily was still dead asleep. She then handed Francisca the one-hundred-shilling note and left.

When Lily woke up, she tried to open her eyes, but she could only see the figures of her mother and Tom without recognising them. Then she fell asleep again.

Tom was distraught. He had to come up with a solution. An idea came to his mind, but he was doubtful if it could succeed. Thinking fast, he copied Juma's number from Lily's phone and walked out of the ward.

Outside, Tom had a lengthy conversation with Juma in which Juma promised to help as much as he could. But he did not stop at Juma's promise of financial assistance. Back in the ward, he excused himself and rushed back to campus.

At campus, Tom called a few of his close friends and Lily's. Geoffrey heard about it when he was smoking; he dropped the cigarette on the floor and let it burn to the end. He had just been discharged from the hospital that day. Together, they discussed Tom's idea of making a proforma for students to contribute moneytowards the bill.

Geoffrey designed and printed the proforma immediately. They made copies and distributed them to students, starting with Lily's and Tom's friends. They moved from one campus to another, department to another, lecture hall to another and from one hostel to another, raising funds for a fellow comrade. It surprised Tom how willing and ready comrades and junior staff were to help withwhatever they had.

* * *

Juma was so touched that, at night, he tried talking his wife into agreeing to help Lily. They spoke at length about it. "What if it were your relative? Or what if we were poor and it was our daughter who needed help from someone else?" Juma begged.

"Juma, how could you even link our daughter to cancer, just because of that slut?" Riziki could hear none of it.

"God forbid, Riziki. I'm not insinuating that our daughter will get cancer. AllI'm trying to say is that that girl didn't choose for herself the ailment. But now

that she is sick, there's no harm in helping her. We have little means, my darling. You never know, maybe one day, we'll also need help."

"Nonsense!" Riziki clicked.

"Riziki, you never know about tomorrow. What if our daughter was to be orphaned? Wouldn't somebody else come to her aid?" Juma asked as Riziki stood up and walked out of their bedroom, banging the door behind her.

After giving the matter some serious thought, Riziki slowly walked back to the bedroom. An hour had passed. "It's okay," she told Juma, "let's help her, but…"she did not complete the sentence.

"But what?" Juma asked.

"I think I need to teach her a lesson once she recovers." Juma just kept quiet.

By agreeing to help Lily, Riziki knew that that would give her a chance to be close to Lily. That would give her a chance to finish Lily once and for good.

* * *

Francisca and her grandson kept vigil at Lily's bedside in the hospital. In the morning, Lily woke up lethargic, but with a less crowded mind. She immediately recognised the charming smile of her ageing mother. Her son was dead asleep beside her.

"Mum, what's happening?" Lily asked with a small faltering voice. Francisca told her everything, including the panic when Dr Esther summoned them. "I'm sorry, mum," Lily said afterwards.

"It's okay, don't worry yourself. Take this, it still belongs to you," Francisca pressed the one-hundred-shilling note in her palm.

"The doctor refused?" Lily asked, smiling. "I thought doctors take an oath never to abandon their patients."

"No, she didn't abandon you. She even paid for your night's hospital bill." Francisca narrated, encouraging her in a soft and low tone. Lily listened carefully,most of the time nodding her head.

On a nearby bed lay a patient with a body too frail; every trace of flesh in her was gone. Lily could only imagine the struggle the patient had been through to remain alive. She could only sympathise, even with the spurts of cough and groans of pain by patients, or the people mourning their dead relatives outside. Perhaps victims of cancer, the killer disease.

Before Lily was discharged, Dr Esther took them to a Counsellor, who was also her friend. Dr Esther had explained to her Lily's situation, and she offered her services for free. So, Lily was counselled and Dr Esther and Francisca would, from time to time, chip in a word of encouragement to whatever the Counsellor said. They encouraged Lily to ask as many questions as she had; then and any other time. They encouraged her to always visit the doctors whenever she felt the need to, and that she should always carry along a notebook and a pen. Reason? They said that once the chemotherapy sessions commenced, she could lose bits of her memory. After all was said and they were all in agreement, Dr Esther showed Lily pictures of how her chest might be after the surgery.

"It doesn't look as bad as I thought," Lily said, encouraged.

"Sure, and with time, you'll get used to it." Dr Esther even volunteered extra information about cancer services and the resources from where she could get more information.

When they went back to the ward to get their stuff, a nurse brought them a discharge sheet on which Lily appended her signature. Attached to it was a receipt of the bill Dr Esther had just cleared. When Dr Esther came to check on her before they left, they were very grateful. And she took a few minutes to encourage Lily and reiterate her earlier counsel.

After Dr Esther left, Lily asked for a glass of water. Then, she leant on her right palm and tears started streaming down her cheek. It was the first time that she was crying after the diagnosis. And Francisca said it was okay to cry. That it shall all be well in God's name.

"In everything, believe in God. Only He knows why it happened," Francisca said to Lily. They were back in her apartment that evening.

"Yes, mama," Lily said, her eyes red from crying. A phone call from Juma distracted her before she could add something.

"You hear me Nekesa?" Francisca asked as Lily turned to answer the call. "Yes, yes," Lily responded.

When Lily got outside where Juma had called her, he held out his arms and pulled her close into a tight embrace. "Oooh, Lily?" he whispered in her ear, still holding her tight in his arms.

"Mmmh?" Lily snivelled.

"Lily, they say each misfortune we encounter in this life carries with it seeds of tomorrow's luck! I subscribe to that school of thought." Juma released her but held on to both her hands. "I'll always be available to help you with anything that you will need."

Juma embraced her again. Lily was overcome with emotion; she melted into his arms, with the tears rolling down her cheeks soaking his shirt. Juma held her tighter, rubbing her back in a soothing consolation as if to say, we are together in this. Lily ignored the intensifying pain in her left breast and held him even tighter. She inhaled the sweet scent of his *Versace Eros* cologne, reminding her of the time when they were lovers.

"Don't cry. It will be okay."

Juma's fresh breath softly swayed the small hairs sprouting at her hairline. And yes, she had to heal. She was not ready to lose either the sprouting hair or the long dark hair that stretched down below her nape, leave alone the breasts below his chest. There must be another way out, she thought.

"Tomorrow, go to the hospital and book a tentative date for your mastectomy. We're arranging for the money." Juma said. His assurance breathed new life into her. She was about to stretch and kiss him but recalled that their affair was over. "Thanks, Juma, thanks a lot!" She said instead.

He also gave her three books on cancer that he had brought specifically for her. "You'll get facts and relevant information there. You can read about diagnosis, treatment, and living a happy and healthy life after treatment." Juma intoned.

"Go well," Lily said and stood by the gate as a cloud of dust gathered behind the car as he drove off. She stood there until the car was safely out of sight.

"Who was he?" Francisca probed.

"Juma," Lily blurted out, "he's just a friend." She picked up a cup and wentto the kitchen.

"Nekesa, my daughter?"

"Yes, mum," Lily responded from the kitchen.

"Come and sit here." Lily returned with the cup and sat facing the TV.

"I know we have problems, but God will create ways for us to get help. Our problems should not push you to go around with men. You hear me?" Francisca's raised voice left no room for discussion. Jim was jerked awake. He had been sleeping on the sofa next to Francisca. He turned, rubbed his face and fell asleep again.

"Mum, he's my laptop repairman." Lily spoke with a tremor in her voice, unsure if Francisca would perceive the lie.

"Whoever he is, my heart isn't at peace. Leave him alone! I hope nothing has happened between you two. You hear me, leave him!" Lily held the cup on the table and rotated it a few times. "Haven't you learnt anything from the words my mouth has been saying all these years?" Francisca was irritated.

That day Tom did not visit Lily. She tried calling him, but his phone was off.

Had he abandoned her? Lily thought as she mopped the living room.

That day, they went to bed early. Lily thought about the lie she had told her mother, and her cancer. She broke into intermittent sobs without a sound until she slept. In her sleep, Lily turned and turned over and over that it woke Jim up. He watched her turn and move her lips in her sleep as though conversing with someone in her dreams.

The electricity token metre kept beeping, producing a dull sound. Jim sneaked out of bed and went to the living room, curious to know what it was. He stoodby the edge of Francisca's mattress spread on the floor and looked at the gadget on the wall. When he got bored, he walked to the kitchen, where the light wasstill on. He turned on the gas and waited to see the yellow-blue flames from the nozzles. There was nothing. He opened the second panel, and still, there was no flame. He waited, patiently, and waited, until the smell of the gas in the house started making him feel dizzy. Getting impatient, he took a matchbox and out of it, a matchstick.

Chapter Twenty-Four

Lily was booked for her mastectomy tentatively in December. It was less than two months away. Even though getting money to pay for the treatment was the only remaining task, she was yet to come to terms with the reality. Not once, not twice, she found herself forgetting to switch off the lights at night or waking up to mop the house even when it was clean.

Lily visited Tom the day Victor Mugubi Wanyama played his first game in the UEFA Champions League. The students, as usual, gathered to watch the match. They would break into cheers whenever the camera focused on Wanyama, but Lily was absent-minded. She didn't enjoy the game as she had enjoyed the one between Ghana and Uruguay. Tom tried to convince her to watch to the end, but she left in a huff for her apartment.

Francisca kept on telling her that it was okay to cry to vent out her emotions, but she had to know that she had a bright future. Just as the doctor had said, the diagnosis wasn't a death sentence. And now that Francisca had already left for Kitale, she rarely cooked. She visited Dr Esther twice to ask one thing or the other. On those visits, Dr Esther encouraged her to ask questions and seek clarification on what was not clear.

Lily spent a lot of time in the mirror looking at her breasts with the painful apprehension of losing them. They had always been part of her. She admired, for the last time, the long black hair that she was sure she would lose because of chemotherapy. But the prospect of death made her accept anything else that would spare her life. She no longer wore lipstick on her luscious lips. She no longer went out of her house. She had even asked for a few days off from her part-time workplace. She no longer attended her lectures; relying on the photocopied notes her friends brought whenever they visited.

Lily retracted herself from the world and would mostly spend time alone. President Obama's re-election for his second and final term did not attract her attention. A week later, her birthday would as well have passed by unnoticed were it not for a text from Geoffrey; *Happy Birthday to you dear, and me.*

Who are you celebrating this birthday with; now that Mary is not there? She texted back.

Lily didn't see Tom for a few days. She now believed Tom had already deserted her in her hour of need. Why and yet I am still in good health? She would wonder. But Tom had rushed to Ahero for two days to register as a voter. He had already set things in place. The fundraising team he had formed with fellow students was still collecting money.

Lily's colleagues at work learnt of her predicament and raised seventy thousand shillings as a down payment. Lily thanked them all profusely when she learnt about the surprise contribution.

Tom visited Lily when he arrived from Ahero. Geoffrey and other friends accompanied him. The students had already contributed handsomely. Lily was happy to see them. Tom had sold his phone to make his contribution towards Lily's treatment. He apologised to her for being inaccessible.

"You'll be fine my dear," Geoffrey said, shaking fear out of his voice. Lately, everyone referred to Lily as 'my dear', but deliberately avoided mentioning 'cancer' in their conversations. It was as if mentioning it would make it more real than it already was.

"Amen!" Francisca interjected. She had arrived that morning from Kitale where she had also solicited assistance from the women's group in her church. Barasa hadalso contributed handsomely. And Milly, too.

The contribution by students was across ethnic and political leanings. Not even regional, gender or religious inclinations were a barrier.

"Lily, this is the little amount the comrades, and the university fraternity managed to raise," Tom said, handing over to Lily a small bag with four hundred and ninety-three thousand, five hundred and ten shillings. Lily fell on her knees, covering her face with her palms.

"May God add where it has come from," Francisca said, kneeling, and prayedfor every person that had contributed.

"Thank you, Tom. Honestly, I don't even know what to say. I'm very very grateful," Lily said.

Francisca had long almost lost hope that her daughter would get money topay the cost of the treatment. "Truly, God doesn't abandon His children," she said, "How miracles work out!" She exclaimed, "I never imagined that this was possible."

"My colleagues at work have already paid a down payment of seventy thousand shillings. I think we should inform Juma about what we've raised. Probably he could also chip in." Lily said softly when she found her voice.

"Okay, Lily, all you need to do now is just prepare and wait for the surgery. I'll be at the hospital first thing tomorrow morning to clear the balance," Juma assured her. Elated, Lily thanked him before rushing to the bedroom to change.

* * *

Lily hadn't slept well since her diagnosis, except when Dr Esther had induced her to sleep. Perhaps she would have slept on the second day too, but her sleep was rudely interrupted by the smell of the cooking gas. Choking, she woke up and rushed to the kitchen just in time. She slapped Jim's hand, and he fell on one side and the matchbox on the other.

247

"Stupid son of a…" Lily shouted angrily but stopped midway. She hoped Jim hadn't heard her, otherwise, he would definitely ask, in future, whose son he was. Lily felt angry at herself, too, for slapping Jim's hand that hard. She knew Jim wasn't to blame for his birth. Neither was he responsible for the rape. It was high time she stopped punishing him for even the smallest of mistakes. It was high time she forgave him for being an evidence of the rape and trauma she had been through. It was high time she visited a counsellor to talk about what she had always hidden within her heart; and that was exactly what she did the day that followed. She wanted to forge a new relationship with her son, at least before she went for her surgery.

A few times Lily would lie on her bed, imagine herself dead and take pictures of herself with her eyes closed. She would then scroll through the photos in her phone to see how she would look if she didn't make it through the treatment. She would then laugh at such wicked thoughts. As much as she was prepared for the mastectomy, she still had doubts. Eventually, she decisively convinced herself that she was ready for it and that it would all be well.

She was beautiful, and she knew she would still be, even after the operation. Besides, she knew there were people experiencing more pain than hers. There were those that died from incurable wounds. Others because they could not afford treatment costs. There were also children with defects abandoned by their parents. There were those in a coma or on life support machines who could not even comprehend who or where they were.

Lily made one more visit to Dr Esther to seek more clarification about the surgery. She then visited Halima and demonstrated to her how to do the BSE just as she had done to Babirye. Later at night, she dreamt of Jim burning them in a house only to wake up and search the darkness.

* * *

A day before the mastectomy, Tom invited Lily out on a coffee date in town. On their way, Lily took a photograph at a studio. "The last picture

248

with full breasts," she joked.

"You shouldn't eat anything from midnight, not now," Tom insisted when she chose to eat just a croissant. But her mind was elsewhere that she instead stuttered an apology for all the wrongdoings she had committed against Tom. She even called Babirye, Halima and Barasa when she reached her apartment and apologised. Her wish was to reverse the wheel of time and atone for her wrongdoings.

"Mum, I'm sorry for my wrongdoings. Please forgive me, mum," she apologised to Francisca.

"My daughter, we're supposed to forgive other people when they sin against us, and our heavenly Father will forgive us too. If we don't, our Father won't forgive our sins." Francisca said, then led a lengthy prayer before they went to bed. Lily stayed awake the entire night. She crept out of bed and sat on the balcony.

At 5:30 am, Juma's phone beeped. It was a message from Lily. He struggled to open his eyes and read:

Hello Juma, there is no way I can ever thank you enough for all the assistance you have accorded me, but I pray that may He who is above us all reward you handsomely. As you well know, I am facing the scalpel today, and there is no guarantee that we'll see each other after I have entered that room. The theatre!

This is why I'm texting you, not only to thank you for everything but also to request you to put me in your prayers, now and even in the days to come; regardless of the outcome. I would also like to emphasise that I highly appreciate your tireless efforts towards my well-being.

I know for sure that whatever the outcome, you'll always be in my heart as a good friend. If I manage to come out alive, I will no longer be the Lily you knew; physically. I hope that won't change much of the way we used to be, the good friends we are now and the good friends we've always been.

Lastly, please ask forgiveness for me from your wife. God bless you. Lily.

Tom, Geoffrey, Halima and the rest of her friends on campus and her colleagues at the airport read edited versions of the same text message.

Tom nowhad a borrowed phone.

Francisca woke up early and prayed. She prayed for her daughter's health and courage, and the doctor's hands and scalpels.

"It's still early for him. We'll wake him up when it's about time to leave," Francisca dissuaded Lily from waking up Jim.

"No, mama. I've just realised Jim never enjoyed his mother's milk. I spent most of the time away from him. He was never breastfed the way he was supposed to," Lily complained. "I want to breastfeed him now," Lily continued deliriously, "Just with the little milk I'm remaining with. I want to breastfeed him until there is nothing left, mama. It'll be the last time I'll be breastfeeding a child, whether I come out alive or not." Tears formed on her lower eyelid. She wiped them with the heels of her hand.

As advised, Lily took a bath using antibacterial soap. She also wore no make- up. Her nails, too, hadn't been polished.

Her procedure was scheduled to start at 10:30 a.m. on 12 December. By 6:30 a.m., when the morning light came in through the white floral blinds, they were all ready. Lily didn't eat anything that morning as earlier advised by the doctor. Francisca intoned a long prayer again before they left for the hospital. Lily noted the hundreds of messages that streamed in her phone. Most were to encourage her, but there was no time to read them.

At the hospital, Lily was again duly counselled.

For the third time, Dr Ogunga, an anaesthesiologist, perused Lily's file to determine the safest combination of drugs and dosage to use. Lily had earlier met Dr Ogunga in Dr Esther's office while signing the consent. She had heard of his reputation and ability, so she felt inspired and confident that all would be well. In no different way the nurses had done, he recorded her age, weight, whether or not she had had any surgeries before, current medication, allergies, previous anaesthetics, and fasting time. He asked her a couple of questions as he made notes on a sheet of paper. Finally, he gave Lily a benzodiazepine as a premedication before Dr Esther took over.

"Do you have any questions, or need clarification?" Dr Esther asked

250

at last.

"No, I don't." Dr Esther then summarised the risks of the procedure and potential side effects.

"Doctor, I am ready for the surgery. I clearly understand the risks." Lily's statement was stern and rife with courage. She was then given a form to read, confirm that she understood the contents, and append her signature.

There was a section that elaborated on the conditions for the treatment and the risks involved. Though she had been told the same information umpteen times, she felt scared signing on the dotted lines that she consented and that she understood that no guarantee had been made that the procedure would improve her condition, even though it would be carried out with professional conduct. The fact that bleeding could occur and that she might be required to return to the operating room frightened her, too. She appended her signature and handed the form to her mother who, with a shaking hand, pressed on it her inked thumb.

* * * Meanwhile, in Kitale, Barasa was praying for her.

* * *

That morning before heading to the hospital, Juma rushed to Lily's apartment to meet the caretaker. He was sure Lily had already left for the hospital at that time. He intended to pay for Lily's rent for six months upfront without anyone knowing. He had also applied for NHIF medical insurance cover for Lily a week earlier and planned to share with Lily about it later. After paying the rent, he quickly drove out of the compound, heading to the hospital.

Outside the theatre, Juma was shocked to find his wife among the few people gathered. He could not understand why Riziki had to lie to him that she was going to work yet she was coming to the hospital. But still, Juma had not asked her to accompany her to the hospital. He had not even mentioned to her that he would be joining Lily's family at the hospital, though he knew Riziki would eventually know.

251

"Darling," he called worriedly, scared about her response and what the public could make of it. "Can I have a minute with you, please?"

He didn't know how Riziki and Lily would react if they finally met there and then. A drama would definitely ensue, he thought. It was evident that Riziki was still angry with Lily, despite her ailment. She had even sworn to teach the *bitch*a lesson.

"Okay."

"Aaah, there comes Lily," Juma said before he could take Riziki aside.

Chapter Twenty-Five

Lily was appalled by Juma's presence, together with his wife and their daughter. An abrupt heavy tension filled the waiting room. Riziki looked at Lily's face, her sparkling eyes, her shiny hair, the ease in her gait as she strode, and the curves of her body. Despite the sadness in her, she was still gorgeous. Feelings of jealousy suddenly choked Riziki, with thoughts of pity and ill wishes for Lily rushingthrough her consciousness all at the same time.

"If you offend someone, ask for a pardon; if offended forgive," the voice of Riziki's priest ran sharply through her mind; but she couldn't expunge the ill wishes from her thoughts. She rose to greet Lily briefly.

Francisca noted Juma's close resemblance with a younger Lubao; especially the ears and eyes. She was meeting Juma face-to-face for the first time, and she was as grateful as she was surprised. She had not expected to meet him.

"You have a handsome boy, Lily," Riziki complimented her, bending down to sweep Jim into her arms. "How old are you?"

Jim was hesitant.

"In what class is he?" Riziki turned to Lily.

"Not yet enrolled in school," Lily said, "You have such a beautiful daughter too," Lily said, touching the girl's shoulder and asking her name.

"*Masha'Allah*, we have such a good couple-to-be; Molly and Jim," Halima said to ease the tension and nervousness. She, too, was still recovering from the shock of the presence of Juma's wife.

"Sorry, Juma and I couldn't get enough money in time for the treatment," Riziki said.

"Yeah, we're...we couldn't get it in time," Juma supported.

"No. That was so much, my children. I thank you very much and may God bless you all abundantly," Francisca said. Lily nodded in agreement. After a brief talk, Francisca switched to Bible verses.

"In the book of Psalms, it's written that '*Many are the afflictions of the righteous, but the LORD delivers him out of them all.*' Amen?"

"Amen," they chorused.

"And it's written that '*A thousand may fall at your side, and ten thousand at your right hand; but it shall not come near you.*'"

"Amen!"

"So, don't sweat it, my daughter, all will be well because God is in control. Okay?" Lily nodded. "In 2 Corinthians, we're told that '*we are hard-pressed on every side, yet not crushed; we are perplexed, but not in despair; persecuted, but not forsaken; struck down, but not destroyed.*' Now let's pray," and they bowed their heads.

"In the name of the Father, and the Son, and the Holy Spirit..." Francisca said, making the sign of the cross.

Lily silently prayed for her surgery and Kenya. Ethnicism had heightened, especially with the ongoing campaigns for the forthcoming general elections that worried her, from where politicians competed in blinding voters into ignorance. For the first time, she thought more of Dr Esther's tribe than her medical expertise. Was she safe under the doctor's scalpel?

Mother and daughter embraced fervently amidst tears that lingered in her eyes for long. Lily smiled and gave the last critical look at them. She seemed to be gaining more strength from their encouragement.

"Mum, please take care of Jim for me. Will you?"

"No, I won't. You'll come out of that theatre and take good care of him yourself."

"Will I, mama?" Lily now brimmed with hope. She felt as if repeating it several times would make it true. It was more of a statement than a question; one thirsting for a strong affirmation. She had always been strong, full of hope for a better tomorrow.

Of course, they all replied on cue, as if they had rehearsed. Lily gleamed with vigour. "My dream of becoming a pilot isn't going to die inside that room, mama," she joked before entering the changing room. Of course, both Francisca and her knew that dream had died long ago!

Behind, in the waiting room, Halima cupped her hands together, before her face, recited a *dua* silently, rubbed her palms together after the prayer and wiped them across her face. "*Ameen.*"

Outside the waiting room, the hospital staff and patients moved up and down the pavements. There was a young man who was being rushed to the theatre, unconscious; his clothes soaked in blood. Halima learnt that the man had been hacked with a machete at a campaign rally after two opposing sides clashed. The wife of the young man ran after them, a young child nestled tightly on her chest. None of the politicians the young man was fighting for trailed behind the young woman.

In the changing room, Lily placed her clothes and other belongings into a polythene bag and put on an oversize buttonless dress, with nothing underneath. She then wore a cap and lay on a gurney.

Two nurses pushed Lily on the gurney, lying on her back, facing the concrete ceiling. A blur of bright fluorescent tubes shone from the ceiling. It was so bright she could count strands of hair on her arms. Finally, a double door swung open, and Lily was wheeled into the theatre where the smell of disinfectant welcomed her.

Inside the theatre, a team of doctors and nurses wore green sterile surgical gowns, green surgical caps, facemasks, latex gloves and white theatre boots.

"Hi," said Dr Esther, then introduced the rest; the anaesthesiologist whom Lily had met earlier, another surgeon, a scrub nurse and another nurse whose name Lily didn't get.

255

They all said their hellos.

"Hello," Lily responded, sitting up on the gurney. "How are you feeling my dear?" One nurse asked.

"Still painful, but I believe I'll be fine in a couple of hours," Lily said. But she was scared.

"You'll be well, *Insha'Allah*," the scrub nurse, Zainab, affirmed. "*Insha'Allah*," Lily responded, looking around. The room was bright with blinding fluorescent lights. Dr Esther, two other doctors and a nurse were setting up a machine next to the operating table. Lily's eyes suddenly became teary. She wiped a tear that stood out in the corner of her left eye.

The nurse then picked up Lily's file and read out loud a pre-operative checklist, her name, her last meal and the vital signs taken earlier that morning.

"So...I would like to take a blood sample." The nurse lifted Lily's arm. "It will hurt a little," she said, wiping the target spot with a piece of wet cotton. Lily felt the cold effect of methylated spirit on the surface of her skin. She then injected the needle- a point at which Lily squinted her eyes as her face crinkled. "Done," Zainab quipped.

The next person to attend to Lily was Dr Ogunga. He injected her with an intravenous anaesthetic drug and then said, pointing to the operation table, "We'll move you there, okay?" Three nurses, two male and one female, helped Dr Ogunga to wheel her to the table.

As the drug took effect, Lily remained anxious, wondering what the doctors were discussing in hushed tones. The nametag strapped around her wrist only reminded her of those placed on dead bodies; hence worrying her. She noted that the nurses were not yet done arranging the needles, gauzes, scissors and other paraphernalia on the silver trays.

They carried her from the gurney to the operating table. Dr Ogunga adjusted the table to a suitable height. Soon, Lily lost consciousness.

An intravenous line was then started immediately, and a breathing tube was inserted. Dr Ogunga placed the endotracheal tube into her windpipe; passing it through her vocal cords with a laryngoscope. Her fingers and arms had already been connected with cables that ran all the way to a machine that displayed her heart's activity, temperature, blood pressure and breathing. There was another machine with bright lights next to the operating table, with the lights lowered to focus on Lily's breasts. The doctors and nurses huddled around the table. Everything was now set, and they were all ready to give her a chance to live.

Outside, everyone silently prayed, and each second looked like half an hour.

Every now and then, Francisca's lips moved in muted prayers that Halima could hear, and Halima would add a silent supplication as a result.

* * *

In a period of four hours, incisions were made around the nipples, the breasts' tissues separated from the muscles underneath, and then the tissues were removed. Then the doctors inserted drains to prevent fluids from accumulating in the areas. Dr Ogunga closely monitored Lily; continuously observed and managed her airways, temperature, and blood pressure, and ensured she didn't regain consciousness.

At the end of the procedure, Dr Esther closed the wounds with sutures while Dr Ogunga removed the endotracheal tubes. Lily was then wheeled to the recovery room.

A few miles away, far from the suffering patients and their concerned relatives, Kenyans had gathered at Nyayo National Stadium for Jamhuri Day celebrations. Images of children's faces painted with the colours of the national flag, dignitaries in perfectly tailored imported suits, low-flying jets and traditional dancers ran on the television.

No one at the waiting room followed the proceedings keenly, except for occasional glances. Top on their minds were their sick family and friends dying for lack of dialysis machines or lack of medication in dispensaries. As political analysts on TV debated about women empowerment, mothers were dying while bringing forth lives because of lack of maternity services in rural areas.

Still, Francisca prayed for the life of her only daughter who was inside the walls not far from the waiting room; walls from within which death was a close possibility.

Halima went to stretch outside and met the lady whose husband had been rushed in earlier. The lady was weeping alone, having lost her husband. Now she was faced with the daunting task of raising a fatherless child. No politician would come to clear the bill or contribute to the funeral arrangements awaiting her.

Finally, Dr Esther emerged from the theatre to brief Lily's mother. She had a promising smile on her face. "She's fine now, already taken to the recovery room for close monitoring. She'll be taken to the surgical ward after, where she'll be for a few days, depending on how fast she heals." Dr Esther's voice was smooth and calming.

"Thank you so much, doctor. Can we see her now?" Francisca asked. Dr Esther advised that they would be informed of an appropriate time to see her because she had to take a rest.

* * *

An hour after Dr Esther's briefing:

"Doctor Ogunga," Zainab, the nurse, called from the recovery room, gently shaking Lily by the shoulders. "Lily, are you okay?" No response. "Lily, are you okay?" Zainab called again. Silence. "Doctor!" She called Dr Ogunga again, who by that time was going through Lily's file.

"Excuse me," Dr Ogunga said as he neared the bed. Zainab paved the way as he leant towards the motionless Lily. He strolled his right hand on her forehead and gently tilted her head back with the fingers of his left hand under her chin.

"Zainab," Dr Ogunga called out, "It seems like we are losing her." Dr Ogunga opened Lily's airways and assessed if there were still any signs of life. He listened to her distant breath as his left fingers felt her carotid pulse at the neck.

"Oooh, No!" Zainab exclaimed.

"Call the switchboard," Dr Ogunga said, pulling the emergency bell next to Lily's bed. An orange light started blinking continuously from the wall. He pressed the heel of his hand at the centre of Lily's chest, over the bandage strapped across it.

"Hello, adult cardiac arrest and critical condition. Wima wing, second floor, recovery room," Zainab quickly said over the phone. She then rushed back.

"Come...continue resuscitating her as I get the..." words evaporated from his mouth as he instructed Zainab to take over. She placed her hand on her chest and compressed the chest, then gently squeezed a bag valve mask twice.

Code Purple, adult, recovery room, second floor Wima Wing. Code Purple, adult, recovery room, second floor Wima Wing. Code Purple, adult, recovery room, second floor Wima Wing. Thank you," the announcement from the switchboard was heard from all the intercoms mounted on the ceilings of the hospital. It was repeated a few times.

Only the staff of the hospital could interpret the announcement that there was a patient at the Wima Wing in critical condition.

Dr Ogunga quickly fixed the mask and Zainab continued with the resuscitation until other nurses and doctors arrived.

With the arrival of more help, defibrillator pads were stuck on Lily's chest just above the bandage, and by the side of her stomach. The cardiac rhythm showing on the black screen with coloured bars, charts and changing figures was not encouraging. They had to deliver immediate shocks with the defibrillator.

* * *

"Hi, I'm Zainab," she shook their hands, one by one, in the waiting room. "We're sorry for keeping you here for the whole day." It was now evening, and Lily's condition had improved. Francisca and a few others were allowed to see her at the ICU.

"How's she now?" Riziki, who had just arrived from her work place, asked.

"Her condition was not good after the operation, but she is now better." They stood up to listen. "She's much stable now; soon, she will be on her feet," Zainab added.

"*Insha'Allah*," Halima quipped.

"Can we go now?" Zainab indicated the way. They went up the stairs; the corridors smelt of fresh disinfectant. At the entrance to the ICU, they wore rubber open shoes and caps, and sanitised their hands before entering. The room was dimly lit with machines bleeping. Many of the patients were on some kind of machine with drips of bottles of drugs and fluids fixed to their bodies. Non- invasive ventilation masks obscured the faces of a few of the patients. Some of those patients would make it. Some wouldn't.

Lily lay on a bed at the end of the room by a wide window. The clean plastic rolling window shades swayed with a slight breeze. The machine next to her bed also beeped with dull sounds. Cords were running from the machine all the way to Lily's body. She was covered with a white sheet. Her face looked pale as if she had been soaked in cold water for a week. Her closed eyes were sunken in their sockets, and her lips dry. There was no movement, except the rising and fallingof her chest.

The transparent oxygen mask aiding her to breathe partly obscured her face. A film of moisture formed where the mask was in contact with her skin. Intravenous tubes dripped drugs and glucose into her veins. Francisca moved closer to get a better view. Lily looked fragile and unaware of her own existence. They all stood motionless watching her without saying a word until they were informed that time was up. Francisca said a short prayer before they left.

"Mama, will Lily wake up from sleep?" Francisca and Jim were back in the apartment at Ngara.

"Of course, Jim," Francisca said, "She'll wake up, and come back home."

"Will she beat me when I go to the kitchen again?" Francisca didn't knowwhat to say. But that night, she prayed a lot.

Halima, too, recited several *duas* and prayed for her friend in her

Isha'a prayer and the following day's five prayers. It was the same thing when she went for her *Juma'a* prayers at the Jamia Mosque.

After her prayers, Halima went to the City Market and bought flowers for Lily. Some students also graced the altar of St. Paul's Catholic Church in Nairobi on Sunday and prayed for her. Halima was pleased when she heard about it.

Tom and Halima visited Francisca regularly at Lily's apartment. They would take food to her and also help with household chores. Three days after the mastectomy - a day they arrived while Jim was struggling to touch his nose with the tip of his tongue - they left together for the hospital. A part of Francisca felt that they would find Lily awake and that her face would not be obscured by the mask. She also imagined how life would be if Lily were to never wake up from her sleep. It was now three days. How would life be if she died? She exorcised the thought.

At the hospital, they walked slowly past a group of relatives praying for their kin on whose door death had just knocked. And since they had passed two relatives weeping in the corridors on their way to the ICU, Tom thought they probably could be kin to the dead patient. Nurses pulled a sheet over the patient's body after the relatives finished the prayer.

Lily's bed was empty. Shocked, they all reconfirmed the number of the bed and looked around the large room to check if by any chance she had been relocated to another bed. Lily wasn't there.

"Mama, where is Lily?" Francisca had no answer for Jim. None of them had.

Chapter Twenty-Six

I may not tell you as often as I ought to, but I need to let you know how much I appreciate your presence in my life. And I love you; that's why I married you; Juma sent Riziki the message from his office. *Why did you cheat? When were you planning to let me know of it? What influenced your choice and decision to cheat? What has changed? These are questions I keep on asking myself*; Riziki replied.

Still, the breach of trust the infidelity, betrayal and deception had brought about was still deeply seethed in Riziki. It had even stained the picture of love she had once created in her mind. And when Lily remained unconscious, Riziki prayed for her to be phased out of the world. Babirye had a similar feeling.

Nonetheless, life went on as usual, except for the emergence and disappearance of ICC witnesses regarding the 2007/2008 post-election violence. The 2007/2008 post-election violence cases in court, calls by human rights activists for justice, and talk of perpetrators and the identification of witnesses worried Mambo. Though he now lived out of Nairobi, whenever he saw strange faces around his neighbourhood, he thought they were secret police coming for him.

Even when a dog barked, or someone's cow strayed to graze in the compound, he would tiptoe to the window to listen if any footsteps would follow.

He suspected everyone was a Criminal Investigation Officer, searching for him to face justice. This made life in freedom even harder for him. At times, he imagined that his life would have been better serving a jail sentence had his uncle not come to his aid. But still, Mambo regretted what he did to Lily.

After being freed, Mambo spent months looking for Lily without any success. He only found out that after Lily left Nairobi in early 2008 for Kitale, she had given birth to a boy. Mambo was informed by the same neighbour, Ndanu, who Lily met after leaving the hospital in Mathare North. The neighbour had given Lily her number before Lily left for the Chief's camp. Lily had called the same neighbour using Milly's phone and confided in her that she had given birth to a baby boy. At that time, Ndanu didn't know that Mambo was the real rapist until he (Mambo) quarrelled with Myche. Annoyed, Myche made the secret public. Unfortunately, by that time, Ndanu had lost Milly's number and there was no way to either confirm the allegation from Lily or inform her.

Since Mambo met Lily again after Juma had sent him, he had been contemplating the best way to confess to Lily and claim his responsibilities as a father. As the rapist. He saw their meeting as fate and wished Juma could send him more often for he wanted to get reasons to see Lily every single day, yet he kept imagining how Lily had been able to stay so well for all that time and take care of the child who he hadn't seen yet and yearned to.

Mambo yearned for forgiveness. He even toyed with the idea of approaching the TJRC, but he was not gutsy enough to face them, so he abandoned the thought. Instead, he made several visits to the hospital to see Lily, but every time he reached the entrance to the ICU, he would change his mind. The watchmen at the gate kept wondering why he came with bouquets only to go back with them.

At times, he just sat outside and watched Jim with Francisca or Tom or Halima come and go. By now he had come to know Lily's mother, and so when he saw Jim with her for the first time, he was so sure it was

Lily's son. Jim resembled him in so many ways. He wished he could move closer and pull Jim aside and just say, "Hello!" But he had no guts to. He could only watch them from a distance and also to avoid raising any suspicion. A few times, he went close to them but instead weaved through an ocean of people coming in and walking out, past Francisca, and kept on looking back at them when he was sure they weren't seeing him.

* * *

"Did you have to leave in my absence?" Francisca asked the bed as if expecting an answer. Tears formed in her eyes as she pictured a future without Lily. Halima too shed a tear. Only Tom, who was holding Jim in his arms, displayed no obvious emotions, but deep inside, he felt like wailing.

"Why, Nekesa?" Francisca whispered.

"Good morning?" Zainab's voice interrupted them. She wore a wide smile. "She improved and is now in the surgical ward. Please come, let me show you!" she informed them. They were all relieved and followed Zainab.

* * *

That Saturday when Francisca had found Lily's bed empty, Mambo was at the entrance and saw Lily being wheeled out of the ICU. He carried a bouquet of red and white roses, which he wanted to give to Lily. Afraid to deliver it by himself, he had given it to a nurse who was preparing her hand-over report.

"Hello, Sister! Please, give these flowers to Lily," he beckoned the nurse. "Why don't you just take it by yourself?" she asked.

He tried to give excuses, but they only made him look shy to deliver the flowers by himself, which still played well to help him have her deliver.

"Okay, then," she took the flowers and added, "and whom should I say brought the flowers?"

"Don't mind, she'll just know." Mambo offered. The nurse didn't bother to probe further. She took the flowers to Lily's drawer and informed the nurse taking over the shift to tell Lily, when she woke up, that the flowers were from a secret admirer.

* * *

Lily was still asleep when Francisca, Tom, Halima and Babirye got into the room. She seemed more restful than they had seen her before. Pale traces of the oxygen mask showed on her cheeks, upper chin and across the bridge of her nose. A breeze swept across the room through the wide, open window. Half asleep, Lily pulled the bed sheet to cover her face from the breeze.

They didn't stay there for long before Lily woke up. Halima was standing by the window, reciting her *misbaha*. The first thing Lily did was lift the white sheet, and raise her head to look at her chest. She felt discomfort at the point of entry of the two drains when she raised her hands to remove the sheet. White gauze bandages went across her chest, and she felt a tingling pain. Her eyes looked wan, and her mind felt blank. She had no recollection of how she had gotten there, or how long she had been unconscious.

"Mama," she called in a tired whisper, wiping a tear from the corner of her eye. Her voice was low; she also spoke slowly – one vowel at a time – as if she were drunk. "Am I alive, mama?"

"You are, my daughter," Francisca moved closer to help her wipe her wet eyes. "We thank God, you are." Jim sat next to Francisca.

"Are you alright, Lily?" Jim brushed his small soft palms against her face. "I am," she replied with a smile. She could now feel love for Jim. "*Alhamdulillah*, we thank God. How are you feeling, dear?" Halima asked.

"You look beautiful, likc always," Babirye said. Lily smiled, a pair of dimples showing.

"Could you please help me adjust the pillow? No...just under the neck. Yes, yes. There...Thanks." Francisca was helping her adapt her posture.

Juma, Dave who was there on behalf of students, and a few of Lily's workmates arrived to check on her progress. They brought food and cards wishing her a speedy recovery.

"Thank you all for your prayers and everything, may God bless you," Lily smiled. The nurse on duty came by for the normal routine check and they excused her. She checked her blood pressure and temperature, and then gave her tablets to swallow.

"You'll feel better," she said and left.

"You'll be alright, my dear. We thank God for you," a colleague said.

Tom visited again only to find Lily dead asleep. With unrelenting hope, he looked at Lily; the only lady whom he truly loved. He pictured her out of bed; without her breasts and hair. She would still be as charming as she had been, and his love for her would always remain boundless. His zeal to fight for his future and love remained strong.

"Keep encouraging her," Dr Esther whispered after calling him aside. It gave him more hope, and he knew that he meant something to Lily.

Alone at night, Lily thought of her new life and sobbed, but was grateful to have seen a day many others did not. She thought of her future and the mistakes she had to correct.

"Hi, Lily," how are you feeling now?" A night-shift nurse interrupted her thoughts. She pulled a chair and sat by her bedside.

"I'm fine, Maggy," Lily said after reading the tag, but Maggy could tell from Lily's voice that she wasn't. With her many years of experience, Maggy was able to decipher voices of untold pain from those of forlorn despair. She had attended to many such patients; some who'd survived and some who'd passed on.

"Glad to know you are improving."

That night, Lily dreamt of men coming to her bed and trying to rape her. In the dream, she saw Zainab helping them hold her legs, while Maggy tried to help her. The men then disappeared. When she woke up, she couldn't remember the exact spot where she had seen the men disappear in that elusive, fleeting dream.

After the holy mass that Sunday morning, students proceeded to the hospital. Lily had woken up to find another bouquet, but she didn't think much about it. She talked with Halima about how much they had missed each other's companyin their hostel room.

When Dave came, Lily was on a phone call with Juma who had travelled outof town.

"And you are stunning," said Dave.

When Geoffrey came, happy to see her doing well, his new girlfriend was carrying flowers nicely wrapped in a transparent polythene bag.

"Do you still miss Mary?" Lily whispered into Geoffrey's ears when his girlfriend walked out to receive a call.

"Very much!" They both laughed it off, in low voices not to disturb other patients. "But I'm disappointed that I'm not the one who brought you the most beautiful flowers," Geoffrey pointed at the bouquet of roses by the bed.

"I'm disappointed, too, that I can't figure out who it is." "Isn't it Juma?"

"No, they're out of town.""Tom?"

"No."

"Then we have a secret admirer somewhere." It pleased Lily to imagine a secret admirer somewhere; someone who loved her the way she was.

"Look at that nurse; she's shooting her patient," Geoffrey changed the topic when he saw his girlfriend approaching. Three beds away, a nurse was taking a patient's temperature using a Non-contact Forehead Infrared DigitalThermometer, pointed at the patient's forehead.

The nurse placed the thermometer on the trolley, recorded the readings, took the patient's blood pressure and gave her drugs. She then silently moved to the next patient. Even before the drug could reach the previous patient's stomach, she held her throat and began to cough. She coughed until she threw up the small amount of watery substance her stomach had carried. Lily turned to look at Geoffrey's girlfriend.

"Your ward is clean and the linen spotlessly white," Geoffrey's girlfriend noted.

"They change the linen twice daily. That's one of the things I love about this hospital."

Over the next two days, many students and her workmates visited her. Tom would also prop Jim on his shoulder and take strolls on the campus, Jim's legs bouncing on his chest as they walked. Sometimes they would walk side by side in town or within the hospital with a fruit, or a bar of chocolate gripped in Jim's small hand.

"Tom, will Lily be fine?" Jim would ask him.

"Sure, very soon. She'll be fine, okay?" Tom would say, and then pinch him softly on the leg or thigh. Tom would buy him candies and small gifts. They would carry plenty of fruits for Lily on their way back to the hospital.

By her fourth day in the ward, Lily's condition had stabilised, and even the pain in her wounds had drastically reduced. Dr Esther showed her how to exercise routinely to prevent shoulder stiffness. She, however, emphasised that some of the exercises should only be done when the drains had been removed. Before being discharged, they once more discussed her chemotherapy and what to expect.

"When you get home, there are things you should be keen on," said Dr Esther. "Yes."

"Take care of the bandage over your incision as I told you earlier and the surgical drains too." Dr Esther made a few notes on Lily's file then proceeded, "Whenever you suspect any signs of infection or lymphedema, call me immediately. But don't worry about the stitches; they'll dissolve over time. There will be no need for removing them. Okay?"

"Yes, Doc."

"And these are your painkillers. You'll take one tablet twice a day, but if you feel a lot more pain, take one tablet thrice a day. If you no longer feel pain, do not take them." Dr Esther gave Lily a cocktail of painkillers and other drugs. She also advised her to take rest often, surround herself with friends for social support, and to be taking a shower with soft sponges until the drains had been removed.

"And when will I be able to shave my underarms?" Lily joked.

* * *

A day after Lily was discharged, Francisca left for Kitale. Lubao had been left alone for almost one and a half weeks. It wasn't good to leave him alone for that long; they had both agreed.

Tom escorted Francisca and Jim to Machakos Country Bus Station to board the Kitale-bound evening bus. Juma had secretly given Lily money for Francisca's shopping and bus fare. Lily had in turn given Tom the cash to help Francisca to shop.

"If she asks, tell her that it's the students who contributed," Lily whispered into Tom's ear.

* * *

The first surgical drain was removed four days after being discharged. Tom escorted her to the hospital. After removing the tube, Lily was surprised by the length of the part that had been inside her skin. The second drain was removed three days after the first, on a Christmas Eve. Tom accompanied her again, but he was to travel that evening for Christmas with his family in Ahero.

For a couple of days after leaving the hospital, Lily had wanted to go to the mirror and look at herself. But every time she reached the bathroom mirror, she turned back and went to bed. She even stopped brushing her teeth from the sink next to the mirror.

"Looking at the new me will be my early Christmas gift today," Lily boldly told herself. Tom watched her in silence. She moved from the bedroom to the kitchen, to the living room, to the bedroom again and back to the living room.She was completely uneasy.

That went on for almost ten minutes before she said, "No, I can't do this when you're here."

After Tom left, she locked her door and drew the blinds on her windows. Then she switched on all the lights and removed all her clothes. When she felt she was ready, one step at a time, she strode slowly to the mirror. She gave her image a stern look, and thereafter, every breath she exhaled fogged the mirror, blurring the image of the tired woman whose reflection she was seeing in that mirror.

That entire afternoon, Lily sobbed from her bed.

For two weeks, Lily didn't see Tom who had travelled home, but they frequently talked over the phone. She saw him when Tom arrived back in Nairobi. They met outside her apartment in the parking lot. Lily was coming from the caretaker's house. She had gone there to plead with him about the delay in paying rent, but was pleasantly surprised to learn that Juma had already paid her rent six-months upfront!

"Welcome, Tom, glad to see you. Happy New Year too! How was your holiday? Aaaha, lovely! Sure, I'm optimistic about this year, but I hope, this year, and those to come, you won't sneeze a cloud of bacteria into my face." They both broke into laughter, and then shared their new year's resolutions that they hoped to abide by.

"By the way, that was then. I was just a naïve *fresha*!" Tom thought for a few seconds then asked, "You remember our first lunch at Arziki?"

"The day I had just dropped my inter-faculty transfer application?"

"Exactly."

"What about it?"

"What was it that you picked from the collar of my shirt?"

Lily gave Tom a smile that was big for her face, and then served him tea and bread and went to the balcony to make a phone call to Juma.

"Thank you, Tom, for coming," Lily started, "Being a new year, I want to apologise to everyone I wronged. I want to start a new phase in my life." She added, "I want to, with utmost humility, ask for your forgiveness for all the bad things I've done to you."

Tom remained quiet for a few minutes, thinking of how she had uttered the words, *ask for your forgiveness*, almost as though the forgiveness was a shirt, as though he could pick it from his wardrobe and give her, and she would use it until she felt like returning it, then she would wash it, peg it out to dry, return it to him and borrow it again at a time that she so pleased.

For a second time, Lily called Barasa and recounted her ungratefulness and insult, then asked him for forgiveness. "I'm sorry," she said, and Barasa said it was okay.

"I forgave you long ago," Barasa added and went silent. She was quiet, too. And she checked to see if the phone was still connected before listening in. There were sounds of crickets chittering in the background.

Since *blessed are the peacemakers, for they will be called sons of God*, Lily also called other friends.

Lily went for a confession at the St. Paul's Catholic Church. She knelt inside a wardrobe on the opposite side of a grille, ready to share her innermost secrets and contrition. There was silence, except for her heaves and the priest's breathing as he waited for her to start, "Bless me, Father, for I have sinned."

"How long has it been since your last confession?" "Two years, Father."

"Okay. So, for what is it that you're asking God's forgiveness?"

"My God and my priest, I have sinned a lot, and I've committed the following sins…" Lily mentioned most of the wrongs she had done, and then added, "For those and others I may have forgotten, I ask for penance and forgiveness."

* * *

Lily's focus now shifted to chasing her dreams. She had missed many lectures, but she made up for them by photocopying and reading notes – on whose pages faint sentences ran across – until late in the night.

A week before she started her chemotherapy sessions, Lily underwent,

271

among other tests, an echocardiogram, pulmonary function tests and a dental check-up – which surprised her. She didn't see any connection between her teeth and her flat chest or the chemotherapy that she was to start.

"This is just to ensure that there'll be no dental bleeding problems caused by chemo drugs," the dentist explained.

With the advent of the general elections creeping close – in a month's time – there were ethnic groupings and tension was building up. And no country wanted to be directly involved in the Kenyan elections. Even a senior US State Department official said the US was not endorsing any candidate in the upcoming Kenyan election, but warned Kenyan voters that *choices had consequences*, words that would soon feature in every political speech.

Lily was scared now that she was alone in her apartment, just like she had been in James' when she was raped.

Chapter Twenty-Seven

Lily arrived at the hospital at 8:10 am. She walked silently along the gravel path past the parking yard towards the silent and cold corridors of the Cancer Centre Wing. As she waited for the lift to descend; 5, 4, 3, 2...her heart pounded. 1, and finally G, the elevator's door opened and a cleaner silently exited as Lily went in.

At the Cancer Centre, there were not many people. Lily pushed the door open and squeezed her weaned self inside. She ambled to the receptionist. Few patients were waiting on the black leather couches; quite diverse in their age, gender, race,and sophistication, among others.

"Hi, my name is Lilian Nekesa. It's my first time here."

"Hi, you're welcome, Lilian," said the nurse. "Do you have an appointment?""Yes, I do."

"Great," the nurse smiled. She had a beautiful smile that exposed only her upper white teeth; her shiny cheeks bulged with the smile. Her round face was beautifully wide. "Then give me your card."

Lily handed her the card as she admired the nurse's large braids held with a black hairband just above her nape. Her silver earrings dangled from the lobes as she turned to her computer from where low-volume gospel music played. Stickers of the accepted insurance companies and

VISA branded cards were stuck on a small noticeboard at the reception.

The nurse took some time feeding Lily's information into the computer and finally printed a receipt for her. "Here you go." She handed Lily the receipt. On her wrist was a small, gold-coated wristwatch.

"Thanks," Lily said, taking the receipt.

"Please, sit on the couch over there. We'll call you once everything is ready."

After fifteen minutes of waiting, Lily was called into the triage room. A nurse drew her blood and took her vitals. Before starting the process, they had to ensure that her white blood cells, platelets and haemoglobin counts were good enough for the chemotherapy.

"We also have to be sure that your kidney and liver are functioning properly," the nurse attending to her said, and whose name had to be Zawadi, a *gift*, for indeed she was warm and pleasant to Lily. "We'll be carrying out these tests everytime you come for subsequent sessions."

Tom arrived just as Lily was getting out of the triage room. He wore a crisp navy-blue suit.

"Good morning, beautiful one?" His breath was fresh and his cologne sweet. "Morning to you, how are you?"

"Pretty well, my dear, I missed you!"

"Excuse me," a nurse interrupted them; they had blocked the way. "Sorry," Tom said, and they moved to the couch.

Lily's results were sent to Dr Esther, who approved the treatment after going through them.

The chemotherapy room was the size of Algeria and was rife with reclining beds. Around each bed were whirring machines, a side table with magazines and books or drinks, and a small chair for a guest. Nurses buzzed in and out in their white uniforms, fixing tubes to patients while others set up the machines.

Already, there were some patients on the beds with intravenous tubes dripping chemo drugs and protein receptors into their veins. The patients kept themselves busy by watching movies, listening to music, reading or just talking with friends or relatives who had accompanied them. One patient was sleeping with headsets on, near the entrance to the room.

"Which bed do you prefer?" asked the nurse.

"There," Lily pointed to a bed by the window next to where a doctor with a stethoscope around his neck was studying an X-ray slide and making notes.

As Lily waited on the bed, they discussed with Tom the political re-alignments that were taking place in the country. Lily's chemotherapy drugs were being mixed at the pharmacy, two rooms away.

"I can't wait to watch the first-ever Presidential Debate tonight," Tom said. "I look forward to it too."

"Maybe we should watch it together?"

"That's a good idea. I'll prepare supper earlier before the debate starts."

Thirty minutes later, it was time for Lily to start her first chemotherapy treatment. Her heart beat faster when the nurse pulled a large machine over to her bed. A plastic bag containing her drugs hung from the machine. The nurse eased a cannula into the vein of her hand and carefully taped it in place with a clean, transparent surgical tape. The nurse bent to inject her with diphenhydramine and a mixture of other relaxation drugs.

Lily felt the smell of the nurse's hair relaxer. The scalp at her hairline shone with oil, and her name tag hung from her chest pocket as she gently squeezed the drugs into Lily's veins. The nurse then connected a set of plastic tubing to the cannula and the top of the tubing to the hanging plastic. Slowly, the drug solution started dripping into her vein through the intravenous infusion.

Lily looked away from Tom; her eyes teary. The drug started flowing into her veins and eventually through her entire body. She felt its coldness and smell. A nurse was preparing a patient's port on a central line just above the patient's chest on an adjacent bed. Lily looked at the patient's cleavage and hidden breast with a mixture of jealousness and admiration. Before Lily could even think of how she would never have such, she was slowly swept to slumber, and Tom was left reading the magazines and watching over her.

"Your next session will be on the eleventh of March," the nurse told her after the day's session was over. That would be a week after the General Elections. Lily felt the taste of sickness in her throat, and nausea crept from her innards. The smell of the drugs was everywhere. Even in her sweat. She felt weak, too.

They left in a taxi. All she wanted was to sleep. Everything she set her eyes on looked like her bed. She slept all the way to her apartment. Once at her apartment, Tom paid the taxi driver and led Lily up the stairs while she held onto his shoulders.

Tom prepared lunch, but Lily couldn't eat.

In the evening, Tom brought her packed food from a restaurant, but still, she didn't eat. After persuading her and ensuring she had eaten something, Tom left early that night to join other students in watching the Presidential Debate.

That night, Lily felt a little depressed and her insomnia was at its best. She tried watching the debate on her TV, but she couldn't manage more than five minutes.

The following day, Tom visited Lily very early in the morning before going back for lectures. Lily paced lazily across the living room to open the door for him. He carried milk and bread, and quickly rushed to fix breakfast. They discussed the performance of the candidates during the Presidential Debate.

Lily could visualise all students standing up in the TV room to sing the national anthem before the debate commenced. She pictured how every student's lips had sung praises to applaud Abduba Dida, a former teacher, who was now one of the fringe presidential candidates. He had stolen the show with his witty but comic responses to questions.

After Tom left, Lily dashed to the toilet to throw up. She could still smell the chemo drugs in her urine hours later.

For the two days that followed, she developed painful mouth sores.

Tom and Halima visited Lily frequently and helped her with house chores. A few times, Babirye would pass by. They would find dirty utensils scattered in the living room or stacked in the kitchen. There were also clothes scattered on her bedroom floor. Sometimes, they would find the house clouded with the smell of over-soaked clothes. They helped as much as they could. They also continued to bring her lecture notes, revision papers and other relevant reading materials.

Apart from occasionally watching TV, Lily read the Bible a lot. On Sundays, she followed the summons by televangelists on TV. Sometimes, she found herself raising her hands or touching the TV in obedience to the calls for miracle healing.

"Amen!" Lily would respond after every word uttered.

On the eve of the Election Day, Tom visited Lily; the air in the room was heavy with the smell of drugs and sickness. She had actually woken up but did not feel like getting out of bed. Tom helped her to the sitting room sofa, hastily cleaned the kitchen and prepared her porridge that had a distant smell of ground *omena*.

"I have to rush and catch the bus," Tom told Lily after serving her the porridge and giving her a book on coping with chemotherapy.

"Take some porridge, please. You have a long journey." When Lily persisted, Tom took only half a mug.

"Stay well. I'll keep in touch." Tom said as he stood to leave.

"Safe journey," Lily told him, the cup of porridge cupped in her hands and held against her raised chin.

Tom boarded the bus whose destination was Kampala via Kisumu. He was surprised to find Babirye on board, and after some persuasion, the passenger he sat next to agreed to swap seats with Babirye.

"And where are you going?" Tom asked Babirye.

"Home, of course. You never know what might happen after tomorrow.

Aren't you running away because of the same fear?"

"No. I'm going to vote." But in actuality, Tom was running away. In the previous general election, he had lost his mother in Nairobi during the clashes. And it was because of the same worry that his father had insisted that Tom goes home. Throughout the journey, he kept calling Tom to confirm he was safe.

"Okay," said Babirye.

"Aren't your leaders doing a good job?" Tom prodded, but Babirye brushedit off.

"But it's good you've always been peaceful even when you are unhappy with your leader." Tom said and added, "On the contrary, I'm not sure if we'll not fight again this time around. I pray not. I lost my...." He realised he didn't wantto talk about his mother. "I lost a close friend in 2007. He used to run a business in Kisumu. He was a nice guy. Karanja. Joseph Karanja."

"Sorry for that," Babirye said and added, "Despite the politicking, at least your current government has done something. Your infrastructure is good! The first time I travelled to Nairobi, this road looked like an animal track in thebush."

Nakuru town was less busy; most businesses had closed. People still nursed fears of what would happen after the elections. It had been one of the epicentres of the 2007/2008 violence because of the multiplicity of ethnicities that inhabit the town and its environs. The driver pulled over the bus at a petrol station for passengers to relieve themselves.

Babirye slept for the better part of the journey until Tom alighted at Ahero.

On election day, Tom was in the voting queue by 3:00 a.m. "The third liberation is here at last!" Someone shouted in the line. Millions of other Kenyans also queued for hours to vote. Tom ended up voting shortly after 8:00 a.m. He nursed optimism in the yet-to-be-formed devolved governments. But he didn't return to Nairobi after voting. He was sceptical about violence erupting, especially nowthat it was taking long for election results to be released.

Lily's parents were equally worried. Her mother kept calling her to find out if she was safe. Lily worried about them and her safety. But Lubao nursed optimism as well. For the first time, he had changed his mindset about women in leadership and cast his presidential vote for Martha Karua of Narc-Kenya. *Women have played an essential role in my life*, he thought.

Lily didn't vote. She hadn't registered as a voter. She watched the preliminary election results to distract her mind, but it kept taking her to the events of 2007/2008. Her nights before the results were released were long, and she was sleepless. She followed the announcements from polling stations across the country but was sceptical about the results from Tharaka Nithi; a constituency widely spoken of during the 2007/2008 post-election violence. It had been claimed that massive vote-rigging had taken place from there.

On the day Lily was going for her second chemotherapy, Halima went to escort her. The room was stuffy with the smell of rotting food. In the kitchen sink, the pan Tom had prepared porridge with was full of frothy water. Halima cleaned the house and washed the utensils, then she stood by the washroom door and stared at Lily, who was sleeping on the sofa, and she couldn't believe it was the same roommate she once had.

"Alhamdu lillahil-lathee afanee mimmab-talaka bih, wafaddalanee ala katheerin mimman khalaqa tafdeela," she made *dua* on Lily's situation. *All praise is for Allah Who saved me from that which He tested you with and who most certainly favoured me over much of His creation.*

Lily, whose eyes were bleary, turned on the sofa and found Halima staring at her. "Thank you, Halima. Thank you very much for your help."

A day after her second chemo, Lily noticed that so much hair had broken from her temple. She requested Halima to help her shave. So, she sat on the brown carpet at Halima's feet in the living room. As the scissors raked and dug into her hair, tufts of it fell around Lily's hips on the carpet, and on her thighs too.

After Halima had finished, Lily went to take a bath. When she came out of the bathroom, Halima couldn't tell if Lily's eyes had turned red from soap or crying. Lily then took a mirror and went to the balcony from where she refused to cry.

"Look at this *handsome boy*," Lily was speaking to her image in the mirror. Halima watched Lily turn sideways to see if there were any curves on her chest.

"You are beautiful," Halima said, moving closer and leaning her chin on Lily's shoulder as her arms wrapped around Lily from behind. They looked at their faces in the mirror – both their eyes moistened – and Lily laughed, and then Halima laughed along.

When Halima left, Lily sat on her bed – with sheets rumpled up – and flipped through her photograph album, reminiscing on the memories each photo carried. She took more than enough time on each and even flipped through a second time.

With time, nausea and vomiting, insomnia, sudden bouts of depression, exhaustion and loss of appetite became part of Lily's life. Everything she tried to eat left a distasteful metallic aftertaste on her palate. She would throw up as soon as she tasted any food. At times, she would go to the kitchen and stand by the door thinking of what she wanted, or open the fridge door and stare at the contents without remembering it was water from the dispenser she wanted. Mood swings slowly became part of her as well.

Lily's menstrual cycle became irregular, and her sweat and urine smelt of the drugs even more. She was becoming so delicate that she started avoiding crowded places and covering her hands in gloves and her mouth and nose in a mask for fear of any slight infection.

With a lack of appetite and eating less, the flesh on her body started disappearing slowly. A few friends and classmates who visited her would console her with praises for her new lean figure. But of course, she doubted their compliments because she eavesdropped on people talking about beautiful socialites, but her appearance was anything but close to them. As her flesh further sunk against her bones and her skin started wrinkling, the friends conveniently chose not to mention anything about her weight. Her clothes drooped on her shoulders, and the elasticity of her inner garments loosened around her thighs and waist. She became distressed, but her friends were always there to give her hope. She slept less and thought more.

Tom did not wave the white flag on her, a fact that gave Lily hope. She didn't want to disappoint him because of his tireless efforts to help; and Francisca too for her endless prayers. She didn't want to let down the many friends who had raised money for her treatment and were still helping. Their efforts made her feel like her life was something worth living for. The only option she had was to be a good patient, take her drugs on time, force herself to eat and make it to appointments on time and without fail.

"I would like you to encourage her, too," Dr Esther requested Tom one evening. On her desk were various brochures and magazines targeting cancer patients and survivors. Most of them were distributed at social gatherings or given as handouts during cancer awareness campaigns.

There were also fliers about entertainment joints and hotels staging poetry nights, karaoke or medium-cost jazz concerts. Dr Esther encouraged Lily to join a support group. When she did, Tom always accompanied her to the meetings. Tom also accompanied her when visiting Dr Esther, and would at times take notes for her. He would note important dates such as appointments for chemotherapy sessions, visits to the doctor and the support group meetings. Halima would also join her, once in a while.

The members of Lily's support group met once a week; venues were communicated from time to time. During the meetings, members introduced themselves, starting with the name, age, diagnosis, and the treatment they were on. Some would then share their personal experiences and how they were coping. When sharing personal experiences, members talked in turns about their battle with cancer and from where they drew their strength to get by each day. They also shared best practices and encouraged each other, especially against feelings of emptiness. In the end, they held hands and one of them led them in prayers.

Lily found hope and a sense of belonging; she empathised with some patients who were more affected than her. Jane was one such patient. Lily became closer to her than any other member in the group.

Lily and Jane started sharing their personal stories and experiences. They also talked about their families and relationships that Lily told her about Jim, Barasa, Tom and Juma. She also spoke about Marto.

Jane also confided in her, and together, they planned what they would do once they fully recovered. At times, they would just sit under a tree in silence as they connected with the rhythm of the earth. They became more of sisters than friends; the sister each one of them never had.

When Jane went for chemotherapy, Lily was always by her side. They talked endlessly about themselves, the twists and turns in politics, and how Kethi Kilonzo, a young lawyer, had impressed them with her sterling performance at the Supreme Court during the hearing of the presidential election petition. At the end of their conversation, Jane sang her favourite song by Matchbox 20:

She says it's cold outside and she hands me my raincoat

She's always worried about things like that

She says it's all gonna end and it might as well be my fault

And she only sleeps when it's raining

And she screams, and her voice is straining
And she says baby
It's three a.m. I must be lonely...

Then Lily picked;

...When she says baby
Well I can't help but be scared of it all sometimes
And the rain's gonna wash away I believe it
She's got a little bit of something, god it's better than nothing
And in her colour portrait world she believes that she's got it all
She swears the moon don't hang quite as high as it used to
And she only sleeps when it's raining
And she screams, and her voice is straining

And she says baby...

And Jane joined;

...It's three a.m. I must be lonely

Oh, when she says baby

Well I...

Mambo continued to keep an eye on Lily. When he came to know about Lily's friendship with Jane from Lily's Facebook page, he thought it was time to move in for the kill. And since Mambo had been friends with Jane on Facebook, and they'd even had chats years back, he had faith his plans would work. Yes, they didn't know each other in person, but from their previous chats on Facebook, Jane seemed approachable. He secretly approached Jane and revealed the secret he had kept for so long. He requested Jane to arrange a meeting between Lily and him.

"I promise; I'll do so once I get an opportune time," Jane promised, though she felt like strangling Mambo to death for having done such cruelty to Lily.

Of course Lily didn't know about it, and she also didn't know that Tom was among the CORD supporters that thronged the city centre with banners and placards chanting opposition slogans. They gathered around Tom Mboya's monument on Moi Avenue and sang the national anthem mentioning *Raila, Kalonzo* and *Wetangula* in the stanzas. The CORD supporters also mourned near the statue of Dedan Kimathi on Kimathi Street. They then proceeded to the Supreme Court, with their clothes soaked in smelly sweat. The supporters gathered at the Supreme Court's gate and chanted that *democracy was on trial* for the better part of the day, hoping that the proceedings going on at the court would favour their candidates.

Chapter Twenty-Eight

Lily went for her third chemotherapy session, on the Monday that former British Prime Minister Margaret Hilda Thatcher died. The nurses reserved her favourite reclining bed for her. The nurses, in deep calming voices, taught her more about cancer and shared encouraging Bible scriptures.

"I feel like the IEBC has failed us again, especially with the hopes we had after they conducted the 2010 referendum on the constitution freely and fairly!" Tom complained. They had just arrived an hour earlier in Lily's apartment from the hospital.

"What if CORD had won, would you say the same thing?" She asked as sheblew her nose into an old handkerchief.

Tom kept quiet.

Lily tried to reposition her frail body on the sofa. Tom rushed to help her. Her eyes had sunk into their sockets, and her peeling lips were dry. Her scalp was bald, and her eyebrows had long vanished from her face.

"What should I prepare for lunch?" Tom asked, diverting from Lily's question. Lily didn't like Tom doing everything for her. She didn't like it when her legs – which seemed like they didn't belong to her anymore – couldn't carry her around to do chores by herself. Life was becoming hard for her, and she could see herself almost resigning to fate. She no longer thought of a future.

*** * ***

"I'll be having a meeting in town tomorrow," Tom told Lily. He had brought her chips and chicken, but she couldn't have any meat. It was a Good Friday; the day the Lord had been crucified. Tom didn't visit Lily the next day. After cleaning his room, he went to a hotel in town opposite GPO along Kenyatta Avenue. Students' elections were approaching, and they had to deliberate on which candidate they would support for Chairpersonship. Many students from their home region had declared their interest.

That afternoon, the Supreme Court gave the verdict on the election petition. Just after the unanimous decision by the court judges giving Uhuru Kenyatta his first mandate, protests ensued in different parts of the country.

Lily watched on her TV. She was terrified when she saw the protests, and the police beating people. Police fished some people out of their houses while others were being clobbered in the streets where protesters burnt properties and blocked roads, harassing motorists. Again, images of 2007/2008 post-election violence were conjured in her mind.

Meanwhile, with the turn of events, Tom's meeting in town came to an abrupt end. "Lily, are you okay?" He placed a call as he watched from the balcony of the hotel the police chase down protestors in the streets, back and forth.

Almost all of the businesses were hurriedly closed down. The city was like a ghost town, especially the CBD. Police had been deployed everywhere and they patrolled the entire city in their lorries.

"I'm okay, Tom," Lily said. Raila Odinga's voice boomed on the TVs mounted on the walls. He was Uhuru Kenyatta's main contender.

"Are you okay?" Lily asked. Tom disconnected the call quickly to catch up with what Raila was saying. He was addressing the nation from his office. "Raila is my President," Tom said bitterly when the address came to an end. As he walked back to campus with three fellow students, he kept repeating the last words from Raila's speech; *Justice be our shield and defender.* A few times, Tom would add his own words, *"History will judge them!"* The fellow students couldn't tell if the *them* implied the Supreme Court judges or the newly elected government.

Tom was only bitter for a few days; he later acknowledged that, indeed as a Kenyan, his only President was Uhuru Kenyatta. Even when Uhuru Kenyatta was sworn in as President, Tom was among the cheering crowds at the Kasarani Stadium; a place that had too many red flags – perhaps an indication, a red flag that the incoming government would plunge the country into a grave of debts. It was the same venue where the political marriage between President Moi's KANU and Raila's NDP had taken place. That day, William Ruto who had once defied his suspension as Minister was sworn in as Deputy President.

That evening, Lily's mind revisited her primary teacher's sentence that bore the weight of three presidents. *Listen, class, President Moi has already vouched for the first President's son, Uhuru, for the Presidency!*

Twice, Tom and Lily had found a bouquet in the support group room with a card addressed to her. That had made Tom feel insecure. So, he planned to buy Lily a beautiful bouquet and an expensive ring, as if he would insure her finger. So, after he left Kasarani, he went to a jewellery shop to get one but thought it wasn't a good idea to. They had never dated, so it wouldn't make sense. So, he decided that he would only buy a bouquet which he would give to her on her fourth chemotherapy session. It was during that time he intended to ask her to be his girlfriend. He didn't care if she would say no or yes. But just a day before Lily's fourth chemo, Jane was stricken down by a sudden infection. It took with it Jane's strength. She was rushed to the hospital on whose reception's wall Kibaki's portrait that previously hung on had already been replaced by that of Uhuru Kenyatta. In Siaya, there was a standoff when the Governor showed his loyalty and allegiance to Raila by putting up Raila's portrait instead!

By the time Lily went to see Jane, the infection had snatched her. It had just left her breathing body. Lily tried to talk to her; to remind her of the pleasant stories they had shared in the recent past and the future plans they had, but Jane couldn't even tilt her head. Lily sang her favourite song;

She says it's cold outside and she hands me my raincoat

She's always worried about things like that

She says it's all gonna end and it might as well be my fault

And she only sleeps when...

But halfway through the song, Lily ran out to cry. A nurse was detaching an intravenous tube from Jane's arm when she came back. Jane was no more. She had left Lily. She had gone with a secret, and the promise she had made to Mambo, unfulfilled.

Tom had bought a black suit, white shirt and pink necktie. He woke up very early and rushed to the barber's shop in Hall 5 for a clean shave. It was his day, their day; a day he finally intended to ask Lily to be his girlfriend. He even informed his friends.

"Should I trim this one?" The barber asked as if Tom could stop the trimmer that was already working on the moustache. The barber's hand smelt of methylated spirit.

Shortly, Tom left for the hospital with a few students.

Reaching the hospital, they alighted from the taxi and sauntered into the chemo room, the bouquet delicately nestled at his arms and a soft breeze lifting his necktie. Tom had earlier informed the doctors and nurses about his plan, and they had given him permission with the only condition that they would be swift and quiet.

They found Lily asleep on her bed. People in the chemotherapy room stared at them with intriguing eyes. Tom knelt next to the bed, still holding the flowers in his arms. Just then, images of Jane and Lily joking and laughing in the support group flooded his mind. *This isn't the right time to do it*, he thought.

"Lily," Tom whispered. There was no response. "Lily," he whispered again, a little louder now. Lily turned to face his direction, opening her sunken eyes. There was a network of veins that ran under her pale skin like a thousand tributaries. Deep in those sunken eyes, he still saw Lily's immense beauty.

287

"Yes, Tom," Lily whispered. For the first time, Tom looked more handsome than her eyes had ever seen before. She opened her mouth, but couldn't say a word. She wasn't sure if Tom would believe that she now felt love for him.

"Lily," Tom whispered soothingly. The anticipation and excitement of other students around Lily's bed were suppressed. Tom held the flowers to her but didn't say the words that had brought him and his friends there. He had changed his mind. *It wasn't the right time*, he had convinced himself.

"Yes, Tom. I can hear you," Lily's voice was weak, and her hand trembled as she tried to receive the flowers with a genuine smile on her face.

"You are beautiful, and all of us here have come today to let you know that you are," Tom said and stood up slowly, gesturing at the rest. It was then that Lily realised that many other students were around.

That day, Tom's friends were disappointed in him. But neither Dave nor

Mwangi nor Halima nor Geoffrey mentioned to Lily what the initial plan was. Babirye had cut links with most of Lily's friends and, thus, didn't attend. And Lily was happy to have been visited by friends, and also elated that Naisula, her inspiration in empowering the girl-child, had been nominated to the Senate.

Lily adhered to her medication and the remaining chemo sessions consistently. She attended lectures when she felt a little stronger. Her fifth chemo was on the 3 June. The day before being an International Mothers' Day, she had called Francisca and thanked her for raising her and sacrificing a lot for her. She had also prayed for her at St. Paul's that morning. She also called her after the chemo, just to repeat the same thing.

Lily was now stronger than she had been when she started the chemotherapy sessions. In the afternoon, she decided to just pass by the library since she was alone, as Tom had gone to meet a certain Governor together with his friends from SONU. It had been a while since she was at her favourite basement spot in the library. As she got in, she found students crowded around a desk, reading news of Nelson Mandela being in a Pretoria Hospital in critical condition and the world praying for him.

In the evening, Tom surprised Lily with a proposal to go out to a cinema. After persuading her for a long time, she gave in.

She wore blue jeans, which were folded at the waist. On her head, she had a heavy woollen cap. To conceal her thinness, she stuffed her hands into the pockets of her jeans as they ambled to town. They walked so close to each other that the jumper, which appeared loose around her frame, kept brushing against his left arm.

Tom bought Lily her favourite ice cream. She refused to eat it. "It's freezing," she said. He then bought popcorn that they ate slowly as they enjoyed the 3-D movie. Halfway through the popcorn, Lily suddenly started throwing up. She profusely apologised to the people around on whose clothes she splashed the vomit. But they clicked and murmured curses and insults at her. Those in the front seats turned to look at the commotion. It didn't auger well with her. She wished she hadn't come to the movie.

"I'll handle it," Tom told her. Tom apologised to the people and went for a mop to wipe the mess. They watched the remaining part of the movie in silence.

Lily was jittery. Once it was done, he looped his arm into hers and they strode to their favourite exquisite restaurant along Kimathi Street, with Lily keeping her head down. The lights of the restaurant reflected a golden glow on the cream wall. The place was almost full, but they located an empty table and sat opposite each other.

"Hello Tom," a tall, pretty waitress greeted them with a beautiful smile planted on her face.

"Hey Emmy," Tom responded, "How was your day?" "Superb! Hope yours too."

"Sure," Tom said.

"I meant plural, *your*," she joked, forcing Lily to smile.

"We had a great one, except this evening..." Tom pinched Lily softly on herlap before she could finish the sentence.

"Oooh, sorry! What's up, my dear?" Emmy asked.

"I meant we had a *great* one, but this evening is turning out to be *greater*." "Wow, nice to know. I'm happy for you." They smiled. "So, what can I offer you to make this evening the *greatest*?"

"Hot chocolate for me," Lily said, turning to Tom and added, "And a mango shake for him." Lily knew his favourite drink. She had missed the hot chocolate that was always served with a flower or heart pattern on its spongy cream foam.

"Anything else?"

"Not for me. Maybe just to add that you look lovely today," Tom complimented the waitress. There was a sudden jerk on Lily's face. Tom noticed. He had also noticed recently that Lily started showing so much affection to him, and it was evident that she was finally falling in love, if not in love yet. To avoid the questions showing in Lily's eyes, he looked at a guy at a table next to them. The guy was sipping his tea audibly while his disgusted female companion watched, idly rotating her glass of iced water at one spot, round and round.

"Nothing more for me," Lily said, and Emmy left. Lily's eyes followed thestraps of her dangling brown apron. There was silence at their table, except for the sounds of spoons on plates, talking, and the sound of chewing and swallowingaround them.

Tom reached across the table and held Lily's hands. "It was just a compliment. They go through a lot in a day serving us. A little compliment can go a long wayin cheering them up."

Lily opened her mouth to say something but changed her mind. "Thank youso much for helping me at the cinema," she said after some time. She pulled her hands and rushed to cover her mouth, almost vomiting, but she swallowed back the nauseating saliva.

"Any time, my dear, though I feel like there's something more you wanted to say."

"Don't mind..." Lily left her sentence hanging, and then went silent with asurly expression even after their order came.

Still, after their drinks, they walked in silence towards the campus. Somewhere along Loita Street, she caught Tom turning to glance at a tall, beautiful lady in green jeans trousers and a floral maroon blouse. Her hair was long, dark and shiny, and her cleavage shone with the bright illumination of the street lights.

"What's that, Tom?" Lily asked in a low voice. She couldn't believe it herself that the affection she now bore for him made her feel jealous.

"Pardon?"

"Nothing," Lily said, then remained silent for the rest of the evening before going to her apartment. *Did Tom have to compare the lady's breasts that swayed with her every stride with my bare chest?* Lily also thought of that lady's hair and the wide hips of the waitress in the restaurant.

Lily finished her chemotherapy four months before her university graduation. Their final examination was to start in a week, and she had passed her continuous assessment tests very well. She had as well resumed her job at the airport. Though one of her final examination papers coincided with a day she was to have an appointment with her doctor, she knew she would be given a special examination. She was sure she would pass just the same way she had passed previous ones.

Lily had saved some money for her gown and for food and refreshments for her parents and friends; all in preparation for the graduation. Since her father wouldn't be able to sleep in her house, she had also saved some amount for his accommodation. She even pictured how it would be at the graduation square with friends and family.

Lily's appointment with Dr Esther was on a Friday morning. By 8:00 am, she was already at the office waiting with bated breath. They had a warm chat sprinkled with breaks of laughter, and she underwent the same tests she had before her diagnosis. She was then asked to go back on Wednesday for the final results.

Dr Esther had felt sorry for Lily's struggles, which had reminded her of her own childhood; being brought up in dire poverty. Her family had struggled to educate her, and she had always found fulfilment in saving lives as a doctor, and in touching lives through many charities

291

she contributed to. But since she had suddenly become fond of Lily, she thought it good to do everything that she could to give Lily hope and make her happy. Anything that could call for a celebration. So, this was the time to celebrate Lily's victory. She slept over the idea and decided it was the best she could do. She shared the idea with Juma, who had always constantly called her to check on Lily's progress. They both agreed that Lily was to be kept in the dark about the plans.

Chapter Twenty-Nine

Tom was given the task of receiving Lily's parents, Jim and Milly. On arrival, he was to take them straight to a hotel Dr Esther had booked.

The bus they had taken went to drop off some passengers at Eastleigh before heading to town. It glided through the streets awash with dirty water. Whenever it encountered submerged potholes, it splashed water to vendors and hawkers who lined the streets. From the dry Sergeant Kahande Street where the sewage spillage hadn't reached, a whirlwind swept a cloud of dust. It swept the dust across the street, through the bus to the opposite side of the First Avenue where traders, mainly of Somali origin, sold assorted perfumes, *kaimati* and dates wrapped in clear polythene bags. The wind carried with it dried elements of raw sewage that usually flooded the streets with potholes, and phlegm often spat on the streets.

The bus was leaving Eastleigh for town when there was a very loud bang. Lubao didn't hear the bang, but he felt a slight tremor. A minibus had been ripped apart a distance away. It had been reduced to mere wreckage by an incendiary device.

A woman's body lay there in a pool of blood. Lubao saw a young child run towards the wreckage. A man tried to grab the child to safety.

Petrified, people pushed against the flow of humanity. A young man shoved an elderly woman aside as he ran. His pocket was filled with a black polythene bag of *khat*. The elderly woman almost fell on a vendor's table full of perfumes. A second young man with his inner lips greened by pellets of *mogoka* - a type of *khat* - shouted to nobody in particular, "Run!" as he pushed past. There was commotion, wails and stampede.

"What's happening?" Francisca asked, more to herself. Shops had instantly been closed and the area was deserted. People were running away, and even their bus driver was accelerating fast from the area.

People gathered at a distance from the explosion scene and watched the smoke coming out of the wreckage. The smell of a mixture of perfumes and sweat choked them. Police had arrived. Some were securing the scene with black and yellow- striped tapes. Some, together with paramedics, were rescuing victims from the wreckage. Open shoes, handbags, pieces of cell phones, a burnt ID card and other stuff were scattered on the bloody road.

"Another grenade attack by Al-Shabaab!" Someone mourned loudly.

"Where's this Kenya heading to? Where is the government we voted for?" asked a passenger seated next to the driver.

"Why send soldiers to Somalia if our own country is not safe?" Another lamented.

Outside, a man was crying, his hands clenched into a fist and his neck veins popping out. He was mourning the death of his wife, whom he had just seen off minutes earlier.

Ambulances with sirens on and even private cars helped to transport the victims to hospitals. Inside them lay people who were fighting for their lives. Pharmacies around the area donated boxes of latex gloves for use in the rescue mission.

* * *

Much the same way she had done it before, Lily was at Dr Esther's door by 8:00 a.m. that tranquil Wednesday. Though Dr Esther had hinted

294

to her that she had responded impressively well to the chemotherapy, Lily was still a little worried about what that day's appointment was about. She wondered what would happen if she was to be told that; *unfortunately, Dr Esther had wrongly observed her response to the chemotherapy and the medicines were not working for her.* What would happen to her family? Questions filled her mind, all scrambling for answers.

"Hello Lilian," the receptionist, Ciku, welcomed her with a warm smile, extending her hand. "Let's go to the Cancer Unit please; Dr Esther must be waiting for you. She's attending to some patients, and instructed me to take you there when you arrive." Lily couldn't understand how different that day was from the other days when Dr Esther attended to her patients from her office.

Ciku led the way with Lily trudging behind, perturbed. Ciku's hair reminded Lily of her former self.

When they reached the door to the reception of the Cancer Unit, Ciku asked, "Are you really ready to see Dr Esther?"

"I wouldn't be here if I wasn't," Lily's lips quivered. She couldn't wait; whatever the outcome. She had even carried a present to give the doctors in appreciation for the good work so far. Ciku's right hand was already on the handle of the door. Looking directly at Ciku, Lily took a long deep breath and emphasised, "Yes, I am ready, Ciku."

Ciku flung the door wide open. The room was adorned with balloons and flowers, and it smelt of a sweet fragrance. Lily's eyes were first met with the cheerful grin on her son's face. He held out a bouquet for her. On his head was a pink cap with the words, *You are Cancer-free, Mum.* Lily upped her face in disbelief! Everyone else wore either a pink ribbon or a pink wristband.

Just behind Jim were Francisca and Lubao. Old age had shrunk Lubao's flesh against his bones. Lily hadn't seen him for a while; he seemed half his former size and older than the 74 years he was. His deeply ingrained brow told of a person who had traversed through decades of forlorn hope for a better life than he had lived.

"Dr Esther, I'm cancer-free?"

"You successfully completed your treatment regimen, and the tests have confirmed that indeed, you are cancer-free," Dr Esther said, smiling broadly. She and the entire team that had worked on Lily, except Zainab, were there. She wore long black trousers, a few inches above her ankle with golden lip-gloss on her lips.

Lily didn't believe her. "Is my cancer gone?"

"Yes, Lilian," Dr Ogunga intervened, the fluorescent light from the bulbs above reflected on his clear lenses.

"Is the endless list of tamoxifen, taxotere, trastuzumab, doxorubicin, palonosetron and other drugs past tense?" That question was more to herself than anyone else.

"Sure," a nurse said, smiling.

How different would it feel if Jane were here? How would we feel celebrating together; both of us being cancer-free? Lily thought. A sharp scream, like a whistle, rented the air and the next second, she was on the floor crying. Francisca wrapped her in her arms.

Juma, Riziki and their daughter Molly were also present. Juma wondered if Riziki had come to confirm that Lily had healed so that she could start her revenge mission. He didn't want to imagine that was her motive.

There was some unexplainable force Lubao felt when his eyes locked with Juma's. There was something he felt about Juma that he couldn't explain. And so, he meant to ask Juma where he came from before the day was over.

Geoffrey was in a wheelchair next to Mary; his long-lost girlfriend. Were it not that Lily was still overwhelmed, she would have asked him where the other girlfriend was. Geoffrey had been admitted to the hospital after a fight with a man over a woman in a nightclub. A large piece of broken beer bottle had been sunk deep into his innards. He had also been diagnosed with gonorrhoea, but his close friends suspected HIV/AIDS.

Lily's colleague, Pauline, her friend Milly, and the staff at the Cancer Unit were there too. Only Tom was absent because he was sitting for an exam. Barasa and Babirye were also missing. When Lily hugged Lubao, she felt their lean bodies shaking, and the pulse in their chests intensified. There was a smell of old age in him. He felt how thin his daughter was, and how sharp her shoulder blades were. She shed tears that dripped on his lean back.

After moments of crying, soothing, hugging, congratulating and presenting gifts to her, Lily started, "If words were food, then I'm totally malnourished! I don't think I'll ever get adequate words to express my gratitude for the scope of human generosity you've drowned me in. I can never be able to repay adequately for what you've done. Only God can."

She wiped a film of tears and continued, "And in the fullness of my joy and gratitude, I would like to share with you two of my stories; stories that only a few of you might be aware of." Again, she wiped a drop of tears and turned to Lubao.

"This old man here is my father, and this is my mother."

"*Masha'Allah*," Halima said, and they all clapped regardless of their incomprehension.

"They've sacrificed all they had for me. I thank you, mum and dad," she paused to search for the next line. Lubao couldn't get what she was saying. "They had waited for a child for too long, and when I was brought forth, they were so happy and grateful." There was an eerie silence.

Meanwhile, Milly was updating Barasa of the party over text messages. Tom rushed out of his exam room. He ran down Prof. Mourice Alala Road to his room and picked his gift for Lily.

Francisca nodded in agreement and struggled to explain to Lubao in sign language what Lily was saying. "That happiness tickled my father's philanthropy, and he gave my mother this note to buy with it whatever she pleased," Lily fished out the one-hundred-shilling note.

"Wow," Pauline exclaimed; they all broke out in laughter as they clapped.

Dr Esther wrote a note for Lubao. After reading the note, Lubao quickly threw glances at the note Lily was holding and then puzzled glances at his wife with a coy surprise. He had long forgotten about the note. Francisca conveniently ignored his glances. Everyone laughed.

"Yes, that was the amount my father had, and besides, it was quite a

297

lot of money back then!" She said when the laughter died down. "So, my mother kept it well, intending to pass down the gift to her daughter as a wedding gift. And the note seemed to have stuck in a time warp if the judgement of its texture is anything to go by." She rubbed her fingers against the fabric of the note. She told them how her mother opted not to keep the gift for too long and gave her, "...the day I was reporting to campus." Claps from Geoffrey interrupted her; claps that were very infectious that everyone else joined in.

"Wow," Geoffrey responded. There was a smell of tobacco in his breath. He had wheeled himself to the parking yard, tapped at a packet of cigarettes, lit one and sent clouds of tar down his windpipe. His eyes were sunken, and his almost fur-like hair was somewhere between black and tan.

"And, when I was growing up, I knew I was the only sibling to myself. I never knew God had created people who meant more than the elder or younger brothers and sisters I would've loved to have. But I now know that I need to thank God; to be grateful for my life and to pray and thank Him for you all. It was never about which ethnicity, faith or political affiliation but about a human being in need. I can never thank you enough. I owe you all and all those who haven't made it here.

Lily's mind for a moment focused on the entire fundraising team, and the endless and selfless support they had given. She thought of Tom, and how the love she had always conveniently ignored was strongly re-emerging. The love for Tom, which he was not aware of.

Lily's voice and words swept the room to silence. "And to my second story... after being diagnosed with cancer, I read a lot into the night. Not that I even recalled the previous pages' contents. I just wanted to beguile some of the time. However, there are two things that I remember vividly from the books." There was still silence. Jim pricked a balloon and it jerked a few of them with its bursting sound.

"Marcel Proust asserts in one of the pieces that 'Let us be grateful to the people who make us happy; they are the charming gardeners who make our souls blossom,'" Lily said, and added after a pause, "The same is emphasised in a different book; that we should always let

298

gratitude be the pillow upon which we kneel to say our nightly prayers. And that we should let faith be the bridge we build to grapple with evil and welcome good."

She wiped her eyes. "And today I'm incredibly grateful not because they say we should be grateful, but because I am grateful. Forever and sincerely! And this one-hundred-shilling note that I present to Dr Esther is just a symbol of my gratitude to you all! My gratitude to you is boundless and endless as the horizon of the sky." She fell on her knees before Dr Esther and stretched both her hands as she gave her the note.

Juma was planning to leave with Riziki because he imagined her causing a scene if she remained behind. In his small briefcase, there was a letter summoning him to face a disciplinary committee at the Ministry of Health. It was a long letter in response to his corrupt deals as reported by his wife which he had no idea about, yet.

Juma walked to Lily, Francisca's eyes following him, and whispered in her ear. She whispered back. Juma said to them all, "Sorry family, I have to leave. I have an urgent meeting this afternoon. Have fun tonight; we've organised a thanks- giving party. I'll be joining you then. But most importantly, thank God for His goodness." They all clapped for him.

"Before Juma leaves, I want to conclude that...and it's not because he's leaving. His leaving just coincided with the end of my speech." Some smiles flashed across the audience. "Lastly, I would like to conclude that I value and appreciate everything, small or big, that you have done. The things I took for granted and those I didn't. Looking at life with appreciation and valuing the role each one of you played in ensuring I lived to see this day, I thank you all. And if there is anyone whose path I crossed and left sour feelings of hatred and annoyance, I say sorry. Above all, I thank God."

As they were having soft drinks and cakes, Mary joked to Geoffrey that she would only marry him if he changed to be a 'good boy' like Tom. Geoffrey laughed it off and suggested a joint birthday party for him and Lily in November.

Tom bumped into Lily, who was on her way to the washrooms. She pulled him to the wall along the corridor, took his cheeks in her hands and pressed her lips passionately against his, oblivious of the cleaner scrubbing the pavement or the old man that was being pushed in a wheelchair in the corridor.

In those few seconds, her feelings were a far cry from what she had once felt with Marto or Juma. She felt an electrifying surge in her nerves and a soothing feeling of someone who had finally found what she had been missing for years.

Barasa, Juma and Marto would just remain her treasured friends. Yes, she had made mistakes in the past, but she knew a new future awaited her. In those few seconds, she felt okay to imagine Marto taking someone else to Morocco.

"Where are you from, brother?" She imagined the driver asking. "Kenya."

"Aaah, the land of Kibaki?" "No, Uhuru Kenyatta."

Perplexed, he would ask, "I thought his name was Jomo?" Marto would laugh, and then say, "No, he's Jomo's son."

"Ahaaa," he would say, and then drive for a mile before adding, "And have you heard of Joseph, the son of Laurent Kabila?" Marto would say, "yes." Then the driver would ask if he had heard of Ian, the son of Seretse Khama, or Ali the son of Omar Bongo, or Faure Essozimma of Togo, and Marto would curtly say, "Yes, I also know of John Quincy, the son of John Adams and George W. Bush the son of George H. W. Bush."

A gush of blood rushed through Tom's body, but she released his cheek once she noticed a change in his breath. It was deep and heavy. "Thank you so much, Tom. I'm cancer-free!" She held him firmly on the wall. "Tom, may you have all the joy your heart can hold, all the smiles the days can bring and all the blessings life can unfold."

"I see the smile on your face, and it makes me more thankful. I've longed to see it since it disappeared many months ago. It makes you look like a thirteen- year-old." Tom smiled amidst tears. Bound by the sudden twist of fate in her life, his unsparing dedication and love had always amazed her. "They say that beauty is the promise of happiness, and I see so much joy from your beauty. You're beautiful, Lilian Nekesa. I love you; I always have! Can you be my girlfriend?" He finally asked, forgetting they were in a hospital, and then brought her lips closer.

"Yes, Tom, of course!" Lily held his hands, fighting back the urge to kiss him again, and instead said, "If I'm to honestly bare my soul to you, I love you, Tom. I'm not just saying I love you back because you've said so, but I always have! And I count myself lucky to be truly loved by one person whose comparison I've failed to cite." An overwhelming feeling stretched throughout his body.

Despite the temptation to throw her hands around him and hold his nape tightly, she again snubbed his second kiss attempt. He dropped his gift bag on the floor and rubbed a teardrop on her eyelids with his thumb. With his hands on her cheeks, she felt breathless and charged in a way she had never felt before. With an impish wink, she said, "Join the rest inside, and remember we have a celebration tonight!" She then rushed, past a man hobbling around on crutches, to the washroom; to milk out all the tears out of her tear glands.

"Yes!" Tom punched his fist in the air and picked up the gift bag.

"How could he still love me in this state?" Lily asked herself, looking at her image in the washroom mirror.

Chapter Thirty

"What do you have to say about the corruption allegations whose evidence we have with us?" A committee member fighting to pin Juma down asked; a question whose answer Juma fumbled with.

The questions and answers were thrown on the floor, and the session went on for the entire afternoon. Some members of the committee became personal, and so did Juma. He was even ready to battle with them in court - if it came to that.He was sure he could bribe his way out of the mess. It was apparent that most members were determined to ensure stringent punishment was met upon Juma. When the session ended, all that Juma wanted was to be alone. He had also been informed that the many pieces of evidence they had against him were given to them by his wife. By going home, he was sure he would end up harming his wife or doing something terribly bad that could make him regret for the rest of hislife. So, he thought it wise to be alone for that day and confront his wife the day that would follow once he had cooled down. He called Lily to inform her that he wouldn't make it to the party. He then booked himself a hotel room, went in and switched off his phones.

* * *

At the party, Lily promised her father that once she graduates, she would ensure he got a cochlear implant. An ENT specialist had once suggested that that wasthe only solution if Lubao was to get his hearing back.

"How is it going with your aviation career?" Lily asked Mary.

"It's good. I enjoy it," she placed down her juice, a pink mark of her lipstick planted on the glass.

"Aaah, that's nice," Lily said and continued, "Growing up, I wanted to be a pilot."

"Maybe your son will be a pilot," Mary said, reaching for lipstick in her pouch.

"I hope that's what he'll like," Lily said and added, "...by the way, I once promised Geoffrey that I would get you for him. I'm glad that things just worked out and you met today."

At the next table, Tom was talking about how County Governments were allocating tenders wrongfully.

"Most of these people getting tenders are either relatives to the Governors or their cronies," Mwangi opined.

"You don't get tired of discussing politics?" Lily asked, pulling the chair nextto Tom.

"How can we keep quiet when some Governors are buying ballpoint pens at five million shillings a packet? Pens that cost one hundred shillings per packet!" Tom complained.

"We can't, especially when the same Governors are suffocating from a miasma of stale ethnicity! They demand that the universities and colleges within their jurisdictions admit only students from their tribes! Is that what our liberators fought for, or what we voted for in the 2010 Constitution? Remember..." Mwangi paused abruptly, checked around, and then whispered, "He who goes to bed with an itchy anus wakes up with smelly fingers!" He thrived on throwing in his conversations, phrases, proverbs or aphorisms.

"We can't afford to sit down and watch them steal our money and

303

invest inforeign countries," Dave argued.

"Okay, let me leave you to discuss your politics; I don't have the energy to contribute," Lily said.

Dr Esther and other doctors left the party mid-way, some to resume their duties as others retired to their homes early. Lily joined Francisca, Lubao and Jim at their table.

"Do you have a boyfriend?" Francisca asked Lily after they had talked for a short while.

"Mum!" She paused to absorb the question. "Ok, I'm not sure whether I'm seeing someone or not. Are you enjoying the party?" Lily asked, cleverly trying to change the topic.

"I like that young man called Tom," Francisca broached, further searching Lily's eyes. *How would she react if I took someone else home?* Lily wondered. *What does she now think of Barasa?* Barasa's parents had visited their home several times. He had also given foodstuffs and offered other help, including financial, to her parents many times.

"And I hope you remember my advice; that you stop seeing that man Juma," Francisca interrupted Lily's thoughts.

"I remember, mum. Can I serve you more juice, please?"

"No, thanks. I'm full." Francisca said, pausing to search Lily's face once againfor signs that she was speaking the truth. "He's a good man," Francisca continued, "He's helped us a lot, but don't come between him and his wife. Okay? Good.Then, lastly, where does he, Juma, come from? You don't know? Okay, try to find out...and what of his parents?"

Lily felt intimidated by Francisca's flurry of questions and admonition. "Okay, I hear you," she said, biting off a piece of meat and continuing to chew in silence.

As she retired to bed very late that night, Lily thought about her mother'sadvice and the questions.

The next day, Lubao and Milly were headed to the bus station to catch a bus home. Francisca and Jim were to remain behind for a few days.

"Always be a good boy to Grandma. Okay?" Milly joked to Jim. "Yes, I will."

"Good."

"Mum Lily?" Jim turned to face Lily. "Yes, my dear."

"Where is Baba?"

A turgid silence ensued, with all of them exchanging glances. "We're getting late, Nekesa. They have to board the vehicle. It's almost leaving," Francisca said to defuse the situation, softly brushing Jim's head. But Lily now knew it was that high time for her to seriously start looking for Jim's father.

* * *

Lily visited Tom the following day; a Friday afternoon. She arrived in Hall 10 before the fragrance Tom had sprayed in his room had diminished. She spent the afternoon with him just listening to music, chatting, and eating snacks. Tom chose a soothing playlist that made Lily forget about the past and the world outside.

"Wow, your room is sparkling today!" Lily observed. Tom just smiled because her face was glowing with renewed hope. She wanted to tell him about her urgent intention of looking for Jim's father but instead said, "I want to start a group that can sensitise young girls on the need to have frequent breast cancer screening. I will first target secondary school girls."

"That's a brilliant idea," Tom exclaimed happily. "When do you intend to start?"

"In less than two months. During the Breast Cancer Awareness Month of October to be precise."

They discussed the concept. Lily imagined herself making a presentation: "If a close family member has ever been diagnosed with breast cancer before menopause, you are at high risk than those with no history of cancer in their families. This should make you suspicious. If your periods started before age twelve, you too are at an increased risk." She imagined switching from one slide to the next and her audience intently listening. She would then mention ovarian and cervical cancer

305

and link them to breast cancer.

"What about the funds?" Tom eventually asked.

"You remember the proposals you used to help me write to NGOs...with theaim of helping disadvantaged girls across the country?"

"In our second year?"

"Precisely," Lily said, stretching on the small bed.

"That was long ago! I had even forgotten."

"So had I, until one of them reached out recently. They said they are interested, but they want to concentrate on breast cancer issues." Tom's face suddenly brightened. "So, when they asked if I'm interested, I quickly said, 'Certainly!'"

"That's what we call double blessings," Tom said, leaning to kiss her on the cheeks. "Congratulations!" He then picked a remote and increased the volume of his Ampex music system that was playing Fadhili William's hit song *Malaika*.

"That song reminds me of my childhood. I hear it was released even before I was born..."

"Late 1950s, to be precise," Tom curtly said with tinges of pride. "I also like *Todii* by Oliver Mtukudzi, and *Amka Kumekucha* by Maroon Commandos." There was a slight pause. "*Malaika, nakupenda malaika*..." Tom sang along, leaning over her and expressing his affection.

"Now," Tom said in a serious tone, "Tell me more about the NGO proposal." He joined her in bed and they lay side by side. They talked in whispers, listening to Tom's playlist. He ran his thumb along where her hairline used to be, softlyblowing his fresh breath on her temple, and rested the hand on her neck. Her beautiful face and eyes were gradually closing. He looked at her, listening to her carotid pulse until she fell asleep. He turned down the volume of the radio andstretched to cover her feet with the duvet. Tom admired her closed eyes, lips and face before pulling the duvet to look at her flat chest. He still loved her; he wascertain.

"I look forward to watching next year's FIFA World Cup with you," Lily saidwhen she woke up.

"I look forward to it too, and many more other things." "You remember the match between Uruguay and Ghana?" "I'm surprised you still do," Tom said.

"How can I forget? We had such fun cheering our own African team. Wherewill next year's World Cup be hosted?"

"Brazil."

Then they kissed. She then pulled up her top and showed him her bare chest.

"You still look very beautiful despite the scars," Tom said and added, pressing the tip of his finger on a birthmark above her small navel, "You're an embodimentof beauty." It seemed as if treasures were hidden below the navel; treasures that could easily send him on a spending spree. The hem of her panty showed on the waistline. He thought of pulling down her trousers and removing the panty. He tried to bring his hand to her trousers' button and zipper, but she pushed him away.

Lily started dancing, and when the song ended, they curled under the duvet and watched movies from his smartphone and cracked jokes. He cradled herhead in his arms. They didn't touch a book despite both of them having examsthe following Monday.

They strolled to the Arboretum that evening, after which they went to Ufungamano House for a karaoke. A young man strummed a guitar, and another sang in high pitch, bringing back memories of their secondary school drama and music festivals. They talked a lot about local dances like *nyatiti* and *isukuti* as they enjoyed the show.

Back in the room, they had supper. "Why don't you stay for the night?" Tom pleaded, holding both her hands.

"Why do you want me to stay?" She asked, though she knew she had to goto work that night.

"Your presence just makes me more complete and secure," he interlocked their hands and held her close. Their foreheads and noses touched. He pleaded with her, but she didn't give in.

307

Before they parted, Lily fished out of her pouch an audio CD and pressed it into his palm. "Listen to it and have a goodnight," she said.

He watched Lily make strides then rushed and pulled her from behind. He hugged her, sniffed her shoulder for her perfume and said, "Goodnight."

And they longed for each other the moment each went their way.

On her way, Lily decided that she would finally take the bold step and go back to Mathare North after finishing her exams and ask around for any leads about Jim's father. If she found him, what kind of conversation would they have? Would it be in a restaurant or at Jeevanjee Park? She thought.

When he returned to his room, Tom sent Lily a message telling her how grateful he was for her time. He then inserted the CD in his music player and took the remote. He switched off the lights, pulled his duvet, slid into it and pulled it up to his chin, braced his head on his soft pillow, and pressed the "play" button on the remote. The CD had only one song, *Love you in the morning* by Gregory Isaacs. She knew he loved Gregory Isaacs' songs.

Lily called to tell him that she had arrived at her apartment, and later when she got to her workplace. "Good night," she said.

Tom held on to the phone long after Lily had disconnected as if they were still conversing. His thoughts switched to the events of the day; the dancing, resting in bed and just everything.

"Hello, Tom," Lily's second call interrupted his thoughts. He was still listening to the song on the CD.

"Talk to me, sweetheart." For the first time, he called her *sweetheart,* which surprised them both, as though they were witnessing the sprout of civilisation in Mesopotamia.

"Someone has just called me. He says he's Jim's father." Her hand trembled, and her voice was shaky.

"Calm down," Tom said, thinking of what to say next. "What else did he say?"

"Nothing else," Lily said, "He ended the call after saying that. And I

308

couldn't call back since he called from an unknown number. But his voice sounds so familiar. I strongly feel I've heard that voice before, and very recently."

"Maybe his phone's battery went down..."

"Can we discuss it tomorrow?" Lily curtly asked.

"Of course, why not?" Just then, Tom heard Lily heaving so heavily. "Are you okay?" he asked Lily.

"Yes, Tom. If I'm not, you won't miss the headlines. It's only that I'm rushing to finish up some work. My supervisor is coming. Goodnight."

"Goodnight," Tom said, then sat on his bed holding the phone and waiting for sleep.

The tranquillity of that Saturday morning was interrupted by a phone call Tom received at about 7:30 a.m. "Lily's apartment collapsed last night," the caller, a classmate, started, "...and rescue efforts are underway."

"What!" Tom shouted, jumping out of bed. Gregory Isaacs' song was still playing. When the building collapsed, Francisca struggled for air in the pitch- black rubbles, groping for Jim while trying to call for help without success. She tried to stretch her legs, but there was no space. Heavy blocks were pressed against her chest; she tried to scream in desperation for help, but no voice came out. She called out Jim's name but nothing could be heard. She tried to scream again when she heard faint voices outside the rubble, but her own voice failed her. The reality of facing her death crept closer, and the air became thinner until she lost consciousness.

Tom arrived at the scene short of breath. He tried calling Lily's number but it was off. The police, the army and the Red Cross officers were in their rescue efforts. Civilians also helped in carrying the injured into the ambulances. The City Council Fire Fighters arrived late just as it was the norm for government agencies to respond poorly to emergencies. The sight devastated Tom.

Several bodies had been recovered from the debris and wrapped in body bags, and more victims were being pulled out of the debris with severe injuries. Tom, tangled and sweating, moved closer to the rescuers, past people craning their necks to get clear glimpses past the area cordoned by police. He moved past young girls taking *selfies* and videos of the scene to upload on social media, past a cluster of journalists clicking their cameras and interrogating witnesses to where the army, in orange reflector jackets and blue helmets, and Red Cross volunteers in red reflector jackets and white helmets, were. He walked around, desperately, peeping through the ambulances' windows as the injured were put on board to be taken to hospitals. But he couldn't see clearly through those windows. He couldn't see what he was looking for. Yet, in one of them, Jim was being given first-aid. He rushed near the debris where he could see more clearly, but still, he could not see the people he knew. He dialled Lily's number again. It was still off.

Then Tom saw one more victim being removed from the rubbles and rushed there. It was Lily's mum. He scanned around to see any other victim, hopefully Jim, being pulled out, but there was none. He made a wide stride, then a second one, and lastly, he started running alongside them towards the ambulance.

Strapped on the stretcher, her right leg was splinted; it had a bandage soaked in fresh blood. "Please pave the way," one of the rescuers shouted at Tom, waving his right hand.

"I know her," Tom shouted back with a slush of anger. He ran alongside the stretcher. "Mama Lily," he called out, leaning towards her head. He called four times. No response. "And there's also a young boy…. his name is Jim!" He shouted to the rescuers, tears lingering in his eyes.

"Then pave the way and follow us into the ambulance!" "What about Jim?"

"Rescue is ongoing. He will be rescued." One responded.

"How old is he? A boy has just been rescued five minutes ago, and is in an ambulance on the way to the hospital!" Another one shouted.

They rushed into the ambulance and once inside, with the doors closed, the ambulance took off at high speed. They quickly fixed a plastic medical collar around Francisca's neck and wiped the streaks of thick blood.

"You can sit there, please," the ambulance attendant pointed next to a student paramedic.

"How's she?" Tom asked, an intense apprehension building up in him.

"She has suffered serious injuries. Her chances of survival are quite..." The paramedic realised he was about to say something unprofessional. He connected her to cardiac monitors with black and green numbers flickering on the screen. "She will be fine. We'll do the best we can." The paramedic took her blood pressure and started fumbling with the oxygen saturation readings.

"She will survive, right?" Tom asked, choking on saliva. They attached black, white, red and green cords to her; they had to read her heart rhythm and check for any heart event.

"Mom," Tom leant closer to her. He held her palm. Her finger folded, clutching around his. Her fingernails were short. "Can you hear me?" He asked. She slightly moved her head, and he smiled, a film of tears forming on his unwashed face. "Can you hear me, Mom?" No response. Tom turned to look outside the window to hide the tears that lingered.

Outside, a crowd of onlookers stood by the road, making it hard for the driver to join Thika Superhighway. Some even came to the window of the ambulance trying to peep inside as it slowly moved past a heap of garbage where street urchins basked around burning cartons. A crowd of flies swarmed around the urchins as the ambulance passed.

Traffic was stagnant on Thika Superhighway. The President, the Minister for Internal Security and his counterpart for Transport's convoy were heading to Jomo Kenyatta International Airport where a building was on fire. It was a long convoy with the lead car blaring a siren and several motorcades and dark chase cars following.

Had the President gotten news of the building that had collapsed not far from where they were now passing? Tom wondered. Perhaps the media hadn't given it much attention, or those concerned had conveniently ignored it.

If he had known, he would have stopped by to console the victims and the affected. Maybe his deputy, or a Cabinet Secretary, or an MP, or a

Permanent Secretary would have extended a hand of help to the victims, in addition to just saying, "sorry." There would have been no traffic deadlock that resulted from blocking other motorists, including ambulances from using the Superhighway.

Francisca's grip tightened around Tom's fingers. Her heart was palpitating under her chest as her lungs struggled for air. She opened her mouth slowly and whispered, "I...I..." She felt immense pain as she tried to whisper. Tom leant further close to her. "I...I...am..." she paused to take in a gulp of air and then struggled to say something, but could not. She made two more attempts but ended up just coughing, choked by the air trapped in her throat.

She tried to open her eyes, but they closed immediately. "I...I..." she could not utter a word. Her grip loosened around Tom's fingers, and her hands gradually became cold. The paramedics tried to deliver shock on her, but she remained completely inanimate.

The attendant wished he had the authority to say, "We're sorry, we've lost her." If he had, Tom would definitely have shouted, "No!"

Tom squeezed her hands. She didn't show signs of feeling any pain. "Mom!"he shouted in desperation. *Had she died? How? Why?*

* * *

A crowd rushed to wave as the Presidential convoy whizzed past Ngara. Among the people waving were beneficiaries of free maternal care his government had introduced. Others were optimistic that maternal care would work just like free primary education, even though the huge appetite for tuition fees and unnecessary levies by school heads still bothered them.

The people were optimistic civil servants would perform their duties without prejudice, impunity, corruption or favour, but with fervour. With a law-abiding civil service, they were confident that no bribery would thrive, and no more buildings would collapse. They would be assured of no accidents on the roadsdue to speeding, reckless driving or driving unroadworthy vehicles. They wished the President would give a stern warning to other landlords, or even form a commission of inquiry. But they were aware of the findings of many commissions that either sat on the shelves or were never heard of.

* * *

"Maybe if there was no traffic, she'd have made it," Tom said with a mixture of brute shock and anger. The President's convoy had already passed and they were almost approaching a nearby hospital.

"Maybe. Maybe not," the student paramedic said and added, "God has a plan for every one of us. We just don't know our day." The ambulance attendant gave the student a stern look that immediately muted him. The student knew that he had questions to answer at the office later as a result.

"Life is like a shadow and mist; it quickly passes by," Tom said, and bent down to sob. If only he could reverse the hand of time and glue himself in the depth of the past days.

Tom would mark that Saturday, 17 August 2013, as one of the coldest days of his life.

Chapter Thirty-One

Lily's limbs became bulky and her tongue too heavy when she got home and got the news of her mom's death. *Was it not just last night we were chatting and laughing?* She muttered under her breath. But after the news sank in, she broke into wild wails, and well-wishers rushed to hold her, or mutter a prayer. She had not only lost everything she possessed, but also a pillar in her life; her mother. Fortunately, Jim had survived, though he was in critical condition in the hospital. The news had even gotten to the village, and it was being dispatched to their relatives.

"Take heart," was all Tom could say when he met her at the hospital compound where she had just arrived. He hugged her so tight and for so long. He had come out of the children's ward to meet Lily at the entrance. At the children's ward, Halima was watching over Jim as they waited for Milly and Lubao to start another journey back to Nairobi. They had just arrived in Kitale when Tom called Millyto relay the sad news.

"I'll see mum first," she finally spoke, tears in her eyes, and Tom led her through corridors crammed with patients. Some were on wheelchairs, some tended by relatives while some were all by themselves. The morgue was at the far end ofthe hospital, so they went straight past doors with large plastic signs, through corridors smelling of sickness and whose walls had been scored by gurney frames. When they got to a sign that read 'Children's Accident Ward', where Jim was, he thought Lily would change her mind and opt to see her son first, but she didn't.

Lily's heart leapt. There was silence as they stood at the heavy double doors waiting for the attendant to swing them open. By the look of flakes of paint remnants on the morgue's wall, it hadn't been painted in ages. When he finally opened the door and a draft of air full of formaldehyde hit Lily's face, there was more silence. Deafening. Sadness. A flux of energy left Lily. Her throat dried. Then they heard a distant painful sob of another person who had also come to view the remains of their relative.

"Lily?" Tom whispered. Lily didn't hear. Her mind was elsewhere with a haze of disbelief, and tears heating the back of her eyes. Tom wanted to tell her something calming. Anything. He wanted to tell her that they were all, as human beings, mortals with one definite destiny of death. That Francisca would always watch over her from the unseen world, and that she would be happy to see Lily strong through that agony. That he would always be there for her. But there was still silence, and he could only judge himself at how terrible he was at consoling and mourning. At how terrible he was at the language of mourning.

When Francisca's remains were pulled out, Lily shook her head and lost all her strength. Tom held her before she could touch the floor.

"It's all my fault…. I could've done something…." she murmured. Tom wiped her tears and whispered that there was no ounce of fault on her.

When Tom helped her out of the morgue where she sat on a bench and wept some more, and requested to go see her mum alone, they granted her. She weakly walked in, leaving Tom outside, worried. They pulled Francisca's body for her for the second time, where she stood in silence viewing the body for long, until the attendant told her that time was over. She walked out without uttering a word.

"Hold this for me," she gave Tom her phone. "I'm going to the ladies. I'll be back in a few, then we'll go to check on Jim." She strode towards the latrines hidden behind the morgue, and when she was out of sight, she walked past the latrines. That was the last time she was seen.

* * *

They had searched for Lily everywhere for a whole week, but they could not find her. So, they decided to go ahead with Francisca's burial plans. Fundraising was organised and two buses were hired to transport her body, some of her relatives and friends, and Lily's friends from the university.

The long trip from Nairobi commenced at the crack of dawn. It was a quiet and non-stop drive, except at Sachangwan, a place where slopes were steep, corners sharp and heavy trucks trundled, and from where accidents had claimed many lives.

The buses stopped there briefly as if to honour the souls of the many people who had perished there. As other students shouted out to sugarcane vendors, Halima sat still, her hands clasped together and her voice intoning a silent prayer, "*I-a'tasamto beka yaa rabbe min sharre maa ajedo fee nafsee faa'simnee min zaaleka.*" "Oh, my Creator! I seek Thy shelter from the mischief of the danger that's linking in my heart, protect me from it."

Other than gnawing off sugarcane peels, and the *sssss* sound of sucking the sap from the pulp, all was quiet. Only a few times did Tom point out and say, "That road connects to Molo town" or "This one can take you to Ahero, my hometown, then Kisumu city," with an imperceptible emphasis on the word *city*.

In Kitale, a crowd of youths came to welcome them home. Most of these youths were members of groups Lily had once been supporting financially while some were members of Francisca's church or friends and Lily's former schoolmates.

Some of the students, who had been napping, like Halima, woke up. They quickly shot their eyes above the seats and the heads of the students seated in front, to get a view. They had a clear view of the crowd

316

that welcomed them. Halima wished she could comprehend the songs the crowd danced to passionately and vigorously, their shoulders and chests moving in tandem with the drumbeats.

The crowd led the buses a long way down ragged roads that snaked into the village. They broke stems and leaves from roadside trees to wave in the air as they danced and chanted. The synergy of energy and emotions that drove them surprised the students inside the two vehicles.

Along the narrow paths, bicycle riders and pedestrians had to give way for the buses. Some were forced into the maize farms to pave the way while others just stood by the roadside. A few placed their hands over their heads as a sign of empathy. One sat on the tip of a hoe's shaft that dug deep into her butt, yet some drove their cattle into the bush. Many children, in school uniforms whose colours couldn't be easily placed, and who were barefoot, scampered to the roadside to watch or scuttled after the buses with hopes of getting a lift. From one of the homesteads, an older sibling with a high-pitched voice hurled insolence at a boy - whose toes poked through a dusty pair of black shoes - in an attempt to summon him home for his evening bath. The sun was receding behind the huts and maize plantations, and a mountain of cold awaited the students.

Later that evening, the *isukuti* that roared on, with residents dancing in circles as they thumbed their feet hard on the ground, bore memories of an evening with Lily in Nairobi, a week earlier, when Tom had taken her to watch a karaoke and had discussed local dances. He wondered where Lily was. He wondered if she was alive, or had she taken her own life from a place nobody could discover? To get rid of such thoughts, Tom joined the *isukuti* dancers and danced until he felt a reprieve from all the energy, simmering anger and disappointment life had thrown his way. He then joined other students seated around the bonfire set outside the hut, near the tent. He was tired because of the dance and from the long journey they had made for that whole day.

Tom sat close to the crackling tongues of fire with exhaustion that had settled in with the advent of darkness. Occasionally, he smiled at the memories of meeting Lily. He was gratified to have enjoyed her charming company and seen her dimpled smile, a smile that was always present even amid tears. Meanwhile, elders gathered in Lubao's hut to discuss Jim's fate.

"Namwalo," Okumu addressed Agnes by her clan name, the fragrance of incense smoke chasing away mosquitoes that buzzed around his ears. "What plans do you have for *Omwana we indasimba*?"

There was silence.

Okumu took the last swig of his drink. The remnants of the tea leaves were now gathered at the bottom of the plastic cup. He sucked traces of unstirred sugar from the tea leaves, spat the dregs behind him and turned to look at Agnes. Silence hung over the room, with a sharp wave of estrangement rushing across her face. A lantern placed on top of an inverted *kinu* – a wooden grinder – lit the room, from the centre of the semi-circle they had formed. It was made from a *Blue Band* margarine tin that had a picture of a young boy Jim's age. The image of the boy showed him having a piece of his bit-off toast with a broad smile, as if telling Agnes, "It will all be well."

Agnes would have been honest and repeated to Okumu that she didn't care about their kinship, that she didn't need them, and that in 1 Timothy 5:8 it's written that, *Anyone who does not provide for his relatives, especially for members of his household, he has denied the faith and is worse than an unbeliever.* But she opted not to. Perhaps she knew they would tell her she was first a Luhya before being a Christian. "*Omwana we indasimba...*" the words stuck up in Agnes' throat. *Omwana we indasimba*, a name given to a boy born and raised in his maternal land, and probably fatherless, was, in that case, Jim. And since Halima had also come to Francisca's funeral, Lily's friend and colleague, Pauline, was taking care of Jim at the hospital.

At last, the elders promised to exploit all possibilities to eliminate Jim from their progeny, even using witchcraft.

"I'll keep him, and you'll find a way to be okay with it!" Agnes swore.

"Namwalo, please leave us to whisper together and we'll get back to you with our final decision," an elder tried to cool down the situation before Agnes stomped out of the hut.

"The best way to eat an elephant in your path is to cut him up into little pieces," Okumu said, unashamedly concluding the unending discussion on Jim's fate.

Outside the hut, mourners kept arriving. Some went to the coffin, bowed, and walked to their seats, in silence. Some mourners gathered around the bonfire while the women group from the church sang long dirges at a high pitch from the tent.

Occasionally, female relatives shot up and wailed behind the tent, interrupting the choir. They walked around the compound crying and stamping their feet on the ground, throwing their arms up and down, cursing the fiend that had snatched their loved one, wiping tears with their bare palms, and slapping their thighs or throwing their heavy hands in the air. One old woman sang dirges in vernacular in alternating tones. She cried as she sang, and even paused for a few minutes before picking up the song again. Everyone mourned in their own ways, perhaps not to contradict Jesus' counsel that *Blessed are those who mourn, for they will be comforted*. Tom broke a twig into small pieces and tossed each piece into the fire. Unawares, Tom watched the last vestiges of the twig turn into ash at the hearth and wondered if Lily was thinking of him or her family wherever she was; if she was still alive. He watched the dying flames till the warmth from the burning logs swaddled him to slumber. Tom woke up at dawn to find himself wrapped in a Maasai *khanga*, the bonfire gone, except for the embers that blinked with the blowing breeze, and Halima watching over him.

It was an overcast Saturday, August 24, 2013. A beehive of activity was going on in the small compound. At the periphery of the compound, a small group of youths surrounded a middle-aged man slaughtering a goat. He concealed a knife from the goat's view, said *"Bismillah, Allahu Akbar"* and gave the goat precise, swift and deep incisions at the throat while facing Mecca. Presenting it before the Maker.

Young men, with shirts clung to their sweaty backs like a second skin, split logs into fine pieces of a woodpile. From behind the hut where a temporary makeshift kitchen had been made, female relatives squatted and fed the fire with the firewood, cooking fowls that had fallen victim to the occasion. The air was crisp, except for the ribbon of smoke billowing from the fire. As the women knelt to blow the fire, their behinds raised to the sky, the smoke curled into the air with incredible ease, and plumed with a breeze like a solemn ghost.

Children hovered around the cooking area in torn dresses. "*Cha era! Go away!*" One of the relatives half-shouted, choking from the smoke, as she waved them away. But the children stayed put, looking forward to small pieces of roast meat being thrown their way. They stared at the women, as they listened to the tales they were recounting about Francisca. Not even the noise the cooking spoons made against the soot-smudged pans could deter them from eavesdropping.

By noon, people had settled in the tents. Halima and other students sat thigh to thigh on benches sourced from the nearby church. There were slight tit-tat sounds as the plastic beads of her *misbaha* slid in between her fingers in flawless twirls. She sat at the end of the bench. "*Subhan Allah, Alhamdulillah, Allahu Akbar,*" Halima repeated each thirty-three times.

To Halima's left sat Lydia. Tom was sandwiched between Lydia and Dave. A middle-aged woman – with a sleeping child wrapped on her back in an old *khanga* – sat next to Dave. At the other far end of the row was an average-built, tall and dark man. His eyes pierced through the crowd. He was the only person who knew about Jim's conception. He knew every detail. Weakness drilled into every cell that nourished his body. His heart was almost bursting with remorse for his past sins – sins that he hadn't atoned for. He could still see how it had happened that day – five years, eight months earlier – as if it was just yesterday.

Meanwhile, as they were mourning Francisca in Kitale, other affected people were sending off their loved ones too; loved ones who had only left nostalgic memories and photographs. Others were gripped by grief and fear; the fear that the buildings they stayed in could be next to collapse. Nonetheless, the government officials charged with such duties to ensure citizens lived in safe buildings were still enjoying naps in their cosy office chairs waiting for their hefty salaries. Only a few junior officers had been suspended, albeit wrongly, to appease the relatives of the victims demanding answers.

"The ruins of a nation begin in the homes of its people!" A victim's relative had said in a television interview when asked to comment on the suspension of the junior officers. "These are just sacrificial lambs!"

"And before I invite the priest to lead us in the final prayers for our departed mother as we escort her to her final resting..." the speaker interrupted Tom. Juma had also just arrived and a villager had vacated a seat for him right behind Agnes' seat.

Tom looked up to see the speaker pointing at the grave. Next to the grave were bicycles of mourners tied on the tree under which Lily and Francisca had sat the evening before she left for university.

Mambo suddenly jerked from his seat and made strides towards the front of the tent. Juma was shocked not only to see his driver but to see how Mambo's sudden reaction made everyone turn to look at him. He was now making strides towards the speaker. He stopped midway and decided he wasn't going to let out the secret he had lived with for years now. It wasn't time yet.

"Would you like to say something, sir?" the speaker asked, not so much surprised, for it was at funerals where unknown children born out of wedlock, creditors and debtors, predators for deceased's property, and all sorts of characters emerged. Because it was only at funerals that such characters had the opportunity to let out whatever they had. It was only at funerals that one could spill a secret, reveal a will; spoken or otherwise, and claim property or relation.

"No, I.... I....." Mambo fumbled. "Please, feel free to say what it is."

"Actually, that man there is my boss," Mambo pointed at Juma, who was still visibly shocked. "I have seen him do so much for this family, and I request you give him an opportunity to say something..." A murmur swept through the crowd of mourners, shifting their glances from Mambo to Juma to the speaker and back. "That was all... Thank you," he said before eyes and murmurs escorted him back to his seat. Still, heads would keep turning to steal a glance at him.

321

After a few seconds of consulting the elders seated at the front row, the speaker finally said, "Our dear family, friends and mourners, a friend in deed is indeed a friend. As some of us know, and as you've heard with your own ears, this kind gentleman here has indeed done so much for us as a family; way from the time our lost daughter got cancer. He is not just a family friend, but we consider him as one of us, and it will only be fair if he is given a chance to pass his condolences as rightly requested by the gentleman over there – whom we thank for his kind reminder." Many heads nodded in the crowd, and some turned to look at Mambo. "Mr Juma, please," the speaker invited him. At this time, Juma had already made a decision to call Mambo to his office once they got back to Nairobi and have a sit-down with him about all that embarrassment. A disciplinary action awaited him.

Behind the hut, cooking continued. If at the end of the day some goat meat remained, it would be distributed among the relatives. Two mature *chidaywa,* cocks, had also been slaughtered for the priest and his team, and other special guests like Barasa's family. The gravediggers had been given the third one, as per custom, to slaughter and eat by themselves.

In three minutes from then, unknown to Juma, police in Nairobi would be searching for the landlord of the collapsed building after arresting a university student linked to a corrupt deal involving the construction of the same collapsed building.

"I greet you all," Juma would clear his throat and say how sad it was to learn of Francisca's death. He would convey his heartfelt condolences and that of his family, and he would then promise to be with Lubao's family then and in the days to come. In four minutes, he would say how he hoped Lily was still alive and reassure the mourners that the search was still going on with the relevant government officers and among Lily's friends. He would also mention that Lily once shared with him her dreams of building her parents a decent house. "For that,

I'll personally build a house for you Mzee Lubao as an honour to our deceased mother. I'll as well provide your daily basic needs, and most importantly, try to help you in reclaiming your land which Lily had also mentioned to me…"Applause would cut into his speech.

In five minutes from then, news of a Member of Parliament, Hon. W., having gone into hiding would be gracing newsrooms. But back in Kitale, there would be a layer of hope in Juma's promise and an assurance that not all was lost. Lubao would recall the day he had rushed Francisca to the hospital to deliver, hoping the child would be a boy; a son he had even pictured growing up and constructing a house for them. But now, it would be someone else's son who would. Not Francisca's.

"I will ensure he gets back his land. Dr Esther, her team and I will also take care of Mzee's cochlear implant operation and Jim's welfare. And if by any chance we ever learn of Jim's father, I promise we'll use all legal means to ensure he pays the ultimate price for his criminal act! And as I've mentioned, the government is working to find Lily. We've been to relevant offices and they've promised to put more effort into the search," Juma would add.

In the next five minutes, as Juma would be addressing the mourners, his boss at the Ministry of Health would be holding a press briefing to terminate Juma's services on the grounds of corruption, misconduct and abuse of office. In the next thirty minutes, Samantha would be arriving in Lubao's homestead.

But before then, Juma was still giving his speech.

"As I was saying," Juma continued, "We'll ensure he rots in jail." He paused for the mourners' mumbles to subside. A few people still turned to look at Mambo.

Above them, the clouds were low in the sky, and anytime, the rain would fall; washing clean the green vegetation before soaking the soil. Definitely, mother earth was also mourning her daughter. And the rain would fall to escort her, seeping deep into the grave. And Samantha, who was on her way to Kitale with Riziki, was driving fast to get to the funeral before the rain started.

When Juma chased Riziki out of their house for reporting him to the ministry, she went to stay with Juma's mother. So, after telling Samantha that Juma had travelled to Kitale, they planned to join him in mourning Francisca to appease him. But Samantha had even a bigger motive in that trip to Kitale.

Samantha's plan was to stay back with Juma in Kitale after the burial; a period within which she would help him trace his roots. She didn't know precisely where the funeral was or Francisca's home. But she planned to call Juma and ask for directions, once they arrived. She didn't know whether Juma's father, Justus, was still alive or not. But she was sure they wouldn't miss a relative if by any chance he had died. If only she knew what awaited...

What if Lily was never to be found? Halima wondered.

"Where is grand-mama?" Halima imagined Jim asking someone. But most importantly, she was praying that Jim gets well so soon.

"Grand-mama went on a very long journey. We don't know when she'll come back." Someone would respond.

"And where is mum Lily?"

Halima imagined kilogrammes of dark brown soil and gravel being thrown down the grave, moulding the earth to cover her roommate's mother. She pictured the scene after the burial, and everyone leaving the graveside – one by one – never to see Francisca again. But she would remain by the graveside to give her last prayer. Then she thought of Lily and how long and quiet the journey back to Nairobi would be.

And, she felt bitter that authorities of the land assume citizens live in peace and utmost bliss if, in reality, fear about substandard buildings collapsing was there. People lived in misery, insecurity, and hunger, while hefty salaries and allowances were the order of the day for corrupt government officials who enjoyed them with impunity. Citizens experienced road accidents daily, high cost of health services and increased terrorist attacks. The rate of youth unemployment was rocket-high, while ethnicity in job placement had become the norm. Candidates who fit the bill are never given employment opportunities just because they are not of this or that tribe! Didn't all Kenyans pay taxes? Was it not true that as they struggled to cope with the high living standards, the politicians struggled to steal even the smallest portion remaining? Some supply 'air' to ministries and loot billions in return!

While Halima thought through all that made her bitter, Mambo was still burning in spasms of guilt. He wondered what would happen after he revealed himself, especially now that Juma, his boss, and the rest were already in the picture. He was thinking of what to say as fast as he could because, if the priest started the final prayers, he wouldn't get another chance.

"And we urge our sisters and mothers to go for consistent check-ups and screening for early detection of cancer…"

Juma's phone buzzed, interrupting his speech; it was Samantha, his mother. Juma ended the call; he would call her after he was done. So, he continued, "With modern technology in healthcare, we shouldn't be scared that cancer diagnosis is a looming mortality. It is treatable, and the earlier it is detected, the better."

Juma's phone vibrated again; it was Samantha. "…May Mama Francisca's soul rest in peace; we'll surely miss her," Juma summed up and went to receive his mother's call from behind the tent.

Tom was slowly beginning to believe that Lily would never be found. That he would never again set his eyes on her. He was beginning to think of how different life would be after that, and how he would handle it. He began to realise one might have big dreams, but without the will of God, the dreams were nothing.

And he would start his life afresh. It had been long since he had gone to church, and he wasn't exactly sure when that Sunday was. But he was sure that the following day – 25th August – if he would still be alive, he would rush to St. Paul's Catholic Church immediately after he arrived in Nairobi.

Images of him replaying, at loud decibels, Morgan Heritage's *I'm coming home* or Gregory Isaacs' *Love you in the morning* all the way to Nairobi flooded his mind. Or he would be asking the driver to play Musa Juma's hit:

Nilikimbia Nairobi mama, sikuoni Nilikimbia Malaba mama, sikuoni Nilikimbia Mombasa mama, sikuoni

And as the song played in his mind, he pictured himself looking for Lily in Nairobi, Malaba, Mombasa, Busia and Port Victoria, without finding her. Eventually, with only the memory of Lily, he would accept

325

the finality, resign and settle on starting a new life. Maybe he would search again, everywhere, but in the end coming back to where he had started, and his love for Lily would remain constant. Maybe. Besides, was it not true that love was a sweet tyranny for he would just choose his torments willingly? But first things first, he decided to start with the church.

Before the master of ceremonies could invite the next speaker, Mambo shot up from his seat. "My name is Mambo...Mambo Magu, and I am the father of Jim. His blood and flesh are my blood and flesh." Mambo shouted brazenly in a loud audible voice.

Acknowledgments

My siblings; Zaituni, Jamilah, Faizah, Musa, Mariam, Juma, Fatuma. I would never have been who I am, were it not for you and your unending love and support.

Mr Lucas Wafula, your wise words gave me the encouragement to come up with this book. You made me believe in my capabilities.

My editors; Verah Omwocha who never gave up on my manuscript from the word go! To Benson Shiholo with a very professional touch, Mercy Mwende Kyalo, Flor-ence (Brenda) Kimuyu and Scholar V. Akinyi with keen eyes and magical touches that ensured everything was right. It's your contribution that scaled my creativity toa different sphere.

Jackline Muthoni Mboi (JM^3); you were a constant source of energy and encourage- ment. Thank you.

Wakah William, Emmanuel Mwikwabe, Preston Kedohe, Otiato Guguyu and Gabriel Dinda; I'm always grateful for your encouragment. Special thanks to Preston.

Jacinta Njeri Wanyoike, Christine "Shi" Wanjiru, Daniel Okumu and Powell Omollo, thanks for spending your valuable hours dissecting the manuscript of this book. The way you people infuse law, science and language into your creativity inspired me as well. Your contribution was immense.

Roy Tanga; thank you, nephew, for your intellectual insights. And for the tea. And the mahindi choma. You ensured I had enough glucose during the initial stages of this long process! You were the best. Hildah Nakhama: You were always ready to read my raw manuscripts and continued encouraging me. Uncle says, thank you.

My early readers; Verarita Nanyanga, Brenda Brestaris, Steve 'Snape' Nzeki, Mary Muriithi, Edith Kegengo, Mupa Nzaphila, Trizah Kilonzo, Sheilla Barasa, Jessicah Ki- mondo, Brian Otieno Nyandega (Yobrah), Ken Mumo (Kimondyo!), Claire Jahenda Kihamba and Esther Wambui; it was fulfilling enough just to have you read through the manuscript. Your feedback is what made this book what it is now. For Ashley Khadija, thank you for the small writing challenges you gave me, and for being an inspiration.

And for all those I may have missed your names; I thank you all for your valuable contributions.

Made in the USA
Columbia, SC
27 February 2023

12975967R00198